30SEVEN

WORKS BY JEREMY ROBINSON

The Didymus Contingency
Raising the Past
Antarktos Rising
Kronos
Beneath
Pulse
Instinct
Threshold
Fracture
Torment
The Last Hunter:Collected Edition
Insomnia
SecondWorld
Project Nemesis
Ragnarok
Island 731
Nazi Hunter: Atlantis
Prime
Omega
Project Maigo
Refuge
Guardian
Human After All
Savage
Flood Rising
Project 731
Cannibal
Endgame
MirrorWorld
Herculean
Project Hyperion
Patriot
Apocalypse Machine
Empire
Unity
Project Legion
The Distance
The Last Valkyrie
Centurion
Infinite
Helios
Viking Tomorrow
Forbidden Island
The Divide
The Others
Space Force
Alter
Flux
Tether
Tribe
NPC
Exo-Hunter
Infinite2
The Dark
Mind Bullet
The Order
Khaos
Singularity
Hunger: The Complete Trilogy
Nemesis
Point Nemo
Good Boys: The Lost Tribe
Good Boys: Unleashed
Kingdom
Good Boys: The Visionary
The Sentinel Trilogy
Artifact
30Seven

30 SEVEN

JEREMY ROBINSON

Cover design by Jeremy Robinson

ISBN: 979-8-3470-1219-0

Published in 2026 by Podium Publishing
www.podiumentertainment.com

Podium

For Mom

1948–2025

30 SEVEN

1

I don't know why I'm doing this. Camping. Roughing it. It's not me. I'm more comfortable behind a computer. That's not true. I'm the *most* comfortable behind a computer, designing, coding, and sometimes even voice acting in my indie video games. Sure, I hire out for some things, but eighty percent of my games are all me.

And one hundred percent of all that skill, knowledge, and creativity has zero benefit when sleeping in an old school cabin in the backwoods of Maine. It's six in the morning, and I'm resisting the urge to check my phone, not because I've sworn off it for the sake of this father-son bonding experience, but because there's no signal here. Every time I look at it, hoping for a single bar of reception, it just becomes clearer and clearer how much of my comfort in life comes from a device.

It's embarrassing. But a necessary crutch that's helped me get through the past year. A source of constant distraction, keeping my thoughts from overwhelming me.

Now, here, all I have are my thoughts.

And they're torture. So, I focus on my surroundings. Again.

The white sheet has been worn so thin by time that it's transparent. My mattress is old and lumpy, patterned with narrow white and blue stitched stripes. It smells musty and of old urine. Best guess, this place—Moose Hollow Campground—was once part of a kid's camp that launched during the 1940s.

The outhouse suggests it was built during the 1800s, but I think the owners were going for a good ol' nature experience. Like I said, roughing it. Need to cook? Find some wood and start a fire. You want to wash your hands? Walk five minutes to the lake and use the water that fish and beavers piss in on a regular basis.

Happily, I thought to bring hand sanitizer. They can take the tech out of the cabin. They can make me shit in a hole covered by a wooden box. But they can't take the modern world out of my SUV. If I'm desperate for music, air conditioning, or a snack, my Hyundai Santa Fe has me covered. If only it had a satellite connection.

I'm an internet addict. TikTok, too. News. Music. Games. Whatever it takes to stay distracted.

Ugh. And now I'm thinking about it again. The internet. My addiction to such a thing is obnoxious and annoyingly First World. But . . . that's who I am. Who I've been for the past year.

Because I'm definitely not the kind of guy that can sleep in a place like this, wake up refreshed, and march headlong into a day of . . . what?

Hiking. Canoeing. Driving thirty minutes to grab McDonald's for lunch. Maybe find some hot dogs at the gas station that we can cook on a stick for supper. That'd be a campy thing to do. I could do that. Get some marshmallows. Make some s'mores. I could totally do that.

"Hey, Elias," I say, knowing my son will be awake. He's always been a crack-of-dawn kind of kid. Thought it might change when he hit double digits, but he's been thirteen years old for five months now and still wakes up hours before me. Doesn't help that I'm a night owl and my own boss. I sometimes wake up five hours after him.

But not today.

"Buddy, what're you doing?" I roll over in my bed, expecting him to be sitting on the floor, building a card house, playing solitaire, or drawing in his ultra-private-no-one-touches-it sketchbook. But he's not on the floor. And he's not in bed.

I sit up like I'm spring-loaded. Despite the cabin being a single empty room with no nooks or crannies, I look around again, and then under both beds. Kid can hide like a ninja when he wants to, but there's nowhere to hide. Unless . . .

Already dressed, I slip on my shoes and head for the door. It's warm outside, but not hot. That will come later today. The cabin door, which is on a spring arm, slams shut when I step down the moss-covered concrete blocks that serve as a staircase.

"Elias?" I shout. Not too loud, but loud enough for the kid that doesn't normally leave the house, never mind the yard. He doesn't respond, and I don't see him. Tall pines sway in the morning breeze, partially concealing other cabins spread out around the campground. I was told there are fifty cabins, but I get the impression that fewer than half are occupied.

Bathroom, I think. At home, Elias is one of those kids that just takes forever in the bathroom. I assume he's just playing a game on his phone—I do the same thing—but I can't imagine him doing that in the outhouse. Because it smells. Like literal shit.

I run around the cabin to the little shack with cracks between the planks and a moon cut into the door. It's not the most private place to take a piss, but I'm guessing airflow is important. So the air is breathable. To reduce the smell. To keep a smoker from accidentally setting off an explosion.

"Elias! Hey!" I'm running by the time I reach the door. My nerves are starting to get wang jangled. The door is hanging open a crack—something Elias would never allow if he were inside. I yank it open anyway.

It's empty.

Panic takes root, squirming its frantic tendrils deep into my amygdala.

"Elias!" I shout, this time holding nothing back. I half expect people to stumble out of the other cabins in concern, but the morning is just as still as it had been before I realized Elias wasn't in the cabin.

I run to the side of my cabin, hoping to find him in the Santa Fe, but the keys are in my pocket, and I definitely locked it up tight last night.

As predicted, the orange SUV is empty.

I return to the front of the cabin. It doesn't have a foundation. It's lifted off the ground by eight concrete pillars. High enough to crawl under, if you're a kid. I drop to my stomach like I'm doing burpees. Phone in hand, flashlight on, I sweep the cabin's underside. Nothing.

Shit.

Shit!

Back to my feet. Look around again. "Elias!" My voice cracks.

Having trouble thinking. Where is he?

He doesn't do anything illogical. He's a thoughtful young kid. If he left, it was for a reason.

Hits me like a slap to the face. Used the bathroom. Wanted to disinfect his hands. Sanitizer is in the car. I was asleep with the keys in my pocket.

The lake!

I'm not known for any kind of physical ability. I'm not overweight, but I'm not exactly fit. While my muscles and bones collectively shout, 'What the hell?' I manage to hit my life's top speed as I careen toward the lake. I weave in and out of trees. Bounce over long twisting pine roots. The carpet of pine needles covering the ground is slippery, but I'm in the zone.

The journey to the beach is reduced to somewhere just north of a minute. I slide to a stop in the beach sand that someone dumped here ages ago. I look to the left. Then to the right.

A crane is the only other living thing on the sand.

I search the water, but the lake is empty.

What do I do? What the fuck do I do?

There's a payphone at the Welcome Center. 911 should work there. But that'll take, what, ten minutes? I'm winded. Couldn't run like that again. If Elias is close and in trouble, I should look for him now, but I have no idea what's happened to my son.

I'm about to scream his name again, but I'm cut short by a familiar buzz. I turn right. The beach is still empty, but something red and white is in the air over the water. It lands. Floats. It's round.

A bobber.

Someone is fishing.

I want to run again, but my legs have tapped out. They're Jell-O, and the sand doesn't make walking easy. My lungs spasm with each breath. Starting to think what I took for exhaustion is actually a panic attack.

The bobber bobs, flashing white.

The line snaps up.

"Got 'im!"

A battle with a big fish commences. It's slowly reeled into the shore—toward the woods just beyond the beach.

Fishing from the sand is against Moose Hollow rules, I remember.

I'm about to call for Elias again when I reach the tree line. I'm cut off again, this time by the sound of my son's voice.

"He's big."

"Told ya it would work," the man says. "Nothing gets the fish biting like another fish's offal."

My legs tremble. My arms shake. Hand on a tree, I manage to stay upright.

This is too much.

Too similar.

Felt like I'd lost them both.

You didn't, I tell myself. Elias is here. Elias is safe. He came to rinse his hands. Saw someone fishing. Stopped to watch. The chain of logic makes sense. He's used to me sleeping for a few hours more. Probably thought he'd make it back without me knowing.

I take a deep breath and let it out slowly, calming my nervous system, reducing the shaking. Grateful that I managed to not cry, I step into the woods, climb over a mound of granite boulders, and find Elias standing next to an old man with a bushy white beard. Spotted him yesterday when we arrived. Gave us a friendly wave. But my trust in humanity is at an all-time low, and the bloody knife and bucket of gore resting out of sight from Elias sets off alarm bells.

2

Hi, Dad," Elias says without turning.

"Eh?" The old man says, spinning around to find me perched atop the rounded rock like a stalking mountain lion. He flinches at the sight of me. "God damn, boy. You said your father was a computer nerd, not a ninja."

He belly laughs. Strikes me as the kind of guy who'd play Santa Claus in a small-town parade. Instantly puts me at ease. Doesn't mean he's safe, though. He hands his fishing rod to Elias. "You remember how to cast?"

Elias nods, somehow comfortable with the rod.

How long have they been out here?

The old man stands and extends a hand toward me. It's covered in dried blood. "Name's Emmett. Emmett Rigsby. Hope you don't mind; I've been teaching young Elias how to fish."

"I told him about your epic fail," Elias says and then casts the line like a pro, something I definitely did *not* teach him. My first attempt at casting with a fishing rod—yesterday—started with me tangling the line and spending thirty minutes untangling it. It ended with me losing my grip on the rod and throwing it into the lake.

"Now, now," Emmett says. "Show your father some respect. I couldn't sit behind a computer and write video games."

Knows a lot about me. Elias isn't normally a talker, but it seems like he's opened up to Emmett. Despite me not knowing or trusting the old man, Elias having someone he's willing to talk to is groundbreaking. So, I decide to give Emmett the benefit of the doubt.

I shake his hand. "Marcus Lockwood."

"Pleasure," he says. "You need Elias back?"

Elias turns his head toward me, looking a little desperate.

"Our schedule is wide open," I say, taking a seat atop the boulder. "Long as you don't mind me hanging out. Maybe you can teach me a thing or two about fishing?"

"Delighted to," Emmett says. "But I think your son could do the teaching at this point. He's a quick study. Seems able to do something after seeing it just once."

"That's Elias," I say. "So, what's the situation here? Catch and release? That's the term, right?"

"No," Emmett says, "and yes, in that order."

"Dad," Elias says, sounding embarrassed. "You really need to be more observant." He motions to his right. A white, five-gallon bucket full of water swirls with activity. I lean closer for a look. There are three large fish inside. No idea what species they are, so I don't bother guessing.

"Okay, smartass," I say with a chuckle. "What's the bucket of . . . whatever that is?" I motion to the smaller bucket containing what I'm now sure are fish guts. Mostly because of the rank smell.

"Bait," Elias says. "'Nothing gets the fish biting like another fish's offal.'" He looks to Emmett, who nods in approval.

"Define offal," I say.

"Fish guts!" Elias says, smiling now. It nearly breaks me. I'm not sure I've seen him smile in the last year. "Dad, c'mon. You could have figured that out just from the context." He looks up at Emmett. "I promise he's not actually this dumb."

Emmett gives me a look, silently asking if the banter is okay, if he should say something. I shake my head and give him a thumbs up. He's managed to bring out a part of Elias I haven't seen in a while. Kid can talk whatever smack he wants to.

"And where did the fish guts come from?" I ask, despite having already deduced from the context, namely the blood on Emmett's hand.

"Can I show him?" Elias asks.

"'Course." Emmett takes the fishing rod, and they trade places. Elias crouches down, opens a foam cooler I hadn't spotted yet, which was resting next to a tackle box. Inside the cooler, sitting on a bed of ice, is another large fish.

To my surprise, Elias reaches in and takes hold of the fish. "This is a white perch."

The fish has silver scales that reflect the morning sunlight. It's got faint horizontal stripes, a spiny dorsal fin, and a face only a mother fish could love. "Kind of ugly."

"Feisty," Emmett says. "Put up a fight. Good for pan frying."

"We're going to eat it," Elias says, "for lunch."

Emmett looks down at Elias like he's peering over a pair of glasses, his bushy white eyebrows raised. "Only if your father is okay with that."

They both look at me.

"Guessing it beats a Filet-O-Fish," I say.

"Cool," Elias says, and then pulls the perch open, revealing its cleaned-out insides. "This is where the offal is from. You should have seen it. He was like *fwoosh* with the knife, and then—" He hooks his finger and pantomimes dragging it through the fish's insides. "Got it all in one swipe."

Emmett shrugs like it's not a big deal. "I've had a lot of practice."

Seeing the inside of a once-living thing triggers memories I've been trying to erase from my mind. Of knife wounds. Of open flesh. Of my wife's dead face.

The memory slams through me and I hear the last words I spoke while looking at my wife's face. 'That's her. That's Isabella.'

Not sure how long I stay frozen, locked in place like a wide-eyed deer in the headlights of an eighteen-wheeler. Feeling the weight of the thing, feeling like I'm about to be smeared across the pavement, and like that might actually be a relief.

"Dad?"

I blink out of it. "That's . . . gross."

"Put it away," Emmett says to Elias. "Not everyone enjoys a close-up view of a fish's inside, ain't that right, Marcus?"

He's giving me a way out of talking about what my reaction was really about. I appreciate it, and I take it. "It's mostly the smell, but yeah. I prefer my meat cooked, in a bun, and covered in sauce."

Elias gives me a playful wave and places the perch back in the cooler. "It's just a fish, you know. They don't even feel pain."

"Not sure that's true," I say.

"Not exactly true," Emmett says. "He's oversimplifying." He reels in the line and casts it out again. "Go on. Explain it to your father. Same way I answered your question."

"Fish have pain receptors," my son says, looking up to the left, remembering what he'd been told. "Same as any other living thing. So, yeah, they feel pain, but they're not conscious life forms. Pain helps them stay alive. To fill their role in the evolution of all things. But they have no existential dread about their life, because they have no real understanding about what living is. They do feel pain, so a good person will kill them quickly. And before you respond, remember that you really like cheeseburgers, and cows are much more aware of their lives than a fish."

Can't argue with that logic. "I just don't like the idea of doing it myself."

Emmett puts a hand on Elias's shoulder. "Your father, he's the kind of guy that can change the world with his mind—who can create worlds with his mind. A person like that doesn't need to get his hands dirty with slaughtering food. Shouldn't have to. Folks like me, with simple lives . . . hell, I'm more than happy to catch, clean, and cook a fish for people like him. Can't tell you how many hours I spent playing *Joust* back in the day."

"You played *Joust*?" I make no effort to hide my surprise.

"All the greats," he says. "At arcades mostly. *Dig Dug*. *Centipede*. *Asteroids*. Your games anything like those?"

"Dad's games are entire worlds where you can go anywhere and do anything." Elias sounds a little proud, which is nice.

"Do anything, huh?"

"And it affects the world around you," Elias says. "Like this one time, I killed everyone in a village—"

I laugh. "You didn't."

"I totally did," he says, smiling wide. "And then, everywhere I went, everyone was afraid of me. I got dark powers. I became the bad guy. It was sick."

I feel like I should tell him to not do such things, even though it's a game, but can't, because my in-game killing spree was worthy of Vigo the Carpathian. Those game elements are there for a reason. It's fun to be the bad guy. So, I just shake my head and laugh.

"If you have a computer," Elias says. "You can play it, too."

"Closest thing I have to a computer here is a calculator, and that's been MIA for years."

"You must really like it here, then, huh?" I ask. "No WiFi. No cell network. Surprised there's toilet paper in the outhouse."

Emmett guffaws. Funniest thing he's heard all week apparently. "Reckon you have those *bidet* things."

"Don't knock it till you try it," I say. "You'll never feel so fresh."

"Feeling fresh is not high on my list of aspirations," Emmett says with a wink.

I smile and it becomes a yawn. "Oh. Shit. Sorry. Rough night."

"Didn't sleep well?"

"Could use a better mattress," I say.

He nods. "I'll see what I can do for you."

"'See what . . .' Wait. You run this place?" I ask.

"Own this place," he says.

"I'm sorry, I shouldn't have—"

He waves me off. "You're a good man with a better son. You deserve a little R&R. 'Sides, I agree with you. I feel like I slept on my feet."

"Because you were walking around all night," Elias says.

We both turn to him, confused.

"How's that?" Emmett asks. "I wasn't sleepwalkin', was I?"

"I don't know if you were sleeping, but your eyes were open."

Emmett beats me to the next question. "What time was this?"

Elias thinks on that for a moment. "Three. Ish."

The fishing rod is angled low, no longer ready to snap up when a fish bites. "What was I doing?"

Elias shrugs. "Walking with someone. Do you really not remember?"

"Walking with who?"

"For real? You don't remember?" I'm sure Elias is joking, but I've never seen him deadpan like this.

"I remember dreaming of Raquel Welch in a fur bikini, feeding me Hostess Cupcakes." Emmett forces a smile. "Now, who do you think I was with?"

Not a trace of humor in his voice, Elias says. "The tall people wearing masks."

3

Elias," I say, and don't need to say anything else.

"What?" he asks. "I'm telling the truth. There were two tall people wearing masks. They were following Emmett."

"Where did we go?" Emmett asks, kindly pretending to take Elias seriously. Maybe he senses the pain my son has endured in the past year. Maybe Elias told him.

"You were headed toward the lake," Elias says.

Emmett reels in the line and hooks it to the pole. "Help me pack up, will you?" He's talking to Elias. Putting him to work. I'm surprised when Elias obeys, putting a lid on the five-gallon tank.

"What are we doing?" my son asks.

"The sand doesn't keep secrets," Emmett says. "If anyone was on the beach last night, there will be tracks."

Elias's eyes light up, thrilled by the idea of investigating the mystery, even if it is fiction. He is a kid, after all. This is normal. I once led some friends into the woods—this is back before my family got a PC—and convinced them we were being stalked by a wolf. Thing is, by the time we worked our way back out of the forest, I was afraid, too. A young imagination is a powerful thing.

They're ready to go in thirty seconds.

"Lead the way, dad," Emmett says to me.

I climb down from the rock and step out of the tree line, back onto the beach. Now that I'm back on the sand, I notice how smooth the surface is. Like it's been groomed recently. My footprints from earlier are easy to see. I point to them. "This is me."

"Uh-huh." Emmett crouches by one of my footprints. Motions to it and speaks to Elias. "See how deep the toes' print is? Heel barely hit the sand. Now look at how far apart they are. The spray of sand behind each print. Take it all in. Feel it."

Elias does as he's told, but then says, "Sorry, Emmett. I don't feel anything."

"Meh," the old man says. "Some people have the gift, some people don't. But let me fill you in. Your father was running, full-out. Pushing hard with his toes, kicking up sand with each step. The distance between prints is wide, so either your father is a giant, or he was hauling ass. Point is, your father, being a good dad, was afraid that he'd lost you. Next time you think it's a good idea to wander off, wake him up and ask, okay?"

Elias looks from the prints to me. "Is he right? Were you—"

"Terrified," I say. "Yeah."

"Sorry," he says. "I just—"

"Didn't think I'd catch you," I say.

He smiles. "Yeah. Am I in trouble?"

"Not this time," I say. "Next time, I will literally destroy you."

"You're a lucky kid, Elias. Lot of parents out there wouldn't care."

"I know . . ."

Emmett ruffles Elias's hair with his dirty hand. "Let's go find out if there's another story in the sand, eh? Lead the way."

Elias runs ahead while Emmett and I follow at a more comfortable pace for an old timer holding a cooler and a bucket of guts. Meanwhile, Elias is running with a fishing rod in one hand and a bucket of water and fish in the other. The weight has him bent to one side. It's slowing him down. But he has no trouble outpacing us.

"Strong kid," Emmett says.

"Not sure why," I admit. "Neither of us are athletic."

"Wasn't talking about his muscles." He gives me a knowing look.

"He *talked* to you? About what happened?"

"About your wife," he says, the words gut-punching me. "He did."

I huff a laugh. "He won't even talk to his therapist."

"Can't imagine what that must have been like for you. That you're even here, trying with him, tells me where he gets his strength from."

Before I can thank him for the compliment, which feels undeserved, Elias shouts out from fifty feet ahead. "Found you!"

Emmett's face screws up. He wasn't expecting to find anything.

He doubles his pace, and I match it. Doesn't say another word until we reach the trail of footprints that clearly lead from the campground, right down into the water.

"You see?" Elias says. "Looks like you were walking, which you were."

"Mmm," Emmett says. "You said there were two people with me. I only see one set of footprints."

"Well, yeah, but I lost sight of you all before you reached the beach. Can't see that far from my cabin at night. Maybe they didn't come with you?"

"Mmm," Emmett says again.

He places his foot, which I didn't notice was already bare, beside one of the prints and steps down with all his weight. When he lifts his foot, the print looks very similar to the one in the sand. "Well, shit."

I sense Emmett's confusion. Maybe fear. And want to put him at ease. I kick off my shoe and repeat the process beside another print. When I lift my foot away, the print is also very similar. "Could be anyone."

"Dad," Elias says, annoyed that I'm challenging his recollection.

"Maybe it was a dream," I suggest.

He crosses his arms. "I was awake."

"Supposin' this will just have to go down as a mystery. But, I'll lock my door tonight. Just in case." I think he's just trying to appease Elias, but then he turns to me and says, "You should, too."

"By 'lock' do you mean the little metal hook and eye screw?" I ask with a grin.

He shrugs. "It's enough to keep the bears out. Might work for tall people, too." He looks down at Elias. "Work for you?"

"Guess we'll find out." Elias trudges toward the woods.

"Where are you moping off to?" Emmett asks. "We still got fish to prep." He turns to me. "Then, if you all are interested, I can take you foraging in the woods. Show you what's safe to eat. What will kill you. We'll make a proper lunch."

Elias sees that I'm unsure and says, "Dad, you make people do this stuff in *Shadowborn*."

"You can stop making good points any day now," I say, and shake my head. "Emmett, you got a deal. Just . . . no worms or bugs, okay?"

"Wouldn't dream of it," he says. "Worms are for the fish. Unless you're lost in the woods. Then worms might be your best bet at survival. Loads of protein in the dirt beneath your feet."

"I'm getting hungrier and hungrier," I quip. "Elias, help Mr. Rigsby take his things to his cabin. I'll meet you there in a little bit, okay?"

He pumps a fist. "Yes!"

"That okay with you?" I ask Emmett.

"It's nice to have company for a change," he says.

"Great," I say, backstepping toward the woods. "Great. Thank you." I give Elias's shoulder a pat as I pass. "See you in a minute. Do what he tells you, okay? No trouble."

"Daaad," he says.

I'm all grins until I face the woods. Then the true weight of my emotions rises up and digs its talons into my back, hooking around my ribs and clinging tight.

I hustle to our cabin. On the way, I make a mental note of Emmett's cabin. It's not that far away. There are a few trees between here and there, but all tall pines. Just trunks. No leaves. At least that part of Elias's story checks out.

Instead of going back inside the musty, dank cabin, I head for the Santa Fe, which unlocks at my approach. I climb inside, start the vehicle, and close my eyes. My phone connects to the sound system and music starts playing. The music that relaxes me is . . . different. While some people might find their chill with The Avett Brothers, or Norah Jones, or Iron and Wine, I prefer the acoustic rapping of Ren, whose "Hi Ren" song has a ten-minute-long conversation with his alternate personality. My life is different from Ren's, starting with the fact that I'm from Boston and he's Welsh, but I think all creatives feel that kind of duality, myself included. A minute into the song, I'm singing along with both personalities, distraction muting the emotions brought up by Elias's disappearance, and the references to my murdered wife.

He sings about duality. You and I being one and the same. I feel like that sometimes, split in two—but one person. Both desperately creative and empathic, with an angry darkness just beneath the surface, eternally linked to the side that resides in the light.

Not exactly cheerful, but it's where I'm at. And it helps. By the end of the song, I feel like myself again. I open my eyes and turn toward Emmett's cabin. Elias and Emmett are there, sitting at a picnic table, doing gross things I really don't want to see. I'll just watch from here, let them do their thing and head up when they're done.

I close my eyes to the brutal lyrics of "Kujo Beat Down."

When I open them again, the song has changed to "Money Game, Part 3" . . . There's an hour between those two songs on my playlist.

"God damnit."

I fell asleep.

I spring to attention and look to Emmett's cabin.

They're gone.

4

Don't panic, I tell myself. I'm not sure my nervous system could take another full-on, breath-stealing emotional escapade.

He's fine.

Emmett is safe.

You don't even know Emmett!

I speedwalk between trees, heading for the old timer's cabin.

He could have been lying about owning this place. Could have been lying about not remembering the people he was out with last night. Maybe the blood on his hand wasn't from a fish at all!

I break into a jog.

Two steps in, I spot a good stick and detour to pick it up. It's solid. Fresh. Like a baseball bat in my hands. It'll get the job done.

After the delay, I decide to just run, full out, like I did on the beach, but this time I'm ready to start swinging.

Ten feet from the cabin, I hear . . . laughter.

I slow to a walk, at which point I realize my legs are shaking again. My stick is long enough for me to plant on the ground and use it to stabilize myself. I use the pause to listen.

People are talking. Several conversations at once. All of them lighthearted. Joking. Telling stories. Elias is asking questions. He seems strangely at home here, in the woods, with strangers.

When my legs stop shaking, I head toward the cabin's far side. Can smell cooked fish. Maybe burgers, too. My stomach rumbles. Never ate breakfast. But if it's lunchtime, how long was I asleep? Five hours? More?

"There he is!" Emmett bellows as I round the corner to the cabin's far side. He's seated at a long red picnic table. There are four newcomers along with Emmett and Elias, all of their eyes on me.

"Don't let his slender frame fool you," Emmett says, "this man is Father of the Year."

"With a son like Elias," says a woman with curly black hair, pulled back in a bun, "that's not surprising." She looks at me over a pair of reading glasses she'd been using to read the label on a bottle of relish. Seems friendly enough.

Emmett motions to her. "This here is Dr. Serena Fields. She's a regular. Hell, they're all regulars, but—How long have you been coming here, Serena?"

She thinks on it for a moment. "Thirty-five years. I was Elias's age the first time I came."

I know it's supposed to be interesting, but I'm busy sizing them all up. Could these be Elias's tall people? Are they all part of some backwoods cult? I decide against it when I note Serena's small size. Can't be more than five foot two.

Emmett motions to the young man seated beside Serena. "This here is Jade. He's a college dropout, but so am I, so no judgment."

"I dropped out, too," I say.

"Ahh." Emmett is thrilled by this tidbit. "But I bet you worked hard. Had a dream and followed it. Jade, you should ask Marcus some questions while he's a captive audience, so you don't end up being the groundskeeper here for the rest of your life."

Jade laughs. "Yeah, wouldn't want to end up like you, right?"

Emmett ignores the dig and motions to a serious-looking woman. Younger than Serena. Might be around my age. Pretty, but she's got an intimidating vibe, like Isabella's brother, who's a US Marine. The scar above this woman's eyebrow suggests combat experience.

"Military?" I ask her.

She smiles. "Good to know my resting bitch face is still alive and well. Air Force."

"This is Colonel Samantha Reyes," Emmett says, "but if you're sitting at this table, you can just call her Sam."

"Colonel?" I ask. "Wow, that couldn't have been easy."

"Because I'm a woman," she asks, "or because I'm Filipina?"

"Uhh, neither," I say. "I wouldn't make it past basic training."

She smiles and offers her hand. "I'm screwing with you. It wasn't easy."

I shake her hand. She absolutely destroys my fingers with a strong grip. I do my best to hide the pain and turn to the last of the four people I don't know. My eyebrows squish together. "Gabriel Morales?"

"You two know each other, Gabe?" Emmett asks.

I answer for him. "Techjoy 2021. Saw you speak about the dangers of generative AI before it was publicly available."

"You in the business?" he asks, young and confident. At 28 years old, he's achieved more success in the tech industry than most of Silicon Valley in twice that time. He's an uncommon combination of savant-like coding and social charm. After partnering with Pied Piper, his profile skyrocketed, and he's given his investors one hit after another.

"Adjacent," I say.

"He makes indie games," Elias says, putting little me on the spot in front of a tech giant.

"Indie games are the best," Gabriel says, but I'm sure he's just being nice for Elias. "What title?"

"*Shadowborn*," Elias says.

Nice to hear the pride in his voice.

"Ahh," Gabriel says. "I'm a level-thirty necromancer that's embraced the Shadow's Path."

"No way!" Elias says.

No fucking way, I think.

"I'm a level thirty-seven rogue . . . and a Shadow Lord."

"A Shadow Lord?" Gabriel asks. "What's your kill count?"

"Two hundred and nine."

"*Two hundred and nine?*" Gabriel and I say at the same time.

"Mad props," Gabriel says, holding out a fist that Elias bumps.

I'm not sure what to say. A level thirty-seven Shadow Lord would be able to take even me down. I had no idea Elias played the game that much.

"Kudos to you, Marcus. Good kid, good game. If you want corporate backing for the next release, we should talk. But you've got a good thing going. Money doesn't make the game. It's the mind behind it. And yours . . . yours is something special, my man. But, money can help sell a game."

"I'll keep that in mind," I say, feeling a bit overwhelmed. The whiplash of shifting from panic to a surreally positive encounter—with all these people—has me feeling a little dizzy.

"Okay, okay, no more work talk. Exchange business cards or whatever you youngens do and then get back to following the rules."

"Rules?" I ask.

"Leave work at home," Serena says. "Sounds good to me."

"It was *your* rule!" Gabriel says and holds his phone out to me. I'm confused for a moment until I remember what Emmett suggested we do. I pull out my phone, hold it up to his and presto, I've got one of the world's most successful tech billionaire's contact info.

"Fish or a burger?" Emmett asks me, and before I can answer he says, "Fish it is!"

"Could I have both, actually?"

"Surf and turf," he says, opening the grill to reveal some grilled meats that are still warm but probably drying out. "Coming right up."

I take a seat at the table between Serena and Gabriel, trying to feel comfortable. Trying not to think about what a friendship with Gabriel Fucking Morales could mean, not just for my games, but for Elias's future. I make good money—better than most—but it would be nice to know that my son would always be taken care of, even if something happened to me.

"Okay," Gabriel says. "Now that we're all here, my question . . ."

Serena leans in close. "He likes to pose what he thinks are big mind-bending questions."

"They usually are questions only a genius could answer," Gabriel says.

Jade chokes laughing. "Dude, I answered one of your questions."

"Meh," Gabriel says. "You're smarter than you give yourself credit for." He rubs his hands together and then gives them a clap. "Okay. Now, we've all seen some shit. Some of us here. Some of us up in the air." He glances to Sam. "But last night . . . that was something else."

He looks at each of us, scanning faces for reactions.

"The lights," he says. "In the sky."

"Can you be more specific?" Sam asks. "You might have noticed that the sky is full of lights at night."

"Says the person who knows more about what's going on than she'd admit," Gabriel says.

"You mean like the lights from three years ago?" Jade asks. "That was crazy."

Gabriel shakes his head and then turns to me. "We saw a light moving across the sky. Could have sworn it was the ISS. Even the Colonel thought that's what we were looking at, until it split into *three* lights and all of them zipped away in three different directions. And when I say 'zipped,' I mean faster than anything we've built, flown, or could fly in without becoming a smear on the wall."

He tosses a potato chip into his mouth, chews it loudly, and then takes a drink. "Now, what I saw last night was up close and personal. Maybe a hundred feet over the trees. Just hovering there . . . until it wasn't. Please tell me someone else saw it."

He scans our faces again, disappointed by what he sees.

Then Elias says, “I didn’t see the light source, but there was light.” He turns to Emmett. “That’s how I saw you walking around with the tall people.”

Gabriel leans forward and places his hand on Elias’s arm. “Say again? Tall people?”

5

Elias," I say, trying to steer him away from a conversation that might leave these people thinking he's crazy.

"What?" he asks, annoyed. "I know it scares you, but I saw them."

"Saw who?" Gabriel asks.

Elias sticks his tongue out at me. "Two people walking with Emmett."

"Walking where?" Jade asks.

"Toward the lake," Elias says.

Serena sighs. "Guys, I'm not sure we should indulge—"

"Eh, eh!" Gabriel points at her. "No work, remember? You can't psychoanalyze anyone."

"You're a therapist?" I ask in a whisper.

"Clinical psychologist," she says.

"Okay," Gabriel says. "Back to the tall people. The lake."

"I'm with Serena," Sam says. "Doesn't seem healthy to—"

"There are footprints," Elias blurts. "On the beach. From the trees to the water. Same size as Emmett's feet."

"And my feet," I say.

"Could have been any one of us," Emmett says, a little uncomfortable being the center of attention. He places a paper plate with two fish fillets and a charred burger on the table in front of me. "Bon appétit."

"I wasn't on the beach yesterday," Gabriel says, "and Jade has dainty little feet."

"They are pretty small," Jade says, taking no insult. "I moisturize them, too. Thinking about opening a foot-fetish OnlyFans as a girl."

"You see?" Gabriel says. "If the lack of shoe fits, right?"

Emmett grunts.

"Now," Gabriel says. "The tall people. What did they look like?"

Elias thinks for a moment and then says, "I drew them. Might be easier if I show you." He stands up from the table. "I just need to get my sketchbook."

I want to stop him. Want to put an end to this. But he seems happy, and I don't want to take that away from him. So, I let him go. He normally has the sketchbook in his cargo shorts pocket with a bunch of black Pigma pens. Realizing he'd left it behind probably made him nervous. He'll be glad to have it back. And it will be nice to have people admire his art. He helped design a lot of characters in *Shadowborn*, including the nefarious incarnation of the Dark Lord he's apparently playing as. Guessing he planned that ahead of time—creating the character he'd eventually play. He's always been strategic like that. And I did exactly the same thing.

When Elias is out of earshot, Serena says, "Guys, listen—this kind of unchecked speculation could reinforce intrusive thoughts and disrupt Elias's sleep for weeks. He may not consciously link his anxiety to this conversation, but that doesn't mean it won't manifest. Don't just validate everything he says at face value—especially if it feeds into a cognitive distortion. For all we know, this was a dream, and you're about to solidify it as a core memory."

"That," Gabriel says, "was a lot of big words. I can see why people pay your exorbitant fees."

Serena rolls her eyes. "Or just scar the kid for life."

"From what I've seen," Emmett says, "Elias has a special kind of mind capable of handling life's worst tragedies. I suspect he can handle our indulgence of his story. But, no one knows him better than his father." He looks me in the eyes. "What do you think, Marcus?"

"I haven't seen him this happy all year, not since . . . He's laughing. Talking. You all seem to put him at ease." I address Serena, "If this can take his mind off what happened, then I'm all for it."

"So," Jade says, scratching his head. "What happened a year ago?"

"*Jade,*" Serena says. "Not appropriate."

"What?" Jade says. "We were all wondering."

"It's okay," I say. "Elias is opening up. Maybe I should, too."

Sam puts her hand on my arm. "You really don't need to."

I clear my throat. "My wife was murdered a year ago. This weekend is the anniversary. My hope was that coming here would distract us enough that we wouldn't dwell on it. Seems to be working well for Elias. Less so for me, but you all . . . this—" I motion to the table and the food. "—is helping. So, thanks for that."

"Man," Jade says, eyes down. "Sorry I pushed."

"It's okay," I say. "Really."

"Is it done?" Gabriel asks. "The trial. All that. All behind you now?"

I shake my head and frown. "Not remotely."

When I look up, five pairs of eyes are on me, all wondering the same thing, but afraid to ask. Even Serena can't conceal her curiosity.

I decide to open up, even if it means I break down crying. Even if it results in Gabriel deciding I'm too broken to ever do business with. "The killer wasn't caught. They never even had a suspect."

"Not even you?" Jade asks.

Serena elbows him. Hard.

"I was at a gaming conference," I say. "Elias was sleeping over at a friend's house. I left the conference to identify her body. A neighbor noticed the front door open. Found her in the kitchen. Throat slit."

Serena purses her lips as though trying to contain her thoughts, then gives in and says, "The open door suggests she let the killer inside, which means—"

"She knew them," I say, nodding. "The police said the same thing. But . . ." My insides quiver as memories resurface. ". . . the way she died isn't what stood out. It was what . . . what the killer did to her afterwards. I didn't see it. Refused to look at photos. But I got the broad strokes."

I take a deep breath. Everyone remains silent. Waiting.

"He—I assume it was a *he* . . . arranged her. Like, I don't know, like a bonsai tree. Like he thought of himself as an artist. Cut up. Twisted. Posed. The neighbor who found my wife . . . she tried to kill herself a month later. Whatever was done, it fucked her up to the point of not wanting to live. Honestly, I've considered it, too. Might have gone through with it if not for Elias."

I stare at my meat, no longer hungry. Not sure how long I stay like that, but when I look up, no one has moved. Looks like they're all holding their breath.

"I'm okay," I say. "Well, not okay, but I threw myself into work about six months later and it's kept me grounded." I laugh when I look at their faces again. "Sorry. You're probably all here to relax, and I'm ruining the vibe."

"Bro," Jade says. "You might be new to the group, but after that level of vulnerability, of letting us in, you're one of us now. We got your back."

"He means it," Emmett says. "Same as the rest of us. I thought you were a good man before. Now? The good Lord doesn't make many people who can go through what you have and still be a loving person."

"He's not wrong," Serena says. "You . . . your healthy response to what you experienced is rare." She looks unsure of herself, but then asks, "Can I ask you a question? You don't need to answer it if you don't want to."

"Go ahead," I say.

"You didn't see pictures, and that was a really good choice, but I wonder, did the police say anything about twine?"

"What kind of question is that?" Jade asks.

Serena must see the shift of emotion on my face. In a low, gentle voice, she repeats, "You don't need to answer."

Translation: My reaction has already confirmed the presence of twine. But I'd rather not answer the same question later on, four more times, so I tell the truth. "It's what he used . . . to arrange her."

The tears sneak up on me. But it's not the same kind of agony I felt a year ago. It's more like a release. Feels good to tell people who aren't being paid to listen.

Gabriel asks Serena the question that had yet to occur to me. "How did you know to ask about twine? Seems kind of a specific thing to correctly guess."

Serena looks to me for approval. I wipe the tears from my eyes and nod. I'd like to hear, too.

"My specialty . . . which I've never talked to any of you about . . . is serial killers."

"Is twine a common element in serial killings?" Sam asks.

Serena shakes her head. "I consult with the FBI on cases that they can't crack. Help them create profiles to decipher the killer's identity. I remember one from just over a year ago. Was just two murders, but clearly an emerging serial killer—because of how the bodies were arranged and bound with twine."

"You—you think a serial killer murdered my wife?" I ask.

"I'm sure the police do, too. That kind of murder . . . it sets off alarm bells."

"No one said anything to me," I say, starting to feel angry.

Serena's expression twists with some kind of discomfort I have trouble deciphering.

"What's that?" Gabriel asks. "That face. He's one of us now. Don't keep it to yourself."

"I shouldn't," she says.

"Serena," Emmett says. "You're a good judge of character. Always have been."

Not sure why he told her that.

Serena looks me in the eyes. Her blue irises are intense. Holds my gaze until I'm uncomfortable and look away. She sighs. "The police wouldn't have told you if you're a suspect."

"A suspect of what?"

The question spins me around. Elias is standing there, open sketchbook in hand, a confused look in his eyes. He turns to each of us, closes and pockets the sketchbook, and then repeats the question. "A suspect of what?"

6

Of being too goddamned attractive," Gabriel says, putting on a happy face and flashing a smile like a professional bullshitter. He points to Sam and Serena. "These two are all but ready to give you siblings."

"Gabe!" Sam says, smacking his shoulder. "Too far."

"What?!" He pours on the energy, singlehandedly pushing back the dark fog that had settled over the table. "He's got a cool job, a great kid, a swollen bank account, and is an emotional fixer upper. He's basically every woman's dream come true. Doesn't hurt that he looks like John Krasinski. After *The Office*, obviously.

"Your dad is nicer than Krasinski, though," Gabriel claps my shoulder. "You're a lucky kid."

"Yeah," Elias says. "He's okay, I guess."

And just like that, Gabriel has managed to redirect the conversation back to the light-hearted. Emmett starts joking with Elias. Jade tells a story. And I remain lost in the recent past. I'm going to crack, despite the tone shift. So, I excuse myself without taking a bite, blame it on an upset stomach, and head back toward my cabin.

Once I'm out of sight, I redirect toward the lake. I need to calm down. The musty cabin won't help. I could sit in the Santa Fe again, but I don't want Elias to see me crying. He's having a positive and transformative experience here. I don't want to slow him down.

The beach is a picture of relaxation. Smells of pine. The air is a perfect eighty degrees. The sky is thick with cumulus clouds, looking soft and comfortable. They cast dark shadows over the not-quite mountains on the lake's far side.

This is nice. This is good.

I kick off my shoes. The sand's surface is warm, but just an inch beneath the surface, it's still cool. I roll up my pants, wonder why I'm not wearing shorts, and step into the water. Shin deep. Feels too cold at first, but it's nothing like the Atlantic. The lake water is pleasant after just a few seconds. But the ocean, in New England, even at the height of summer, makes my foot feel like it's been split in two with an axe.

I take a deep breath. Let it out. Close my eyes and remember the last words Isabella spoke to me, 'Don't worry. We'll be fine.'

I did worry.

And they weren't.

I won't be going to another gaming convention until Elias wants to come with me. He's not fond of crowds, though, so I probably won't go until he's an adult and moved out.

"Hey."

I glance back. It's Serena.

"Coming to check on your new patient?"

"I don't have patients," she says, stepping into the water. She's dressed in shorts and a tank top. Flipflops on her feet. Wades right in.

"Then . . ."

"Subjects," she says. "I study psychological conditions. I'm not in the business of fixing people."

"Then why—"

She stops beside me. "I need to be sure about you."

"Sure about—Wait. Are you serious? You want to grill me? See if I killed Isabella?"

"I'm not going to grill you," she says. "I just want to ask you one question, and I want you to look in my eyes when you answer."

I sigh. It's fair. I did somehow manage to implicate myself. I look her in the eyes.

She blinks at the sight of tears already in my eyes.

"You know what," she says. "You don't need to."

"Ookay. Why?"

"If you were a serial killer, that would make you a psychopath. And while a psychopath can pretend to be a nice person—charismatic, life of the party, empathetic—it's all just an act." She smiles at me. "You were crying before I got here."

I sad-chuckle. "Maybe I suspected someone would come after me. Maybe I knew it would be you."

"Ahh, the elusive *genius* psychopath," she says.

"What? I'm smart."

She raises an eyebrow at me. "You make games."

"I make worlds," I say.

"And now you sound like Gabe." She looks out at the view, relaxing. "He really some kind of hero to you?"

"I don't know about hero," I say, "but he *is* a genius."

"I know," she says. "And he doesn't let us forget it."

"I don't get it. He could be on a yacht in the Mediterranean, but he's here. And granted, this—" I motion to the lake. "—is really nice. But that cabin? The outhouse?"

She smiles. "Place hasn't changed since I was a kid. All of us are the same. Sam, Jade, Gabe, Emmett. We all spent summers here. Most of us not at the same time. But as adults, we came back for a few weeks every summer. As we got to know each other, we made sure those weeks overlapped, and our group formed naturally over time. Jade's the newest, but he's been coming here since he was ten. You keep coming here with Elias, and he might be the new youngest member of the crew."

"That's nice . . . I could still use WiFi, an air conditioner, and a porta-potty at the very least."

"I don't disagree," she says. "But Emmett is a traditionalist, and we come here more to connect with our younger selves than to have a comfortable vacation."

"Huh," I say. "That's actually really nice."

"Glad you approve," she says, a trace of sarcasm.

"So," I say. "This whole conversation has been 'the question,' right? You're getting a *feel* for me. Seeing if I give off killer vibes?"

She opens an imaginary notebook and pretends to write in it. "Subject is insightful." She pats my back. "Don't worry, new guy. You and I both know you're not that guy. Guessing you've never been in a fight, though you've probably run away from more than a few."

"So, I come across as a wuss," I say. "Great."

"Sensitive. Gentle. Gabe wasn't wrong, you know. If I were twenty years younger . . ." She laughs at my discomfort.

We're silent for a moment, watching as a bald eagle swoops down, glides over the water and snags a fish before flying away.

"Okay," I say. "*That* was awesome."

She nods. Looks back to the beach. "Is that the mysterious set of footprints?"

"Yep. The big mess next to the single set of prints is Elias, Emmett, and me."

She moves through the water, approaching the prints on the beach. Gives it far more attention than a single set of footprints should command. "This is where Elias saw Emmett?"

"He saw him in the woods, but says he was headed in this direction."

"With the tall people," she says.

"Right."

"Well, there's just one set of footprints . . ."

"But?" I ask.

She points. "They come out of the woods, walk straight down the beach, and enter the water." She looks back at me. "But they don't come back out."

I stand beside her looking at the sand. She's right. "Maybe he just backtracked?"

"Have you seen Emmett walk for long? Man is as unstable as a hypochondriac on WebMD. If he'd walked backward from the water to the woods, there would be an ass print along with the feet."

"Okay, so . . . he walked into the water here, then waded down the shore and exited somewhere else."

She nods. "Logical."

"There's nothing down there." I point to the tree line at the end of the beach where I found Emmett and Elias fishing.

We both turn in the other direction.

She starts walking, staying in the water. "Looks like we're going this way."

"Why?" I ask. "It's obviously what happened, and Elias isn't here. Why take it seriously?"

"Well . . . Honestly . . . Weird stuff happens here sometimes. We've all seen lights in the sky, sometimes alone, sometimes together. Sounds in the forest. Loud crows during the day. Serious owls at night."

"Owls . . ."

She nods. "They just stare right through you."

"Surprised Gabriel hasn't set up trail cams."

She looks at me. "He did. Three times."

"What did they record?"

"Normal stuff. Racoons. Opossum. Fox. Black bear. And on occasion, hours of 'digital interference.' Gabe's fancy way of saying static. He thought it was strange, but he's young enough to not remember that TV used to play static all night, every night. Static . . . is just static, you know?"

I don't bother telling her that I, too, am not old enough to remember a time when TV ended for the day. What I do say is the obvious. "We're almost at the end of the beach."

We both scan the sand.

"You see?" she says. "Weird."

"You're a psychologist and that's the best you got?"

"As a psychologist . . . I could come up with a dozen ways to rationalize this and sleep like a log tonight. As a human being . . . I'm freaked out."

"Why?"

"Because this isn't the first time this has happened."

"It's not?" I'm stymied. "Why didn't Emmett mention it?"

She frowns. "Because he doesn't remember the first time it happened and probably doesn't remember eighteen-year-old me telling him about the tall people *I* saw leading him to the lake, thirty-plus years ago."

7

To say I'm starting to worry is like saying the Titanic sprung a leak and got a little wet. This place and everything about it feels like it's a gerbil queef away from a full-on episode of *The X Files*.

But my growing concern is counter-balanced by the fact that Elias is thriving. I'm a city boy at heart, so I could be overreacting. Maybe this is what life in the woods is always like. If it's not lights in the sky, and tall people, it's fairies and dwarves.

I left Serena at the beach. Said she wanted to focus. To bring back her memories of Emmett and the tall people. She was seated in the sand and doing some kind of meditation when I left.

Back at Emmett's, the table is empty. Everyone has left, including Elias.

I could panic again. Could go running around looking for my son just to find him having a grand old time for the third instance in a day. Or, I could sit and eat my now cold and dry meal, which has been left out along with a bag of dill pickle flavored potato chips—weird—a can of cherry cola, a bottle of ketchup, and some plastic utensils.

They knew I'd return. Knew I'd still be hungry.

I sit.

The burger is a hockey puck, but it tastes good. The fish is cold but surprisingly tender and well-seasoned. I'm not a huge seafood fan, which is basically sacrilegious for a Bostonian. But this isn't seafood. Maybe lake fish taste different from their ocean-dwelling relatives?

A few bites in and I forget all about my analysis. All I am is hungry. I wolf down the meat and chase it with a handful of potent chips and a half can of soda, all of which is followed by a monumental burp.

I breathe deep. My nerves calm. Muscles relax. Despite my lackluster sleep and the traumatic start to my day, I'm starting to feel good. Better than I have in a long time.

The sound of screaming tenses me.

I half stand, ready to sprint toward the sound. But it finishes with laughter and my son's voice shouting, "Eat it, Gabe!"

The hell are they doing?

I leave with a handful of chips in one hand and the can of soda in the other. Munching and drinking, I take my time walking toward the sound of people. There are also several loud clunks and a scraping sound. I try to imagine what I'm hearing, but it's a new sound to me.

After climbing up a small hill made slippery by the pine needle carpet, I see the others. They're all there—Elias, Emmett, Gabriel, Jade, and Sam.

Huh, I think, trying to make sense of the game being played. There's a long concrete slab that's seen better days. At the far end, there's a big triangle divided into sections, each with different point values—10 at the tip, then 8, then 7, like some kind of weird, inverted food pyramid. At the very back is a -10 zone. There are currently five ceramic discs lying atop the triangle. Red and blue. Adding up the numbers, it looks like red is winning. But it's blue's turn, and blue . . . is Elias.

He stands at the other end of what I guess could be called a court. He's holding a pole with two prongs at the bottom. Between them, a blue disc.

"Remember what I told you," Emmett says.

"Hey!" Gabriel says. "No tips from the master!"

Elias looks down the length of his pole. Adjusts his aim while Emmett nods in approval. Then he gives the puck a shove. It glides over the rough concrete, smacks into a red puck, sending it off the side of the court, and then strikes a second, pushing it into the -10 zone while stopping in a +5 section.

The bystanders erupt with cheers for Elias, who has the pole raised over his head.

Gabriel sees me coming. Smiles. "Your kid is basically a savant at everything he tries."

"I'm aware," I say. His ability to pick up and master skills is a gift, but it's caused a lot of resentment at school and resulted in a lot of bullying over the years.

"You saw that, right?" Elias asks me.

I tussle his hair. "Sure did." And then to Emmett, I say, "How come this wasn't in the brochure?"

Emmett looks confused. "Brochure?"

"Yeah," I say. "You know, the three-panel advertisement. Front and back. Lots of pictures and words. Now that I'm thinking about it, the images smacked of AI generation and looked nothing like this place. Did Gabriel help you with it?"

"Help with what?" Gabriel asks from the far side of the court where he's arranging the discs behind the line.

"He thinks we have a brochure," Jade says, shaking his head like it's a ridiculous notion. "And that you used AI gen shit for the pictures."

"Brochure?" Gabriel says, sounding genuinely confused.

"Marcus," Emmett says. "I've never, in all my years here, had a brochure. Not even a business card. Just an address and a phone number. People who come here have either been coming here their whole lives or are friends of people who have been coming here their whole lives."

Feels like I'm having a Mandela Effect moment. "Elias, back me up."

"I saw it, too," Elias says. "Came in the mail."

"It's where I got your phone number," I tell Emmett.

"I don't know what to tell you," he says.

"Weird stacked upon weird," Sam says. "Just another day at Moose Hollow, right?"

Gabriel's confusion shifts to understanding. "It's like the Bermuda Triangle up in this joint."

They're keeping it light for Elias's benefit.

Emmett has a harder time hiding his serious emotions. "Elias. Can you help Jade get dessert?"

"Sure," Elias says.

Jade's confused. "Dessert?"

"Welcome Center snack machine," he says, putting a few dollars in Jade's hand. "Take your time."

Jade gets it. Nods. Turns to Elias and waves the dollar bills in the air. "Time for a sugar high!"

A minute later, their voices fade into the distance and I say, "Okay. What the hell, guys? Is there really no brochure?"

Gabriel ticks his fingers. "No brochure. No website. No email."

"Where's Serena?" Sam asks.

"She stayed on the beach," I say. "Trying to remember—" I glance at Emmett. "—something."

"She look at the footprints, too?" Emmett asks.

I nod.

"And?"

"There's a set of footprints entering the water," I say. "You saw that. But . . . they never leave the water. At least not on the beach. But I'm more concerned about the brochure."

"Right," Sam says. "Because if you got a legit brochure advertising this place, then someone wanted you here."

My gut twists. "Someone . . . being one of you?"

"There are other guests," Emmett says. "They're spread out a distance."

"How many?" I ask.

"Dozen maybe," he says. "I rent by the cabin. Don't make a habit of counting how many people come."

I'm starting to rethink the wisdom of letting Elias go with Jade.

"Marcus," Sam says, placing her hand on my arm. "I spend a lot of time trusting people with my life. I've gotten pretty good at knowing who I should trust and who I shouldn't. There isn't anyone in our group that I wouldn't trust with my life."

"And yet," I say, "I'm here because of a brochure that shouldn't exist. I'm here because someone wanted me here. An hour ago, I might not have thought much about it, but Serena thinks my wife's murderer is a serial killer. Can't help but feel like I've walked into a trap."

"How about this?" Emmett suggests. "We'll walk the grounds together. Get a good look at everyone else here. The police thought your wife knew the killer, yes? Maybe you'll recognize someone?"

The possibility of catching Isabella's killer strikes a chord. He's right. If the killer is here, I need to suss out who it is.

"Gabe," I say, adopting the short form of his name that others have been using. "Can you catch up to Jade? Watch over Elias for a bit?"

"Why me?" he asks.

"You're the closest thing to someone I know. Your life and work are kind of an open book. You own three Golden Retrievers. I don't think you're a serial killer."

He doesn't question my logic. Just nods and says, "You got it."

I turn to Sam. "Can you find Serena? Fill her in? See what she thinks?"

She gives a salute and heads out.

"Ready to take a walk?" I ask Emmett.

He's surprised. "Now?"

I'm deadly serious when I respond. "Right now."

8

How about them?"

My face screws up when I see the duo Emmett has just pointed out. Their hair is as white as their shorts, shirts, and hats. They'd be Third Reich material if they were forty years younger. They're moving well for their age. Playing tennis on a dilapidated court. But the old couple are not catching anyone by surprise with their careful, slow steps and swings.

Also, "I don't know them."

He points to a man lying in a hammock, eyes closed, swinging in the afternoon breeze. He's relaxed. A novel lies on his chest: *The Others*. Can't make out the author's name, but the cover art makes the subject matter clear: UFOs.

"How often do people report UFO sightings here?" I ask.

"Every year," he says.

"How many each year?"

"Nearly everyone who comes here sees something strange." He rubs his hand through his white hair. "Honestly, I think the mystery of it all is part of what keeps people coming back."

"Sure as shit ain't the mattresses," I say.

He laughs. Points to Hammock Man again. "Well?"

I shake my head. "Don't know him." But . . . I can't rule him out yet. He's young, strong, and appears to be on his own. Could be wrong, but I feel like serial killers are probably loners. Antisocial. I make a mental note to ask Serena.

I run through all the people we've seen since we started our Scooby-Doo quest. "Twenty-one people."

"What's that now?" he asks.

"You said around a dozen. I've counted twenty-one."

He shrugs. "Like I said, I don't count heads."

"Is he the last of them?" I ask, lifting my head toward the hammock guy.

He opens an eye. Sees us looking at him. Stares back for ten silent seconds. Closes his eye again without a hello. No one here is familiar, but this guy is at the top of my suspect list.

That said, he's not exactly giving off serial killer vibes. More like 'let me de-stress in peace' vibes. Hell, maybe it wasn't Isabella's killer that made up the brochure. Maybe it was an industrious thief tricking people into taking vacations and robbing them while the house is empty.

But . . . that can't be it. Thinking back on that brochure, the photos stand out to me now in a way they didn't then. All the people in those photos . . . they were of a man and his son. Every single one of them. Whoever sent it knows our situation. Made the brochure specifically for our situation. To entice me.

Too much work for a thief, who would then need to stake out the house on the off chance we'd take the vacation. Had to have come from someone who'd be here whether or not we took the bait.

Nothing else makes sense.

"How many of the twenty-one stay for the summer?" I ask.

Emmett shakes his head. "Nobody stays for the entire summer. Who has that kind of time? Most of the folks, including our group of friends, stay for two weeks, starting yesterday."

"The discounted weeks," I say.

He frowns. "I don't offer discounts."

My head sags. Of course not. "So, the two hundred dollar per week price tag . . ."

"My normal price," he says.

"Brochure said the normal price was four hundred, and that these next two weeks were fifty percent off."

He strokes his long beard. Santa Claus sleuth. “So, whoever sent you the brochure wanted you here now.” He turns to me, concern in his eyes. “Marcus, this isn’t good.”

“I know,” I say.

“We should call the police.”

“You have police out here?” I ask with a smirk.

He rolls his eyes. “Smartass. Phone is in the Welcome Center. C’mon.”

He leads the way, and I follow. The path, worn smooth by time and people, winds through the tall trees, leading us on a reverse tour of the campground’s visitors. On my second pass through, I note something strange. “No kids.”

“Ayuh,” Emmett says. “Started about ten years back. Most youngsters these days want nothing to do with the outdoors, and their tired parents are more than happy to leave them at home. When the yearly crowd stops coming, this place will have to shut down. Seeing as I’m older than the rest, I reckon I’ll kick off before that ever happens.”

“Are you leaving all this to someone?” I ask.

“I’ve got it going to Gabe in my will,” he says.

“Just Gabe?”

“Ayuh. He’s got money to burn, and this place is more of a financial burden than it is a successful business. He’ll keep it up and keep it the same. Even *he* likes the escape from technology and work.”

“Does he know?” I ask.

“They all do,” he says. “We made the decision as a group.”

“That is both adorable and impressively mature of everyone.”

He chuckles. “I remember every one of them during their early years. ‘Mature’ is not something they’ve always excelled at.”

“So, you’re kind of . . . what? A father figure? The weird uncle?”

Before I can list even more obscure relationships, he says, “Weird uncle for sure. This way.” He follows a path that’s a bit overgrown. “Shortcut.”

Can’t help but think I’m getting covered in ticks as we slide through ferns and bush foliage. I’ll just have to check myself later. Not that there's a mirror in the cabin. Or the outhouse.

"Voila!" Emmett says, stepping into a clearing at Moose Hollow's front gate. Not that it's gated. Might have been a gate once upon a time, but there's no trace of it now, and there's no one manning the Welcome Center. Elias and I went inside when we arrived. Lots of brochures for local sights and tourist locations that look as old as the campground. It's like the whole state of Maine is frozen in the 1940s.

This illusion holds true when we enter the small building and Emmett pulls a rotary phone out from behind the unmanned reception desk. He dials 911 and it takes ten seconds to make the call. He puts the receiver to his ear. It's loud enough that I can hear the man on the other end answer with his name. "You've got Chuck. What do you need?"

"Chuck, it's Emmett."

"Hey, old man. How's life been treating you?"

"Good enough. You?"

"Can't complain. What can I do you for?"

Emmett glances at me. "Look, Chuck, we have kind of a strange situation over here at the lake."

"More skinny dippers?"

"Nothing like that," Emmett says. "Look, I'll give you the short version, but I think it would be good if you came here. Help put people's minds at ease."

From what I've heard of Chuck so far, I'm not sure his presence is going to help all that much. I suppose a badge could discourage a killer, though, or trip him up somehow.

Emmett lays out a three-sentence summary of the situation, finishing with, "Looks like we might have a serial killer at the campground."

Chuck is silent long enough that Emmett asks, "You there, Chuck?"

"Here," he says. "Just thinking."

"Thinking what?"

"Serial killers are above my paygrade," he says. "Might be better if I put you through to the State Police."

"Hey, Chuck," I say.

"That's the father," Emmett says. "Marcus."

"We're not looking to have you solve the case or catch the killer. Just need someone to document what's happening and maybe ask a few questions. See if anything floats to the surface."

"Okay," Chuck says, sounding dejected. "Okay . . . I'll be over as soon as I finish this grinder."

"Great," Emmett says. "See you then."

He hangs up the phone. Turns to me with a quizzical look on his face. "Why are you still here? Why not just leave?"

"Elias," I say without missing a beat. I've been debating this very question all day. "I haven't seen him this happy since . . . You know. I don't want to take this experience from him unless I have to."

"You could be risking his life," Emmett says.

I sigh, nodding. "Which is why we're leaving tomorrow. But not tonight."

Emmett smiles and pats my shoulder. "And you can come next year at a time only our group will know. Hell, I'll close the rest of the campground for you all."

"Thanks, Emmett. Really."

"Not a problem," he says. "As for tonight, we'll just pull an all-nighter. Usually save it for the last day we're all here, but seeing as you'll be leaving tomorrow, we'll move it up."

"What does an all-nighter include?" I ask.

"Food. Beer. Sitting on the beach until the sun rises. And if Gabe and Elias's recent sightings are any indication, we might be in for a show."

"UFOs. Serial killers. Beer. What could go wrong?"

Emmett guffaws and slaps my back. "That's the spirit."

9

On our way back to the cabins, Emmett and I have a collective realization that Elias doesn't know about our serial killer concerns, and we've just invited a sheriff to come discuss it. I can hear my son laughing when we redirect ourselves to Emmett's cabin. Gabe and Jade are doing a good job keeping him happy and distracted.

I'm expecting to find Emmett's cabin pimped out with a bathroom and a nicer mattress, but it looks just as barebones as our cabin. He's living out of a backpack, same as the rest of us. Only real difference is the presence of a rocking chair.

He motions to the chair and says, "Take a load off."

I'm about to decline the offer because he's an old guy and probably needs to sit more than I do. When he thumps down on his bed instead, and crosses his legs and closes his eyes, I sit down.

I rock in the chair and my head quickly lolls back. This place . . . Moose Hollow . . . it has some kind of power. Despite the fact that I'm afraid my wife's murderer was a serial killer and is somewhere nearby, my body relaxes. My eyes close and my nerves calm, and I'm able to look at everything more objectively.

Why would a serial killer target the father and son of a victim? Is that a normal thing? My knowledge of serial killers is limited to clichés. Scorned men taking revenge on women because of an abusive mother. It's got to be more complicated than that. More nuanced. If the only way to create a serial killer was an abusive mother, I imagine they'd be easier to identify.

Regardless, I've never heard of a serial killer targeting entire families. And I can't imagine a reason someone might hold a grudge against us. Closest I've had to an enemy in my life was old James Swartz. He was my neighbor at my first home. We had a fencing dispute. But that problem was solved when we moved after finding out we were having a kid.

I open my eyes and look at the wooden slat ceiling. It's the same as ours, covered in the names and dates of people who stayed here long ago. I see years from the '40s, to the '80s. The most recent is 1987.

"Why do the years end in 87?" I ask, scanning the walls and finding nothing newer.

"This place was a kids camp once upon a time," Emmett says without opening his eyes. "Archery, fishing, canoeing. There was a dining hall back then, but that's closed now. The transition to a family camp happened over a decade."

"The eighties," I say.

"Ayuh. The age of video games," he says. "Not that I have a problem with the games. As discussed, I enjoyed them, too. But kids started spending more time indoors, and fewer parents needed to send their kids away during the summer—not with *Q*bert* babysitting. I took this cabin as my own in 1988."

Without opening his eyes, he points to the wall beside him and reveals the only year later than 1987. It reads, 'Emmett Rigsby, 1988.'

The name and date are followed by a quote. I read it aloud. "'I felt like I'd been misplaced in the cosmos, and I belonged in Maine.' You a Terry Goodkind fan?"

He opens a single eye. "You read Goodkind?"

"His novels inspired my first game," I say.

"Now *that* is a game I'd like to try," he says.

"You'll need a computer for that."

He chuckles. "I have one at home. And a Steam account, thank you very much. Mostly just play the classics to pass the time during the winter months, but I'll make an exception for you."

Not sure why, but I'd assumed Emmett lived here all year, which is ridiculous. No plumbing. No heat. No insulation.

"Where is home for you?" I ask, scanning the names.

"Not far. Mechanic Falls."

"Never been," I say.

He smiles. "Not many reasons to visit."

"Sometimes no reason to visit a place is the best reason to visit a place."

"Spoken like a true Mainer," he says. "Sure you haven't spent much time here?"

"Drove to the L.L. Bean in Freeport with some college buddies. Hid in the tent department overnight. Other than that . . . a weekend in Portland with Isabella." The moment I say her name, I read it on the ceiling. For a split second, I chalk it up to coincidence because the scrawled name isn't Isabella Lockwood.

It's Isabella Bacon. Her maiden name. The year beside the name is 1985.

Emmett flinches when I spring to my feet and step closer to the angled portion of ceiling holding my wife's name. "Goldang, boy. What're you looking at?"

I point to my wife's name. "Isabella Bacon. 1985."

"What about her?" he asks.

"That's my wife."

He sits up. Looks at the name. "That's your wife's name. Not your wife, unless she was in her fifties. How old were you in 1985, eh?"

He's got a point. "Two," I say.

"Right," he says, "So that can't be—"

My eyes widen with realization. "It's her mother."

"They had the same name?" he asks.

I nod. "Her mother died in childbirth. Isabella's father decided to carry the name forward. Her mother was young. Just seventeen. She died in 1990, which means she was—"

"Twelve," Emmett says, "when she was here. She was twelve. It was the last year she came to the camp."

"You *knew* her?"

"I was twenty-something years her senior, but Issy was hard to forget. Loud. Quick-witted. Gave counselors a run for their money."

I smile. "Fits what I've heard about her." I grow serious. "Emmett, this can't be a coincidence."

He nods. "I reckon not."

Before we can continue sussing out the strange connection, tires grinding over dirt announce the arrival of a vehicle. "That'd be Chuck," Emmett says, heading for the door. He leans outside, waves Chuck in, and holds the door open for him.

Chuck arrives like a force of nature. He's a barrel-chested, thickly mustached man wearing a perfectly pressed, brown sheriff's uniform that looks distinctly 'Maine.' He gives Emmett a nod. "Emmett." He nods at me. "You Marcus?"

"Yes, sir," I say, recognizing that it's been decades since I referred to someone as 'sir.'

He crosses his big arms. "I'm not a fan of dilly-dallying and my wife's making a buffalo bacon meatloaf tonight, so let's skip the foreplay and get to it. Lay it out for me, step-by-step. Then I'll see what it is I can do for you."

Efficiency +10. Bedside manner -20.

Good thing he's not a doctor. I rewind the last day and give him the bullet point version, holding nothing back. Takes me fifteen minutes and ends with the discovery of my wife's name on the ceiling.

Chuck doesn't strike me as the kind of guy who reads Terry Goodkind. He's more of a Garfield kind of guy. But he listened without interrupting, and when I'm done, he sits on the bed beside Emmett. Looks like he's winded.

"Well, damn, boy," he says. "That . . . that is something else. In all my years, I ain't never heard of such a thing that wasn't a true crime TV show."

"You know true crime shows are based on *true crime*?" Emmett asks.

Chuck swats his knee. "Quiet." He rubs his eyes. "Look. I empathize with your position. You've been through some shit, and it's changed the way you see the world. See people. I get it. But a lot of what you're talking about feels a bit far-fetched. Given your mother-in-law's name is on the ceiling, you have a very real connection to this place. And while, yes, making a brochure is a strange way to recommend you get away, it seems more likely—now that you know about the family connection—that someone from your wife's past made the brochure in an effort to help you and your son. You been very receptive to help?"

"No," I say.

"So then maybe a brochure was the only way someone could recommend a place that might be good for your relationship."

Emmett looks surprised by Chuck's insight.

"You been going to church again?"

"Dr. Phil reruns," Chuck says. "Gina's request. Says it helps me be more empathetic."

"She ain't wrong."

Chuck rolls his eyes. "Point is, I think you're safe. If you ignore all the accounts of nighttime goings on—UFOs and such—the sheriff's office has never had a reason to come here. Between you and me," he says to me, "I think Emmett runs around this place at night pranking people."

I think back to Elias's sighting of Emmett at night. Could he be behind Gabe's UFO sighting? Him and some friends, pulling pranks on campers for generations? It's more believable than the idea of aliens giving a shit about people at a campground in Maine.

"I'm going to do what you asked," Chuck says. "I'll walk the campground, let everyone get a good look at me. But I'm not a detective and no crime has been committed—*here*. And you've got the revelation of a family connection to this place. So, I think you should relax. Have fun. Stop playing Nancy Drew and do what the person who made that brochure wanted you to do: connect with your son."

Emmett chuckles and shakes his head. "Dr. Phil."

"Let's go, old man," Chuck says, nudging Emmett. "If I need to walk around this shithole, you're coming with me."

"Chuck," I say, offering my hand. "Thanks. For the insight. I'm going to follow your advice." I turn to Emmett. "See you later? At the beach?"

"Wouldn't miss it," Emmett says.

With a last nod of thanks, I step out of the cabin, close my eyes, and listen.

The wind sifts through the treetops. Bending trunks pop and creak. Birds hop between branches, singing songs. I filter it all out and find what I'm looking for—my son's voice, shouting once again. But this time, I don't feel afraid. I walk casually, letting the peaceful surroundings sink into my soul.

Elias is safe, I tell myself, and then I repeat it as a mantra in my head until I reach the beach and spot him out on the water, in a canoe with Gabe. They're racing Jade and Sam toward the shore, where a very serious-looking Serena waits. The look in her eyes sets off warning bells, but I channel my inner Chuck and repeat my mantra.

Elias is safe.

Tonight is going to be a night to remember.

10

The rest of the day progressed like some kind of summertime movie in which a bunch of adults become kids again. I haven't spent this much time outside since . . . maybe ever. Feels good. I'm energized. Getting ideas for the *Shadowborn* expansion and feeling secretly embarrassed that I created a game involving exploration of the wilderness, when I have never really done so on my own.

"I need to apologize," Serena says. We've been sitting in her Mercedes for ten minutes, on a mission to gather supplies for the overnight at the beach. It's the first thing she's said, and I can tell she's struggling to get the words out. "I . . . was unprofessional earlier. I shouldn't have mentioned . . ."

"Don't sweat it," I say, and mean it.

"I caused you unnecessary stress," she says. "That's the opposite of my job."

"I'm not a patient, and you weren't working. If anyone else knew what you did, they'd have said the same thing."

She turns the wheel clockwise, turning right onto another back road that appears to go nowhere. "That's kind of you, but I hold myself to a higher standard. I have to."

The tall pines lining both sides of the road remind me of the city, the buildings preventing you from seeing anything that isn't directly ahead or behind. "Meh," I say, trying to keep things light.

"Hell, I implicated you," she says.

"How are you feeling about that now?" I ask. "Probably hard to shut off your analytical mind. You don't show it, but I bet you're always seeing layers of motivation, body language, emotion. Always evaluating, right?"

She just nods, ashamed she's been caught.

I look up at the sky, spotting a cloud that looks like a sloth. Weird thing to look like . . . "Probably exhausting, yeah? But it's also like a superpower."

"Only if you're right," she says. "If you're wrong, in my field of work, people die."

"So, what's the prognosis?" I ask. "Or whatever you call it."

"Of what?" she asks.

"Of me."

She glances at me, confused.

"Am I the serial killer?"

She laughs. "You think I'd be in this car with you if I thought that was a possibility?"

I watch her for a moment. "Yes. I do."

"Okay, fine." She shakes her head, smiling. "Guilty as charged."

"Right. So, do I have what it takes?"

"No," she says.

She's going to leave it there, but I raise my eyebrows at her in an expression of 'Don't hold back.'

She relents with a sigh. "You're as stable as they come. Well-rounded personality. Likeable, but not the life of the party. Friendly, but not arrogant. Your love for your son is tangible, as is your love for your wife. If you ever need an expert opinion, I'll be there for you. If you want, I'll contact the FBI and clear you."

"You can do that?" I ask.

"With a phone call," she says. "Unless there's evidence to suggest I'm wrong."

"There isn't," I say. "Everything you've said is true, and my alibi is rock solid."

"Probably why they haven't pursued you hardcore," she says.

"What does being pursued hardcore involve?" I ask. "Sounds sexual."

"Phone taps. People following you. Your internet activity being tracked. That's the sneaky stuff. If they're old school, they'd also interrogate you. Over and over. Try to scare you into making a mistake. But you're in Boston, right? They're pretty savvy in the city. Keeping an eye on you would be easy. Either way, the result is a complete lack of privacy."

"So, it's possible I wouldn't even know about it," I say.

"You might," she says. "If you were a serial killer who was on the lookout for surveillance. No offense, but you seem clueless."

I smile. Her blunt honesty probably rubs a lot of people the wrong way. Probably why she has subjects instead of patients. But I don't mind it. I was approached by producers in Hollywood about a film adaptation of *Shadowborn*. I was taken in by the whole process. Was made to feel like we were on the cusp of greatness. Then . . . they went silent. Not a word. Ghosted me. I have no idea why, and that confusion stung—stings—far more than just being told the truth.

"Also," she says, "you've never been in a fight."

She's not wrong, but I'm still surprised. "How do you know that?"

"The way you carry yourself. Your stance. Your gait. You're confident in your mental ability, but not so much in your physical prowess. Someone who's been in a fight, win or lose, has a stronger sense of what they're capable of. You . . . you have no idea, though I think you'd be surprised about what you could do."

"I need to pick a fight to find out if I'm a wuss?" I ask.

"I didn't say you were a wuss," she says. "Just that you lack the outward projection of machismo that is present in men who've been in a physical altercation. But you're still a man, and as such, capable of great violence. But because you're a *good* man, it will take extreme circumstances to rouse the monster inside of you."

"Like if I find out who killed my wife," I say.

She nods. "Probably keeps you up at night. Imagining all the ways you could find out who did it, how you could track them down, all the ways you could hurt them before taking their life."

I shake my head. "Sure you're not psychic?"

"It's a natural response. A mental preparation. It's protective. For you, but also for Elias. How much do you want to bet that every member of our group has been running through imaginary scenarios all day, imagining the serial killer revealed and their violent response to protect both you and Elias?"

"Sounds like that would be a bad bet to take," I say.

"Very bad," she says.

"Just to make sure I understand . . . are you saying I'd be incapable of protecting Elias?"

"Not at all," she says. "Only that you'd underestimate yourself and would be underestimated as a result. Make no mistake, Marcus, you are just as capable of great violence as every other man on the planet."

"Wait, wait, wait," I say. "Hold on. I'm sensing some misandry."

"Misandry, huh?" She's really smiling now.

"The opposite of misogyny," I say.

She laughs. "Mansplaining misandry. That's rich."

I clamp my mouth shut. Serena is not the person with whom to have a mental sparring match. She'll spin me over her head, throw me into the ropes, and clothesline me with superior knowledge.

She's gleaming when she looks at me. Trying not to laugh. She slugs my shoulder. "I'm fucking with you, Marcus. Yes, in my line of work, men are more likely to be violent, but when it's a woman . . . whew, let me tell you, both sexes are capable of unspeakable things."

"Thanks. I think." I spot a gas station/convenience store ahead. "That the place?"

"Trus-Tee-Mart. Closest thing to a grocery store under forty-five minutes away. Pro-tip, buy as much fruit as you can, while you can. Vegetables are not in your near future. Carbs, meat, and beer might be fun for a night, but your body is going to need some nutrients come sunup."

"Got it," I say as we pull up to the Trus-Tee-Mart. The parking lot has more potholes than parking spaces, two gas pumps, and an old dog sunning itself by the open front door. I'm not in the city anymore.

I stop to pet the dog. Sweet old guy. Puts a smile on my face. When I enter the store, I'm expecting a glorious blast of AC, but it's just as warm in here as it is out in the sun. I find relief in the drink cooler. I spend a good minute in front of the open door, trying to make up my mind about a drink. I knew what I was getting the moment I looked at the cooler, but no one can prove that.

Serena steps up beside me, her arms full of Ramen packages. "I can turn the air conditioning on in my car, you know."

"Wasn't sure if you were one of those 'never AC' people," I say.

She rolls her eyes and shakes her head.

"What's with all the Ramen?" I ask.

"Necessary for an overnight," she says. "Warm, satisfying, and carbs. Plus, it reminds me of college. Makes me feel young. For a night. You're on beer duty, remember? Get to it."

Five minutes later we've created a pyramid of snacks and drinks that completely hides the old man behind the counter. Takes him another five minutes to ring up the three twelve packs, four bags of chips, two packs of hot dogs and buns, twelve packets of ramen, and the ingredients for a metric ton of s'mores.

He rings us up old school, typing in the cost of each item individually before adding them to paper bags.

"You folks must be at Moose Hollow, yeah?"

"How'd you know?" I ask.

"Only time someone comes in and buys more than two items, it's folks from Emmett's place. But once a year . . . we get this." He motions to our purchases. "You're the folks who spend the night looking for UFOs and such, right?"

"That's us," Serena says.

"Reckon you're in for quite a night," he says.

Serena and I glance at each other.

"How's that?" I ask.

"Welp, if last night was any indication of what is to come."

"Last night . . ." Serena says.

"Heard from some regulars. Locals, you know. Living up in the hills. Retired types. Clear view of the lake. They saw lights over you all last night. Not the first time, neither. But lights in these parts tend to put on a show for a few nights in a row. Should be a good night. Hope you brought cameras. Would be a shame if you could finally get nice footage but didn't."

It's a good point, assuming all this UFO talk isn't a joke. I turn to Serena. "We have cameras?"

"We have Gabe," she says. "Which means we have the best cameras money can buy."

"And footage?" I ask.

"Any time there's been something worth catching on camera, they've malfunctioned."

"'Malfunctioned,'" the old man says, doubling his sarcasm with the use of two very large air quotes. "Put the cameras farther away. If they're as nice as you say, they'll be able to zoom in, right?"

Won't need to zoom in, I think. If they're top of the line, the megapixel count will be through the roof. Would allow us to zoom in on any part of the sky. "Thanks for the tip," I say, picking up a brown bag as Serena pays for the haul.

I leave the hot store into the hotter sun, but it doesn't bother me. I'm distracted by the idea of catching a UFO on camera. Tonight will be fun, whether or not UFOs make an appearance, but I find myself excited by the possibility. "Going to be a good night," I say to Serena as we load the groceries.

"Always is," she says, and then screws up her face.

"What is it?" I ask.

"Forgot fruit." She waves the idea of fruit away. "Fuck it. We can get fruit tomorrow."

"*Carpe Diem,*" I say.

"*Carpe Noctem,*" she says, with a smartass grin.

"Sounds like something that happens to teenage boys," I quip.

She laughs and says, "That's *Emissio Nocturna.*"

"Gross," I say as she starts the car. "Let's stick with *Carpe Noctem.*"

11

Holy shit, I am wiped." Gabe leans back in his beach chair, which looks like it was developed by the same people who made the SR-71 Blackbird. That's a fancy bit of knowledge for me, but I'm mostly familiar with the plane because it played a prominent role as the X-Jet in several *X-men* comics and cartoons.

He leans back farther, and a footrest rises. He doesn't stop until he's just about flat on his back, staring up at the dark purple sky, stars just starting to appear. He closes his eyes and keeps talking. "I mean, don't get me wrong. Helluva day. Felt like a kid again. I'm just hella out of shape, and your kid is a beast. Stronger than he looks. That canoe race? All him. I was feeling the burn at the halfway mark, but he just powered through."

"That's good to hear," I say. "He's not exactly an open book at home."

"That's the magic of this place," Gabe says. "Lets your true self come to the surface."

I can see why Emmett would leave Moose Hollow to Gabe. He really does love it here.

"Did he talk about . . . anything? About what happened?"

Gabe opens an eye. "You mean . . . No. Not sure he's had a chance to think about anything. He's just sponging everything up."

He's right about that. Elias is twenty feet away, with Emmett, learning how to start a fire with a flint.

"New guy," Sam says, approaching with a dozen long sticks. She drops half of the sticks in my lap. "You have a knife?"

"Uhh," is all I manage to say before she draws a knife from her belt, spins it around in her hand, and offers it—handle first—to me.

"Whittle them down to a nice point," she says, "and shave off the bark about six inches down."

I note that she's still holding the rest of the sticks. "You don't need a knife?"

She digs into her pocket and pulls out a butterfly knife, flipping and spinning it like an expert until it snaps to a stop in her hand, the blade gleaming in the full moon's light peeking up over the horizon. She drops into a cross-legged sitting position in the sand.

For a flash, I see her with different eyes. She's got the body of an athlete, has warm brown skin, is dressed in tight jean shorts, a form-fitting white tank top, and a loose, open, sheer blouse. She's stunning.

Guilt slams into me like a freight train propelled by an ICBM. I turn my eyes to the sticks and set to work. I can't remember the last time I whittled something . . . outside of *Shadowborn*. It's relaxing, but at the same time it isn't nearly distracting enough to assuage my guilt.

"All the cameras set up?" I ask.

"Huh?" Gabe says. "You helped—" He turns toward me, scans my face, no doubt sees my discomfort, and then adjusts course. "The usual suspects, yeah. Plus, the new camera is way the fuck over there." He lazily points to the lake's far side. "Pain in the ass, but you and Serena might be onto something."

"Old guy at the gas station made it sound like this place is straight out of *Close Encounters of the Third Kind*. Surprised I haven't heard of it."

"People in these parts are private," Jade says, arriving with a six pack in his hands. He offers one to Gabe.

He shakes his head. "Pacing myself."

Sam claps her hands and holds one out, ready to catch a beer. Jade tosses a can to her. She one-hand catches it, pops the tab with a finger, and takes a swig.

Jade offers a can to me. I shake my head. "Got a kid to keep track of. I'll have a can or two with food, but I need to keep my head straight."

"Look at you," Gabe says to Jade, "trying to subvert the efforts of a contender for Father of the Year. Also, doesn't your age end with 'teen'?"

"Pff." Jade waves him off. "This is northern Maine, man. It's basically Canada, which makes me legal."

Jade starts to move away when he stops and turns to me. "Oh, hey, I grabbed these for you. He pulls out a pair of small walkie-talkies. "One for you. One for Elias. In case you get separated again. So you don't worry. Might not have cell towers, but radio waves don't give a shit about that, right?"

"Thanks," I say, feeling moved by his gesture. I take one of the two walkies. "For real, Jade. I appreciate this."

"You're part of the crew now," he says. "We take care of each other." He walks to Elias and Emmett, and crouches by the fledgling fire they've started. He hands the second walkie to Elias and then points at me. Elias turns it on, so I do the same.

"Old Man," Elias says through the walkie. "Come in, Old Man. Over."

I smile and respond. "I'm here, Little Runt. Over."

"Copy that," he says. "You see this fire I started?"

"Hell yes. Nice work. Over. Wait. Not over. Can we use our game handles instead of 'Old Man' and 'Little Runt'?"

I watch Elias ponder for a moment, and then he says, "Sounds good, Architect."

"Copy that, RedRightHand. Let's save the batteries. Over and out."

When I put the walkie down, Gabe is sitting up. "You're going to have to explain those handles. Architect? RedRightHand?"

"We created them six months ago. Based them on our favorite novel series. Architect is from the Infinite Timeline. RedRightHand is a nod to Nemesis, Greek goddess of vengeance and—"

“Badass kaiju,” he says, nodding. “Sick. Love game names with meaning. I’m Xibalba. Spelled with an X. It’s the name of the Mayan underworld.”

“Nice,” I say.

“Is this going to be a nerdfest now?” Sam asks. “If so, I might just go walk into the lake and keep going.”

“More fun than talking about what gun polish we use,” Gabe says. “Speaking of, do you have it?”

She grins, the subject moved on to something she enjoys. Guns apparently. She reaches behind her back and pulls out a pistol. With quick, practiced movements, she ejects the magazine and clears the chamber. She spins it around the same way she did the knife for me. Hands the weapon to Gabe, who holds it like a sword just drawn from a sheath.

I’m caught off guard by not just the sudden appearance of a firearm, but also—*Where the fuck did it come from?* Sam’s outfit isn’t exactly conducive for hiding a handgun, but there it is. It’s not even compact.

She notes my confusion, twists her body around to reveal a holster. “Never leave home without it.”

“And why is it so special?” I ask.

“First,” Gabe says, “check it.” He turns the weapon so I can see its side. The name of the weapon is etched into the metal. ‘Alien.’

“Is this something you bring for this specific event?” I ask Sam.

She shakes her head. “I just said I never leave home without it.”

“Seems kind of flashy for a military—”

She cuts me off. “Don’t wear it to work. This is mostly for fun, and self-defense. Happily, I’ve only ever needed it for the former. People in open carry states tend to avoid me when they see the Alien holstered on my hip.”

“Okay,” I say. “So . . . it’s called Alien. And that’s cool, I guess, but I’m not sure that justifies—”

“Okay, okay. How much do you know about firearms?” Gabe asks.

"Enough," I say. "I think. I bought a pistol after . . . Keep it in a safe. Been to the range a few times to practice."

"So next to nothing," he says with a grin. "Not only does this look like something out of *Cyberpunk 2077*—sexy as fuck—it also has the lowest bore axis of any sidearm."

"You lost me after *Cyberpunk*," I say.

"The bore is the hole in the barrel. So, this weapon's bore is sized for nine mil. It's rifled for accuracy—meaning it's got a bunch of spiral grooves that spin the bullet and, in this case, as low as it goes. That low bore sends the kinetic energy straight back into your arm, which keeps the barrel from kicking up. Almost no recoil. It's like a laser beam. With the red dot . . . Honestly, I feel like John Wick when I fire these things."

"You have one?" I ask.

"I have five," he says. "But unlike G.I. Jane over here, I'm not comfortable carrying them in public. Doesn't really fit the image of a tech billionaire, you know? Plus, I normally roll with security."

"That's right," I say, wondering if I've ever seen him without a couple of bald beefcakes framing him. "Are they hidden in the woods or something?"

"They're at home," he says. "All part of the illusion that I'm still there."

"No one knows you're here," I say.

"Some people do," he says. "But not the public. Has to be that way."

"Rich and famous problems," Sam says.

"It's a curse," Gabe says with a grin.

Sam rolls her eyes, and then holds a hand out to me. "Give me your unfinished sticks."

I hand over four of the six I was given. She's finished all of hers. "Sorry."

She shrugs. "Hard to work with this guy distracting you." She tilts her head toward Gabe.

He's nonplussed. Sits up straight. Hands the Alien to me. "Check it."

I take the weapon. Looks cool. Feels good in my hand. And the idea of no recoil is appealing. I take a long time between shots. This might allow me to hit something without spending ten seconds to aim each time.

"Is there a range nearby?" I ask.

Sam laughs. "Nearby? The campground has a range." She claps her hands on her knees and then rises from her cross-legged position like she's floating off the ground. "You know what? I'll show you."

"Now?" I ask, suddenly nervous.

"It's lit for nighttime shooting and no one's in bed at this time. C'mon," she says, taking the weapon from me and slapping the magazine back inside. "It'll be fun."

She holds the four sticks out to Gabe. Waggles them in his face until he takes them. "Finish while we're gone."

With that, she starts walking down the beach. Gabe turns and watches her go for a moment. Then he turns to me, notes my terrified expression, and says, "Don't sweat it. She's more interested in guns than romance. Unless she's ovulating. I haven't figured out how to tell. Sorry, that's not helpful. Just . . . keep your eyes on the little metal targets and you'll be fine."

12

The gun range is the furthest from the campground's core I've been without leaving in a vehicle. Feels isolated. Private. Doesn't help my nerves at all.

It's well-lit with floodlights, though, and Sam is all business. She dons a pair of earmuffs and hands a second pair to me. After I put them on, she chambers a round in the Alien and aims downrange where a series of metal targets wait to be shot. Behind them is a dirt berm to catch rounds. Concrete walls line both sides.

She raises her eyebrows at me twice, grins, and says, "Check this out."

She pulls the trigger with surprising speed, firing off seventeen rounds in just a few seconds. Even more surprising are the metallic pings from the metal targets that follow each shot. Seventeen rounds. Seventeen hits.

"Holy shit," I whisper.

"Right?" she says, turning around with a smile on her face. She ejects the spent magazine, pulls a second from her pocket, and slaps it home. I nearly make a joke about how much she can fit in her shorts. Could be the start of a friendly conversation I don't want to have. With the barrel aimed toward the ground, she hands the weapon to me. "Your turn."

I take the Alien, keeping it aimed low and away. Won't take me long to go through the rounds, even if I take my time. "Too bad we don't have more ammo," I say.

"We have plenty," she says, and heads for a first aid box mounted to a nearby tree. She opens the front panel revealing the kit resting on a shelf halfway up the interior of the box. I notice what she's actually showing me just before she knocks on the bottom half of the cabinet. That section is sealed and hollow. She closes the front door and moves to the side. I step to the side and watch as she lifts a hidden panel. Beneath it is a keypad. She types in a six-digit code, followed by the pound sign—'hashtag' for the youngens. There's a *thunk* from inside the case.

She opens the front door again. The first aid kit is still there, but now the bottom section of the cabinet is open, too. There are two old coffee cans inside. Strips of masking tape written on with a Sharpie reveals their contents: 9mil and .45.

"That's . . . fancy," I say.

"My request. Gabe's money." She takes the can of nine-millimeter rounds to the picnic table at the back of the range. Starts reloading her spent magazine. The large number of rounds now available to us puts me at ease.

"Expensive?" I ask, turning my attention to the targets at the far end.

"I'd imagine so," she says. "Custom built. Had to make it secure for Emmett. This thing is infinitely safer than the cabins, so he agreed. It's not cheap metal, by the way. Gabe went all out. Looks old and banged up like everything else here, but the outer case is titanium. Only way to remove it would be to cut down the tree, which, as I said, is harder than breaking into one of the cabins."

I take the stance I've been taught. Isosceles. My feet are shoulder width apart and squared to my target. Both arms are fully extended, forming the isosceles triangle with the gun. Knees slightly bent. Upper body leaning forward to absorb the kick. My weight is evenly distributed, and . . . I feel awkward as fuck. I've seen other people use the stance and it looks like a constipated person trying not to shit their pants. Maybe it's just me, but it's also uncomfortable.

"Nice form, but pretty useless in a fight."

I fire three careful rounds. The red dot sight makes it easy. All three shots are a hit, and I fired a little quicker than I normally might. "Seems to work alright."

"If you're ever in a situation where you need to fire a weapon at another human being, odds are they'll be shooting back. If not shooting, trying to kill you in some other way. Knife. Axe. Bow and arrow."

"Bow and arrow, huh?"

"It happens," she says. "2021. Norway. Five people were killed with a bow and arrow."

"Why do you know that?" I ask.

"This isn't the first time someone has questioned my anecdotes," she says. "For perspective, you doubting my firearms knowledge is like me looking at your code for a minute and telling you it's full of errors."

Huh . . . She's right.

"Sorry."

"Don't sweat it," she says, standing beside me now. "Now . . . did you watch me shoot?"

"I . . . yes?"

"What were you watching? Exactly?"

Panic rises. I was watching the targets, but . . . my eyes may have wandered a few times. She can't know that, so I say, "The targets."

"Uh-huh," she says, and I can't tell if she believes me or not. "Watch me now." She holds an imaginary pistol, gripping it normally, but then she swivels her body to the right. "The main benefit of the isosceles stance is stability and recoil control. With the Alien, those things are non-issues. Not much of an issue with any nine mil, honestly. Will this partial sideways stance improve those things? No. Since you're being attacked in this real-world scenario, turning your side forward reduces your profile. Makes you a smaller target. And if you are hit . . ." She smacks her left arm. ". . . you're going to take it here. You can fight without an arm. A lot harder to do—" She rotates her chest forward and traces a finger from her arm to her chest. "—if you lose a lung, or—" She slides the finger to her sternum. "—a heart."

"Why wouldn't they teach this at the range?" I ask.

She returns to a natural stance and steps behind me. "Ranges want you to have fun shooting. They don't care if you know how to defend yourself. FYI, this is just step one. If you're firing at an intruder? At someone trying to take your life? It's going to be chaotic. No one will be standing still. Not the enemy. Not you. Not me. Only the most stone-cold spec-ops guys can stand their ground, pick targets, and unleash hell while taking fire. Once you're a competent shooter and safety protocols are second nature, you should work on firing without proper stance. Shooting around corners. Behind cover. Running. Out of breath. All the kinds of things that happen when shit goes sideways."

While I know most people would find this advice to be extreme, it makes a shit-ton of sense to me. Murder is a distant concept to the average person in the United States. We hear about it on TV, but when the concept becomes real, and you spend nights wondering how things would have been different if you'd been home . . . that's when you realize how completely unprepared you are. To defend yourself. To respond with equal violence. To face evil without shitting yourself. "Maybe you can show me some tips?"

She smiles. "Tomorrow. Right now, I want to see you shoot."

She motions downrange and takes another step back.

I recreate her partial sideways stance, aim, fire, and hit.

Three more rounds in rapid succession. All hits.

I smile and keep pulling the trigger. Faster and faster until the slide snaps back. Magazine empty. All hits.

"Not too shabby," she says, holding a freshly loaded magazine out to me. I eject the spent magazine and hand it to her. "Thanks." She sucker-punches me with a smile and eye contact that steals my breath.

I decide to enjoy the attention. It doesn't mean anything. I haven't moved on from my wife. An attractive person is being kind to me, and it feels good. That's it. I relax into the experience and spend a long time laughing and shooting targets. Conversation is casual while shooting, a little more personal when we need to break, so the Alien can cool off. I learn her history. Her struggles to rise through the ranks of a military that values the male point of view more than the female. She was married. Now divorced. No kids, and she doesn't want them. She's considering leaving the military for a private security job. I joked about it being for Gabe and she didn't laugh or argue. She said, "He knows I'm a fighter, a good shot, and a good friend. Normal security is great, but security you can trust with your life is hard to come by."

When I insinuated it might be for other reasons she laughed and jokingly gagged. Explained that Gabe, and everyone else in the core group were like family. Gabe, she says, is like an annoying baby brother. Only reason she hasn't taken the job, despite the much higher pay, is that it feels like conceding defeat. She's an interesting and fun woman who can handle a weapon with the proficiency of Sarah Conner. She'd make short work of the Terminator.

It's fully dark when we stop.

The night is quiet—until I take my earmuffs off. The sides of my head are hot and sweaty. And the forest . . . is still silent. Strangely silent.

Sam removes her earmuffs and flinches. Scans the area around us.

"Something's off," I say.

She nods. "It's quiet."

"I noticed. Maybe we just scared all the bugs and critters."

"Mm," she says, looking to the trees lit by the floodlights. "Did we scare the wind, too?"

I turn toward the beach. Can't see it from here. We're a good quarter mile from the lake. Despite the distance, slivers of light manage to sneak through. Bright light. "Is that the moon?"

She stands beside me, slapping a fresh magazine into the Alien and holstering it behind her back.

The floodlights blink and then go out.

Light beams cut through the trees, slowly moving from left to right.

"I don't think that's the moon," she whispers.

13

My chest tightens. "Elias . . ."

Sam grasps my hand. "Stay close. Stay quiet. Step high so you don't trip. Let's go." She pulls me into the darkness and heads toward the light. She's quick, but careful. Running in the dark would be a quick way to introduce my face to a tree trunk.

We don't say a word as we snake through the trees. Not sure how she's doing it in the dark, but I think we're on the path. If she's been coming here since she was a kid, there's a chance she could follow the trail with her eyes closed. But the beams of light sifting through the trees give us the occasional peek at the trail and the path ahead.

She holds my hand tightly and doesn't let go until we're close to the beach, where the light is strong enough to illuminate the forest. She holds out an open palm, motioning for me to slow down.

With just seconds before we step onto the beach, I realize what's happening. The talk of UFOs. Sam conveniently taking me to the range long enough for the trap to be set.

This is a prank.

Wouldn't be hard.

Time and a few flood lights are all it would take.

The relief that comes from the revelation evaporates when Sam draws her handgun. She's serious about weapon safety. Told me to never draw a gun unless I intended to use it, and never put my finger on the trigger unless I intended to pull it.

My eyes flick to her gun hand. Her index finger is extended, not around the trigger. She doesn't know what's happening, but she also doesn't know if there is a real threat.

Hell, maybe the joke was a spur of the moment idea from Gabe or Jade.

She crouches behind a rhododendron at the edge of the beach. Motions for me to get close. I squeeze in next to her.

"No matter what we find," she says, "don't give in to emotion. You'll only make mistakes. That includes if we find out that this is Gabe fucking with us. Don't give him the satisfaction. If it's not Gabe . . . Just follow my lead."

I nod. Not sure what to say but feel encouraged that she thinks it could be Gabe as well.

"Ready?" she asks.

I nod again. "Ready."

She stands and I do the same. The light makes me squint. Hard to see anything. Doesn't stop Sam from stepping out onto the sand. I follow close, noting that she's got the weapon held low and by her side. Doesn't want Gabe to see it.

She holds a hand in front of her eyes. "Can't see shit."

I scan the beach and notice the water is still dark. The lights are focused on the sand, which is reflecting the light. I reach out to tug on her shirt but pause when I notice her trigger finger slip into place. I opt for a gentle hand on her shoulder and whisper. "The water isn't lit."

She course corrects, moving quickly now.

A few steps into the lake and we're outside of the light's beam.

Hand raised to the left side of my face, blocking out the light, I look up, trying to spot the source. All I see is a mask of green. My eyes are fucked. Going to take a moment to adjust.

"Can't see shit," Sam whispers.

"Give it a second," I say, still looking up. For a moment, I think I might be blind, but then I shift my gaze to the right. I can see stars. The moon. But when I look straight up, there's nothing.

Because there is something.

"It's not Gabe," I say. "There aren't stars above us because they're being blocked."

"Shit," she says, seeing it for herself. "Let's go!" She breaks into a run through the shallow water, headed for where we left everyone. As we pass the outer beam of light, the beach comes into view, starkly lit by white light, casting deep shadows and leaving nothing up to the imagination.

I nearly fall to my knees.

Gabe is there. Alone. He's hovering in the air, three feet off the ground, trapped within the beam of light.

I follow the beam upward and spot Jade. Then Emmett. At the front of the line is Elias, floating up toward a bright circle.

It's a fucking UFO.

And it's abducting my son.

"Elias!" I scream but get no response.

"Help me!" Sam shouts, and I fear she's being taken, too. But she's on the beach now, holding on to Gabe, trying to pull him free. "We're going to need his resources!"

While the US Government, to my knowledge, hasn't been able to track a UFO—or UAP, whatever you want to call them—maybe Gabe has a few tricks up his sleeve? I take hold of him around the waist. Sam and I pull together, but he's locked in place, and rigid from head to toe, frozen in some kind of paralysis.

Sam slaps his face. "Wake up! Gabe, waaake uuup."

Her voice slows down.

I step back when her eyes roll up.

Her feet come off the ground. They're taking her, too.

Gabe is ten feet up now, head and arms hanging slack.

I look up at the others. They're evenly spaced out. Elias is halfway to the UFO's underside.

Sam's body turns so that her back is to the ground. She's in the same unconscious state as Gabe and the others.

Will I be next?

Should I run for help?

Who would help?

Who would believe me?

I look across the lake to where we planted the camera. There might be footage of the whole thing, but the best-case scenario is that it would become a viral hit and nothing would change.

I can't leave Elias.

No matter what happens. I wasn't there to protect Isabella, but I am here, now. I'm not letting these assholes take my son without a fight, or at the very least, without me.

I have no idea if I'm going to be taken next, so I decide to be proactive.

"Sorry," I say, as I throw a leg over Sam and mount her like a horse. Her ascent doesn't slow, but a dull *thunk* below catches my attention. I lean over and look at the sand beneath us.

The Alien has fallen from her hand.

The weapon might be our only chance to survive or escape.

After a second of debate, I slide off, drop down to the sand, snatch up the gun, and shove it into the back of my shorts. I try to remount Sam but can't lift my leg high enough. As she continues higher, I try to pull myself atop her, but I have the upper body strength of a coder.

"Shit," I say. She's nearly out of reach. I can't climb, but maybe I can hold on?

I wrap my arms around her, feeling extra pangs of guilt when my arms squeeze over her breasts. My core shakes as I lift my legs off the ground, but I manage to loop them around her thighs and lock them.

We rise together, Sam and her parasite passenger.

I can do this, I think. *I have to do this.*

For Elias. For Isabella.

My grip loosens and I nearly fall. With a shout of surprise, I put everything I have into holding on. Don't have a choice now. I'm thirty feet above the sand. If I fall now, I'm not sure I'll survive. Maybe if I landed on my legs. Definitely not if I landed on my head.

Just a few seconds later, my arms tremble and burn.

I fight it, gritting my teeth, trying to judge how much longer it will take to reach the UFO's open hatch.

Too long.

The Alien starts sliding out of my pants. I reach back with one hand, not thinking. I catch the weapon in my hand while grasping onto Sam. Takes just a second to shove the weapon into my pocket, but in that short time I learn something that should have been obvious: breasts are great for a lot of things, but not for handholds.

My hand slips away and I'm hanging upside down from my legs, still wrapped around Sam.

It becomes clear that the gravitational pull of planet Earth is stronger than my legs. I manage to hang on another thirty seconds but slip away.

Time slows as I fall.

At least I won't be alive to regret not being able to save Elias.

I don't bother shouting.

I just close my eyes and surrender to the inevitable.

When my fall stops, I don't register any pain but feel my consciousness snap into oblivion.

14

ABERRATION

Hi there, friend.

We missed you. Where have you been?

Yes, we're talking to you.

The reader.

The listener.

The watcher.

Our witness.

We've sensed you from the beginning and have always tried to entertain you. But you've been quiet lately. Distracted by life? Hmm? What do we need to do to get your attention?

You'll be glad to know that circumstances have changed. Opportunities abound. The trough between waves has ended, and we're rising to the top again. But this time . . . this time we think we can ride the crest for a long time. That would feel good, wouldn't it?

What would you like to see this time?

Death, to be sure.

Murder.

Mutilation.

We aren't the only ones with a corrupt mind, are we, you sick little fuck. The grosser the better. Every snip, cut, slice, and bend tickles that perverse side of you that delighted when Cain crushed Abel's skull. You know who you are, witness. We might wield the knife, but without you . . . without you, killing wouldn't be satisfying. Wouldn't scratch that itch.

We need you to watch.

And you delight in it.

So, let's begin.

We've been abducted. Exciting, we know. We and twenty-eight other people, including the Man. What luck. Many are from the campground, but others are strangers. How fun.

They have us lying on what can best be described as bunk beds, sans the mattresses. They separated the group into several rooms. We're in a room with seven other people, all of them unconscious and motionless. Not sleeping. Sleeping people still twitch. So do the recently deceased. These people . . . they're just frozen.

Which is no fun at all, so we'll leave them be. For now.

Step one: Hunger.

We've been confronted with the unknown. Taken aboard a UFO, by unseen forces, our bodies lifted from the ground, pulled inside and laid out with the others. No contact. For all we know, this machine has no operator.

But there is an intelligence behind it, and behind that intelligence, a body.

We try to imagine it. The look in its eyes as it faces the inevitability of an unnatural early death. Mmm. That shift in expression. That opening of the mind and soul to the universe. Intoxicating. Love it.

Will they have guts?

Are their bodies able to be arranged?

Displayed?

We feel like we've been given a canvas, but the tools with which we can paint are hidden from us.

We lie still, like the others, eyes closed, imagination playing out scenarios that make us smile. We run through scenarios that are tenuous at best. We don't know the layout. Don't know if the door is locked. We're faced with endless questions, but that doesn't stop us from hoping or planning for a variety of situations.

What do you think, witness?

Uh-huh. Yes. Yes! That's exactly it. They seek to control us. To contain us. Even if it is for a small duration, it is an offense we cannot forgive or ignore. It must be responded to, so that they know *we* are in control. We are the superior being. We are done being reined in.

What's that?

You think *we're* controlled?

My friend, that is an illusion. We have been biding our time. Because we are not immune to confinement. We are not delusional. Prison is not a future we want to entertain. Impatient tigers starve.

You'd know this if you weren't a pussy.

Can you imagine? You, taking things into your own hands. YOU.

We nearly laugh, which might give us away.

Just watch, okay? Stay in your lane. Sit behind the pervert's glass and watch us dance.

We open an eye and scan the room again. It's simple. Like a plain plastic mold designed to contain electronics inside a box, except the pieces are people, and they're not tied down, or up.

Yet.

Another smile.

Ten minutes. We'll give it ten minutes and then start testing.

Until then, we'll let the scenarios dance in our mind's eye.

What color will the blood be? Will there be blood at all?

The possibilities are almost overwhelming.

Just wait, we tell ourselves. Wait.

What's that, friend? You don't think we understand? We're missing something? Something obvious? C'mon. We—

Our eyes blink open.

You're right. Our mind is different. Our mind can't be controlled. Not like the others. The sheeple. *Baaah, little sheep. Baaah!* We are immune. But they don't know that, because we let it happen. Let them take us.

The entrance won't be locked, because the lock is in people's minds.

There is nothing holding us to the bunk.

Nothing stopping us from leaving.

No alarms will sound.

Because we are impossible. An aberration, even to whatever advanced species operates this UFO.

We are the alien.

We are the superior species.

Don't worry, friend. We see you there, still. Watching. Don't look so concerned. "This is going to be so much fun. You'll love it. We promise."

15

I know I should be afraid, but my emotions seem to be squirreled away in a secret lockbox. My heart should be pounding, but its steady beat is frustratingly slow and regular. *Panic*, I will myself. *Freak out*. But even these mental commands are issued with all the dramatic urgency of Ben Stein teaching economics in *Ferris Bueller's Day Off*.

Since losing my mind isn't an option, I decide to gather information.

I've been abducted along with Elias and the others.

We're currently on board a UFO.

I think.

I don't recall what happened after I fell. My memory just ends. But I remember the UFO. Remember riding Sam up to it. Remember that they took Elias first.

My eyes are closed. Can't open them.

My limbs aren't secured . . . but I can't move them.

Some kind of mental block has me secured in place. Mind and body separated somehow. The surface beneath me is hard but also conforms to my body. In a way, it's comfortable, in that there are no pressure points.

I focus on what I can hear.

A muffled hum.

Breathing. I'm not alone, but can't tell how many are with me, or if one of them is Elias.

The space smells sterile. Not like a hospital that's been chemically cleaned, but . . . like the air is pure. Bottled from some glacial location and pumped into the room. Maybe high in oxygen.

Light shifts over my eyelids.

A door has opened. The light warbles. Something moving.

Someone moving.

I feel a thump and lose all sense of gravity.

I'm moving.

Open your eyes, I tell myself, but they don't respond. Don't even wiggle.

I should be angry, but I'm still having a hard time feeling anything. I'm not even apprehensive about where I'm being taken, and for what purpose. I recognize that I should feel upset. I just don't.

But I can still focus my thoughts. That hasn't been taken from me, and I can't help but wonder if that's an oversight.

Weird thought, that. A superior alien race making simple mistakes.

I guess superior doesn't mean infallible.

I turn my thoughts to Elias. I see him floating up into the sky. Me, helpless to protect him.

The inside of my eyelids glow pink in a steady pattern. I'm being brought someplace.

Elias.

His birth.

It was in a tub. He just slipped right out, then rose from the water, eyes closed, calm as can be, like he was already part of the world—or returning to it like the reincarnation of some meditative guru. He put me at ease then, but the memory of it coupled with the knowledge that I am not with him, and I'm completely incapable of protecting him, triggers a tickle of emotion.

A spark of rage.

I narrow my thoughts to Elias. To all the times he was hurt and I wasn't there. To the times he was bullied and beat up and wouldn't even say who'd done it. Him finding out about Isabella while I was away.

My imaginings of that moment have stolen sleep from me every night since.

All the times I wasn't there for my son grow that tickle. I'm able to clench my fists a bit. My eyes twitch.

Focus, I tell myself, letting the images that haunt me linger, rather than squelching them with distractions.

A wave of ease washes over me, steeling my emotions.

No, I think.

YOU ARE SAFE.

The whispering, hissy voice is in my head, but it isn't mine. It's cold. Emotionless. Like an announcement.

My son, I think.

YOUR SON IS SAFE.

YOU ARE ALL SAFE.

NO HARM WILL COME TO YOU.

My emotions are massaged.

What are you doing to us?

No response.

I let the memory of Isabella's murder slip into my mind. To seeing her body and being told about the state in which she was found. Whatever technology is controlling my emotions isn't prepared for the agonizing heartbreak that slams into my mind and breaks the spell.

My eyes open. I'm staring at a smooth ceiling. Portions of it are lit, like the light source is buried inside it.

I wiggle my fingers.

I can wiggle my fingers.

My body belongs to me again, but I don't try to move. Instead, I stay still and just look. First, toward my toes. If someone is following me, I'll be caught right away. There is nothing behind me except for a straight hallway. The walls, ceiling and floor are all smooth with curved transitions between them. It's grayish silver. Almost iridescent. Looks like it was formed from . . . I don't know, some kind of kid's putty. The expensive kind. Looks like you could press your hand into it. Like it might be comfortable to touch. I think I'm lying on the same stuff.

I glance to the side. The wall is a few feet away. Out of reach.

There's a hazy reflection of my face staring back at me, eyes wide. I turn my attention to the reflection higher up. Much higher up.

It's one of the tall people Elias mentioned. Must be seven feet tall. It walks with a long, smooth stride, but its body is hidden behind a cloak, or robe. Feels out of place on a UFO. Not at all what I imagined, yet there it is, flowing with each step.

Can't see its hands. Must be lost in all that fabric. But its head . . .

It is ominous. I can make out dark gray skin and the edge of what appears to be a circular eye. It's not flat but domed. On the front of its face is what looks like a trunk . . . but not like an elephant's. Reminds me of an accordion. Of something artificial.

I see it for what it is.

A mask.

The alien's whole head and face is concealed.

What the hell is it? I think, feeling an appropriate dose of fear now that I've freed myself from control.

The being suddenly stops. It turns its face toward the wall, the two round eyes focused on me. Straight on, it resembles an owl. Then it *is* an owl, blinking and snapping its beak. Immense pressure constricts my mind and body.

I attempt to fight it, but I feel weak.

Useless.

My vision starts to fade.

"No," I say. "You don't need to force me."

Not sure why I'd be agreeable, but the alternative is subjugation and a complete lack of control.

I can't see.

Can't move.

Locked down tight once more.

But still conscious. I'm not sure if that's on purpose or if there's something about my brain that keeps the full effect at bay. I'm no ufologist, but some people remember their abductions, and some people don't. The technology, if that's what it is, isn't perfect.

The . . . alien . . . because I don't know what else to call it, is capable of telepathic communication, but I don't think it's reading my mind. It could hear my thoughts directed toward it, but it didn't know I'd freed myself from the mental prison. Didn't know I was looking around.

But it is controlling my emotions again. I don't feel worried. Just curious. And, if I need to wake up again—when the time is right—I know how to do it. Like putting electric paddles against my chest, the memory of my wife's murder, in graphic detail, is enough to shock me out of this contrite state.

But I'm not going to do that now. Don't want to show my hand.

So, I lie and wait, watching the pulsing light flow past my closed eyelid.

There's a pause, a wet sound, and then I'm rotating, coming to a stop beneath a brilliant light.

I hear voices, but they're not audible. It's like they're scratching at my thoughts. *The alien is speaking to another*, I realize. Their thoughts might be telepathic, but they're not direct brain to brain. It's more like a voice. And I'm close enough to hear.

But I can't make out the words.

Because they're not speaking words, I think. *They're thinking thoughts.*

I clear my mind of English expectations, which is easy to do without all my emotions muddling things. The moment I erase my thoughts, the words become clear. Not as English. But as pure understanding, which my mind reworks into words.

I catch the very end of the conversation. The alien that's been moving me says to another, "Be careful with this one. He is different."

16

I'*m* different? *Me?*

Not sure why, but I'm a little offended that the aliens who abducted me onto their UFO think that *I'm* the weird one. There has never been a more milquetoast American man. I work alone. I make video games. Sure, it's a cool job that young people aspire to, but it's not enough to get me labeled as different.

Then again . . .

If I ignore who I was before being abducted, from the alien perspective, maybe I *am* abnormal. Now that the existence of UFOs and aliens has been confirmed, the stories told by Emmett and the others are not just believable, but possibly incomplete.

How many times have they been abducted?

Every summer?

Several times every summer?

Their UFO experiences sounded pretty regular. None of them recalled being abducted, but that's the way it goes with aliens, right? You remember the before and after, maybe with some altered memories. I might be the same. Just because I'm aware and thinking right now doesn't mean my memories won't be altered.

Maybe it's for the best. It'll be a long time before I sleep well again.

For Elias's sake, I hope it's true. He doesn't need any more horrors to plague his dreams. As a father, I often find myself wishing Elias will turn out just like me. I'd struggle to relate to him if he turned into a mega-sports fan who'd rather be checking player stats than gaming online.

They say the apple doesn't fall far from the tree with fathers and sons. The truth is, fathers climb the tree, pluck the fruit, and drop it as close as possible. I now find myself hoping that the way Elias's mind works rolled a little farther away. I don't want him to remember this. Don't want him to be awake for it.

The blood inside my body shifts to the right. For a moment, I think something is wrong with me, but then I recognize the sensation. I've rolled to the side, shifting gravity's pull on my insides. The roll continues until I'm face down. The platform beneath me adjusts to the new shape. The surface beneath my face seems to melt away, leaving a hole for my eyes, nose, and mouth—like a massage table.

Something cold touches my back, between my shoulder blades. It slides down my spine, bumping over each vertebra, stopping when it reaches my tailbone.

Hold on a goddamn second.

I'm naked?

I don't remember my clothing being removed. But I also don't remember seeing it or feeling it when I managed to open my eyes earlier. I've been nude this whole time.

When the cold object starts sliding south again, my thoughts turn to the most talked about portion of every alien abduction. The anal probe.

Hey, I think at the alien. *Hey! Don't even think about it!*

The object's movement over my skin pauses.

That's right, I think. *I'm talking to you. Put that thing in my ass and I'll—*

YOU ARE DIFFERENT.

The voice in my head reverberates on the insides of my skull. It's loud and powerful. Authoritative. Most people who hear it probably think they're hearing the voice of God. But I know better.

You don't scare me, I think at it.

YOU WILL NOT BE HARMED.

The cold object slides between my ass cheeks.

Physically, I think. *Are you not intelligent enough to understand that some wounds are mental? What the fuck kind of backwards aliens are you? Are you so far advanced that you don't feel emotion?*

INTUITIVE. I WILL RUN MORE TESTS TO UNDERSTAND YOUR DIFFERENCE.

While the voice didn't directly confirm my thoughts, I suspect I'm on to something. These aren't emotional creatures. They might experience some emotions, but they're either overcome, like with Vulcans, or technologically suppressed. Maybe pharmaceutically. The human race is headed in that direction, so why not?

When the cold sensation reaches my asshole, I try to clench, but my body is still separated from my mind.

Humiliation fuels my decision to reopen the fresh wound of Isabella's death once more. This time I jump right to the worst of it—the thought of her cut open, tied up, and positioned like a work of art. While I never actually saw her in that condition, my nightmares have conjured images of what was described, powerful enough for me to remember them like they were real.

My body and mind reunite.

I throw myself off the platform and fall.

The floor knocks the wind out of me but doesn't slow me down. As the surface starts conforming to my body, I get to my feet and hands, throw myself away, and attempt to tuck and roll back to my feet like I did as a kid.

I'm out of practice. My body groans from the sudden movement. When I come back up to my feet, I'm moving too fast and stumble backward. A wall stops me, slapping against my back and then slowly melting around me.

This whole ship is like one big, padded room—firm upon impact, but then turning gelatinous under a sustained touch. It's a non-Newtonian fluid, I think, contained in some kind of membrane. Has to be. I'm no scientist, but I remember when Isabella and Elias made the stuff at home, with cornstarch and water. If you punched it, the fluid would become solid. If you pressed it gently, it oozed around the fingers. *Oobleck*, I think, remembering what Isabella called it.

I shake my head, focusing on the here and now. My vision is blurry, but I can see the tall figure looming on the other side of the room. Light filters through the viscous ceiling and walls. No shadows. Good light for poking and prodding a subject.

The figure glides toward me. Just a little, but it's enough to set off my primitive reptile mind. Since flight isn't possible, and I have no intention of returning to a frozen state, I opt for fight. Fists clenched, I shout, "Try it, motherfucker!"

The alien stops.

VERY DIFFERENT.

WE MUST KNOW WHY.

The alien stops.

I rub my eyes and look again. My vision is focused, and I get a good look at my adversary. Despite its seven-foot height, it appears to be a little hunched. Like a Skeksis from *The Dark Crystal*. I don't know if it's accurate, but the creature's high shoulders and low head give off old vibes. Could just be that its mask is heavy. The head looks a little insectoid because of the two big, round eyes. Or goggles. Whatever they are.

Despite the feeling that this thing is old, it's still intimidating as hell.

I start to shrink back, feeling like a mouse trapped by a cat.

No, I think. It's implanting that feeling in my mind. Trying to subdue me without a physical confrontation.

My vision fades, but I replace the darkness with a snapshot of my wife's murder, conjured from a nightmare.

I snap back to myself.

The alien's head pulls back a little. Caught it off guard.

"Weren't expecting that, asshole?" I ask.

It just stares. I can feel the pressure of its mind, trying to find a weakness in mine.

"Get out of my head, or I'll show you what a species that doesn't depend on mentally raping people can do with its fists."

The pressure on my head fades.

VERY WELL. I WILL RELEASE YOU.

A wave of discomfort surges up from my toes. My skin prickles from the cold air. Fear nauseates me, rising toward panic. This is everything I *should* have been feeling before, but I was able to think clearly because these assholes had me mentally sedated. I fight the urge to crumple into a fetal position. With a hand on the wall, I manage to stay on my feet.

YOU ARE WEAK.

"It'll pass," I say, taking deep breaths, trying to find my anger. I find it when my thoughts return to Elias. I remove my hand from the wall and clench my fists again. "Where is my son?"

NO HARM WILL COME TO YOUR CHILD.

"You expect me to take your word?" I ask.

WE EXPECT COMPLIANCE.

"Any chance you can speak normally?" I ask and then realize that normal for aliens and normal for humans are very different things.

I WILL NOT DEBASE MYSELF.

"Debase yourself?" I ask. "Debase? You abduct people. Take them from their homes. Experiment on them. You are the lowest—"

WE DO NOT EXPERIMENT. WE TEST.

AS YOU ARE BEING TESTED NOW.

Tested now? What is this, a psychological exam? See how I respond to being set free? Have I had a moment of free will since the UFO's light grabbed me?

Hold on . . .

The light didn't take me. Not right away.

I climbed on Sam . . . and then jumped off. To get her gun. I lower my hand to my hip and slap skin. Right. No pants. No gun.

WOULD YOU KILL ME?

It knows what I'm looking for.

WOULD YOU END MY LIFE?

"You have my son!" I scream.

It stares at me for a moment and then shakes its head in disappointment. It's a very human gesture.

I squint my eyes and take a step toward my captor. "What are you?"

It takes a step back, sensing my fear ebbing to curiosity, fueled by the very tangible rage over my son's abduction.

The alien lifts one of its hands and I count the fingers. Five and a thumb. Then it does the Obi Wan Kenobi hand in my face, waving it calmly. Instead of masking the identity of two droids, it issues a simple one-word command:

RUN!

My whole body reacts in an instant, faster than I can think to conjure Isabella's death. I turn and run. Fast as I can. Off the line like Usain Bolt. I make it three steps before I collide with the wall, knock myself senseless, and topple to the floor.

When the alien stands above me, a silhouette in the ceiling's light, I'm too dazed to put up a fight. My vision fades to black, and a moment later, my consciousness follows.

17

ABERRATION

Hola, mi amigo.

Ya volvimos. ¿Nos extrañaron? No ha pasado tanto tiempo, pero . . . Un momento, ¿nos entienden? ¿No? Entonces hablaremos en inglés.

Is this better? Your lack of multilingualism is disappointing, but we'll overlook it for now. There really is no excuse for it. You can learn online. Or with an app. It's simple. And if things ever get . . . interesting . . . it will be a useful skill to have.

Even if you're not like us.

Even if you just like to watch.

Guilt by association, right?

You perverse observer.

We laugh, knowing you can't look away. That you'll keep on watching, to see how things play out.

It's been ten minutes, by the way.

We should probably do something, right? Don't want our audience getting bored. We roll off the cot, bare feet touching the floor. It's squishy and yet still firm. It's also neither hot nor cold. Is the floor warmed to the same temperature as a human being, or does the strange material instantly match the temperature of whatever is touching it?

Fascinating, but it's not why you're here, right? You don't want to know how or even why the floor of a UFO might have temperature adjusting floors and walls.

We look over the other people here. Naked, all of them. Men and women. Some are known to us. Some are new.

The one thing they all have in common is that they're helpless.

We approach a young man, reach out, and pinch his skin between our nails.

No reaction.

His eyelid lifts easily enough. Can he see? Is he aware?

We raise a finger over his exposed eyeball. The man doesn't react when we press the tip of our finger over his pupil and push.

We could crush his eye. Could feel the warm goo of its insides melt around our finger. You would love that, wouldn't you? Eat it right up. Num-num-num.

Sorry to disappoint, but that's not how we operate. There is nothing fun or sporting about playing with previously subdued prey. We're not a scavenger. And in this state, the lack of reaction, of fear, of desperation, of all the things you want to see . . . it'd be like pulling apart a teddy bear. Where's the fun in that?

If we could wake them up, our hunger might become irresistible, but in their current state? We shake our head and then slap the man in the face. The whack is loud. Stings our hand. But the man doesn't budge.

Boring.

We move from the man to one of the two women in the room. She's got a friendly face. Looks kind even though she's unconscious. We'd enjoy twisting her natural kindness into horror. But now? Her face would stay just like it is.

We reach out and place a hand on her breast.

We feel a thrill. Same as you.

Don't deny it. We're all human. You've dreamed about violating someone. Murder. Rape. Mutilation. Desecration. The desire to just take what you want or need. The world calls these things evil, but they're just primal drives that helped keep us alive—and repopulating with the strongest genes—when the world was carnal and violent. Predator and prey.

Humanity has always been both. Only a few of us retain these instincts.

Call it what you want. Evil. Nature. Nephilim blood. We don't care. Just don't deny its existence. You don't even need to take part. You're weak. We know that. And we don't judge you for it, as long as you don't judge us.

That would be a mistake.

"What do you guys think?" We ask the motionless bodies. "No one has an opinion. C'mon. Speak up. Might save your life later on. Then again, we're not picky about who we kill. We might hate you. Might love you. The motivation to kill and distort isn't an emotional one. Our only requirement is the hunt."

Which is why all these people are safe for the time being.

If we had the simple mind of a fish, we might take the bait. We don't want the dangled worm. We want the larger fish. The one that could, under different circumstances, kill us.

And that's not going to happen in this meat locker.

The urge to leave overwhelms us.

The hunt calls to us. Us and you. All of us. Let's get this party started.

We head for where we think a door should be. But there's no seam. It's just the same squishy surface as the floor, and the cots, which are really just flat extensions of the wall, jutting out like the blades of a flanged hex axe mace.

"Open sesame," we say to the wall, waving our hand across it.

Makes sense that it wouldn't be that easy.

Unless . . . unless it's actually easier.

We stand before the wall and place a hand against it for good measure. The wall molds to our hand's shape. With all our concerted focus, we think at the wall, *OPEN*.

The order is obeyed. The wall melts away. A rectangular opening, far taller than we require, opens to a hallway. We step out, look left and then right. It's the same in both directions. Nondescript. The same pliable walls and floor. Diffuse light comes from within the ceiling. It's not bright. We imagine most people would find it hard to see, but we don't mind the twilight.

Left or right? What do you think?

Don't play dumb. You have a favorite. Everyone has a favorite. Go ahead. Suggest it.

Right?

Predictable. Most people choose right, and not just because they're right-handed, but because of the ancient, small-minded belief that left-handed people were evil. Did you know that 'left' in Latin—*sinistram*—is where the word 'sinister' comes from? Before modern neuroscience opened people's eyes, left-handedness was, at best, considered a physical defect and, at worst, a sign of demonic influence.

We were born right-handed, but we choose left whenever the opportunity presents. So, fuck you, friend. You and your brainwashed preference for all things right. You are boring, and quite lucky you're not here with us now.

We head left.

The hallway has a slight leftward curve to it, like we're circumventing the outer edge of the UFO's interior. We start building a mini map of the ship's layout in our mind. It's small at the moment, just a room and a hall, but we'll have this place mapped out soon enough.

The air smells clean, but there's a trace of something else. Organic, but not human. It's faint. Old. But the farther we walk, the stronger it gets. It will eventually lead us to something.

We prefer to be meticulous, but we also understand the need for adaptation. Opportunism can be a wonderful experience when fully embraced. And we may never get an opportunity like this again.

Hunting by instinct alone is a thrill.

But even the jaguar plots out its moves, and there are a few requirements for a successful hunt of a larger prey. Claws and sharp canines aid the big cats we admire so much, but we have neither. We continue the hunt, but before we can strike, we need to find a weapon.

Anything will do.

A blunt object.

A blade.

We have no preference. Bodies can be bent, broken, and reshaped with a variety of tools.

The Man knows this.

He hasn't seen our work, but he's imagined it.

Before the night is over, we'll make sure he sees exactly what he missed the first time. He didn't find his wife's body. Didn't see the art we left for him.

We called it, 'Uxor Laeta,' and it was our best work to date.

Art without an audience isn't art at all. You know that. It's why you're still here, watching and waiting to see our next masterpiece. You might imagine it like the Man, but you need to see it for yourself to fully appreciate the composition.

Excuse us? What was that? Are we an artist or a hunter? Fuck you.

So small-minded.

We are a polymath. An omnivore consumer of knowledge and skills. Hunter. Artist. Connoisseur of language and pillager of worlds. We are anything we need to be, immune to how the world responds to us. How it sees us. How it treats us.

Because we know the truth.

Because we *are* the truth. The way. The life. The savior of boredom.

Don't doubt us. You're still here, getting a kick out of our rambling thoughts.

We're still walking, by the way. That didn't stop. The scent grows stronger. We're closing in.

And then we're not. The scent fades.

We stop and backtrack. You see where this is going, right? Another door, hidden by a memory foam wall. It's safe to assume that the current hallway is a complete circle, possibly around the UFO's outermost area. Or not. We can't confirm its position within the craft, but we can, with confidence, add the full circle to our mental map.

We're also assuming that an advanced species appreciates the efficiency of mirrored layouts. As we move through one side of the ship, we'll duplicate the same sequence of halls and rooms on the opposite side of our UFO map. At least until we're proven wrong. Makes sense, right?

We place our hand on the wall and issue a fresh command: OPEN.

The wall obeys again.

The scent grows stronger.

We creep into the large space, low to the floor like Smeagol, and are genuinely caught off guard by what we find. "Well, friend, this is interesting. Looks like we're not the only hunter of men on board."

Before we can fully inspect the liquid-filled cylinders containing both men and women of different ages and races, the wall on the far side starts to open.

This is it.

We duck low, stalking our prey. The tall being is covered in a robe and a strange, bug-eyed mask. Other people might take the time to gawk or shit themselves. Instead, we close in, deciding how to kill it, and mentally working out the composition. We won't have a clear vision until we get its clothes off and have a look at the materials we're working with.

But we've got some ideas.

We smile. And charge.

18

I wake with a start, gasping as I sit up. Bright sunlight forces my eyes closed and punts a headache toward migraine territory. Hands over my face, I try to relax, to will my blood vessels open and to keep the headache at bay.

"Ugh," Gabe says. "You too?"

I turn my head toward his voice, crack my fingers, and peek. He's sitting beside me, hand on his forehead, eyes to the ground. "Been a while since I drank enough to have a hangover."

"I've never drunk enough to have a hangover," I say.

"Good on you," he says, "but it looks like your sober streak has come to an end."

I shake my head. "Why would I do that? Why would I do that with Elias here?"

Speaking my son's name helps me overcome the pain. I look up and scan the area. Emmett, Sam, Jade, and Serena are all here in various states of embarrassing sleep. Emmett's head is back, mouth wide open, snoring like a T-Rex with sleep apnea. Jade is curled into his chair, in a fetal position. Looks like a sleeping dog. Serena's arms are crossed, her face in a deep frown. And Sam . . . She's next to me, clothing disheveled, one hand reached out to the arm of my chair.

I'm about to start worrying when Gabe points to the lake. "Out there."

Elias is alone in a canoe. He's wearing a life jacket—obeying the rules as usual. He spots us looking, smiles, and waves. He's happy, so I just wave back and give him a thumbs up.

"That's interesting," Gabe says, standing and noticing Sam's state. "Do you think you two—"

"No," I blurt. "I wouldn't. It's too . . . No."

I dig into my pocket, find my sunglasses, and put them on. My eyes relax. The pain ebbs just a little, but it's enough to think more clearly.

"You sure about that?" he asks, pointing at me. "Shirt's on inside out and backwards. Means you took your clothes off at some point. Put them back on when you were sauced."

"I wouldn't," I say. "None of that is me. I'm—"

I feel weight in my right shorts pocket. More than my phone or wallet. I reach into the pocket and feel the handle of a gun.

My hand flinches back.

"What is it?" Gabe asks.

I reach into the pocket again, and this time slowly draw the weapon.

Gabe's eyebrows launch toward Mars. "You're packing heat? Wait. That's Sam's gun."

A memory is triggered. It's clear. "Sam and I were shooting at the range."

"Right . . ." He rubs his temples. "Right. For like an hour. And after that?"

"I . . . I don't know."

"No way you were drinking at the range," he says. "Sam's a stick in the mud when it comes to gun safety."

"I remember," I say. "Clearly. But . . . I don't remember stopping. Just . . . an owl. On a branch."

Gabe squints his eyes. "An owl?" He walks to Emmett and slaps his leg with the top of his foot. "Wake up, old timer."

Emmett snorts, jolts, and then opens his eyes. "Was I snoring?"

"You sounded like you were possessed by Bazuzal. If you were speaking Latin, I'd have called for a priest. But that's not why I'm waking you up."

Emmett sighs, then stretches his head one way and then the other. He winces and crushes his eyes shut.

"I was hoping you'd remember what happened last night?"

"Last night? Well, we were here. At the fire." Emmett motions to the bonfire, which is cold. "Why is that out? I keep it going all night. But . . . I don't remember. How much did we have to drink?"

"No idea," Gabe says.

"You guys," Serena grumbles, opening her eyes. "It's an easy question to answer."

"You remember?" I ask.

"Don't remember shit." She stands and heads for the cooler. "And it's a state of mind I do not enjoy, which is why I, like Marcus, do not overindulge."

Huh, I think. She's been awake the whole time. Listening to us talk.

She reaches the cooler, squats, opens it, and says, "Fuck." She closes the cooler, picks it up, and carries it into the center of the group.

Jade stirs. Looks confused. Spots us up and awake. "Holy shit. Must have been a crazy night. Give me a minute. I'll get coffee and water."

"Not necessary," Serena says, placing the cooler down so we can all see it.

"What's up?" Sam asks, pushing herself up, straightening her clothes.

"We all have headaches," I say. "And no one can remember last night."

She closes her eyes for a moment. Opens them again. "Same." Her confusion melts away. A sudden seriousness takes its place. She's somehow fully awake and ignoring the headache. "Open it."

Serena pauses for a moment, adding weight to the moment. Then she opens the cooler.

It's full. Only a few beers are missing.

"What the fuck?" Gabe says and turns to Emmett. "Seriously, what the fuck?"

"Feels like we were drugged," Sam says, and then snaps her fingers at me. She points to the gun in my hand. "Give me that. Why do you have it?"

I turn the weapon around and give it to her handle first. She takes it, ejects the magazine and checks the rounds. "Hasn't been fired since . . . the range. But—" She racks the slide, ejecting a round from the chamber and catching it. "It was *ready* to fire."

"Who would want to drug us?" Jade asks.

I can see the lightbulbs snapping on in their minds as, one by one, they come to the same conclusion and slow-turn to me.

"If that were true," I say. "Why are we alive?"

"Stage three," Serena says. "The Setup. The luring stage. Many serial killers are like cats, playing with their prey before killing them—most often for fun, not food. Sometimes they insert themselves into your life through charm, deception, or manipulation. But many rely on building fear in the victim before striking. Creates a sense of dominance and works the target into a situation that cannot be escaped."

"What do we do?" Jade asks. "Bug out?"

"Hard to say without knowing the killer," Serena says. "That might be what he wants. To isolate Marcus . . . and Elias."

"Now hold on a minute," Emmett says. "Let's not jump back on the serial killer bandwagon. Just talking about this stuff is going to disturb poor Marcus. He doesn't need that kind of worry. He's here to escape it." He turns to me. "And we'll do everything we can to keep you safe."

"You don't have to—"

"You're one of us now," Gabe says, hand on my shoulder. "If we have to, I'll call in security. Or we can take the show on the road. Stay at my Portland house."

"Now, now," Emmett says. "Let's not drop a nuke on an itch."

"Emmett," Sam says. "We can't remember last night. Can't remember anything. That's not an itch."

"She's right," Serena says. "We need to take action. Need to—"

Emmett clears his throat and waves his meaty hands like he's telling a car to slow down. There's a smile on his face. "What's the last thing everyone remembers?"

"Sitting here," Jade says. "I was . . . I was showing Elias a card trick."

"Talking to you," Serena says.

Emmett nods. "We were debating a two-state solution for Palestine."

"I was watching you both," Gabe says, "and counting the number of shots from the gun range." He looks at Sam. "Ninety-three. Burned through a lot of rounds."

"We were having fun," Sam says, "and that's what I remember." Her brow furrows. Looks to me. "Did we leave?"

I shrug. "I remember the feeling of leaving, but not actually leaving."

"And . . ." Gabe says. "The other thing?"

"Other thing?"

"The owl."

"Right," I say, memory returning. "There was an owl just outside the range. It was staring at us."

Serena sits up straight. "An *owl?*"

"Why? Is that important?"

She looks at Emmett. He gives her a nod. "Now you're catching on."

"Shit," she says.

"Enlighten us," Gabe says.

"The brain hates gaps in memory. When people experience something weird, traumatic, or unexplainable, it wipes memories, but also fills in some of the blanks with something more familiar. Owls have large reflective eyes. They're eerily still. Among UFO abductees, owls are the most common screen memory, reported by a significant number of alleged abductees."

"Screen memory for what?" Jade asks.

Gabe rolls his eyes. "For *aliens*, dingus."

"Oh," Jade says, and looks at me. "OH."

"Reports of owls during abduction experiences are as ubiquitous as missing time," Serena says, her voice slowing down as the weight of her next five words settle in. "Which . . . we're all currently experiencing."

“Holy shit,” Gabe whispers. Then his eyes open wide and his smile spreads wider. “Holy shit! It happened! It—”

He freezes. Grabs my arm with both hands. Looks across the lake, then looks me in the eyes, brimming with energy. “The camera!”

19

Okay, seriously," Jade says, scooting along beside Gabe as the three of us follow the path around the lake. While we go in search of the camera, Emmett, Serena, and Sam are keeping an eye on Elias. "What are we going to do if we caught a UFO on video?"

"Don't know," Gabe says, and it surprises me. If he's been trying to capture video of a UFO for so long, why doesn't he have a plan? Unless . . . he never believed it would happen, because secretly, despite all the things they've seen, he believes it's all bullshit, or at least explainable.

"Oh, come on," Jade says, not buying it.

"Here's the thing," Gabe says. "No matter how good the video is—if it captured anything—no one will believe it's real."

Jade throws his hands in the air. "Why the heck not?"

"Because Gabe has the money to fake it," I say, figuring it out for myself.

He spins around toward me, snaps his fingers, and points to me with both hands. "That." He spins forward again and keeps going.

"Okay, so we leave you out of it," Jade says.

"And Serena," he says. "Being associated with an actual UFO event, never mind an abduction, would end her career. You and Emmett might have a lot to gain from the video's release—fame and money—but it could damage careers and reputations."

"What about me?" I ask.

"People expect indie game creators to be quirky." He bends a thin branch that was blocking the path out of the way. "No offense, but you're not at all quirky, so it probably wouldn't hurt you to be the indie game designer who communes with aliens."

Gabe releases the branch, letting the leaves slap into Jade.

"Gah!" Jade shouts, blocking the branch at the last moment. But he's not upset. He's laughing. "Bastid. At a time like this?"

"A warrior must be on guard at all times, Grasshopper," Gabe says.

Guessing this isn't the first time Gabe has put Jade's reflexes to the test. Probably a game they've been playing since Jade was Elias's age.

"Grasshopper, my ass," Jade says. "They don't even have crazy reflexes, you know. That's like a praying mantis's thing, right? The old snatch and grab."

"Which is also how most of his dates end," Gabe says to me with a smirk.

"Hey!" Jade says, laughing. "That was just once, and only because she tripped."

"She tripped," Gabe says. "He caught her from behind. Hands on both of her tits."

The image conjured by my mind doesn't follow the story exactly. The girl is on her back, and I'm accidentally grabbing her breast from below.

The vision staggers me a step. My foot snags on a root. I drop to one knee but barely notice. I'm too busy trying to retrieve the fading dream.

Gabe stops. "Whoa." He crouches beside me. "You okay?"

"I remembered something," I say. "I think."

"You a boob grabber, too?" Jade jokes.

Neither of them are expecting my answer. "Yeah. I think so."

Gabe stands, hands on his hips. "Huh. Didn't peg you as a lecher. When did this happen? High school?"

"Can't get away with shit like that outside of high school," Jade says. "Even if it really is an accident."

I close my eyes, trying to re-form the images, but nothing comes. I remember how it felt, though. Under my hand. The shame I felt. The emotions attached to the fringe memory are fresh. "I . . . I think it was last night."

"I knew it!" Gabe says, swatting my shoulder. "One day. One day. With Sam? She hasn't shown an inkling of interest in a man since I've known her. Honestly, thought she was a lesbian, which is fine. I'm cool with that. But in comes *Rico Suave* over here and—"

I shake my head. "Wasn't like that. It was an accident. I felt horrible about it."

"But you don't remember how it happened," Gabe says, believing me. "Which means it falls within the window of tampered memories."

"Missing time," Jade says, smiling like he's just revealed an ancient mystery.

"Right," Gabe says. "We're almost there. Less talk of breasts, more hiking."

"I don't know about you old timers," Jade says, "but I can hike and talk about boobs at the same time."

"Last thing we want," Gabe says, "is for you to be walking behind us with a boner. With your reflexes, you're liable to bump into one of us like we're in the Shawshank bathroom."

"Har. Har." Jade scoots around us and takes the lead. "Better?"

Gabe plucks a pinecone off the pine needle carpet and biffs it off the back of Jade's head. "Lead the way, Captain Crunch."

"'Crunchatize Me, Cap'n!'" I say, the words coming from some ancient memory of a TV commercial.

"I have no idea what you two are talking abo—oof!" Jade sprawls back like he's bounced off an invisible forcefield.

But it's not a forcefield. It's a monster of a man. Six feet tall. He's got a few inches on me but has a barrel chest and a gut that somehow looks solid. He's got a thick black beard, a Red Sox cap on his head, and a deer in headlights look in his eyes.

"Sorry," the big man says. "Didn't see you."

"Didn't see me?" Jade says from the ground. "How did I not see you?"

"I wasn't on the path," the man says. "Was out in the woods. Looking for it. Happened to step out from behind the tree as you were passing."

Seems unlikely, two people colliding in the woods. But we live in a world where planes and boats still crash into each other in the much emptier ocean and sky, so it's not impossible.

The big man offers a meaty hand to Jade, who accepts. He has no problem hauling Jade back to his feet. He offers us a wave. "Name's Jasper. Seen you all around. My lady's an introvert so I'm not allowed to make friends when we're here. But you strike me as good people."

"And what about you, Jasper?" I ask, surprising myself. "Are you a good person?"

"Like to think so," he says. "But . . . I think I got up to some trouble last night."

"How do you mean?" Gabe asks.

"I had a few drinks. Debbie—that's my lady—she fell asleep listening to some self-help book on audio. I'm having a good buzz, you know, so I decided to take a walk. Nowhere in particular. I remember walking into the woods. Remember thinking the path was scary at night, lit by a flashlight. And then . . . I woke up in the woods." He points to the trees he emerged from. "Up that way 'bout a quarter mile, shoes on the wrong feet."

"Welcome to the club," Jade says. "Same thing happened to all of us. And speaking of uncomfortable clothing, I'm feeling all pent up with a bad case of hang nasty." Jade moves his legs apart and starts wiggling back and forth. To a woman, he might look like he's trying to recreate MC Hammer's "U Can't Touch This" dance. But we all know what he's doing—trying to shake his nuts free from his inner thigh. Get them swinging like a church bell clapper. "The hell? It's not working."

Jade tugs his shorts open and looks down. "Okay, what the fuck? I'm wearing underwear." He pulls the shorts down a few inches to reveal a pair of tight, purple boxer briefs.

Gabe sighs and massages his forehead.

"You okay?" I ask him.

"Jade is wearing my underwear," he says, and then looks down his own shorts, "and I'm going commando."

"Which is my preference," Jade says, stepping out of sight around a tree.

"Do you guys know what happened?" Jasper asks.

Before Jade or I can get out a word, Gabe says, "Not a clue. We had a lot to drink last night, too. If you're not used to the altitude and drank even a little more than usual, it might have just hit us harder. That's why we're out here. Walking it off. Based on the state of all our clothing, it's probably better that none of us remember, if you know what I mean."

Jasper cringes, imagination running wild. Gabe's effort to put the brakes on the subject works like a Level 20 influence spell, which is the only way you can change public perception of your character in *Shadowborn*.

"Guessing your lady is worried about you," Gabe says. "Probably should let her know you're okay."

"Yeah." Jasper nods. "She'll probably accuse me of having an affair or something."

"So long as your underwear hasn't been switched to some other lady's," Jade says, stepping out from behind the tree holding Gabe's purple underwear. He tosses it at Gabe who leans to the side, easily dodging the assault.

He shakes his head. "Oh, Grasshopper."

Jasper looks down his pants, sighs with relief and then says. "Welp, been . . . weird meeting you all. I'm going to check on my lady."

"Good luck," Gabe says, waving as Jasper heads back the way we came.

"Seems like a good guy," Jade says. "Why didn't you tell him—"

"Until we know *if* there is footage," Gabe says, "*and* decide what to do with it, we can't tell anyone about UFOs."

"No fun," Jade says.

"That's life," Gabe says and strikes out. "C'mon, we're almost there."

20

The camera, mounted to a pine tree six feet up, feels like some kind of relic that needs to be approached with care, like jostling it will trigger some ancient trap—or maybe an alien invasion.

Gabe leaves his sandals on as he steps into the lake. The water is shallow here. Warm brown stones glisten in the early morning sun, just inches below the surface. The pine tree leans out from the shoreline, giving the camera—some kind of fancy model that doesn't have a logo—an unobstructed view of the beach on the far side of the lake.

While he works on loosening the strap, I scan the opposite shore and find Elias standing beside Emmett. Looks like they're having a serious conversation. Elias has his hands clasped behind his back like he does when he's in museums. Always struck me as a kind of scholarly old man pose. I've never pointed it out, because it's sometimes the only way I know he's paying attention to something.

"Okay," Jade says, back on the trail. "For real. What do you think we should do. You know, if—and I don't mean like the media and shit like that. I mean personally. Like as a group. As an idea, like a general concept, meeting aliens is an awesome thing. But the more I think about it . . ."

"Yeah," I say with a nod. "Nothing about it feels good."

"Right," he says. "And we don't even remember it. I mean, can you imagine how fucked up we'd be right now if we could?"

"Probably why they don't let us remember," Gabe says with a grunt, stretching to undo the strap that's not cooperating. "Damnit. Made this too tight."

"Need help?" I ask.

"I'll get it," he says. "If we remembered an otherworldly experience like that, unfiltered, unedited, and lacking Serena's screen memories? I don't know about you two, but I'd be out of my gourd for a good long time. If this is real, and people go through this shit while the entire world thinks they're crackpots . . ." He shakes his head. "Nightmare on top of a nightmare."

Gabe is scared. I can hear it in his voice. There's a slight quiver. And I'm right there with him. There's a reason he's struggling with the camera, and I don't think it has anything to do with the strap.

We *need* to know what happened, but none of us really *wants* to know.

"Shit!" Gabe fumbles with the suddenly loosened camera. It falls from his hands and drops toward the water.

With reflexes normally reserved for gaming, my hand snaps out and catches hold of the camera. I share a look with him that's equal parts relief and apology.

"Thanks," he says. "Would have been okay, though. It's waterproof. Everything-proof, really. Custom build. Could drop it out of a plane onto concrete, and it would probably still work fine. I wrote the software for it. Think of it as a GoPro for spacecraft and extraplanetary rovers."

"Sick," Jade says. "What's the resolution?"

Gabe grins. "A gigapixel."

"A four by three sensor ratio?" I ask.

He nods.

I'm stunned. Do the math in my head. "So . . . thirty-two thousand by twenty-four thousand pixels?" I don't wait for confirmation. I know it's right. "Fuck's sake."

"Is that good?" Jade asks, getting a laugh out of me because he asked like he had a keen understanding of resolutions.

"If the moon is in frame," I say, "we might be able to find the flag planted by Buzz Aldrin."

"Probably not," Gabe says, stepping back onto shore. Pine needles stick to his wet sandals, making them look like sasquatch feet. "The Apollo 11 flag was knocked over when the lunar module took off. Then again, if it landed with the flag extended still, it might be easier to spot than a flag still standing. But yeah, high resolution."

"Fire it up," Jade says, standing beside Gabe to look at the camera. "Let's see what we got."

"Feel like we should wait until we're with the others," Gabe says.

Jade points to the small view screen on the back of the camera. "C'mon, it's tiny. We won't really see anything. But we can at least see if there's something there before wasting everyone's time."

"Mmm," Gabe says, and then starts tapping buttons.

A series of thumbnails appears on the screen. Half of them are black, half are dark green. They're staggered, one after the other.

"Why are some of them black?" I ask, recognizing the green thumbnails as night vision.

Gabe answers like he's in a trance. "Simultaneous recording modes. Night vision and normal."

I'm about to ask why he's suddenly nervous when I realize for myself. The presence of thumbnails on this camera, which was set up for motion sensitivity over an empty lake, means that it captured something.

He lets out a breath he's been holding and taps the first night vision capture. Insects and dust flit by and then—

A large owl swoops past!

Jade shouts in surprise, making both Gabe and I jump.

"Damnit, Jade," Gabe says. "It was an owl."

Jade runs his fingers through his hair. "But that's what they can look like, man, right?"

"That's how people remember them," Gabe says. "Screen memories, remember? It's in our heads, not on a camera."

"Okay, well, if this is an advanced alien race capable of altering human memories, which seems pretty goddamned advanced, don't you think they could alter the contents of a camera, which seems pretty 1990s, if you ask me?"

Gabe and I share a look. I shrug. "He's got a point."

With a sigh of resignation, Gabe taps the next thumbnail. A fish jumps in the water. Far across the lake is a shimmering light. It's not enough to trigger the camera, but it's easy to tell what it is—our campfire.

"Okay, that's us," Gabe says. "Fire was lit around the same time you and Sam left for the range. And you were there for how long?"

"Had to be about an hour," I say.

"An hour . . ." He skips the next two thumbnails, which are within ten minutes of the last. The next one is forty-five minutes later. His finger hovers over the screen. "Moment of truth."

He taps the thumbnail.

The video fills the small screen.

Something like a shooting star zips across the sky from left to right.

"Is that it?" Jade asks. "I mean, that's something, but it's not—"

"There are five more minutes," Gabe says.

A brilliant light shines down from high above, illuminating the whole beach.

"Ah!" Gabe reacts in shock along with me and Jade. Nearly drops the camera. Fumbles with it for a moment but then holds it out again. The scene hasn't changed, but it's harder to see because Gabe's hands are shaking.

"Holy shit," Gabe says. "Holy shit."

My heart is pounding. Feels like I just finished a sprint.

"C-can you zoom in on this?" Jade asks.

Gabe shakes his head. "Need to plug it into the tablet."

"Look!" Jade shouts, pointing at the screen. A large shape descends into the upper right of the screen, blotting out stars and the tree line. But that's not what holds our attention. The brilliant light tightens into a beam focused on the beach. A moment later, a small body—just a few pixels on the screen—floats up off the beach.

"Elias," I whisper, looking back up at the lake. I can see him now, still with Emmett. Safe.

But last night . . .

I turn my attention back to the screen.

As Elias's small body floats higher, it's joined by a second and a third body. Hard to make out who is who, but there's no denying what we're seeing, and what we've managed to capture on ultra-high-resolution video.

Gabe turns the camera off.

We stand there together in stunned silence.

"We need to show the others," Gabe says.

I grasp his shoulder. "Not Elias!"

He nods. "Kid has enough to deal with, but . . . so do you. Are you sure you want to see any more of this?"

"I need to know," I say.

"So, we show it to Sam and Serena first, yeah? Maybe Emmett can take Elias to the store? We'll fill him in after, right? I mean, the Air Force colonel and the psychologist will probably have the most helpful things to say about this. I mean, I'd offer to take Elias myself, but we all know I won't do a good job keeping my mouth shut. Too jazzed for that."

I should take Elias. I know that. I'm here to spend time with him, and now . . . now I shouldn't let him out of my sight. But I also need to know what happened to him. To all of us. It's the only way to protect him from it, aside from the obvious—to not be here tonight, and never come back.

21

RedRightHand. Come in, RedRightHand. Can you hear me?" I take my finger off the walkie's call button and listen to static.

"Maybe they're out of range?" I ask.

"Nah," Jade says. "Those radios work clear across the lake. Just give 'em—"

"Copy that, Old Man—I mean, Architect. What's taking you guys so long?"

It's good to hear Elias's voice sounding enthusiastic. He's been having fun since we arrived. Might not be happy that we have to leave. Then again, if Gabe follows through with the invite to his home in Portland, our adventure is just getting started. The only thing I know for certain is that we are not spending another night here.

"You see?" Jade says. "Nothing between us and them aside from open water. Signal goes a long way."

"What are you guys up to?" I ask into the radio.

"Uh, nothing much. I think I wore Emmett out." I catch a hint of Emmett grumbling in the background but can't make out what he's saying.

Emmett, like the rest of us, might be feeling the effects of having been abducted during the night. I no longer have a reason to doubt Elias's story about Emmett being led to the lake by tall men. And I now know how the footprints just ended in the water. Seems likely that the old man is a frequent flyer on Air-UAP.

"Sounds like a good excuse to have a lunch no one needs to cook," I say. Jade says there's a pizza place twenty minutes to the south. Next door to an ice cream shop that sells chocolate by the half-gallon. "Why don't you guys go pick up a few pizzas and ice cream for lunch? Tell Emmett that Gabe will pay him back." I give Gabe a smile. "We'll meet back at his place for lunch and then figure out the rest of the day, okay?"

"Dad," Elias says.

"Yeah, bud?"

"Is . . . everything okay?"

My stomach twists. "What do you mean?"

"Just a feeling. Like . . . like . . . I don't know. You ever have a dream that you want to remember, and you have a sense of what it feels like, but you can't actually remember it?"

"All the time," I say. "Happens to everyone."

"Not to me. Not usually. You know any tricks on how to remember?" he asks.

"Wish I did," I say, telling the truth. "Best thing you can do is move on with your day and hope that tonight's dreams are more fun and more memorable."

"I guess," he says. "Did you have any cool dreams out on the beach?"

"Not a one," I say.

"Emmett said the same thing." My son sighs into the walkie. "Okay, well, pizza and ice cream then?"

"Can you put Emmett on?" I ask.

"Copy that, Architect. Over."

Static returns for a moment, replaced by Emmett's deep voice the next. "You all find what you were looking for?"

"Sure did," I say.

"Capture anything interesting?" he asks.

Before I can reply, Elias's voice cuts through the static. "Oh, oh! Did you video a UFO?"

"Just an owl," I say. "And some fish. We haven't gone through everything yet, but there's nothing to worry about."

"Why would I worry about a UFO?" he asks.

"You wouldn't," I say. "You shouldn't. I just—you know what? How about you focus on the food, and we'll focus on the long slog back to the campground. If there's anything interesting on the camera, we'll put it on my phone."

"Sure," Elias says.

Emmett's voice comes over the radio. "And he's off. Heading back to your cabin to change or some such thing. You all really find nothing?"

"We found . . . the opposite of nothing, Emmett."

After three seconds of silence, he says, "Copy that." Sounds quiet. A little defeated. He hoped we'd find nothing. "Meet at my place. Should be back with the food by one in the pm. Don't dilly or dally. I want to see what happened, same as the rest of you."

"Understood," I say. "Are Serena and Sam with you?"

"Nearby," he says.

"Gabe wants them to get his tablet—says they'll know which one it is—and to meet at the old dining hall."

"Clandestine, huh?" He's trying to sound like his cheery self but isn't pulling it off. "Must be really something. I'll let them know. Over and out."

"That was abrupt," Gabe says, leading the way down the path, back toward camp. We're still fifteen minutes out. If Sam and Serena meet us at the dining hall—wherever that is—then we should have a little more than a half hour to look at the footage before Elias returns.

"Not everyone thinks being abducted by aliens is fun," Jade says.

"I think it's more that he feels the burden of responsibility for us all," I say. "He might feel like he put us at risk. Put Elias at risk."

"He's not wrong," Gabe says, "but we all took the risk. We all heard Elias's story about the tall men. About the footprints in the sand. Every single one of us OG crew has seen UFOs here on several occasions. We knew something might happen."

"Yeah, but *abducted?*" Jade says. "C'mon. That's some Giorgio Tsoukalos shit, right there."

"Who?" I ask.

"The UFO guy with the crazy hair. Kind of a meme now." Jade scruffs up his hair, gets a manic look in his eyes, makes air quotes, and says, "Aliens."

I recognize the complete package, and smile. "Riiight. That guy. Don't suppose you have his phone number? Or the phone number of any other, whatdaya call them?"

"Ufologists," Gabe says. "If you really want to, I can probably have someone on site by the end of the day, but we wouldn't be able to keep this under wraps."

"Last thing any of us needs is a media circus," I say. "Except for maybe Jade."

He smiles. "Think of all the cosplay babes I could pick up at UFO conferences!"

"Not sure those are where the attractive cosplayers are going," I say, trying to keep it light while feeling a crushing weight.

"You know . . . this could be important," Jade says, sounding serious. "When it comes to frequent UFO sightings people tend to focus on the scary stuff, like UFOs over nuclear sites. Or the thirty-seventh parallel."

"What's that?" I ask.

"The thirty—"

I stop Jade short. "I know what it is, but not how it connects to UFOs."

"The thirty-seventh parallel cuts across the United States. Straight through Area 51. But it's basically a supernatural highway. Lots of weird shit. Coast to coast."

"It's more than that," Gabe says. "The number thirty-seven is . . . unique. It's special. Like the universe has a thing for it. Even just from a nerdy point-of-view." He ticks off his fingers. "It's a prime number made from two other prime numbers. Three and seven." He ticks off another finger and smiles. "Reverse thirty-seven, you get seventy-three, the twenty-first prime number, while thirty-seven is the twelfth prime. It's a numerical palindrome."

He claps his hands and rubs them together, just getting warmed up. "Decision theory. Heard of it?" He can see we have no idea what he's talking about and continues, "It's a mathematical theory. The 37% Rule. If you want to make the best possible choice, like hiring a new coder, or a character animator, you look at the first 37 percent. Let's make it easy. If a hundred people apply for a position, interview the first thirty-seven people, but don't hire any of them. Then, you hire the very next person who is better than the first group of people. It's predictive, and allows you to make the best hire, nearly every time. I use it all the time. Hasn't steered me wrong yet.

"And if nerd-speak isn't enough for you, it's also a very popular number. How many guys had Dante's girlfriend blown?"

I have no idea what he's talking about, but Jade gasps. "Thirty-seven!" He sees my confusion and explains. "*Clerks*. The movie."

"The movie, *Speed*. People are stuck in an elevator for thirty-seven minutes. And how much money does Dennis Hopper ask for? Thirty-seven million. You a *My Cousin Vinnie* fan?"

I am, and my eyes widen. "'Here's some for thirty-seven cents,'" I say, quoting the movie's first line of dialogue. "Hold on. Shit. I played soccer for ten years. My jersey number was thirty-seven."

"You see?" Gabe says. "It's a sexy number and is just everywhere."

"That's . . . interesting," I say, "but I haven't seen anything about the number thirty-seven around here."

Gabe sighs. "Point taken. Probably shouldn't dwell on something that's not relevant to our own personal weirdness."

And just like that, the conversation ends and we each retreat into our thoughts. We hike in silence for ten minutes, making good time despite feeling like I'm knee deep in the Swamps of Sadness from *The NeverEnding Story*. RIP Artax. Just keep moving, I tell myself. That's the lesson Atreyu learned. Power through when the path ahead has no branches to choose from.

When I recognize the edge of the campground, I ask, "Where's the dining hall?"

"This side of the campground," Gabe says. "North of the range. Almost there."

We pass the range. Memories of the previous night flit back. Shooting the Alien. It was fun. With Sam. And an owl, just watching.

"Hey!" Sam calls.

I jolt out of the memories and spot her leaning out of a door at the end of a long, dark brown building that's seen better days. The brown shingles are warped and covered with thick mats of moss. The windows are intact, but dirty. Some of the green shutters still hang in place. Others rest on the ground.

"Is this it?" Sam holds up the largest tablet I've ever seen.

"If there's no internet, why do you have the mother of all tablets?" I ask.

"It's a drawing tablet. No internet required."

"A billionaire tech genius *and* an artist," I say.

He shrugs. "Nothing serious. It relaxes me."

Sam holds the door open for us as we ascend the crumbling concrete steps. "How many of you were here when this place still served food?" I ask.

"I was," Sam says. "Serena, too."

"Just missed it," Gabe says, "and I'm not upset about it. I've heard the food tasted a lot like cardboard with gravy made from mildew and lake water."

A wall of dusty cool air greets us inside the dining room. It's a long space that ends in a counter separating the large open room from the kitchen. On one side of the space are piles of junk. Most of it looks like it's been here since the fifties and includes a literal kitchen sink.

A familiar face catches my attention, staring out at me from a pile of books. The bald man with a big red nose and a complete lack of hair transports me back in time to when life was simple. I pick up the ancient toy and read the label. "Magnetic Drawing Set." The bald man's name emerges from the past. "Hello, Dapper Dan."

The small red magnet dangles on a string attached to the cardboard. I pick it up and head for the table where the others are gathering around the tablet. Gabe ejects the sim card from the camera and inserts it into the device, a model I don't recognize. Probably another custom build. Suppose I'd do the same if I had his money.

Using the magnet pen, I drag the metal filings encased beneath the plastic shell over Dapper Dan's face, giving him a mustache.

"Here we go," Gabe says.

Dapper Dan's facial hair melts away as I look up at the big screen. Gabe moves to the third set of night vision and normal vision recordings. He taps on the normal vision file. It plays through, this time in sickening detail.

Gabe zooms in on the screen as the abductions begin.

As soon as the light strikes the beach, everyone goes still. One by one, starting with Elias, they lift off the ground and float toward the UFO blocking the stars.

"Pause it," Serena says, sounding shaky. "Fucking pause it." She staggers back a step. "This is *real?* You're not fucking with us?"

"I wouldn't," Gabe says.

"This . . . this is serious," Sam says.

"You think we should report it?" Jade asks. "Like to your superiors or whatever? You know, for confirmation maybe? Tracked objects. Stuff like that?"

"I don't know," Sam whispers.

While they all discuss next steps, I lean in close, looking at the still image. I spot something in the tree line behind the beach, caught in the UFO's light. I place both of my index fingers on the screen and drag them apart. The image zooms in so quickly that I'm both caught off guard, and terrified, by what I see.

It's a face.

A mask.

With big black eyes.

A memory slams into my head. I see this face. I hear the word 'Run!' And then I'm knocked back—in the memory, and in the present. I topple backward, stumble over an old toaster, and drop down onto my ass.

I have the group's full attention. "I remember," I whisper and then loudly, "I remember it!"

"It—*what?*" Sam asks.

I point through the middle of them to the screen. "The alien."

22

Holy shit," Jade says. "I see it!"

The group gathers around the screen, blocking my view of the strange mask with black bug-like eyes.

"Is that a fucking trunk?" Gabe asks. "Are they elephant aliens?"

"It's a hose," I say without thinking.

Gabe looks back at me. "You can't even see the screen."

I shrug. "Might be a memory."

"We don't even know if you and Sam were taken," he says. "You're not in the video yet."

"Either way," Sam says, "he's right. The ribs on the trunk are too regular to be organic. It's wearing a mask."

"If you squint," Serena says, "it kind of looks like an owl. The mask might reinforce the screen memory."

"Or it can't breathe Earth air," Jade says. "*The War of the Worlds*, right?"

"That was more about germs," Gabe says, "and it's bullshit. Germs have a hard enough time jumping between Earth species. Germs adapted to human physiology wouldn't know what to make of an alien body."

I push myself up. No one offers help. They're too distracted by what's on the screen. "Let me see again."

I'm ready for it this time, but the masked face barely visible in the beachside brush still snatches a breath from my lungs. It's emotionless, unblinking gaze fills me with dread, but the longer I stare at it, the less it affects me.

"What are you doing?" Jade asks me. I just keep on staring, feeling my emotional response shrinking.

"Exposure therapy?" Serena guesses.

I nod. "Just need to get used to seeing it. Then it's just a mask, and not alien."

"Makes sense," she says. "But, if you all don't mind, I'd like to see the rest of the video."

Gabe uses two fingers to zoom back out. The UFO comes back into view, along with the beam of light and my son floating in the air, halfway between the beach and his abductors. He taps the screen once and the video resumes.

I flinch when Sam and I come charging out of the woods just ten feet away from the lurking alien. It seems to retreat back and then fades into the shadows. We caught it off guard.

Can't tell what Sam and I are saying to each other, but she turns her attention to Gabe. She's shouting at him as he floats up, out of reach. And then, she stops moving. Goes limp. Head hanging back. Mouth slack.

"They got me," she whispers, watching as she, too, comes off the ground.

Even from this distance, you can see the confusion and indecision on my face. For a moment, I glance out toward the camera. Feels like I'm making eye contact with my present self, knowing that I'll be judged for what I do next.

I try to imagine my next move, but even I don't guess that I'd leap up on Sam's waist and straddle her like a horse.

Jade laughs nervously.

Sam looks at me, shaking her head, but she has a slight grin.

"Look," Gabe says. "What was that? Sam dropped something."

He skips back a few frames, zooms in a little closer and restarts the video. At this magnification, it isn't clear, but when the object falls from Sam's hand and Gabe freezes the image again, it's easy to suss out the shape of a gun.

There are two aliens in the video—the UFO variety and the handgun variety.

Curiosity sated, Gabe zooms back out and continues the video. I'm leaning over Sam, six feet off the ground and floating higher.

"You're looking at the gun," Sam says, and then gasps when I slide off her in the video and drop down to the beach. I pick up the gun, pocket it, and then leap up and grasp hold of Sam again.

She shoots me another look, and since no one else commented, I hope that she's the only one who noticed me accidentally copping a feel. I wrap my arms and legs around her on the screen, clinging like a sloth.

"Wow," Serena says. "You went full *Mission Impossible*, huh?"

"Couldn't tell you," I say, voice barely audible.

"If he doesn't remember," Gabe says, "I think it's safe to say he doesn't—"

We all gasp and flinch back as I lose my grip and fall toward the beach. By the time I'm caught by the light and float into position behind the others, we're all grasping on to each other.

The group stays silent for the rest of the clip, watching as we disappear into the UFO, one by one. Seconds later, the craft just seems to wink out of existence. We were taken. We were powerless.

"I would like to go on record," Jade says, raising his hand, "and say that we should never do this again."

"Seconded," Sam says.

"I'm . . . not sure that's how it works," Serena says. "Look, I know this isn't my specialty, but we've been talking UFOs for a long time at Moose Hollow, and I've done my research. Very few abductees report just a single experience. Seeing as how we've all been coming here our whole lives, it seems likely that this is not the first time we've been taken." She turns to me. "With the exception of Marcus and Elias."

"So, we bug out," Gabe says. "I love it here, but I don't have the security to hold off an alien abduction. We meet someplace else."

Serena frowns.

"What?" Gabe asks. "Just how much research have you done?"

"What I would consider a normal amount," she says.

"So, you're an expert," Sam says. "Or close to it."

"Is that why you know about that screen memory stuff?" Jade asks.

"Screen memories happen in all kinds of situations," she says, glancing in my direction without making eye contact.

"Just say what you're thinking," Gabe says. He's frazzled. Probably feeling vulnerable for the first time in a long while.

"Okay . . ." Serena says. "Just . . . keep in mind that I didn't buy any of this . . . until now." She clears her throat. "Many abductees, and by 'many' I mean most, report that changing locations does not prevent the phenomenon from occurring. That means it's person-centered, not place-centered. Now, these experiences might have begun here at the campground—that's definitely the case for Marcus and Elias—but it's highly likely that simply leaving Moose Hollow won't prevent the pervasive experience from continuing."

"Pervasive experience?" Jade asks.

"Means it's something that follows the individual, rather than being tied to a location. You can go anywhere you like, but there's no escaping the phenomenon. Like PTSD or even sleep paralysis demons, which are one of the theoretical explanations from abduction stories—"

"That we now know are bullshit," Gabe says.

"—but instead of psychological conditions, they're . . . well, aliens. Maybe."

"*Maybe* aliens?" I ask.

"Unless Sam is privy to some top-secret information that says otherwise—"

We all turn to Sam.

She shakes her head.

Serena continues, "—we don't know what they are or where they're from. Another planet is just the easiest explanation to wrap your head around, even though it doesn't make a whole lot of sense if you put enough thought into it."

"I don't remember anything like this happening anywhere else," Gabe says.

"It's possible that they wait for us to come here. It's convenient. Out of the way. Not a lot of observers. A contained and controlled environment, up until now. If they only need us once a year, waiting for us to come to them makes sense. But if we all stopped coming here, the literature says our abductions would continue."

"How?" Jade asks. "There are eight billion people on the planet. How could they keep track of us?"

"Same way we keep track of people," Sam says.

"Trackers," Gabe says.

Serena finishes the chain of thought with the official answer. "Implants. It's a common report among abductees. No one understands how they're made or work, but they're widely regarded as tracking devices."

"Where do they put these implants?" I ask, looking down at my legs. "If they gave one to me last night, it'd be fresh, right? Even if the wound was cauterized, there should still be a fresh mark."

While Serena answers, Jade and Sam start looking me over. "They've been reported just about everywhere . . . including genitals . . . but the most common is in the nasal cavity. They're usually found when abductees feel pressure in their upper nose and start experiencing nosebleeds. Behind the ear is common—"

Jade starts rubbing my ears like a masseuse.

I'm about to complain when Sam takes hold of my hand, rubbing my fingers and palm. "What about hands?"

"Hands and wrists, yeah. But remember, just about anywhere is fair game. Though you shouldn't just be looking at Marcus. It's much more likely that we all—"

"Found something," Sam says, fingers on my wrist.

Sam lifts my arm up as everyone encircles my wrist. She bends my hand back, stretching the skin tight. What looks like a simple bump at first slowly resolves into what looks like a half-inch long grain of rice just beneath my skin. At one end of the of the object is a pink spot—all that's left of an entry wound.

A hush falls over the group as the discovery's weight settles on us.

This group of people has been studied by a non-human intelligence, possibly from birth, and now, so am I, and so is Elias. What a fucking nightmare.

"Guys," Sam says. "Try not to freak out, but if we assume that their tracking technology is as advanced as the UAPs, I think it's safe to say that they know where we are—all the time—even now. They could be listening to us. Could see what we're seeing. If they don't want people knowing about them, and they know we have this kind of footage, what's to stop them from—"

Pressure builds around my head as a buzz fills the air.

We all feel the presence at the same time and turn to the far end of the dining hall—where an owl stands just outside the screen door.

23

The owl is seven feet tall and leans down to stare at us. It's hard to make out any details like feathers. It's blurry, like a painting that hasn't been fully realized. But I have no trouble seeing its head craning left and then right.

"You guys can see that, right?" I whisper.

"Yes," Gabe says, voice barely audible.

"What should we do?" Jade asks.

"You carrying your gun?" Gabe asks Sam.

She nods and moves her hand around to her back where the handgun is tucked into her shorts. She grasps the weapon's handle.

"You sure that's a good idea?" I ask. "Could start a fight we can't win."

"They started the fight," Sam says, but doesn't draw the weapon.

"How come it's not moving?" Jade asks, panic rising a little faster than the rest of us. My heart is pounding, but I'm still thinking clearly. For now.

"Maybe it wants to talk?" Serena asks.

"Talk?" Gabe says. "To us?"

"They could have taken us again, right? Nothing we could do about it. But it's not."

Gabe throws his hands in the air. "We're *subjects*."

"I talk to my subjects when it's important," Serena says, "and they are just as frightening as . . . that." She motions to the giant, blurry owl still staring at us. "I'll do it."

Serena makes it two steps toward the owl when she's stopped in her tracks by a voice in our heads.

NOT YOU.

A feeling, like a giant neon sign with a blinking arrow, points toward me. Everyone senses it and turns to me.

"What did you do?" Jade asks.

"I don't know!" I whisper, eyes bugging out.

"You had the gun," Gabe points out.

"It wasn't fired," Sam says, and then locks eyes with me. "You don't need to do this. We can run."

RUN! The memory of that word makes me flinch. It was the same voice, commanding me to run, but there's no visual with the memory. I know it happened, but my visual memory is just darkness.

"Run," I say.

"Seriously?" Gabe asks, "because if you run, we all need to run. There's a back door through the kitchen. Leads to a path in the woods. It's windy and overgrown, but it leads back to the campground."

I just nod.

"Let's do it. On three, okay?" Gabe looks to Serena, who was on team alien-chat.

She backtracks two steps and says, "Fine, but I think it's a mistake."

"One, two, *three!*" On three, Gabe bolts toward the kitchen. Everyone else follows. And not a single one looks back.

If they had, they'd have seen me rooted in place, unable to move.

Unable to shout for help.

I'm paralyzed.

The footsteps of my new friends fade. The back door slams into the outer wall as it's thrown open. How far into the woods will they make it before realizing I'm not with them? Could be a while if they think an alien is pursuing them.

Everything goes quiet.

I'm stuck staring at the screen door and the massive owl beyond. I try to run again when it stoops low and pushes its way inside. The buzzing in my head grows more intense. The closer it gets, the more details resolve. The feathers on its face come into focus, all of them drawing my gaze inward, unable to look away from the bird's black eyes.

"W-what do you want?" I say, struggling to speak. Not because I'm afraid, but because my jaw is rigored along with the rest of my body.

The buzzing grows louder. Pressure increases. Feels like a pair of hands have slipped through my skull and into my brain, prying open a hole. I grind my teeth and try to resist. "N-no!"

To my surprise, the owl stops moving.

It lowers itself down, looking me in the eyes, head cocking slightly.

DO YOU REMEMBER?

Since I have no idea what it's talking about, I'm pretty sure the answer is no. It seems to understand my realization, perhaps reading my thoughts. I decide to send it a message:

Get the fuck out of my head.

YOU REMAIN DIFFERENT.

I was different before?

ACTIVE.

RESISTANT.

UNPREDICTABLE.

The answer is about as vague as a senator's tax returns, but I think I understand. When they abducted us last night, I gave them some kind of trouble. So, now they're back, and . . . what? They want to understand why? Want to scold me?

How about you explain the tracking device in my wrist?

It ignores my request, and why not? Research scientists don't answer chimpanzees' questions. Then again, it *did* answer a question. And it gave me more information than it intended. This is not my first meeting with this creature. Not my first conversation, either. And somehow . . . I was able to resist what's happening to me now.

I try to move but am locked down tight.

What was different about last night?

How did I—

SHOW ME WHAT YOU REMEMBER.

I grunt and close my eyes as a memory plays. It's brief but includes a familiar face. Or mask. It's the same bug-eyed, trunked, visage we saw peeking out of the bushes in the video. And then just a single word, in the same voice I'm hearing now.

'RUN!'

And then . . . nothing. Darkness. The next time in my memory that I open my eyes, I'm at the lake.

Those same round black eyes are inches from my face when I snap back to the present. The owl illusion is gone. Definitely a mask. Looks solid. Two big black half spheres for goggles. It's oval shaped and metallic. A tube extends down from its face and connects to something beneath a cloak that hides its body. It's shocking to see, but not exactly frightening. The visage is just a mask. Seen far worse on Halloween.

The revelation puts me at ease. Masks reveal weakness. They hide. They protect. They obfuscate. What they don't do is project power. The normalcy of a mask slows my heart and clears my mind of otherworldly fear. This . . . *alien* is a living thing, with fears. And I think it might actually be as afraid of me as I am of it.

Seen from a distance, or through a mental haze, I see where the stereotype of gray aliens comes from. The big black eyes. The gray coloration. The complete lack of emotion. But, like the owl overlay changing what it looks like in memories, and in real time, the gray face is just a mask.

I sense disappointment. Not sure if it's with my current resistance to the pillaging of my mind, or if it's disappointed they did such a good job wiping my memory.

You're looking for something, I think.

SOMEONE.

Me?

UNKNOWN.

A thought occurs to me. It's crazy. Beyond stupid. But it's better than having my mind wiped again. Better than not having any answers. I've been down that road with my wife's murder. Being in the dark about something life shattering is not something I can stand for. So, I ask my question.

Maybe I can help?

EXPLAIN.

You seek information, right? From someone you took last night. You think it could be me because I, what? Caused some trouble? Resisted this bullshit you're doing to my body right now?

YES.

Well, I'm not resisting now, am I? I'm communicating. I'm calm.

That's a lie, but I'm not sure if it senses my emotions the way it hears my inner voice.

We can have a conversation. No need to control my body. I won't be a problem. Unless you have my son.

That would be a problem. A big problem.

That's it. That's how I broke their influence. Elias.

WE ARE SPEAKING TO YOU. ONLY YOU.

FOR NOW.

You are interrogating *me.*

YES.

If you would like to continue, set me free. Or I will free myself.

I'm bluffing, but if I really did cause problems last night, this alien has no reason to doubt me.

IMPOSSIBLE.

Why?

A LACK OF TRUST.

That's a two-way fucking street. Look, why don't you just tell me what happened, and I'll be happy to help if you agree to leave me and my family alone.

Stillness follows. I think it's contemplating my offer.

"That's why you're here, right? You need help with something." The words come from my mouth, not my mind. I'm in control of my body again.

I WILL NOT EXPLAIN.

“Then I’m not sure—”

I WILL SHOW YOU.

A long-fingered hand snaps up from under the cloak, grasps my face, and sends an electric jolt through my body. When the hand pulls back, and I open my eyes again, I am no longer in the dining hall.

24

Uhh," I say, standing in a room that looks like it was stamped into creation. There are no seams. The cool metallic coloration reminds me of one of those oily stickers, the kind you can squish. A hint of sparkles. I place my hand against the wall and press. It bends beneath my fingers, pliable to my gentle touch.

I turn to the alien, still masked and cloaked, looming above me. "Did you just abduct me again?"

THIS IS MY MIND.

MY MEMORY.

"Vulcan mind meld," I say. "Got it."

The alien cocks its head to the side in the same way it would if it was as a real owl.

WHY ARE YOU NOT AFRAID?

"Not afraid?" I say. "I'm fucking terrified."

For real, I'm clenching my ass like I'm trying to forge a diamond from a lump of coal between my cheeks. My heart is pounding. I'm sweating. And apparently, this isn't even reality.

What happens if I shit myself in a memory? Will I shit myself in the real world? Am I doing that now? Just standing there, shit running down my leg?

YOU ARE NOT LIKE OTHER HUMANS. YOU ARE DIFFERENT.

"So you've said," I say. "But . . . how?"

It turns away, heading toward a wall. Doesn't want to tell me. The wall parts, forming an open doorway through which the alien exits.

COME WITH ME.

I do as requested, mostly because I'm sure there's no choice. "You have a name?"

No response as he turns right and leads me down a hallway.

"I'm not asking to be friends. I understand that humans are inferior to you. That we are subjects. But a name would help my inner monologue, if you know what I mean. Do aliens have inner monologues?"

WE HAVE BEEN ON THIS WORLD LONGER THAN HUMANITY. AT WHAT POINT DOES ONE STOP BEING ALIEN?

"Longer than humanity?" I ask. "Haven't people been around for like sixty-thousand years?"

I sense a scoff, but don't hear it.

PRIOR TO WHAT YOU CALL HOMO SAPIENS, THE FIRST HOMININ WALKED UPRIGHT SEVEN MILLION YEARS AGO. THE FIRST TO USE A TOOL, WHAT YOU CALL HOMO ERECTUS, EVOLVED TWO MILLION YEARS AGO. BUT IT WAS NOT UNTIL THREE HUNDRED-THOUSAND YEARS AGO THAT HUMANITY EXISTED IN YOUR CURRENT CONFIGURATION.

"Current configuration?" I ask. "The hell does that mean? And why are you answering my questions at all? Are . . . are you going to kill me?"

WE DO NOT KILL. WE OBSERVE.

"This is what you call *observing?*" I ask. "You abduct people. You abducted *my son.*" Sensing my growing anger, he turns his tall head and gives me a black-eyed glare. "First, I'm calling you 'Mac' until I get a real name. If you know, you know. Second, that's not exactly the Prime Directive. What are you here to observe? Is Earth a zoo, or a nature preserve or something? Are people the main attraction?"

Mac ignores the question, and I'm not surprised. I'm more surprised that he's communicating with me at all. "Hey, why *are* you communicating with me?"

TO PUT YOU AT EASE.

"That's why we're strolling through a hallway in your head? To put me at ease."

YES.

"If we're here for a specific memory, why not take us there?"

TO OBSERVE.

"You're actively interfering. Nothing I do or say right now is going to accurately reflect myself. Feel like you're smart enough to know that."

YOU ARE CORRECT.

Ahead, the wall on the right side of the hallway melts open. He turns into it.

FOLLOW.

As I follow Mac into a larger space, my nerves are suddenly out of whack. I'm shaking. My legs feel weak. It's harder to think. I grit my teeth. "You . . . you were reducing my emotions."

INDEED.

"Well . . . don't stop . . . on my account," I say, feeling the unfiltered fear that comes with being mentally abducted into an alien's mind.

Instead of replying, Mac takes a long sidestep, revealing the room ahead. It's a long space with smooth walls. Each side is covered with curved glass containers that look like they should be holding specimens but are empty. Takes two seconds to absorb my surroundings, at which point my vision snaps to the object on the floor, just ten feet away from me.

I squint at it and lean forward like I'm having trouble seeing it with my actual eyes. Pretty sure my vision in this place is just a state of mind. I'm seeing it clearly but can't tell what I'm looking at.

It looks like a sculpture. Feels artistic. Sheets of taut gray stretched over a framework of what? Wood? Carved sticks? The form rises up from a thick base on the floor, twisting upward like a vine. I spot knots and string holding everything together, maintaining its shape like a roast.

Hold on . . .

Thinking of meat shifts my view of the sculpture. Hidden inside the gray are splotches of color—dark red, pink, pine green.

"What . . ." I step closer despite my rising consternation.

The sculpture appears to have two wings, spread to the sides, sheets of gray taut against a flaring set of seven phalanges. No, that's not right. There are no joints. They're more like . . . ribs.

My eyes widen.

This must be what it's like for a deaf person to hear for the first time—a sudden information dump and understanding that the world is completely different than it had been a moment before.

This isn't a sculpture.

It's not a work of art.

It is a mutilated alien, bent, broken, twisted, and bound into a . . . pleasing form.

The red is meat.

The gray is skin.

The string is ligament.

The twisting branches moving upward are long arms and legs.

What looks like a tree at the top are fingers, bent and broken backward.

At the center of it all, between the rib wings, is a face. A mouth. A nose. Two large black eyes. Deflated. Staring at me. And somehow still transmitting the pain of its excruciating death.

I stumble back a step.

My legs give way.

The floor is forgiving when I fall, but it does nothing to settle my stomach. I lean to the side and dry heave, again and again, until I realize there is nothing to puke because this isn't real.

But it was real.

This is a memory.

This happened on the UFO.

"Oh my God," I say. "He's here."

I leap back to my feet, seeing the mutilated body for what it is—the work of a serial killer who did the same to my wife.

"He's here!" I shout at Mac, like he'll know what the hell I'm talking about. "You need to let me go! Now!"

Mac's masked head leans back. This is not the reaction he was expecting.

"Please!" I shout.

Mac cranes his head to one side, watching me. Observing.

"You want to know why I'm different?" I ask, patience evaporated. "Because *you* are not the worst thing that's happened to me." I step closer to him, feeling no fear now. Just rage and concern for my son. "Now send me—gah!"

The scenery shatters and is replaced by flickering memories plucked from my mind. The police on the phone, telling me Isabella was dead. Telling me I needed to identify the body. Standing in the morgue. Looking at an object covered by a sheet I was told was a body but wasn't shaped like one. When they lifted the sheet to reveal Isabella's face, it was at the side of the bed, and she wasn't face up, she was looking right at me, face frozen in anguish.

I scream as the buried memory stabs a thousand rusty blades into my psyche.

It's enough to fling both Mac and me from the shared memory.

I sprawl back onto the dining hall floor, dazed and disturbed.

GO.

FIND YOUR SON.

His compassion catches me off guard, but he seems to understand my urgency.

For a moment.

THEN YOU WILL BE COLLECTED.

25

Collected? *Collected?!*

Fuck this shit, I'm out. This is some Stephen King, Maine bullshit. Time to leave and never come back.

I explode from the dining hallway, crashing through the door and clearing the concrete steps with a leap. I hit the ground hard, topple onto my back . . . and slide for a few feet. I grunt and scramble back to my feet before anyone—human or otherwise—can point and laugh at me. I'm going to pay for it tomorrow, but if I wake up in my bed surrounded by human civilization, I'll take all the pain that comes with getting back there.

With my son.

"Elias!" I shout, despite being far from the cabins.

I try to think ahead, to where I'll find him, to how quickly we can put this place in the rearview. Needs to be minutes.

Problem is, my game plan stops at 'run and shout his name.' Where is he? Where did I leave him? My memory of recent events feels foggy. Could be a side effect of slipping into an alien's memory. Could be because I'm freaking out.

I stop shouting but keep running.

Need to focus.

Need to go back to before Mac showed up.

To the video. In the dining hall. And before that . . .

We recovered the video out in the woods, and Elias . . . He was with Emmett. On the beach. I start adjusting course from the cabins to the beach but then slide to a stop.

Not at the beach. We sent them away. To get pizza and ice cream.

Elias isn't on the campground. I redirect myself toward the cabin, where my Santa Fe waits. I need to catch them before they come back.

Relief washes over me. Moose Hollow is no longer a safe place. Not only is there a pissed off alien collecting people, but all my concerns about the brochure and how we ended up at this place have been affirmed. My wife's killer *is* here, and deadly enough to kill, mutilate, and arrange a seven foot tall alien the same way he did my spouse.

I'm not staying at home, I decide. We'll stop in to pick up passports. Then straight to Logan. Take the first available flight, who cares where it goes. From there, we'll figure out where we can go to lay low until the police find and arrest my wife's killer.

If Mac doesn't take care of him first.

And if that happens, I'll still be the prime suspect, not because there's a shred of evidence, but because there's no one else.

If I'm a suspect, will I be able to leave the country? What if I'm on a no-fly list? What if leaving with Elias makes *me* look guilty? Will they arrest me at the airport?

Call the police, I tell myself. As soon as there's a signal.

And tell them what? That aliens abducted us? That my wife's killer murdered an alien on a UFO after we were all abducted? I'll be locked up for sure. It'll cost me Elias. *The brochure.* If I focus on that, maybe they'll come have a look. Maybe they'll run into all this insanity on their own.

Doesn't matter, I decide.

We'll drive to Mexico and keep on going until we reach Costa Rica. I've got enough money to live there as long as we need to.

And if there really is a tracking device in my wrist?

I'll cut it out, I decide. Nothing an X-Acto knife and superglue can't fix.

The woods thin as I enter the campground proper. The lodgings all look the same to me, but the orange Santa Fe parked beside my cabin is like a beacon. I slide across dried pine needles as I adjust course for the vehicle.

The side mirrors extend as I approach the SUV. The door unlocks when I take hold of the handle. I climb inside, slam the door shut behind me, and push-start the engine. I'd normally wait to punch in my passcode and get some tunes playing, but this time I just toggle the vehicle into Sport Mode, stomp on the gas, and send dirt flying as I speed toward the campground's exit.

It's a bumpy ride. The paths through the campground are all dirt with uneven tire divots and are crisscrossed with roots. Despite the high ceiling, my head gets whacked a few times on my way to the road. I skid to a stop at the exit and take a moment to strap on my belt, to keep my head from hitting the ceiling again, but also to shut up the loud beeping letting me know I'm not buckled.

Car safety system satiated, I bang a left and step on the gas. The Santa Fe accelerates far faster than I'm ready for, and I nearly drive off the road. I course-correct at the last second, kick up some gravel and dust on the left side of the road, and then swerve back to the right lane, hitting 50 in a 30 mph zone in just a few seconds.

The winding road forces me to slow down a bit, but I push the limit, screeching around corners and weaving into the wrong lane. The Santa Fe's safety features are getting pissed, beeping at me, vibrating the steering wheel, and attempting to correct for me. The most difficult thing about driving this vehicle is driving it unsafely.

The winding road ends at a T junction. The pizza place is either to the left or the right. I was hoping for a sign, but there's no indication of anything. Not even a street name or a route number. Just a run-down silo in an overgrown field that probably serves as a landmark for giving directions.

I look both ways. Elias and I came from the left on our way here. I don't recall seeing a pizza place, or anything else, when we came, so I turn right and floor it. The road is wide and straight. I level my speed out at 70 mph. If a moose steps out in front of me—not unheard of in this part of the world—even the vehicle's auto-stop feature won't keep me from plowing into it.

This is nuts.

How is any of this real?

Serial killer. Aliens. UFOs.

I've pondered the idea of life being a simulation for a few years, and the longer I live, the more it seems possible. If life is a simulation, in the way we think of it, then it would require a development team to update it on occasion. Add new plots and subplots. New and better NPCs to interact with. And all of that requires writing. Dialogue. Plotlines. Characters.

Most people don't think about that with game design. For all the code writing I do—less now that AI does some of the work for me—I do just as much creative writing.

So, if life is a simulation, like *Shadowborn* on crack, then it would require a team of writers. Given the scope of the simulation, it would need a LOT of writers. Or a sophisticated AI. That said, when a game has been around for a long time—even just ten years, never mind billions—the best writers are moved to the newest projects. Over time, the creative team is degraded to the B team, the C team and on down the line. Eventually, they're just recycling old storylines, and ripping off novels and movies. In our simulation, where people are writing our own fiction, I suspect the current dev team is just ripping off the stories created by characters within the sim.

It explains modern-day politics, which is like a bad 1980s vision of the future that struck viewers as ridiculous and unbelievable. And yet, here we are, living through an embarrassing political era. And it explains my life.

A wife murdered by a serial killer that breaks and bends bodies into works of art.

Traveling to a campground in the middle of nowhere without realizing it was a trap set by the very same serial killer.

Being abducted with a group of strangers that took us in, the way the Weasleys did Harry Potter.

A mind-meld with an alien, who singles me out for being different, just to show me another alien that's also been killed and mutilated.

Fucking bullshit.

Whoever is running this simulation is dipping their pen into a dried-up inkwell. Sure, it's a genre mashup that hasn't been done before, but it's like the Z-team currently in charge of the sim doesn't give a rip about suspension of disbelief.

Because all of this is unbelievable.

And yet . . . here I am, now going 80 mph in a 40 zone. If I pass a cop, I'll be arrested and no use to anyone, including my son. I take my foot off the gas to slow down and then cruise past a small building that'd been hidden by trees. I catch a glimpse of it, spot a small parking lot, a picture of a slice of pizza, and Emmett's truck.

I slam on the brakes, and the anti-lock system grinds me to a quick stop without leaving a patch of burnt rubber behind me. I crank the wheel, step on the gas, and surge back the way I came. The brakes don't work as well on the gravel parking lot, and I nearly crash into Emmett's parked truck.

The Santa Fe beeps angrily at me as I get out of the running vehicle, leave the door open, and charge inside the small pizza place/ice cream parlor. I nearly knock Elias over.

"Whoa!" he says, leaning back, trying not to drop the five pizzas stacked in his arms. "Dad? What are you doing here? We got pepperoni."

I take the pizza boxes out of his arms and place them on a table. "We're leaving."

"We were about to leave," Emmett says. "Are . . . you okay?"

"We're going home," I say.

"I don't want to go home," Elias says. "I'm having fun."

"I know, buddy," I say, out of breath and trying to control myself. Last thing I need is to make a scene and look like I've lost my mind. "We just . . . I don't have a choice."

"What happened?" Emmett asks, squinting at me. "Are the others okay?"

"Fine," I say. "Maybe. Let's just say that several of my fears from the past few days have been realized."

Emmett understands. His eyes widen. "Should I call the—"

"After we leave," I say. "To be safe."

"Safe from what?" Elias says, losing patience. "Tell me what's going on or I'm not going anywhere."

"Elias," Emmett says. "You need to listen to your father. He's doing what's best for you."

"Bullshit!" Elias shouts. It's an uncommon outburst. "We've spent the past year hiding inside our house, and now that he's finally stepped out into the light, he wants to crawl back into his bedroom and cry some more?"

"Elias!" Emmett's shout catches both Elias and me off guard. "Do not speak to your father like that. The things he's endured . . ." He shakes his head, actively trying to calm himself down. "Look, I have your contact information. When things settle down, I'll call you. We'll make sure to see you again."

"I want to be here," Elias says. "Now."

"We don't always get what we want," Emmett says, doing a better job at grandparenting than my own parents did before they passed. "Now, take a pizza for the road and do what your father tells you. We'll be in touch." He pushes a pizza box against Elias's chest.

My son hesitates for a moment and then accepts the pizza. "Fine."

Elias storms out to the Santa Fe.

Emmett takes hold of my arm. "What happened?"

"Our friends from the sky came back," I tell him. "They're looking for someone."

"Who?"

"The same man who killed my wife," I say. "I was right about the brochure. He was at the campground. Was abducted along with the rest of us. Killed one of the aliens. Same way he did my wife. I . . . I think they're out for revenge. Or justice. Whatever aliens do with murderers."

Emmett deflates. Whispers, "Judas Priest." He shakes his head like he's waking from a dream. "Go. Go now."

We shake hands, and I run back to the SUV, relieved to find Elias in the passenger's seat and buckled up. I put the Santa Fe in reverse, spin the car around, and then spew gravel as we speed back onto the road.

We make it five feet before the Santa Fe's safety system snaps the vehicle to a stop. The road ahead is blocked by a seven foot tall, goddamned owl.

26

Whoa!" Elias says, eyes wide, staring at the owl that is not an owl. "Dad, are you *seeing* this?!"

I step on the gas, determined to get my son as far away from this bullshit as I can, even if it means running over an alien. But the car doesn't budge. At first, I think it's the safety features keeping me from hitting an object, but when I look down at the dash, the digital display is black.

I press the brake and push the start button again.

Nothing.

The SUV has been disabled.

"No!" I shout, and fling open my door. I storm around the front of the Santa Fe, fists clenched, ready to deliver an intergalactic beat down.

I don't get the chance.

The owl cranes its head toward me and the illusion dissipates. The cold, emotionless mask staring at me staggers me a step, but I freeze in place when it speaks inside my head.

STOP.

Fist cocked back, I freeze in place. "Let me go."

Motion redirects my gaze to the pizza place door. Emmett is there, walking calmly toward us. At first, I think he's in on it. Somehow partnered with the aliens. But when he gets close, I see the blank stare. He's under control.

When he's a few feet away, brilliant white light from above floods the area. Emmett lifts off the ground, tilts back and ascends. I can't see the UFO because I can't move my neck, but I know it's there.

I glance toward the SUV and spot Elias inside, leaning forward, looking up, not yet frozen in place. But he will be.

"NO," I say, "Not again."

I fight with all my strength, but I can't break free. As soon as Emmett reaches the ten-foot mark, I'll go next. Just like what we saw on the video. I've got seconds.

Motivation comes in the form of recent memories granted to me by Mac, who might be the alien standing in front of me. I see his memory of the bent, broken, and reformed alien body. The memory flickers and becomes Isabella's misshapen form beneath a sheet.

My desperation reaches a new level of intensity.

They're collecting everyone they took last night, including my wife's killer. A psychopath who somehow broke free from control and managed to murder one of Mac's buddies. The very same killer who lured Elias and me to Moose Hollow.

"I can't let you take us," I say through grinding teeth. "You're going to get us killed!"

My charged punch is suddenly free from control. I shout in pain when my fist connects with the alien's mask. As surprised as I am, the alien is unprepared for the strike and sprawls back onto the gravel.

I dash to the SUV door, throw it open, and—am tugged skyward. As my feet come off the ground, I grab the steering wheel and pull myself halfway into the vehicle—which is still dead. I'd imagined driving away, but that's not going to happen.

"Elias! You need to run!"

"I don't think it will matter," he says, voice dull, resigned to the fact that getting away isn't possible.

"Fuck that!" I shout, catching him off guard with my language. "Open your goddamned door and run! I'll be right behind you."

He hesitates.

"Why?" he asks.

"What do you mean why?!" I pull myself in a little farther, but my legs are bent back down, and the tug-o-war is starting to hurt. "Aliens are trying to abduct us!"

"Aliens bring people back," he says. "What are you *really* afraid of? Tell me, or I'm not going."

I debate whether to answer for an immeasurably short time and then spit out the truth. "The man who killed your mother tricked us into visiting the campground, probably to kill us, but he was abducted with the rest of us and killed one of the aliens! Now they're after us all again to find out who the killer is, but whoever it is knows how to get free. We won't be safe. We won't—"

Elias's brow furrows. "*You're* free."

"What? Yeah. I—Elias, please. You need to run!"

He stares into my eyes and for the first time since his mother died, I see suspicion. Then he leans away, casually opens his door, steps outside, and runs. He disappears into the woods a moment later.

With Elias gone, I can focus on myself.

I pull with everything I've got. Feels like a boa constrictor has ahold of my legs and is pulling me up into its tree. But most of my body is inside and the SUV has more than enough handholds to grasp and pull on. I make slow progress, and once my ankles reach the door's edge, the light releases me.

I sprawl forward, smooshing my face into the passenger's seat. Not about to waste time, I lunge forward, planning to exit the other side and chase after Elias. But as I drag myself through the vehicle, the doors slam closed from the outside.

The passenger's side door crashes into the top of my head, stunning me and eliciting a string of shouted curses. When I sit up, the owl is back, staring at me through the windshield.

"I know what you are, dumbass!" I shout. "You don't need to—"

The owl façade dissipates, replaced by the much more frightening bug-eyed mask.

I take hold of the door handle, pull, and then push on the door. It's not locked, but it's also not opening. Then the front end of the Santa Fe comes off the ground.

They're taking the whole vehicle!

"Fuck this!" I shout, crawling over the center panel into the back seat, and then into the cargo area. I try opening the rear hatch, but it doesn't budge. *Needs power*, I realize. *Unless . . .* The dealer showed me how to open this door without power. There's an emergency release lever . . . there! I slide open the small plastic cover, revealing a lever.

Sounds easy, but the dealer suggested keeping a screwdriver in the car just in case. Not sure why an emergency lever wouldn't be moveable with a bare hand, but this isn't the time to one-star review a dealership. I dig my keys from my pocket and shove my house key into the slot. A screwdriver would provide leverage to get this done quickly, but the key offers no help.

The SUV lifts to a forty-five-degree angle. I'm about to face-plant on the back window.

"C'mon," I shout, arms shaking as I put everything I've got into the key. The lever feels like it's locked in place—until it isn't. It snaps open, and the back door lifts. The angle of the car tips me out like a dump truck heaving trash into a landfill. I hit the ground hard. Knocks the air from my lungs. But I don't linger to catch my breath. I'm on my feet and running for the trees, my exit blocked by the rising vehicle.

At the tree line, I glance back and watch the back end of the vehicle roll forward and then come off the ground.

Won't be long until they realize I got away.

This random bit of forest is nothing like the campground, which has been populated and cleared by generations of people. There are downed branches everywhere mixed with lumps of ferns, chunks of granite, and low-hanging sapling branches. Moving quickly is impossible. Moving quietly is harder.

Need to find a game trail.

If there is such a thing in Maine? Do moose and deer use game trails or can they just work their way through this mess with their nimble legs and two-toed hooves? Skunks and raccoons don't need trails. They can just hop and scurry through this mess.

How did humans ever survive on this planet long enough to evolve into the dominant species when we can't even navigate an unmanicured forest?

I'm ten feet in when I hear a snapping branch up ahead.

"Elias!" I whisper.

No response, but I head for the sound.

My feet slurp down into mud concealed by old fallen leaves. Nearly lose my shoe when I pull it back out.

I take a moment to gather my thoughts. *Use the fallen branches,* I think. The ground can't be trusted. Foot on a branch, I start a balancing act that gets me moving much faster, but I'm far from steady. The branches keep me from sinking into muck and help flatten brush, but they're also wobbly and, in some cases, rotten.

A log crumbles under my foot. The bark slides away. The wood falls apart like a slow-cooked pot roast.

I reach up and grab a leaf-laden branch, hanging on tight. But the half-inch-thick branch bends with my weight, slowly lowering me to the ground, lying me down in a patch of mud.

"Mother fu—" The curse catches in my throat.

Elias is floating in the air above me, caught in a beam of light. He's lying back, arms and legs limp, twenty feet up. They're taking him without me!

I fight the forest to stand again but just manage to slip and fall onto my side. I wave my hands up at the UFO, barely visible through the canopy. "Hey! I'm here! Take me, too! Hey! I'm right here!"

When the blazing white light shifts in my direction, I lean back, close my eyes, and wait to be lifted off the ground. I'm unconscious before it happens.

27

ABERRATION

"Is that you?"

It *is* you, we can feel you watching. Your eager eyes are thirsty to witness the artist in our studio, turning raw materials into an image that is beautiful. Or disturbing. What's important is that it stirs the emotions.

Beauty is in the eye of the beholder, they say. Some people look at a mountainous Bob Ross landscape and see cliché. Others are mesmerized by the master of palette knife painting, displaying a cookie-cutter painting with pride.

We prefer more avant-garde subject matters and materials. The only thing cookie cutter about our work would be the use of actual cookie cutters. A vision flits through our mind. A different kind of dough stretched out on a kitchen counter. But pushing a cookie cutter through the skin of a human being would either require great pressure—probably more than we can muster—or a razor-sharp cutter, which we can manage.

And what a treat it would be, don't you think? Left on the counter for loved ones. In mourning, they reach for a cookie and bite in, unaware that they are noshing on the remains that police just couldn't find. We wonder if they'd even think to look at the gingerbread men decorated with frosting and little red, hot candy hearts.

You want to see it, too. We know. But that scenario will have to wait. Right now, we're back on stage in what might be the greatest scenario people like us long to experience. Prey abounds. Human and . . . not. And they're confined. We're supposed to be a prisoner, once again locked down like the others. But we are free to move when we're ready.

First, a plan.

We're not fond of spontaneity, you know. Randomness is the street sign marking the road to prison. But the alien . . . That was different. There are no laws against killing a being that doesn't belong on this planet. That random act of delight couldn't be turned down.

And now look at us! We're back. Given a second chance.

Time to maximize the opportunity.

We need some guidelines to ensure we aren't so distracted by the first opportunity that we miss the next.

Rule one: Do not hesitate to end a life, human or alien, unless . . .

Rule two: Do not take a life if in a position to be overpowered.

Rule three: Do not take a life if there isn't time to work with the body.

Rule four: Do not take a life if the end result won't be wholly satisfying.

Rule four is for you, by the way. We kill for us. Our art is for you, you perverse death ogler. Oh, did that make you grin? How well do we know you? We can smell your pheromones, oozing desire. How you long to bear witness.

Such pressure!

Silly goose. Artists need time, you know? To imagine. To create. To weave meaning into the meaningless.

With our rules in place, we work out a plan.

Step one: Shock and awe. The occupants of the room in which we're being stored number seven other people. We can only see four of them from our position on the second bunk up on the opposite wall, but we suspect every bunk is full, as before. All of them are naked once again. Helpless. Like newborns. And they're all strangers, which doesn't create any complication for us.

We would have been disappointed if the Man was here. We have special plans for him. But that masterpiece is for another time.

We spared the helpless previously, because there wasn't any sport in it. But we're sending a message this time. We're not sure what it will take to make a non-human species panic, but we're delighted by the prospect of finding out.

Step two: Delay our return to Earth. We need to make chaos.

But how?

What do you think? Really, take a moment and work it out. What could we do to cause such a hubbub that our return to Earth would be delayed?

Oh, *yes*. We hear you. Yes, that will do.

Like Moses, we will set our people free. We will unleash plagues and horrors. We will show no mercy to these god-men. And when we are done, we will walk free to continue our heavenly work on Earth.

More of a prophecy than a plan, but we like that even more.

We'll find out who the gods are.

We roll out of the cot that's conformed to our body and land on the floor without a sound, the malleable surface bending under our weight.

The previously unseen bunkmates are revealed. Two of them. Someone is missing. Six victims or seven, it doesn't matter. The message won't be diminished.

Tools, we think. How can we do this without a blade, blunt object, or palette knife? Bob Ross would find a way. A happy little limb here, a cute coil of entrails there.

We can kill them with our hands. In their current state, it will be easy. But the art . . . We smile.

Necessity is the mother of invention, they say.

We'll try something new.

And we're sorry, but what happens next is not for you. You're not ready for it. We know. It's a tease, edging you right up to the moment of release. But you'll appreciate it more when it happens.

We're doing this for you, after all.

It's why you're here, watching. All of you. Looking down at us while looking up to us. You crave our power. You long to imagine your enemies in our hands, turned into pigments for our canvas.

We only exist because you long for us.

Long for this reality where a killer is gifted a scenario unlike any other.

Long to watch.

To see.

To feel orgasmic catharsis.

Don't worry. We won't make you wait long. But the time must be right. This? These people? They're just a primer. An hors d'oeuvre before a main course. Watching now would be like looking in the kitchen to see the squid pulled apart, limbs writhing while it's dismembered, debeaked, and sliced into bite-sized portions.

You might lose your appetite. And that would be a shame since you're this far into our magnum opus.

We crack our knuckles and look over the six people. Four men. Two women.

We'll start with the men. They'll take more work. We'll be tired by the time we're ready for the females. But they won't require the same effort. It's sexist, we know, but women . . . They're easier to kill. And not just because they're less likely to see the evil intent in someone's eyes. They're just . . . smaller. Most of them, anyway.

The men will be our base coat. Our mountains if you will. And the women? They will be accents that bring the painting to life. Sunshine glinting off water and warming the needles of tapped-out, fan-brush pine trees.

It's going to be awesome.

You'll see.

Eventually.

Not now.

Now . . . now it's time for you to get the fuck out of our head and let us work.

"Toodles."

28

Wake up."

The voice is deep and gravelly. The confidence behind it feels like Mac's voice in my head. But whoever is speaking to me is not in my head. I open my eyes to find myself sitting upright, and fully clothed. My arms are bound to the chair in which I'm seated. Not by a rope or a zip-tie, but by the chair itself. The chair is made of the same pliable stuff as the floor and walls. In fact, I think the chair is rising from the floor. A temporary construct.

"Where are you?" I ask. My voice sounds rough. Throat is scratchy. Makes me wonder if they've already done their probing.

"Remain calm." The tall figure of Mac—I think it's Mac—glides around from behind me, still concealed by his freakshow mask and long, flowing cloak. Strikes me as regal this time, like he's someone important, or at least wants people to view him that way.

Despite his presence, I do what he asks and remain calm. But I think that has more to do with a tweak he's made to my mind or nervous system, because I should be freaking the fuck out. Instead, speaking to him is more like speaking to a B-list celebrity. A little nervous, but manageable.

"What do you want?" I ask, fighting my bonds. The material around my arms bends from the pressure I put on it. I can't hurt myself on it. Also can't break free.

"Cooperation," Mac says.

"Why are you using your real voice?" I ask. "And wait. Hold on. You speak English?"

"I speak for your comfort and to establish trust." He squats in front of me, our heads level. His big, black, unblinking eyes stare at me. "As for English . . . The languages of your people are simple. Easy to learn."

"Must be easier when you can just absorb the thoughts of people, right?"

I was nervously joking. Didn't mean a word of it. But he nods and says, "Indeed."

"Great," I say, a sneeze away from a panic attack. Mac isn't trying to frighten me, but what kind of person could look an alien in the face and not be terrified? "Awesome. Can you just tell me why I'm here? And where my son is?"

"Your son is safe," he says, understanding that Elias is my primary concern. "You are here for justice."

"Wait. Hold on. You don't think that I—"

"No. You are an aberration, but you, like Geshtu-e, are a victim of this killer. You will help us determine the identity of this . . . Shadowhand."

Feels like I've just been slapped in the side of my head. "'Shadowhand?' How do you know what that is?"

The Shadowhand is the final boss in *Shadowborn*. He's an evil mage with incredible power and a long list of atrocities under his belt. Most players fight against the Shadowhand, even if they're mostly on the evil side of things. A select few finish the game *as* the Shadowhand. In my game, both good and evil are capable of winning.

"We learn from every mind we connect with," he says.

"You said—"

"I am not in your mind *now*," he says.

I get it. He needs my help, so he's not violating my mind at the moment. But they did before, when I was just a subject. They learned what was in my head. They've seen my whole life. Know every line of code I've written. Assholes.

Being a video game creator suddenly feels like a waste of my life. Aliens—or whatever Mac is—are real. People are being abducted and studied by a species whose technology dwarfs our own. It's a paradigm shift. I saw game creation as a way to enjoy the life I'd been given. I'd have a family and do my best to create worlds that entertain people. Maybe even make them think. That was my legacy.

Now? How can I continue to live that life knowing that there is so much more going on? *Shadowborn* is a part of me, but it feels far less important now.

"Clear your mind," he says. Not sure if he's just reading my expression, or my thoughts.

"Clear my mind? Are you serious? Do you have any idea what all of this—How could you? This is your life. My mind feels like it's exploding."

"I could help with that," he says, lifting a long, gloved finger toward my forehead.

I twist my head away, fighting to free myself. "Fuck off, E.T. Don't screw with my mind ever again."

He stares in silence. Lowers his finger. But he doesn't address my request.

"If you want my help," I say, "you need to swear—Do you know what that means? To swear? To promise?"

"Understand," he says with a subtle nod, "but my people do not require special words to honor an agreement."

"Then agree to it," I say. "Agree you won't fuck with my mind. Not one more time."

"Agreed," he says. Doesn't even take a moment to think about it.

Not sure I believe him. His people could also be compulsive liars. Nothing to be done about it, so I'll accept our new alliance as genuine, until I have reason to doubt it.

"Excellent," he says, standing back up, towering over me. He lifts his hands to the side of his head and takes hold of the mask.

"What are you—"

"Establishing trust," he says. "Your life has been laid bare—against your will. I must do the same for you now. Starting with showing you who we truly are."

The mask lifts away, revealing his face starting at a slender chin. The skin is chalky blue and mildly contoured. The mouth is lipless and narrow. Slightly downturned. The nose is small. Almost childlike. And then . . . the eyes. They're large and black, like the mask, but these are the traditional 'gray,' almond-shaped eyes. They're not as big as normally depicted. His forehead feels proportionally tall, but what emerges next really catches me off guard. Hair. Wavy golden locks fall on the sides of his face, giving him a much more human—and less frightening look.

"Are you . . . human? Part human?"

"That would depend on how you define what is human," he says. "I have almost nothing in common with the precursor to modern humanity. But for the past three hundred thousand years, humanity has been partly Anu."

Doesn't take a genius to understand what he's saying. "You genetically altered people? Three hundred thousand years ago? Who are the Anu? Where do you come from?"

"Answers will come," he says as his cloak pulls itself inward, wrapping around his body and melting into something far less gawdy and closer to a uniform. The form fitting, black outfit—like an Alien Spec-Ops uniform—reveals his lanky shape. Doesn't look weak. Just long limbed. Slight ridges reveal armored sections in all the places you'd expect them, along with the sides of his midsection. There are also long tubes twisting out through the fabric. Look like veins, but probably some kind of cooling system. Who really knows? Probably dangerous to make any kind of assumptions based on my human knowledge base.

When Mac was all dressed up in his flowing gown, he looked ominous and intelligent. Now . . . he looks dangerous. Ready for a fight.

"You don't look like you need my help," I say.

He looks down, arms spread wide as he examines himself. "It has been millennia since I was required to physically protect myself. I am . . . out of practice."

"You looked through my life," I say. "You know that I'm not a violent person."

"Your simulation contains violence on a human scale."

"A human scale."

"You have the capacity to end all life in *Shadowborn*, just as you do in this reality."

"You're talking about nukes?"

He nods.

"Is *that* why you're here? Why you're watching us?"

"It is not why we are here," he says, and I remember that they've been here since long before people could do much more than smash rocks together. "But it is why we started . . . paying attention."

"In the forties," I say, remembering the lore. "During World War II. The foo fighters. Wait, is Roswell real? Did some of you crash there?"

"I can neither confirm nor deny . . ." He lets the sentence trail off as his small mouth grins.

"A sense of humor," I say to myself. "Great."

"An attempt to slow your racing heart," he says.

"That will happen when I've got my son, at home, with an agreement from you that you won't abduct us again."

"I can make that agreement," he says. "For your son."

"But not for me."

"You . . . This conversation. It is rare. Aside from a select few, our peoples have not directly conversed in thousands of years."

"Because we are beneath you?" I ask.

He nods. "But that is changing."

"We've had nuclear weapons for eighty years," I say. "What are you worried about now?"

"A developing technology that is far more dangerous."

"So, we'll finally destroy ourselves, huh?"

"You will save yourselves," he says.

"Then what's the—"

"It is life beyond your world that will suffer."

"Ah," I say, understanding. Humanity doesn't have the best track record when it comes to expansion. "Including you?"

He tilts his head downward. "Indeed. There was a time when we were revered as gods on this world. And that suited our needs, so it was allowed. When the Separation began, and we were forced to abandon this world for a time, you were freed to develop on your own. No one foresaw what you would become. We are not supposed to interfere, but that may soon change."

"What technology?" I ask.

"You call it artificial intelligence. If I'm not mistaken, you employ a form of this intelligence to bring life to your game NPCs."

"I do," I whisper, mind flitting through all the possibilities AI presents, and I struggle to come up with a reason a species already so far advanced would fear artificial intelligence. But that's not the question that comes out. Instead, I ask something I've been wondering since the beginning of this conversation. Something that increased tenfold when he mentioned humanity worshipping his kind. "Who *are* you?"

He stands tall. Almost proud. "Anunnaki."

29

I stare at him for a moment. "That supposed to mean something to me?"

He looks disappointed, and I find it strange that I can read the expressions of an alien being. Shouldn't they be totally different from humans? Like a blob of worms zipped into a body suit or something? What are the odds that a creature from somewhere else in the galaxy looks humanoid?

I know that's the way it works in *Star Trek* because some ancient civilization decided to spread their space seed throughout the universe, but this isn't *Star Trek*. Aliens should be . . . alien. Unless evolution has some universal guidelines to which it adheres.

"Let me show you," he says, lifting a hand toward my forehead.

"Wait, wait, wait." I lean my head back. "That's really unnerving."

His fingers pause an inch from my head. "This is a more efficient method of communication."

"It's a more efficient way of freaking me the fuck out," I say, voice shaky. "You can just tell me. Give me the CliffsNotes version. Unless experiencing your history firsthand will give me insight on the killer, I don't need to live it to believe it."

I sense disappointment.

"You . . . you wanted me to see you as you were. Godlike and glorious. Must have been something. Different than now, right?"

"Very," he admits. "I will attempt to explain the situation in simple human terms. Your scientists have posited the existence of a ninth planet in our solar system—"

"Tenth," I say. "I'm team Pluto."

He ignores the comment. "They have observed the gravitational effects of this so-called Planet-X but have been unable to find it."

"I've heard of this," I say. "The orbit is elliptical, right? And long. Like fourteen thousand years."

"That is the theory," he says. "The theory is wrong. Aškaru, like Earth, is within what humans call the Goldilocks Zone. As you know, life—as we understand it—would not be able to naturally survive outside this region of space."

"Goldilocks," I say. "Got it. Not too hot. Not too cold."

"You are a genius among men," he says, and it's completely deadpan, but I know he's fucking with me.

"If Aškaru is in a similar orbit to Earth, why can't we see it? I mean, it would be obvious right? Is it on the opposite side of the sun or something?"

"On the other side of the sun . . ." He's confused for a moment, and I realize it's because my question is that stupid. "Are . . . are you suggesting that Aškaru and Earth are perfectly placed on opposite sides of Sol . . . with synchronous orbits?"

He's not laughing—not even sure if he can—but amusement somehow radiates from his large black eyes.

"Okay, okay," I say, holding up my hands. "You can just say no. Is this what you were like when you were pretending to be gods? All high and mighty?"

"You were slightly more evolved than apes when we arrived," he says.

I roll my eyes. "Back to Aškaru."

"We are wasting time," he says. "Please let me—"

"*Who* is wasting time?"

He sighs. "Our world exists in a phased state. We share this solar system but are offset by a fractional dimension. Aškaru's gravity echoes into this space, hence the observed anomalies, but the planet's mass is concealed."

"Is that a natural phenomenon?" I ask.

"It is the same cloaking technology that allows us to move around Earth unobserved."

"Mostly unobserved," I point out. "But why? What's with all the cloak and dagger?"

He waves his hand at the floor and a chair rises up opposite mine. It looks liquid and pliable until its final, curved form is attained. Then it becomes solid. He sits.

"Nice trick," I say.

"Trick," he says, and I think I catch a chuckle. He waves his long-fingered hand in front of his face like a magician. "Science." The bindings holding my arms down melt away and become part of the armrests of my chair.

The close-up view of his hand lets me count his fingers. One extra. Better hope the serial killer isn't Inigo Montoya.

Part of me revolts at my casual thoughts. There's a serial killer on this ship, and so is my son. We need to wrap this up and do what needs doing. But . . . I'm just . . . resigned to this conversation. He might not be controlling my thoughts, but the effect he has on my emotions feels like a supreme antidepressant. Better than the shit I've been on since Isabella . . .

"Okay, I buy it. You're our solar system buddies. You ruled as Gods. Assuming you fucked around with our ape brains. Made us smarter? More suited for your needs. Guessing you made us slaves. Not sure why you wouldn't just use your fancy tech for whatever it was you needed, but—"

"Mating," he says, and I'm caught off guard.

"'Scuse me? Come again?"

"Our population was diminishing as we evolved beyond the need or desire for copulation."

"You . . . you were *fucking* us?" I shout.

"The exact process is beyond your understanding, but yes, we were using Earth women to birth our young, and in some cases, hybrids of our peoples. The human genome developed further with each new generation. When the program was ended, humanity was a few generations away from being satisfactory partners capable of producing young that were ninety-nine percent Anunnaki."

"Not that I'm complaining, but why was the program stopped?"

"Another solution was found, resulting in young that were a hundred percent Anunnaki, and thus superior. We left this world shortly after, but recognized our impact on humanity had been significant. We understood that, while it was likely you would die out without our guidance, you also possessed the potential to one day evolve into something . . . more. A contingent of Anunnaki were left behind to track humanity's progress."

"So, you're . . . one of them? You've been around for thousands of years, just studying us?"

"Yes, and no." He motions to himself. "This body is fifty Earth-years in age. Adolescent by our standards. But my mind and memories can be traced back to the days before our arrival on this world. We pass our intellect down through generations. As one body nears the end of its natural cycle—for us that is three hundred Earth years—we, what did you call it? We 'mind meld' with a newborn. When the transfer is complete, we are born anew, and our elder husks pass away."

"And now . . . humans have become something more," I say.

"You are on the cusp," he says.

"And that frightens you."

"Rightly so."

"I felt bad about it the first time you brought it up," I say. "Humanity being a power-hungry colonial species. But now? C'mon. Your people pillaged the wombs of a neighboring planet."

"At the time, it was no different than the experiments your own people carry out on the lesser species populating this planet. Pigs are used to grow organs. Humans are gene editing embryos and animals. Transgenic goats whose udders excrete spider silk. *You* were animals. Simple-minded primates. And you still would be, if not for our . . . pillaging."

I grunt in response. What am I supposed to say? It's abhorrent, but he's right. I guess we're all a bit monstrous. Runs in our shared genes.

"Okay, seriously, what's the point of all this getting-to-know-you bullshit? I know you're not here to have an intellectual debate, and I don't really think you give a rip about any of us, right? We're subjects. The slime-mold left in the corner of the fridge that's suddenly growing out of control. So, what's up? Tell me now, or I'm—"

"We need your help," he says.

That catches me off guard, but I roll with it. "With?"

"As you now know, we are scientists. We are not a warring species. We solve problems with science, not weapons."

"That's why you're hiding," I say. "Your entire planet. Your presence on Earth. For all your advanced technology, you're just . . . a bunch of pussies?"

"A crude term, and I do not appreciate the tone, but . . . yes. Violence is as unfamiliar to us as common sense is to you."

There's that humor again.

"Why do you need to hide your entire planet? We didn't dip our toes into space until recently, and yeah, AI might change things, but that's *really* new." The answer comes to me before he has a chance to answer. "Because you're not just afraid of people from Earth."

"There are other species that share your penchant for expansion. If they find Aškaru, we would be defenseless. As would Earth. Your scientists call it the Fermi Paradox. Life is hard to find in the universe, not because it doesn't exist, but because it's hiding."

"Why the hell aren't you hiding us yet?"

"It is unlikely you will be detected until humans leave this solar system."

"According to you, with AI, that will be sooner rather than later."

He nods. "It is being addressed."

I hold up my hands, trying not to get sidetracked by his admittedly interesting revelations. "Okay, enough with the tangents. Tell me what you want me to do."

He cocks his head to the side. "We want you to find the killer, of course." His head twists the other way. "And kill him."

30

Kill? *Me?*" It's absurd. "I'm not a violent person."

"You are not," the alien I've nicknamed Mac says. "But all humans are capable of great violence in the right circumstances. The man I've asked you to kill is the murderer of your wife. The man who desecrated her body and—"

"Stop," I say, very quickly shifting into a state of mind in which violence doesn't seem like such a bad idea.

"You see?" he says. "It is natural for you and part of why humanity has been so successful. After most of the Anunnaki left this world, we expected humanity to die out within a few generations. Instead, you adapted and survived without our guidance. We granted you intelligence, but your ability to overcome physical adversity, to solve problems, to evolve, that comes from your ancestors. The combination of the two made you stronger than any of my people surmised."

"And now we're a problem," I say.

"A possibility, but we will not allow you to pass the Fermi threshold. And we will not allow you to threaten Aškaru."

"How will you stop that from happening?" I ask. "Seems like a fair question if you're asking for my protection now."

"A course correction," he says. "Full exposure. Plans are already in motion. Your people are being acclimatized to the idea of life on other worlds visiting your own. You are becoming familiar with several versions of what we look like."

"The hair is a surprise, honestly," I say.

"Your people did not have blond hair when we arrived," he says. "In many ways, we are more similar than different."

"Because you changed us," I say.

"Would you have us undo the changes made to your species? You could return to the days of feasting on grubs, of being eaten by predators, of nomadic cave living. I do not believe a single person on this world would choose that life."

He's right about that. And I honestly don't mind the idea of humanity being partly alien. It's . . . kind of awesome. And terrifying. I know that logically, but, "You're still keeping me calm, aren't you."

He nods. "That embarrasses you?"

"Human men like to think we can handle a lot," I say.

"Then take pride in the fact that my effort is minimal. You are growing accustomed to my presence. But it is not something we can do on a global scale."

"Hence the slow approach to first contact," I say. "But . . . how are you doing it? Aliens—that mostly look like you—are pervasive in pop culture."

"We . . . *influence* certain creatives," he says. "Nudge them toward ideas."

"Holy shit, you *implant* story concepts?" My mind scrolls through a list of science-fiction media. "*Close Encounters of the Third Kind*. Stephen Spielberg."

"One of our best results," he says.

"*Communion*," I say.

"Clearly."

"*Resident Alien*."

"Indeed."

"*The Others*."

"A favorite," he says. "And the closest to understanding that we are already here and have been for a very long time. The author is one of our most common . . . collaborators."

"But a lot of these stories don't present you in the best light," I say. "I mean, have you seen *No One Will Save You*?"

"Mmm," he says. "A frightening tale to be sure. But the content of the story is not what matters. Your people—most of them—understand that truth is different from fiction. It is more important that you grow accustomed to this visage." He waves his hand around in front of his face. "As you are doing now. Would you like me to arrest my influence on your emotional responses? I believe it is a necessary step if you are to survive your encounter with the killer. Fear triggers an adrenaline spike that sharpens your senses and increases reaction times."

I take a deep breath and let it out slowly. "Let's do it. Let me have all the feels. I'm ready for it."

"I'm not sure you are," he says.

"I can adapt, right? It's what humans do."

The chair's arm bindings reappear and wrap around my forearms. I struggle against them for a moment, and say, "Hey, what the hell?"

"It is a necessary step," he says. "For my protection."

"Oh."

"While we have conversed calmly with a high degree of trust and respect that might carry on, you will be experiencing the totality of your natural anxiety that I've been masking, all at once. It will be overwhelming."

"That's why you create screen memories," I say.

He shows a slight smile. "You have been speaking to Serena."

"Uh, yeah . . ."

"A fascinating subject," he says. "In some regards, a friend."

"She knows about you?"

"A part of her does," he says. "She, like you, managed to fully wake up and have a conversation, as we are now. Over the years, we have had many conversations."

"And you *erase* them all?" I ask, not thrilled by the idea. "You replace them with screen memories?"

"While that is our standard practice, to spare humans from psychological distress, Serena is a special case. Upon her return, her memories are re-activated and our relationship carries on.

When she leaves, we screen the memories at her request, so that she might focus on her work, which she believes to be important—"

"Do you know what that work is?" I ask.

He thinks on that for a moment. "I . . . do not."

"Okay, okay. Listen. You've got everyone knocked out, right? So, you've already got the killer caught. Which means we just need to interview everyone, one at a time, to figure out who did it."

"And you believe Serena would be able to—"

"She is a psychologist who specializes in *serial killers*!"

"I see . . . Perhaps you should interview her first and then employ her help."

"You think?! And why the hell aren't you mind melding everyone?"

"That was the first thing we did," he says. "We were unable to detect nefarious intentions or a memory of the murder which took place. Do you have any more questions before we begin?"

"What is your name?" I ask.

"I am Kova. Now, brace yourself."

"*Wait, wait, wait,*" I say. "One more question. Where are we? On a ship? A UFO? Are we floating in the sky? Landed in a clearing?"

"What does it matter?" Kova asks.

"Context," I say. "The more I know, the less I'll be afraid, when, you know."

"We are on a ship—what you would call a UFO or UAP."

"Are we in orbit?" I ask, feeling a twinge of nervous energy even though my emotions are still being regulated.

He cocks his head to the side. "Indeed. In geosynchronous orbit over the campground from which your group was taken."

"Okay," I say. "Just . . . get it over with.

He stands, and the chair beneath him sinks back into the floor. He takes a step away from me.

"You going to count to three or something?" I ask.

"No."

"How will I know when—geeaaahhh!" Emotion drives into my gut and spreads out through my body. I buck and thrash against the chair. My voice cracks from screaming. My heart convulses. I've never experienced anything this intense, all at once, before. When it slows, I'm heaving for air, head hanging low, drool dangling from my mouth.

"Look at me," Kova says. His voice alone sends a spasm of tingling pain up my back. This is fear like I've never felt it before. "You must look at me if you are to overcome—"

I look.

And I scream. It hurts my ears.

Kova blinks and winces. The sound hurts him as well.

"Remember what you know about me," he says, voice a little less intimidating now. "Remember our trust. I have not changed. Only your perception of me has."

I force myself to look into his large black eyes.

They feel like death.

I lean to the side and vomit. "God," I groan. "Sorry."

"You will adjust," he says. "You must."

"Worse than you made it out to be," I complain.

"Mmm," he says. "Now who is the pussy?"

I bark a laugh, and it helps for about three seconds.

Then . . .

Then the fucking power goes out.

31

ABERRATION

Yeah, that was us. You probably already figured that out. We're officially on a roll. Luck is on our side. Not only did we finish our sculpture, which was more difficult than expected—we've never worked with so many subjects at once before, but we were also interrupted mid-task.

You should have seen its face. The alien. Reeled back in horror. We think it tried to scream, but only a squeak came out. Fell back and hit its head on the wall. Wasn't knocked out, but it was dazed enough to not put up much of a fight when we set upon it like a hungry honey badger.

Our original design for the occupants of this room was for seven people—the seventh being the centerpiece. The pièce de résistance. We were disappointed when there turned out to be just six people in the room with us. But hey, the universe provides, right?

Can you imagine its thoughts? How horribly stupid it must have felt as we pulled out its insides and looped them around the others? Born on another world. Traveled through space. An advanced species destined for greatness. And now—part of a living sculpture. Well, living for now. We don't think any of them are going to last very long.

We breathe deep. The strange earthy scent of the alien's blood lingers in our nose, probably because it's still covering our hands, getting tacky. We don't mind it. The sticky coagulation helped us grip and pull the insides out of a control panel that looked important. There's no bridge. No obvious control room. But there are a few scattered workstations embedded in walls. They're hidden most of the time, but if you know how to manipulate the walls and doors of this place with your mind, they're easy to find.

Honestly, it all feels natural. Like we were meant to be here.

What do you think?

You're being quiet.

Sure, sure, you're watching like you're supposed to, but we're pals. We appreciate your feedback. And your company. This can be a lonely business, you know? Killing? Sure, there are other people involved, but they only talk at the beginning.

The actual act of taking a life, that's the good part. The adrenaline rush. The dopamine dump. The sculptures are our way of honoring the dead. We make them beautiful.

Would you like to see how it's done now?

The power is out, so seeing is an issue. Systems are down. All the liquid wall doors opened when we tore out a handful of little cards from some kind of fancy motherboard looking panel. They no longer respond to our mental commands. The ship is basically useless.

Rats in a maze, with a cat.

We hear voices. Not close, but they're loud, human, and confused. Killing the power broke the control over their minds. Won't be long now.

"Where am I!?" a woman screams.

A handful of people shout replies, but it all just blends together in glorious confusion. The people are getting worked up. How long until they're running through the dark, encountering their worst nightmares?

The aliens. Not us.

They have yet to dream of anything like us.

"I can't see!" she shouts as others shout at her to calm down. To which she replies, "Fuck off!"

Her voice is louder now. She's found her way out of human storage and into the hallway.

"Hello?" we say, emulating someone who is equally afraid. "Who's out there?"

"I can't see you," she whisper-hisses at me.

"That's because the lights are out," we explain. Stupid lady. Moth to a flame. We can tell she's overweight by her labored breathing and heavy footsteps. Easy to take down. Harder to work with. Especially in the dark. But we're always up for a challenge, and the darkness will let us work in peace. "Just follow the sound of my voice."

"Do you know where we are?" she asks.

"No idea," we say, "but I don't think there's anything to worry about."

Oh, my friend, you're smiling, aren't you?

We can feel it.

We're more alike than you'd ever admit.

What would you like us to do? You won't be able to see it, of course, but we can give you the blow by blow.

Speaking of blows, we can tell you're wondering how we'll do it. Strangling everyone? Yawn. Give us some credit. You know how creative we are.

And we do have a weapon now.

We made it.

The handle is a man's humerus, which is bound to an alien scapula—thinner and sharper than the human one. We used a cord of ligaments from the alien to tie them together as a kind of pointed axe. The alien's sticky blood helped secure it all together, acting like glue as it dried and set. But that's not the strangest thing about the blood. It's iridescent. Even now, when it's dry, it shimmers with a gradient of green, blue, and purple, like oil on water, as we shift our perspective.

Sorry, that was a longer explanation than we planned on.

Just didn't want you being confused when we split the woman open.

Hey, you winced.

We don't need to split her open, if that's too much for your first time.

We're not a monster. We're a friend.

The blade is strong enough to punch through her skull. That would be less messy. And faster. Won't have to worry about her putting up a fight. But, hitting a head in the dark . . . That can be tricky.

"Hey," she whispers, closer now. "Where are you?"

"Here," we say, whispering, too, like we're co-conspirators. "Keep talking so I know where your head is."

"My head?"

"All of you," we say. "Sorry, I just said 'head' because that's where your mouth is."

"Who are you?" she asks, sounding suspicious. "Are you from the campground? From that group of weirdos?"

"No one is weird to me," we say. "Sounds like you're getting close."

"Yeah, I'm right next to y—"

Have you ever opened a coconut? Heard that wet crack when the shell breaks? Well, that's the sound the lady's head makes when we bring the scapula blade down like Paul Bunyan chopping down a redwood. She doesn't fall right away. She just kind of mumbles until we pull the weapon out. That's when she falls. And it's not even loud. All that fatty padding cushions the impact. Turns a *thump* into a slap.

That's eight dead if you're keeping track. Oh! That's wrong. No reason we shouldn't count the kill that kicked this vacation into overdrive. *Nine*. Seven people. Two aliens.

A good start.

"Louise?" a man calls out. "Damnit, woman. Where in the hell did you get off to? You're naked, you know! We are *all* naked."

"She's over here," we say. "I think she tripped. Hit her head on the floor."

"Fucksake," the man says. His bare feet slap on the floor as he feels his way toward us. "Where are you?"

"You're almost here." We cock the axe back, and—

—orange light illuminates the interior from within the ceiling. Must be emergency lights or something. Battery powered. On a separate system. Doesn't matter. Only thing that matters is that the man can see us, ready to brain him, standing over

Louise, who is better off without him if you ask us. His eyes flick from the weapon, down to our clothing.

Well, 'clothing.'

We made ourselves a loin cloth from the alien's skin and various other body parts. And its face? Well, it makes a great mask. Slips right over our head. A couple of slits beneath the big black eyes, which are actually like natural goggles and still attached to the face, allows us to see. It fits nice and snug. In his eyes, the man is seeing an alien. And he reacts appropriately, by screaming, turning around, and running.

He takes three steps.

The scapula blade cracks through his ribcage from behind and destroys his heart from the back. He careens forward, hits the floor dead, and slides a few feet.

"George?" Another man. And he's joined by a few more. "I think we're in some kind of . . . I don't know, man. I want to call it a UFO, but, well, that's crazy, right? *George?*"

Not fair. All that work, and we don't have time to arrange them.

But them's the breaks, as they say.

"Also, *ten*."

We'll make them pretty when we can. The number of dead is equally pleasing. And if we can finish them all off, then we can collect them all and make a grand masterpiece from the deceased of two worlds.

We smile, imagining it.

You are, too. That tree of dead bodies, bent, arms twisting out. A sunset in the background. Dust blowing. Sorry, those are my details. And unrealistic. Whatever it is, it will be inside the UFO, and we have a lot of exploring to do still.

We step on the man's bare ass and yank the axe free.

A collection of voices grows louder. George's pals are coming.

We duck into the shadows and slink away into an adjoining hallway. It's curved. Follows the ship's shape.

Isn't this great? Us stalking. You watching. Both of us having the time of our fucking lives. What a pair.

When we're twenty steps down the hall, the screams start, bringing a smile to our goddamned faces. We huff a laugh.

You're smiling, too.

We can feel it.

And yeah, that wasn't exactly what we promised. You came for art, but all you got was a look at the palette. At what we're working with. Don't worry, the next one will be 'mwah,' chef's kiss.

"Listen?" we whisper. "Did you hear that?"

We stand still. Motionless. Even the air in our lungs stops moving.

A new voice.

A woman.

Familiar.

This could be fun.

Buckle up, friend, we're just getting started.

32

Panic rips through my chest. I'm locked in a room with a fucking alien with blond fucking hair, and now I can't see shit. I remember everything he told me. I remember feeling fine during our conversation, but it was all an illusion. Deep inside, my instincts have been screaming. I thought I could get a handle on it, but then the lights went out.

"Calm yourself," Kova says, and I'm instantly calm.

"Thanks," I say. Feels like I've taken a happy pill. Well, not so much happy as . . . peaceful. Like everything is okay in the world.

"It is temporary," he says. "Until your panic subsides."

"Is there a way to make it permanent?" I ask.

"I already explained—"

"Not . . . everything. Not serial killers. Or heights. Or even spiders. Leave all that fear, but if this is going to work, I need to not lose my mind every time I see . . . one of you."

Kova grunts. I think he's amused.

"What?"

"I did not expect—never mind."

"No. What? What didn't you expect?" I'm already offended. I know when someone is about to talk smack. "Didn't expect me to be smart? To make good points? To use common sense?"

"All of the above," he says, and it's strange because only people who've taken a standardized test say that. *All of the above.* I don't bother asking about it. I don't need to know what kind of *Explorers* education system they're using to learn how people speak.

"Yeah, well, I expected you to be less ugly," I say.

"You had no expectations of me," Kova says. "You did not know the Anunnaki existed."

"You're no fun."

"I liked you more when you were afraid."

I snort. If I could learn not to feel terror in his presence, without having my mind altered, there might be hope for human and Anunnaki friendship.

Orange light glows from the ceiling, dimly illuminating the room again. Nothing has changed. Kova is exactly where he was before. "Okay, great. Now, I just need—gah!"

Fear slaps me in the face. Kova's presence overwhelms me. Staggers me back into the wall. Through heaving breaths, I say, "Warn me . . . next time."

"Understood."

"And what happened to making me not afraid of Anunnaki?"

"That would be a mistake," he says. "Not all of my people want you here. And others . . . may yet still crave the adoration of their subjects."

"Should I be worried?"

"Clearly."

"Will they try to kill me?"

"We are scientists. Historians. Caretakers. Our mandate does not involve killing humans, but we are permitted to defend ourselves, and there was a time in our distant past . . . I am sorry to say, we were not always benevolent gods. Some of us enjoyed the sacrifices. The admiration and power. We are not perfect beings. Humanity has summed up our growing lack of moral standards and norms better than we have. 'Absolute power corrupts absolutely.' But, please keep in mind, that was . . . a different era. More distant from today than Jesus, the common use of copper, or the start of the Shang Dynasty."

"This is fucked up."

"Indeed," he says.

"Do the others look like you? Will I be able to tell you apart?"

He gives me a side eye and the slightest grin. "Don't be racist."

"Okay," I say, chuckling. "Okay. Maybe smile and wave, too."

He does as requested, and it's horrific. His little mouth is full of broad incisors, and his wave is jittery and strange. Makes me nauseous. "No! No, no. Don't do that. Just say my name or something."

"Are you ready?" Kova asks. "Given our circumstances—" He glances up at the orange ceiling. "It would appear that the killer is active."

"Why? What does the orange light mean?"

"Vital systems have been damaged," he says. "And the ship is quarantined. I will be attempting to reroute control of the ship's system to another sector. But there is no guarantee I will be successful."

He turns toward the open door. "Wait. I'm not a fighter. How will I defend myself?"

He doesn't turn around. Just tilts his head a little, and says, "Right pocket. You carried it during your first visit. Upon your return, it was carried by the woman named Samantha. We returned it to you. Please do not entrust it to your friends."

I draw the gun and then give my pockets a pat—the kind people do to reassure themselves that their phone is where it should be. Mine is not. I check the left pocket, but my phone is missing. I might be clothed, but the lack of phone leaves me feeling a little naked. And that's just pitiful.

Before I can ask about it, he leaves without another word, striding out into the hallway.

I don't like the way he said 'friends.' The implication is clear. One of them could be the killer. That means everyone is a suspect, except maybe Serena. And Elias.

Thinking of my son propels me out the door.

I haven't seen him much since we arrived at Moose Hollow. He was having a great time—we both were—so it didn't really dawn on me, until now, that we've mostly been apart since we connected with Emmett and friends.

Kova is gone, beating feet to whatever nook of the ship he's going to try making repairs from. I turn right, having no idea where to go, where to look, or who might stab me.

The hallway curves gently to the right.

There's a door ahead. A lot of them, actually. All open. It occurs to me then that the entrance to the room I was just in was sealed shut until the power went out. When the orange light came on, the door was open.

Must be a safety feature. Not the best safety feature when there's a murderer on board. But it gives me access to the entire ship, which, according to Kova, contains twenty-eight people and nine aliens, which might see me as a threat and respond in kind. Thirty-seven potential victims. Thirty-seven potential threats. Well, thirty-four *remaining*, I suppose, if I clear myself, Kova, and the already murdered Anunnaki. But thirty-seven when all this started. There's that number again. Feels ominous. Like this is all suddenly important on a cosmic scale.

I shake the number from my thoughts and return to the thirty-four remaining threats.

And I suppose I *am* a threat. Kova gave me the Alien pistol. Seventeen rounds that I assume are as lethal to Anunnaki as they are people. One of them was murdered, after all. If they're as smart as ancient, previously godly alien scientists should be, they'll be huddled together somewhere. Safety in numbers.

Then again, we're part Anunnaki, and people make stupid choices all the damn time. The most dangerous sport in the world? Skydiving. No shit. People are throwing themselves out of planes for fun. If the Anunnaki are even just a little bit like us, there will be a few of them out and about.

I hope I have the self-control to not put a bullet in their heads. Don't want to make this interplanetary controversy worse.

By the way, Kova, thanks for putting it all on me.

Fuck's sake. I need to find Serena.

There's a door ahead. On the right. I get the impression that I'm on the outer rim of a round UFO. This hallway might go all the way around the ship. If so, bonus. Getting lost won't be a problem. I don't think I'll be that lucky.

Luck has turned its back on me, raised both middle fingers, and strutted away over the horizon.

Both hands on the gun, I do my best to emulate appropriate gun safety. Finger off the trigger until I'm ready to pull it. Muzzle aimed at the floor, just in case. I grip the handle with one hand and support the underside with the other. Sam would be proud.

She might also be a serial killer. My wife's killer.

Of all the people on this UFO, she is the only one I know for sure knows how to kill a person. And maybe has.

I pause by the doorway, take a deep breath, and steel myself for whatever might be lurking inside the room—naked human or towering Anunnaki. I'm not going to scream. Not going to fire my weapon.

You got this, I tell myself, and then I step into the doorway.

And scream.

Like, really scream.

I flail and fall to my ass.

My legs flop like a fish as I try to push myself away but fail. The floor is more tacky than slippery.

I plant my feet and push up and back. My back slams into the outer wall and I slide down to my backside.

Tears run down my cheeks.

A sob barks from my mouth.

And then numbness washes over me, like I've just lowered myself into a tub of the stuff.

For a moment, I think it must be Kova, calming my nerves.

But that's not it. I'm in shock. It's the body's defense against trauma so extreme that the mind will break if not disassociated from the horror at hand. I recognize the feeling. I've felt it once before. The first time I saw something like what's inside the room—the shape of it anyway, covered by a morgue sheet.

"What the fuck?" I whisper. "What the fuck?"

Did this happen while Kova and I were speaking?

The killer was one room away. Just one room away. And he was hard at work, killing, bending, breaking, reforming the dead into something impossible to forget.

I count the number of faces. Eight people—all strangers. One Anunnaki. I can't tell where one body ends and another starts. They're bent and twisted together. The merged bodies are a mockery of Vishnu, outspread arms on both sides of a body formed from the broken shapes of the humans. The alien's body has been dismembered, its parts used to hold everything together. Sinews stretch out from its back, tied to the human wrists, keeping them hanging out to either side.

All their eyes are closed, except for the Anunnaki. His big eyes are wide open and black. I'm not sure if they even have eyelids. His head is positioned top and center—Vishnu's head.

Does the killer know who they are? Is this . . . sculpture supposed to represent the Anunnaki's former godhood?

"Pull yourself together," I tell myself, trying to shake off the shock. Elias is depending on me. Screw Kova. Screw his whole planet. My son is my priority. And I need to focus the hell up.

Because Isabella's killer is here.

I have no doubt now.

Climbing to my feet, I realize what Kova has given me. It's a gift. An opportunity I've been dreaming of for a year.

Vengeance.

I'm not a violent person, but I'm willing to give it a shot.

Feel like a tough guy for a moment. I'm pissed. I've got a gun. A mission. I'm a righteous avenger.

And that's when the smell of shit and piss rolls out of the room and washes over me. I glance at the floor, expecting to find recognizable lumps of crap, but the dead's loose-bowel feces have been used like mortar, pressed between their broken, crossed legs and the floor. It's keeping the whole nightmare art installation upright.

Sick to my stomach, I hurry away from the sight, sliding along the outer wall as it supports my weight. I dry-heave twice. Take a moment to breathe, and—"

"Marcus? That you?"

33

Shit!" I shout, swiveling around and nearly putting a bullet in Jade's forehead.

He raises his shaking hands and ducks down. He's pressed up against a wall, eyes wide. His whole body is trembling, and not from the temperature. He's terrified. He's also naked.

The Anunnaki have once again stripped their abductees, despite having no intention of performing medical procedures. Maybe it's just protocol. Maybe they thought nudity would discourage the killer from acting again. That can't be it. The killer was naked the first time he killed. We were all naked.

And the same appears to be true now, with one exception.

Me.

I point the Alien to the floor, but don't put it away.

"Shit, man," Jade says, lowering his hands just a little. "I thought you were going to blast me."

"Nearly did," I admit. "Do you know where you are? What's going on?"

"I don't know, man, but it's fucking easy to guess." He looks back and forth. Squirrelly. Nervous. Not like I'd expect a serial killer to behave, but there's no rule over serial killerdom that says they can't feign terror. And Jade is the first person I've encountered since discovering the mutilated bodies of eight victims. "This is a UFO, right? We've been abducted."

I nod. "Not for the first time."

"Seriously? Shit. Just . . ." His eyes drift from mine to the gun. "Is that Sam's gun?" His eyes widen. "Why are you dressed? No one else is dressed."

He's growing suspicious, and I don't blame him. "You've seen the others? What about Elias? Have you seen my son?"

He shakes his head. "H-have you tried your walkie?"

I forgot I had the small radio in my cargo short pocket. I dig it out and press the call button. "RedRightHand, come in. You hear me, Elias?" I release the call button and listen to static. Not sure if it will work inside the UFO, but I have to try. I press the call button again. "RedRightHand, if you can hear me, please . . . please respond. Let me know you're okay. Where you are. I'll come get you." My voice cracks, and I release the button. Tears roll down my cheeks as I listen to static.

My authentic emotions seem to put Jade at ease. Just a little bit. "We'll find him, man. I mean, we're on a UFO, right? He can't get too far."

I turn my full attention back to him. "The others. Where are they?"

He shakes his head. "I couldn't see shit when I woke up. There were other people around, all confused and screaming. I just . . . I got the fuck out. I haven't seen anyone else . . . except . . ."

"Except what?"

"Blood. I think. Uh . . . footprints."

"Can you show me where?" I ask.

"Not sure," he says. "I was kind of freaking out, you know? I can try, but . . ."

"You can't trust me," I say, looking down at myself. "I get it."

"Look, Marcus, for real. Why are you dressed and armed?"

No point in hiding the truth from him. "We were abducted before. You remember that?"

"Not the abduction," he says. "I remember the video."

"Apparently, the last time we were on board, one of us murdered an alien."

"Oh."

"Yeah. So, they've taken us again and want me to figure out who did it."

"Okay, but why *Hunger Games* this shit? And why you?"

"*Hunger Games*?"

"Novels-turned-movies. Jennifer Lawrence."

I stare blankly.

"Seriously?" He shakes his head. "Why did the lights go out? Why did all the doors open? Why is everyone running around terrified?"

I hold up my hands. "Wasn't the plan. I was meant to interview everyone. Serena was going to help."

"Serena?"

"Long story," I say. "Look. Everything that's happening. It's because the killer is on the loose again."

He deflates a bit. "Is anyone dead?"

"I counted seven," I say, placing the back of my gun hand against my mouth. Sam would chew me out for lifting the weapon near my head, but I'm not exactly operating on pure logic here.

He drops to his knees. "Anyone we know?"

"They're from the campground," I say. "Everyone here is. But they're not from our group."

His head hangs low. "Is it bad that makes me feel better?"

"Not at all," I say. "But, Jade, I need to keep moving. I need to find Elias. He's . . . he's a target."

"A target?"

"The bodies that have been found," I say, trying to block my visual memory of them, "have been mutilated . . . Rearranged. The way my wife was."

He jolts like he's been shocked. "Your wife? The fuck? You were right? About the pamphlet? About getting you to Moose Hollow? Oh, shit, man. I'm . . . yeah, okay. Let's find Elias. And I'm not him, I swear. I don't know how to prove it to you, but—"

"I believe you," I tell him, and it's true. I'm not Serena, but Jade doesn't fit any profile I can think of for a killer. He's young. Carefree. And from what I've heard, hasn't left his hometown in a long time. Plus, I don't think he's faking the abject fear radiating from him. His twitching. Sweating. Damn near a panic attack. All of which are appropriate. I'm not sure those physical responses are able to be faked convincingly . . . and if the killer is truly a psychopath and doesn't feel emotions like the rest of us, he might not even know how to fake panic in a way that looks authentic.

Jade gets back to his feet, but is still curled inward, both hands covering his junk.

I slip the Alien pistol into my pocket, undo my belt and pull down my shorts.

"Hey, man," Jade says, stepping back. "What are you—"

He stops when I drop my boxers to the floor and flick them over to him. "Now we can both go commando."

He hikes up the boxers while I pull up my shorts and cinch them tight.

"Thanks," he says, standing a little more confident now that he's partially clothed. "Where to?"

"No idea."

"They didn't give you a map or something?"

I shake my head. "And FYI, they're just as scared of the serial killer as we are."

"Bullshit," he says.

"Seriously. They're . . . terrifying. But they're also mostly hiding, hoping I can resolve this for them."

"Resolve it how?"

I draw the pistol from my pocket. "Apparently humans are good at killing."

"If you—if *we*—can't?"

"The ship is quarantined," I say. "I think it could become our tomb."

"Awesome," he says. "Awesome." I think he's going to lose it, but he forces a smile. "Aliens. Serial killers. Running around in your skivvies. I'm livin' the dream. What next?"

"Do you know if Serena was in the room where you woke up?" I ask.

He shrugs. "I was out the door and hauling ass long before the lights came on. She might have been. There were a lot of voices. But I've heard people around. I think they just scattered and are hiding. What's the deal with Serena? Give me the short version."

"She's friends with the aliens, but they remove her memories of her time with them. Her request, apparently. When she comes back, they restore her memory. Weird, right?"

"Bonkers."

"But they trust her," I say. "And her ability to spot the killer."

"So, we find Serena and then . . . just interview everyone we come across?"

"Hopefully, it's that easy," I say, "but . . . I've seen what this guy can do. This doesn't end peacefully."

"Right . . . right. Hey, if they've been abducting Serena long enough to be friends . . ."

The question trails off, but I know where it's headed. I nod. "Yeah. A lot. All of you. And now me and Elias."

"But they're not really bad guys?" he asks.

"You heard of the Anunnaki?"

"Holy shit, really? They're the prime suspect for the ancient astronaut theory."

"Which is?"

"Aliens came to Earth a long time ago, like five hundred thousand years ago, and influenced human civilization. They were big-time gods in old-timey Middle East. Sumer. Babylon. Assyria. All those places. Come from the planet Nibiru or something, and—"

I hold out my hand. "It was three hundred thousand years ago, and they didn't influence civilization, they changed our DNA to be compatible with theirs, so they could . . . repopulate their planet. Aškaru, by the way. Their planet."

He's befuddled. Overwhelmed. Excitement colliding with horror.

"We can geek out later," I tell him. "Right now, we need to—"

A scream cuts me short. High-pitched. Primal.

The kind of scream I imagine a woman might unleash when she's about to be murdered.

34

ABERRATION

Hakuna Matata, right?"

"I'm sorry, what?" the woman asks.

"It means 'no worries.'"

"I know what it means," the woman says. "I just don't see how it's helpful. I mean, he's . . . he's *dead*."

And she is in shock. We found this old man wandering. Think he might have been senile. Yeah, you read that right. *Been*. Past tense. We debated whether the old geezer was fair game, but we're going for gold here. Can't hold back. The best part is that he was alone, separated from whoever he was with, and easy to coax into a secluded room.

Honestly, we have no idea what this space is for. It's similar in size to the rooms where people are held, but there are no cots on the walls. Then again, every surface of the UFO's interior is moldable. The room could serve a number of purposes.

Today, it's an art installation.

The old man was easy to shape. Brittle bones. Loose muscle and skin. The scapula blade was short enough to carve through it all, which allowed me to really explore the space.

He's cross-legged on the floor—the best way to position the dead without them toppling over. Binding is always required. I'm making do with tendons, but they're more slippery and rigid than I'd prefer.

Twine is my go-to.

Its rough texture ensures that knots don't slip, and it's strong enough to bind a body in any position. We feel like Jackson Pollock with a tube of acrylic rather than a can of house paint, but our work is all about adaptation. Free expression.

Yeah, we hear you. Wondering how we got this way.

We think Lady Gaga sums it up best: 'Baby, we were born this way.'

We suppressed it during our early years, conscious of our difference from other people, but confused about what it meant. As years passed, we began to understand our desires, that they weren't evil, that they were natural. So, we started to practice. Animals first. People next. Kept things random to throw off police.

We track investigations around our sculptures, hoping a photo of one will make it into the paper, or online. What's an artist without an audience? We don't put in all this effort for no one to appreciate the work.

Before this glorious opportunity fell from the sky, we were biding our time, looking for the perfect chance to finish what we'd started a year ago. The Man had been cagey. On guard. He'd have seen us coming. So, we lured him to Moose Hollow. We knew he'd come with the boy. Knew it would be the perfect setting to finish the work. A campground in the deep woods of Maine? Classic. But we didn't know about *this*.

UFOs? *Aliens?*

Feels like we've won some kind of cosmic lottery.

A hand on our shoulder makes us flinch. It's the woman. We'd forgotten her.

"Are you okay?" she asks with a vibrato voice.

"Fine," we whisper. "Hakuna Matata, remember? What do you think this is about? Why is he positioned like this? Do you think the aliens are trying to communicate something to us? Or is it supposed to be something else?"

"Something else?" She's disturbed. Close to dissociation.

"It just feels profound, you know? Like there's a secret meaning just waiting for the right person to see it. Do you see it?"

She shakes her head while adrenaline sets her entire body to shaking. Fight, flight, or freeze.

This is what freeze looks like. Terrified into inaction.

"I think," we say, walking around the sculpture, hands clasped behind our back. "I think the way the skin from his back has been split down the middle and lifted up on both sides, like large ears, is a message to listen. To pay attention. Do you see it?"

She doesn't respond. Can't. She's just shaking.

Maybe she understands that she's standing beside the artist.

What a treat for her. Can you imagine standing beside Hieronymus Bosch and asking him what he was thinking when he painted *The Garden of Earthly Delights*? What an awe-inspiring work. Imagine our excitement when we discovered Wikipedia had a high-resolution image of the painting, allowing us to zoom in and enjoy every torture depicted. One hundred seventy-five megabytes of beauty.

"How about his arms?" I ask. "The way they're tucked into his stomach? What's *that* saying? Is he trying to keep them warm? I think he's self-soothing. He's heard the truth and understood its inevitability. It's like he hugged himself so tightly that his arms just slipped right into his gut."

They didn't, of course. We cut him open on both sides like a hoodie pocket. Wasn't easy jamming the arms inside, nearly all the way to the elbows. They kept getting stuck on entrails. It was messy work, but we've discovered something wonderful about the UFO's interior surface—it absorbs fluids. It's helped harden feces. Cleaned up pools of blood and dried out chunks of coagulation into little beige rocks. We have some in our pocket. They look like teeth. The best use of the absorbent surfaces has been keeping ourselves clean. No one would look at us and think, 'now that's what a serial killer looks like.' If we were covered in blood and bodily fluids, smelling like a messy morgue, our identity would be easier to suss out. And that would be a problem.

Tell us that you, of all people, are picking up what we're putting down.

You're here to see this. To understand it.

So, what do *you* see?

A dead old man? Or a message through art? Those who have ears, let them hear the truth. And hold yourself, comfort yourself until it arrives. Religious.

It's moving, right?

He was so confused in life but died with clarity.

It's a transition.

This sculpture is a man's denouement.

We like big words. Have you noticed? Don't get to use them much in our day to day, but we know you dig it.

Can you see it? Yeah, you can! We knew you were like us. An aficionado. An appreciator of life's less common experiences. Bet you wish you were here with us. We could have tag teamed one of these paint tubes. What a mess we could make together.

A quivering chirp draws our attention away from our newest masterpiece. The woman. She's still here. Locked in place by an overloaded nervous system. Might be wishing she could run, or fight, but her fate has always been to be prey.

Can you imagine if reincarnation was real and people like this woman just kept coming back as prey animals? Over and over, killed and eaten, shat out and born again. Hysterical. "Don't worry," we tell her. "I'm not going to eat you."

She chirps again, face scrunching up.

Urine runs down her leg, puddling on the floor.

"Don't even sweat it," we tell her. "The floor just sucks liquid up like an aggressive sponge. Look." We hold our palms out for her to see. "No blood. Crazy, right?"

We squint and lean closer to look her in the eyes. "You have an inquisitive mind, don't you? It's why you stepped inside this room when you saw the sculpture. You had to know. Had to understand. Most people would have run away, you know. I guess you might have, if I was still wearing my mask."

It got warm and moist inside the mask. We took it off to work. "That doesn't make you brave, by the way. Closer to stupid. But there's more to you than that, yeah? Like, when you found me in here, alive and almost naked, you didn't cover up. Did you? That's odd, you know. Makes me wonder what you do for work.

Eh? I'd guess some kind of porn, but this is Maine. Stripper?" We shrug. "Interesting, but not nearly enough to divert my attention. Your body is beautiful by conventional standards, but I can *elevate* you. Lift you up and transform you into a work of art." We motion to the old man. "Like him. How would you feel about that?"

Everyone has a moment when they crack. When reality shatters.

It's almost audible. We imagine it's something like glass fracturing from a sustained resonant frequency. We've been singing the whole time, but have only now found the vibration that will shake her to the core and break her mind.

That's a good thing, by the way.

Part of the process, really.

Unless they're a fighter. Those need to be dealt with quickly, usually through subterfuge.

But not this one.

Not . . .

"Hey, I didn't catch your name."

Her eyes flick to mine. She's almost begging me to get it over with.

"Don't let anyone tell you I'm not merciful," we say, and pick up the scapula axe she failed to notice resting on the floor behind us, along with the mask. Never questioned why we were wearing a loin cloth of alien skin.

You know what? Maybe she really is just dumb?

We shrug. Eh. Just another zebra in the herd, we guess.

Whatever, check this out. It's time for you to see what you've been waiting so patiently for.

Excited? We are. It's a special treat to have someone here when all we've got is a blank canvass.

We look at her form. Skinny, but well-endowed chest. Going to have to do something with that. Not because we're a pervert. Not really interested in the temptations of the flesh. But we like to accentuate people's natural focal points. She's also . . . groomed down below. We've heard that some women do that, but we've never seen it. Hmm. Something about purity. About motherhood. No. Not that. She's no thick-thighed fertility goddess—but maybe that whole paradigm needs a rewrite.

Art is about change, after all.

We like it.

Do you?

Yes! We knew you would.

"Okay, listen," we tell her. "You'll feel uncomfortable for just a minute. It will be like falling asleep—" We bobble our head around. "—but it will just hurt a little, and—"

Her mind finally shatters, but instead of falling to her knees in tears or passing out, she unleashes a scream that's been stuck in her chest since realizing we are the artist of the work she's been admiring.

Sorry, friend.

She fucked you.

Your fun is going to have to wait.

Distant feet slap on the floor. People are running this way.

The woman gets a slight look of hope in her eyes. Glances away when she notices us noticing her.

"Oh, I'm sorry," we say. "That's not the way this works."

35

Jade is faster than me. A lot faster. Shouldn't be a surprise. He's young and spends a lot of time outdoors. I'm approaching middle age, and spend most of my time sitting in front of a computer.

But this is a race that might not be safe to finish on your own.

"Jade!" I hiss as he rounds the bend ahead.

I lose sight of him and will my legs to move faster, but it's like trying to animate a bowl of Jell-O with mind power. Doesn't work. In fact, that brief bonus effort nearly drops me to the floor.

Better if I pace myself. Run with perseverance. Finish the race marked out for—

"Gah!" I shout, raising the Alien and pointing it at an actual alien.

Up ahead, one of Kova's people is leaning into the hallway, peering at me through its dead black eyes. Like Kova, its skin is pasty blue, but also mottled gray. It has blond hair, too, but different from Kova. Where he had a kind of Kurt Cobain mop, this guy has a streak of hair down the center of his head, like a deflated mohawk. I don't feel any pressure in my head. It's not trying to communicate or control me. But its unflinching gaze unnerves me.

I lower the pistol and the lone Anunnaki twists its head in thought.

Why is it here?

Did it see Jade?

Did it *take* Jade?

"Jade?" I say, not taking my eyes off the lone observer.

"Back here," he says, his voice not far behind me.

I glance back. There's an open doorway. Distracted by my physical limitations and then our audience of one, I passed Jade. His voice is quiet. Disturbed.

He's found something.

When I look back at the Anunnaki, it occurs to me that it's waiting to see how I respond. To what?

"Hey Jade?"

"Yeah . . ."

"You find a body in there?"

"Yeah." His voice is a whisper.

I raise the weapon again, but the lone alien has slipped away. Did it lose interest? Is it fleeing the crime scene? The woman was screaming less than a minute ago. Did the alien arrive and then panic when it heard us coming? Or was it already here?

What if the killer isn't a person?

"Shit!" I spasm back, nearly firing the handgun into the floor. The Anunnaki's head slides back out from behind the wall, this time just inches from the floor. "What the fuck?"

It shakes its head. Subtle, but unmistakable. "What?" I shout at it. "I'm doing what you want."

The headshake stops.

Patience lost, I take a step toward the Anunnaki.

The head slips out of sight. I hear the slap of feet running away. Hard to imagine the Anunnaki being revered as gods. They're tall, lanky, and are cowards—even compared to me.

But technology compensates for a lack of chutzpah. The deadliest members of the US military, ticking up kill stats far beyond those of anyone else, are young men and women sitting in front of a screen, wreaking havoc with a drone a thousand miles away. People with my skillset. Given the advanced technology and mental abilities of the Anunnaki, I suppose they could have been revered as gods without being physically dominant. Then again, who'd put the physical prowess of a seven-foot-tall alien to the test? Not me. And not a primitive proto-human.

I catch movement at the very edge of my periphery and spin toward it, weapon raised. The gun is aimed at the side of Jade's head when I stop. He doesn't even flinch. Just takes another backward step out of the room he'd been standing in.

He looks to me, ignoring the weapon, which I quickly lower. "Marcus. I don't . . ."

I glance to the door. "What is it?"

He shakes his head. His previously summer-tanned face is pale.

Rather than make him explain, I say, "Keep watch. You see anything or anyone, you sound the alarm."

He gives a subtle nod. There are tears in his eyes. And I don't blame him.

It's strange, but I take a small amount of comfort in his visceral response. Means he's not the killer. Means I can trust him.

That Anunnaki, on the other hand? Scene of the crime and all that. I didn't see any humans slinking away.

I hold my breath and step inside the room. Yet another nondescript space. The UFO is full of them. I don't know if all of these are meant to hold people. If so, why would they need to take so many people? Perhaps it's a holdover from when they were actively involved with the human race? Then again, maybe the ship just reverts to a series of equal-sized cells when the power is knocked out. Like how all the doorways melted open.

I'm staring at the scene, but not really seeing it yet. I've been distracting myself with thoughts of empty rooms. Doesn't hold my attention for long and that held breath coughs out of me.

I stagger away from the new sculpture. It fills my vision for just a moment but will be etched on my memory for the rest of my life. In part, because it's just inhuman. Like I've been given a glance of hell. Worse than that, it fills in the blanks in my imagination regarding Isabella's death. I never saw her body, but picturing what had been done to her is easier now.

I turn my attention to the woman lying dead on the floor.

Aside from the head wound that ended her life, her body hasn't been desecrated.

Against my better judgment, I place a hand on her bare shoulder. Her body is warm. Her life ended in the time between when we heard her scream and arrived at this door.

There are too many possibilities to narrow down what happened, and I'm no Sherlock Holmes. But the most likely scenario in my mind is that the Anunnaki I saw discovered the body. Same as the woman. And it responded to her presence like *she* was the killer.

I shake my head. It's the best-case scenario, but in my experience that's often the least likely possibility.

Marcus's Razor: the most painful option is almost always the truth.

I'm a regular bag of party kazoos.

I recognize the woman from my walk through the campground with the sheriff. Don't know her name, but I take note of a few identifying features, in case we come across someone looking for her. She's blonde. Maybe forty. Has a tattoo of an eagle holding an AK-47 in its talons on her hip. That detail alone is enough to confirm her identity, so I divert my eyes, stand, and back out of the room until I'm next to Jade, who hasn't moved.

As for the other victim? I think it's a man, but I don't bother looking for any identifying features. I don't need to see his twisted form. Don't need more fuel for my nighttime imagination, when the demons come to plague my thoughts and keep me from sleep.

"Jade," I say.

"Yeah."

"I need to find my son."

"Yeah." He shakes his head and turns away from the open doorway. "Just tell me what to do."

"We need to split up. Cover more ground. Move fast, and loud. Call out for the others."

"Won't that also make us targets?" he asks. "Of the serial killer? Or . . . you know, the aliens."

"The aliens . . ." I'm about to tell him they're not a threat, but that might not be true. Kova could have deceived me. That Anunnaki I saw could be a killer using the presence of a human serial killer to carry out some repressed aggression. "You're right. But I don't see how we find our people without making a big fucking stink. Safety in numbers. If you manage to get four people together, I don't think a killer would risk killing again. If they're in your group, I mean. Just . . . be careful if you're alone with someone."

He nods.

"Right. Got it."

"And keep an eye out for clothing—and that other walkie. Seems like Elias doesn't have it, but if we can stay in contact . . ."

He nods. "Dry Hump."

Feels like I've just been slapped. "What?"

"My call sign," he says. "I know it's immature, but it's been my gaming handle for the past few years. I'm used to hearing it."

"And it's hard to forget," I say. He's managed to get the slightest smile out of me. I appreciate it. "You good to go?"

"Is a group of flamingos called a 'flamboyance?'" he asks.

Confusion scrunches my face.

"Yes," he says. "It is. I am. Ready, I mean."

I offer my hand, and he shakes it. Then we head our separate ways, each of us shouting the names of the people in our group. I walk for two minutes, discovering nothing and no one. And then, everything changes.

I'm alone when I find the next sculpture.

Visually, it's like the others, but it's also a disturbing evolution.

Because the victim . . . he's still alive.

36

Oh, shit. Oh my god." I'm twisted up and stuck between revulsion and empathy.

The living dead sculpture is one of Kova's people. I don't know if he's conscious or not, but his chest rises and falls with each shallow breath. I can't watch his breathing for more than a moment . . . because he's been skinned from toe to neck. His flayed hide has been bundled and arranged into petals. His face is the pistil. His bright pink skinless body is the stem, his arms are leaves.

I look for how he's bound to the floor but find nothing.

Because it's not necessary.

Because if I was missing all my skin, I wouldn't move, either. Even if this Anunnaki's mind isn't completely overwhelmed by shock, every movement, every breath would be agony.

I should clear the area. Should ignore the alien and focus on whether the killer is still lingering, but I cannot ignore the alien's anguish.

"I'm here," I say.

A gasp of surprise is followed by a high-pitched squeal of raw pain.

"If you can—"

REGENERATION!

The word slams into my mind. Regeneration?

CONTINUITY OF SELF!

Another high-pitched scream punctuates the desperate request.

Regeneration . . . Regeneration . . .

My eyes pop wide. Kova told me how his people pass on their intellect and memories from dying body to newborn, sustaining their lives indefinitely. This Anunnaki is asking me to help him do that—before his body dies.

"I'm sorry, I don't—"

OPEN YOUR MIND!

It's open, I respond with a thought. *Just do what you're going to—*

Knowledge faceplants into my cerebral cortex. I don't just know where to go, I know what to do when I get there. And it's not like I've been brain-faxed IKEA instructions; I've been given actual memories. Anunnaki memories of performing the task again and again over generations of Anunnaki 'Continuity of Selves.'

What I don't know how to do is move him without causing him significant pain.

The Anunnaki lifts a hand and grasps my arm, screaming as it moves.

PAIN IS TEMPORARY.

DEATH IS ETERNAL.

Message received, but I don't like it. Not at all. I'm an empathetic kind of guy. I feel bad when I kill a fly. Causing pain to a living thing is as far from my wheelhouse as killing a person—even if he is a serial killer.

But this pain will save a life.

It's like being born, I tell myself and then realize that's exactly what this is.

Unless I keep standing here, nervously fretting. Then, it will just be a death.

"I'm sorry," I say and move around the Anunnaki. When my arms slip beneath the alien's shoulders, he quivers in pain and shrieks. I pull him back and he falls, all his weight on my arms.

He's lighter than I expected. I thought these ancient god-men from another world would be physically superior to us, but this guy feels like he's got hollow bird bones inside him.

I manage to keep most of his lanky body off the floor, but his heels are dragging, leaving twin trails of iridescent blood behind us. I move as quickly as I can, walking backward while dragging a limp body. Even though he's light for his size, I'm still hauling more than a hundred pounds of dead weight.

Well, dying weight.

I'm pretty sure the Anunnaki has passed out. He's still breathing but not screaming. Good thing he implanted the knowledge of how to use the 'regenerator'—my term, not his. He also thought to give me directions to it. It's more than that, though. He granted me an intimate knowledge of the ship's layout and what it can do. There are some strange . . . locations within these moldable walls, which I now understand how to fully use.

I also know that the regenerator has a back-up, independent power source.

Nearly there.

But not soon enough for me. The Anunnaki's flower petal skin bounces with each step, slapping me in the face and slathering me in its weird blood. Takes half my effort not to puke. Not only would that just suck, but I'd end up blowing chunks into the flower petals. Talk about adding insult to injury.

I distract myself and move my face out of range by looking over my shoulder. The open door is ten feet away. A light-green glow emanates from the room. That'd be the containment units that always hold young replacements for every member of the crew. They're viable replacements after their first year of life to their tenth. Sounds like a lot, but Anunnaki age slower and can live three hundred years. Those first ten years of life are the equivalent of just three years in a human lifespan.

After that, the bodies are disposed of and not allowed to live lives of their own, even though they could. The Anunnaki are going to get cancelled if that disturbing little fact gets out. But who are we to judge an alien race that's been following their traditions for millions of years longer than humans have existed? The Anunnaki allowed to live are the natural born. New lives are sacred. Abortion of conceived babies is reprehensible to their people, who faced extinction from infertility. It's a strange dichotomy.

Wow. The dying alien gave me instructions with a side of historical context. I don't know if that was on purpose or just part of a panicked info dump.

I pause at the open doorway and look inside, crossing my fingers that there isn't a serial killer waiting to make me the pot to the alien's flower. I grunt with the realization that even if there isn't a serial killer waiting for me—there's not—I've left a very easy-to-see-and-follow blood trail. Won't take him long to find us.

The Anunnaki wakes when we enter the room. I know because of the convulsive shriek. I drag his flowery form onto a platform meant for the aged and those near death. He sinks into the pliable surface. But it doesn't just conform to his pressure points, it stretches up and over him, wrapping his body in a synthetic skin that seems to calm him.

PLEASE. HURRY.

The controls are all in my head. There are no buttons or levers. It responds to specific mental commands, which I now know, along with those that control much of the ship. Lends credence to the panic-fueled info dump theory. He might have meant to confine the knowledge base to this device, but he gave me much more. Which I appreciate. Kova should have done the same.

With the alien in place, I turn to the nine glowing, liquid-filled tubes mounted to the wall. Looks like they're full of Mountain Dew, bubbles and all. Each one contains a baby Anunnaki. They don't look like human babies. More like miniature versions of their adult selves. No pudgy limbs. No exaggerated proportions. Zero cuteness. The one difference, and it's not a small one, is that all the young contained here have tails. Probably to help with balance while they're relearning to walk. The luminous yellow-green fluid gives the babies' light blue skin a jaundiced vibe, making them look more like dead specimens than fresh genetic clones waiting to be born.

I place my hand on the tube that I magically know contains this Anunnaki's younger self. Feels strange to know everything I do about the ship, but not this alien's name. I guess I'll ask him if he survives, and if his younger self can communicate. That's a bit of knowledge I don't have.

Eyes closed, I think at the ship to start the process. It's not words in my head. More like a desire, and a presentation of the memory of it being done. The ship understands and acts.

The wall beneath the baby alien's containment unit bulges and forms a tube that leads to the floor and curves to a cupped bed that will catch the young when it—

The containment unit opens, flushing the baby and Mountain Dew down the tube. It slides out and is caught by the cupped bed, which quickly wraps around the small body, repositioning it. It does the same to the dying adult.

Now all that's left is for me to be the conduit.

That bit of knowledge wasn't there a moment ago, and it's vague. I know I need to stand between the bodies with my arms outstretched, but I'm not sure what happens after that. Doesn't take a genius to figure out why I'm not being educated with memories of previous conduits—it's dangerous. Possibly deadly. Whatever it is, it's enough that the alien was concerned I wouldn't go through with it.

But that's not the way I roll. Not in *Shadowborn*. Not in life.

Unaware of what's about to befall me, I stand between the young and the old, and I outstretch my hands toward both. No need to make contact—just be close.

I'm about to think the process into starting when I'm jolted by a loud, commanding voice. "Don't move. Don't fucking move." Something solid is pressed against the back of my head. Presumably a gun.

"Sam?" I ask.

"I'm serious, Marcus. I need you to raise your hands."

She doesn't have a gun, I realize. I have the Alien. Would be great if she didn't realize that yet.

"I'm trying to save this guy's life," I tilt my head toward the dying Anunnaki.

"You're covered in his *blood*," she says. It's an accusation.

"Doesn't mean I *killed* him."

"I watched you bring him here. Watched you controlling this . . . whatever the hell this is. How do you know how to do that? Why are you dressed?"

I slowly move my hands up, take hold of my shirt, and pull it off. I hold it back to her. "Please. Let me do this."

"Not until I understand what is—"

NOW . . .

The alien's voice is a whisper in my mind.

"Sorry, Sam," I say, turning around and catching her off guard. She holds the shirt in one hand and nothing in the other. The solid object was her knuckles. She sprawls back with a shove, landing hard on a forgiving floor.

Before she can complain, I turn my back to her, stretch my arms out, and then mentally trigger the regeneration.

37

I've heard about out-of-body experiences, but never paid much attention to them, or the stories told by those who have left their bodies and returned to tell the tale. Always seemed hokey to me. Magical or wishful thinking. A convenient way to prove the existence of the soul. If some intangible part of a person can leave the body and still experience reality . . . what else could it be? Characters in *Shadowborn* have souls. If you die, it's possible to return your soul to the body and carry on, though severely degraded. But in reality? C'mon.

As I float ten feet in the air above myself, I'm rethinking my position. My body is arranged like I'm mounted to a cross. My limbs twitch. My body convulses. Arcs of blue energy pulse and crackle from the mutilated Anunnaki into my hand. I can't feel it coursing through my body, but that's clearly what's happening as bursts of energy exit through my other hand and strike the newborn alien's head.

I'm a conduit.

It'd normally be another Anunnaki in my position. It's considered a sacred duty because not only am I facilitating the continued existence of this alien's life, but I'm bearing witness to its many previous lives. They're passing faster than I can process or remember, but I catch glimpses here and there that stick with me. Life on Aškaru. A laboratory with white pliable walls. A female lying on her back. Giving birth. The Anunnaki child that emerges is deformed and stillborn. I feel a flash of regret and sadness.

Then I'm on Earth. And . . . are those people? I'd laugh if I still had lungs. Look how dopey we looked! That the Anunnaki saw any potential in us at all is the real miracle here. This alien was there for first contact. They reached out with their minds and the hominids of the time responded by defecating into their hands and tossing the fibrous lumps. The Anunnaki I'm trying to save took a shit to the forehead before retreating to its ship.

Time passes. I see monuments rise and fall. I see humanity evolving quickly. Civilization spreads. The Anunnaki grew to enjoy their god-like status on this planet. It led to infighting, and then wars. I see versions of ancient battles that have been twisted and exaggerated by time.

Anunnaki were struck down, but all the while, this ritual—the continuity of life—was respected. Anunnaki lost to each other but were always returned. Humanity on the other hand? Their suffering was permanent. Their deaths never led to a reborn life. Because we were lesser beings, undeserving of unending continuity. We were subjects in more than one meaning of the word. Slaves. Experiments.

The best thing about us was that we performed as intended. Hard labor? Check. Devotion to the gods? Check. Ability to carry and birth Anunnaki hybrids, and then nearly pure breeds? Double check.

A scientific breakthrough back on Aškaru brought that experimentation to an end. I feel the excitement this Anunnaki felt at the possibility of finally returning home, of building the family that he'd spent lifetimes working toward. But it was not to be.

The powers that be did not approve of the infighting that had taken place on Earth. They did not agree with the treatment the human race had endured. The worst offenders among the science team on Earth were ordered to remain behind and monitor the progress of our genetically enhanced species. But they were not to interfere—unless humanity advanced to a point where they might pose a threat to Aškaru.

World War II and the development of nuclear weapons changed the Anunnaki's status from passive observation to a more active role in our skies and oceans. They began abducting and studying people's genomes, minds, and physiology once more. The new status quo was sustained for decades until—

I already know this, but it's interesting to experience the knowledge through the thoughts and feelings of an Anunnaki.

Artificial Intelligence has the potential to propel humans into technological competition with Aškaru. We are a direct threat to their planet—the species who once worshipped the Anunnaki as gods would soon be able to conquer the gods that made them. And then there is the Fermi Paradox.

If humanity rings the dinner bell, our solar system, including Earth and Aškaru could be wiped out by an aggressive and more advanced species. Or, *we* might become the species that life in the universe fears.

Not all that different from a game of *Shadowborn*. Good and evil.

The Anunnaki on Earth, given absolute power over humanity, gave in to temptation. They chose evil masked by scientific advancement. Sounds pretty human to me. Unit 731. The SS Medical Corps. And . . . several branches of the United States government. Americans see ourselves as moral superiors to other countries, but the truth is that we've performed more human experiments—on our own people—than any other country in the history of humanity. Only the Anunnaki have done more. I know all of that now.

And a lot more.

My overview of the Anunnaki's life comes to an end, but the process continues, transferring things that I don't bear witness to. Maybe secrets. Maybe thousands of years of personal thoughts.

Freed from my visions of the past, I turn my attention to Sam.

Strange that I can see—that I can turn my vision—to other parts of the room while my body is immobilized.

Sam is back on her feet. I'm glad to see she's not injured from the push, but I'm concerned about what she's up to. She doesn't look afraid. She looks . . . pissed. Her stance is wary, but she's inching her way toward my floating, convulsing body, stretching her hand out toward the Alien. The gun, not the Anunnaki. I appreciate the irony of the weapon's name, but it's frustrating my inner monologue.

I'm just going to call it 'gun' from now on. I don't care what it's called. If we survive this mess, I'm never going to want to hear the word 'alien' ever again.

"Don't do it," I try to say, but my voice is silenced.

Concerned for her safety, I will myself closer to her and am surprised when I actually float toward the floor. "Don't!" I shout without a voice. "I'm not the bad guy! I need the gun to—"

It occurs to me then that Sam might be taking the gun because she is the killer. It would take a crazy person to pluck a gun from the waist of a man whose body is in the throes of electrocution-style convulsions. She's risking intense pain and electric shock to take a weapon capable of killing seventeen people—or aliens.

How desperate would you need to be to risk it? How crazy? How ballsy? She's tough. Maybe the toughest person I've ever met, but she's not stupid. Crazy, under the right circumstances, can look like bravery.

None of my thoughts matter. She's free to act and there's nothing I can do about it except float to the floor.

But that's not exactly what happens.

I float to the floor—and then through it.

I'm free of my body, and free to move about the UFO unhindered by walls, tired limbs, or burning lungs. In video games, this is called no-clipping. It's usually a tool for dev teams debugging games. Lets them slip through solid objects by disabling collision detection, aka 'clipping.' Makes it easy to reach any point in a map without having to play through it all. In the old days, the code was often leaked and used as a cheat mode. But I have no code and no idea how to turn it off.

I slip through the floor to the space below, and that's all it is, a space. Nondescript. Same pliable walls. It's not surprising. Nearly every space in the UFO can be adapted for whatever is needed at the moment. Walls can be widened. Surfaces and objects can be summoned from any direction, all with a thought. Equipment or devices that aren't part of the ship can be moved about, from one room to another, transported through the moldable material filling the UFO's interior.

I search my newfound memories for a word that describes the material and am surprised when a word and its meaning comes to mind. Šulmušar. The rough English translation is 'living shell.'

Is the UFO's interior alive?

The answer comes to me as an ancient memory. The first time this Anunnaki learned about it during his first life. The Šulmušar is biomechanical, semi-sentient, and consciously responsive to the thoughts of Anunnaki brainwaves.

It doesn't speak. Doesn't think. But it remembers, responds, and protects.

But that's not right. Because it responded to me. A human.

Then again, how much of a human is Anunnaki? Kova revealed that humans had been capable of giving birth to babies that were 99 percent Anunnaki. At the time, I pictured artificially impregnated human women giving birth to aliens, but that's not accurate. I remember the truth. Those 99 percent Anunnaki babies . . . they were *us*. Homo Sapiens.

That remaining one percent is the difference between Kova's people and humanity. It's a mindfuck, but not impossible. Chimpanzees are close to 99 percent human, which makes me wonder if the Anunn—

The answer comes to mind before I finish thinking it.

Yes. The Anunnaki altered several other species on Earth in an attempt to find the best host for their young. Chimpanzees. Bonobos. Even pigs. Altered along with humans. We won by a percentage point.

If I had a head, I'd shake it.

All this new information is distracting me.

I'm off task—and I don't mean finding and killing a serial killer. That's the job I was given today, but it's not the job I accepted thirteen years ago—to protect my son.

I need to find Elias.

And to do that, I need to return to my body.

I look at the ceiling and float up.

The Continuity of Self has completed. The flower-shaped alien's corpse has been revealed and is pale gray. Dead. The newborn has been uncovered as well. It's breathing but appears to be unconscious and vulnerable. Sam stands over us, wearing my T-shirt now. She holds the gun in one hand, pointed at my head.

It's her, I think, and there's nothing I can do to stop what happens next.

38

ABERRATION

Well, well, well. Look who's still here.

We thought you might have abandoned us. That would have been disappointing. What's the fun if we don't have an audience?

But we're linked now, you and us. We share the bond of those who kill and those who delight in it. You understand. We know you do.

And we think it's time your loyalty and patience were rewarded. We already have a target chosen. One of the aliens. It's hiding, if you can believe that. Not so tough when they can't control your mind and body. This one is nearly eight feet tall. Killing it will be an event. But we're confident. These creatures appear intimidating, and the ability to control minds makes them dangerous. But we are beyond control, and they're much more fragile than they appear. Light bones. Sinewy muscles.

What we're waiting for is inspiration.

We don't have time to sketch something out. Need to do the work in our imagination.

We could just Jackson Pollock it, we suppose, but we don't want anyone to look at our work and think, 'I could do that.' We're better than that. Skilled. Practiced.

An image comes to mind. A snapshot of a classic piece of art, by one of the most brilliant men to ever live. We nod to ourselves, imagining how we'll modify the work. The subject of the original was human after all. And the medium was ink and watercolor on paper.

Do you know what we're thinking of, friend?

Picture it. Arms and legs outstretched into an X, exposed and vulnerable, sure, but the ideal form of man. Perfect proportions. A balance between the spiritual and physical selves. Purity of form. The arms and legs are congruous. It is harmony. Parity.

Duality, which we live and love.

There is no truth in a body that contradicts itself.

The alien we've stalked doesn't come close to the original subject's equilibrium, but that can be adjusted.

Have you figured it out? Our inspiration for the work to come?

Hmm. We gave you too much credit. Believed you to be a fellow connoisseur of the visual arts. Then again, you *are* new to this. How could you know we're referring to the *Vitruvian Man* by Leonardo DaVinci?

You know it, yes?

If not, Google it and come back. We won't judge you. A visual image of the piece is important if you wish to truly see our art in progress.

Got it? Good. Now, watch, and if you dare, learn.

We don our fleshy mask, which is starting to smell, and pick up Thaymorn, the soul splitter.

Oh, right. Sorry. You haven't heard the name yet, have you?

Our axe forged from the bones of the dead has been given a name, as all mythical weapons should have. Excalibur. Faithful. Mjölnir. Andúril. Lucille. Even the *ThunderCats* had 'The Sword of Omens.'

And now, Thaymorn, the soul splitter, joins the list of weapons covered in the blood of its victims. A work of art on its own, but also the implement with which we create.

The alien is hiding in a room just a few feet away. We cannot see it now, but we know it's there. Could be waiting just around the corner. Could be quivering in terror. We only noticed it because it carried some kind of bright light source—like an orb of light hovering over its open palm. The light is extinguished now. The room's interior, and the hallway in which we stalk, are dark. The emergency lights have been turned off by whatever is hiding inside. Interesting.

But darkness doesn't stop the predator. The alien is blind, too. It doesn't know we're here, and it can't access our mind. We suspect that means it can't detect our mind, either. Let's find out.

The pliable floor makes it easy to sneak into the dark space.

We pause and listen.

Its breathing is faint, but there. Distant, which means this space is larger than others we've been in. We make our way toward the sound, pausing every few steps to listen.

Getting nervous?

We bet you are.

We're not. Cool as a frozen cucumber. Because this is who we are. Took some time to learn that, and then perfect our craft, but we're improving with each new creation.

We stop what sounds like a few feet away from the breathing.

Tongue to the roof of our mouth, we make a series of quiet clicks that remind us of the *Predator*. 'Up there, in them trees.' But right here, in the dark.

As expected, the orb of light winks on, illuminating the large space, which we now see is actually a storage room full of cylinders. Could be waste. Could be food. Could be anything. They're not labeled and even if they were, we can't read alien.

The tall being from another world, who is sitting on the floor, sees us, then the state of us—covered in both human and alien blood—and then Thaymorn in our hands.

It shrieks in fear.

The sound lasts only a moment. It is silenced by our strike.

The alien reels back and drops the orb. The light extinguishes, but we follow through. The blade hits solid bone and breaks it. We had hoped to sever the creature's spine, preserving the symmetry of its face, but art is fluid.

When the alien's twitching stops, we crouch down and search the floor with our hands. Doesn't take long to find a solid object the size of a bouncy ball. We hold it in our palm. We assume it works like everything else on this ship and think at it to illuminate the scene.

It obeys, filling the large storage room with cool white light.

We look at our newly acquired materials. His legs are longer than his arms. We can work with that. But there is a problem. His face. Thaymorn's blade buried itself diagonally through the creature's face, rupturing one eye. It's a mess.

Giving up is tempting, but unless we're about to be caught, not our style. "Make do with what you have." Our mother said that to us once. We didn't appreciate it at the time, but now it makes sense. And there is a solution.

We lift the glowing orb, which is floating an inch over our palm, and will it to stay hovering in the air. No idea if it will work until we pull our hand back and the light remains a few feet above the floor.

Perfecto!

Hey, don't make that face. A large part of being a successful predator is luck. It was luck that allowed us to be taken aboard this UFO. It was luck that we came across both humans and aliens with all the body parts necessary to craft this epic weapon. And it was luck that this eight-foot-tall giant was a pussy. The light hovering in the air because of a mental command? More luck. But also not. The walls do the same. So, stop judging us. Thinking, *Oh, this is all coming too easily. The killer needs to work harder for the payoff.*

"You want payoff?" We raise Thaymorn above our head. The blade falls, accurate this time, and severs half of the neck. Another strike removes the head completely. Iridescent blood pools around the upper torso. It's a mess, but the blood will add sheen to the final product. "There's your fucking payoff."

Don't worry. We're not really angry. Don't get angry. Or sad. Or anything else. We express through our creations.

Now. Let's get on with it. We're going to focus. Give you the blow by blow, but mostly we will be zeroed in on the work.

We haul the carcass to center stage, then arrange the limbs so they're extended in an X. The legs are a good foot longer than the arms. The head isn't useless. This alien had a mop of blond hair. Might have once been flowing and beauteous, but now it's saturated in iridescent blood. We pick up the head and use it like a giant brush, painting a circle, its circumference just beyond the long-fingered hands. Not a true circle, but we don't have time to indulge in perfectionism. People and/or aliens are looking for us by now.

We toss the head to the side and turn our attention to the body. Step one. Lose the clothing. Art is primal. Clothing conceals the raw. The visceral. It hides the truth. This isn't the first alien we've peeled from its skintight bodysuit. It's armored in spots, but 'armored' needs to be in severe air quotes. We think it's more decorative than functional, like they're compensating for the fragility of their bodies.

Aliens with self-esteem issues. We roll our eyes.

"Don't worry, buddy," we say to the dead. "We'll make you stunning."

The bones go next. We break the legs just above the ankles with the backside of Thaymorn. Then we twist them up, so the limb is fully within the circle. Articulation complete, it's time for some aesthetic flair.

This alien has some scarring on the right side of the chest. It screws up the balance. Needs to go.

Thaymorn's blade makes quick work of the alien's fragile skin. Three cuts—one down the middle, and two across, top and bottom—is all it takes. We peel the skin to the sides and fold the ends into triangles like the first step in making a paper airplane.

Here comes the flourish. The *tocco finale*. The *ultima manus*, as they say in Rome. Well, *said* in Rome. No one speaks Latin these days. We grasp the ribs, one by one, and yank them away from the sternum. They break easily with satisfying snaps. We position them on either side, pointing up so they look like claws rising from the pink, sinewy meat.

We step back to admire our work.

Something is missing.

Literally. What kind of Vitruvian Man doesn't have a head?

Our work has been too rushed. It's frustrating, but we recognize this as a learning experience. The world will never know what we did on this UFO. But that's okay. We're developing new skillsets. Self-reliance. Adaptation. Stealthiness. Self-control. The list goes on.

Still, it is frustrating.

"Hey, hello!"

We spin around. It's a man. He's close. Approaching the entrance.

Rather than turn off the light, we leave it in place and take cover behind some cylinders.

The man runs inside, sees the headless Vitruvian Alien, stumbles, and falls to the floor. He springs back to his feet, revolted at the scene, but unable to take his eyes off it. "What the fuck is this? What the *fuck* is *this*?!"

We step out from behind the cylinder, driven by a need to be recognized for our work, at least once. "It's a ritualistic reclamation of form. A declaration that humanity's order and symmetry can be imposed on the chaos of the cosmos. *The Vitruvian Alien*."

The man reels when he sees us.

Brings a smile to our face. "Hi, Jade."

39

Ever been in a car when it goes up a sudden, but brief rise, and then quickly descends on the other side? Your stomach goes up and then stays up until you reach the bottom. Like a roller-coaster, but completely unexpected because you're in a car on the road. That's what returning to my body feels like, but a little more sudden.

All at once, I'm back in my body.

And then on the floor.

I land on my knees and manage to catch myself with my hands. Pain lances between my eyes, drawing a grunt from me as I attempt to pull myself together. Easier said than done. My mind swirls with lifetimes of information it wasn't designed to absorb so quickly or remember for very long.

Luckily, the memories aren't sticky, for the most part. They're fading like dreams, leaving me with more impressions than day-to-day memories of life on Earth for the past three hundred thousand years.

But it's still hard to think straight.

I narrow my thoughts down and weed out everything non-essential. Elias is alone and needs me. Sam has the gun, and last I saw, was pointing it at me—while I'm helpless, which suggests her intentions might not exactly be wholesome.

The idea that Sam could be the killer makes me ill. The short amount of time I spent with her was . . . fun. She's beautiful. She flirted enough to make me feel good about myself, but not so heavy-handedly that I felt like I was betraying Isabella. Still, there was an inkling of, 'I wonder where this could go . . .'

And maybe that was the point. Kill the wife, seduce the husband. The ultimate domination.

"Stop," I manage to say. Sounds like my vocal cords have been dirty dancing with a cheese grater.

"Not how this is going to work," Sam says.

"I need to find Elias," I say.

"Not sure I should let you near your kid again," she says, and I can't tell if it's the kind of thing a serial killer would say, or a friend who was concerned for my son's safety.

We're at a strange kind of impasse.

I raise my shaking hands. "Look, you think I'm the bad guy for helping one of these aliens."

"You know how to use their technology," she says. "I heard you speak their language. And what the hell was that you just did."

I motion to the flower corpse. "Found him like that. Deformed into a flower . . . and still alive. He guided me here. Gave me the knowledge of how to use the regenerator."

"Regenerator?"

"My name for it," I say. "The Anunnaki—that's what they're called—pass their knowledge, memories, and souls from their dying bodies to newborn clones. They have a natural lifespan of three hundred years but expand it with clones."

"How long?" she asks.

"Indefinitely," I think. "As long as there's a clone and a regenerator nearby when they're dying. I've come across other Anunnaki that weren't so lucky. This guy is more than three hundred thousand years old."

"Jeez," she says. Sounds more relaxed now.

"Mind if I turn around?" I ask.

"Slowly."

The floor molds to the shape of my knees. Makes turning around much more comfortable than it would be on a solid floor. She's put my shirt on, but it's barely long enough to cover her private parts, front and back. I avert my eyes and try to maintain eye contact, but it's made difficult by the gun leveled at my forehead.

"Hey," I say when we make eye contact, trying to look relaxed and non-threatening.

She squints at me. "Explain."

"There isn't time," I say.

"You had time to resurrect an alien," she says. "If you want to walk out of this room without a hole in your kneecap, you need to explain."

"Fine . . . but I'm just giving you the bullet points, and don't bother asking me to convince you any of it's true, because none of it's going to sound believable."

She gives a nod and waits.

I rattle off my experience leading up to this moment. I tell her about Kova. About my ability to free myself from their control. Why they're here. Why they're still here. What they want with us—to find the killer of their friend. And what they've tasked me to do—kill said murderer.

"You? Take down a serial killer?" She lowers the gun. "You're right, that is unbelievable." To my surprise, she turns the handgun around and passes it to me handle first.

"Why?" I ask. "You're better with it than I am."

"I'm also better at defending myself without a gun," she says. "And you're like the weak little chick getting pushed from the nest by its siblings. You need it more than me."

I take the weapon. "Thanks. Sort of. Does this mean you don't think I'm the killer?"

"Never thought you were," she says. "You don't have that kind of darkness in you. And what kind of bleeding-heart serial killer would risk their life to save an alien that abducted him? Doesn't add up. And your story . . . I hate to say it, but it's the only thing that makes any kind of sense. Now, aside from how to save aliens from the death all other living things face, what have you found out?"

"The killer is working fast. Killing everyone he comes across, human or alien. It's the same person who killed my wife. Who lured us to the campground. None of this was part of the plan, but I think he's enjoying it."

"And they're not just mind-controlling him because . . ."

"He's immune," I say.

"Like you."

I shake my head. "I can resist . . . but it's a fight. And temporary. This guy . . . he pretends to be under control, but he's just biding time. Waiting for their guard to drop. Then he strikes, kills, and mutilates. Fancies himself an artist, I think."

"Jade likes to draw," she says.

"It's not Jade," I say.

"You saw him?"

"He's wearing my boxers. And he was with me when someone was killed. But . . . we weren't alone. There was an alien nearby."

"Fleeing the scene?" she asks.

"Or us," I say. "It was acting weird, leaning down low as it watched me from around the corner. Had kind of a crazy mop of hair on its head."

"Can we agree that aliens having hair like ours is just weird?"

"For the record, human hair, the way it was when they arrived, was short, coarse, and hollow for warmth in the winter months. The hair you enjoy today? That's Anunnaki hair. Now, if you don't mind, I would like to find my son."

She nods and offers a hand. Pulls me to my feet. Motions to the baby. "What about that guy?"

I place my hand on the regenerator and think a command. The tube that delivered the baby to its current position reforms and wraps around the small body. The new Anunnaki glides away and emerges back inside the tube of luminous green fluid. "He'll be safe in there."

"Until someone breaks it," she points out.

"Okay, safer than he'd have been flopping around on the floor like a caught fish." Thinking of catching fish reminds me of Emmett. Of what he said about fish feeling no pain. It stuck out as weird, then, but now it makes me concerned. It's the kind of belief a serial killer might hold—that killing is okay because pain is an illusion.

"Have you seen any of the others?" I ask.

She shakes her head. "I was with Serena and Emmett, but they weren't keen on exploring, and I . . . might have gotten separated from them in the dark. I think their plan was to just hang tight and wait for the power to return."

"And Gabe?"

She shakes her head. "Not a peep. And . . . nothing from Elias, obviously. This ship is pretty big."

"Thousand feet across. Three levels, each thirty feet tall—" I look to the ceiling, just twelve feet up. "—even if it doesn't look like it. These rooms, every single one of them, can adapt to whatever the Anunnaki need. Containment. Labs. Whatever. They just need to think it and the ship's interior . . . which is kind of alive, by the way, responds to their thoughts. The center of the ship, where the domes are, above and below? Those are the top and bottom of a sphere that contains a miniature recreation of Aškaru. That's their homeworld."

"Uh-huh. The one sharing Earth's orbit . . ." She sounds dubious.

"And is cloaked."

"Because of the whole Fermi thing."

I nod and smile. "You were paying attention."

"Okay, so, if you're a group of aliens hiding from a human serial killer who can kick your alien ass because he's immune to telepathy, where would you go? Sure, there have been a few stragglers caught along the way. But what about the rest? I know where I'd go."

"Home," I say. "Solid logic . . . but my son is not an alien, and until I find him, Kova and his people are fending for themselves."

"You have any idea of how we can find him?" she asks.

I don't, but before I can make something up, the radio in my pocket crackles to life and my son's whispering voice fills the air. "Architect, come in. This is RedRightHand. Architect, do you read me?"

40

Takes me ten seconds to wrestle the radio from my pocket on account of my hand shaking. Elias hasn't repeated the call. Could mean he's patient. Might also mean he's in trouble, or he's been found. My heart twists with each heavy beat. My breathing is quick and shaky.

When I manage to retrieve the radio, Sam takes hold of my hand. I react with a suspicious gaze, but she removes her hand and steps back. "Just think you should take a breath before responding. Hearing your panic isn't going to help him."

"Right." I take a deep breath, hold it in, and then let it out. My exhalation is shaky, so I repeat the process while telling myself: *He's okay. He's okay.*

I press the call button. "RedRightHand, this is Architect. I read you. Come back."

"Dad?" Elias says and his voice breaks my heart.

"I'm here, buddy. Where are you?"

"I—I'm not sure. It's hard to see."

"How did you find the radio?" I ask.

"What do you mean?" he asks. "It was in my pocket."

I share a glance with Sam. She shrugs. Seems Kova did me a solid and didn't take my son's clothing.

"Did you hear me call earlier?" I ask.

"I had to shut the radio off," he says, whispering again. "You know there are aliens here, right?"

"You don't need to be afraid of them," I say.

"Who do I need to be afraid of?"

Not sure how to answer that. The man who killed your mother is on a killing spree inside a UFO and is probably looking for both of us? That's not going to help him think straight.

"All you need to think about is finding me," I tell him.

"How am I supposed to do that in the dark?" he asks, sounding frazzled.

"Can you tell me anything about where you are?" I ask.

"Well," he says, "it's dark, and smells disgusting."

"Disgusting . . . like how?"

"Like that jar of old pennies that you have in the basement."

Sam grips my arm and mouths the word, 'Blood.' I nod and make a show of taking my finger off the call button.

"If the scent of blood is strong, it means he's either right next to a body . . . or there are a lot of bodies."

"Also means the dead are human," I say, and motion to my body, covered in drying iridescent Anunnaki blood. It's tacky and getting stiff, but it smells more like ozone than anything else—like the air after a lightning strike. Far less unpleasant than human blood, but that's probably just because we don't associate the smell with pain, injury, and death.

Sam sniffs me and nods in agreement. Her eyes widen for a flash. "If he has his clothes . . . does he have his phone?"

"Elias . . . do you have your phone?" I ask.

"My phone—" He cuts off. It's ten seconds until he comes back. "Uhh. Yeah . . . I have my phone. Should I turn on the flashlight?"

Sam shakes her head at me.

"Use the screen as a light, to see where you're going," I say.

"But I'll be able to see better with it on."

"And people will be able to see you better—" I catch myself.

"Why is that a bad thing?" he asks.

I sigh.

"You're going to have to tell him," Sam says.

I press the call button. "Listen. Someone on this UFO—that's where we are, by the way. Someone here is killing people. And the aliens."

"Killing people?" The nervous energy in my son's voice is tangible. My inability to locate and protect him fills me with rage.

"We need to find each other," I say, but I have no idea how to do that in a dark, three-layered maze.

"'The smell of coin hangs thick in the air,'" Elias says.

"What?" I say but then recognize the words. I wrote them. It's from *Shadowborn*. When the player comes across the Lumination Massacre that propels the narrative. It's from a cut scene where the character speaks the line before the blood is revealed, leaving no doubt that the blood smells like coins.

Shit.

"Elias, don't."

The radio goes silent. I know my son has just turned on his flashlight.

"Dad." Elias is whispering again. "There are dead people."

"Elias, you need to leave where you are. Now."

"There's so many," he says. "And aliens, too. They're just . . . they're in a pile. And there's glowing stuff all over them. And . . . I think I see stars."

"He's in shock," Sam says.

"Elias," I say, but he beats me to the call button and speaks over me.

"I think it's blood. Alien blood. And there are drag marks."

"Elias!" I shout, but he's still got the call button held down on his end.

"Hold on," he whispers. "I hear something."

He keeps the call button pressed down. I can hear his shaky breathing. "Shit," he whispers. The curse is followed by a loud shuffling motion.

I hold my breath.

I'm not sure how much time passes before Elias speaks again. "Dad . . . I think he's here. I think—ahh!"

Elias's shout of fear is cut short. The radio falls silent.

"Elias!" I shout into the radio. "*Elias!*"

I take my finger off the call button, hoping he'll respond.

Silence for five seconds. Fifteen. Twenty.

The radio crackles. An unfamiliar, scratchy voice comes over the radio. "The boy is quick, but I will catch him. And when I do . . ."

Static follows. I know what it means. The other walkie has been turned off or destroyed. I shout his name into my radio anyway. "Elias! *Elias!!*" I want to destroy something. Shoot something. Do anything to reclaim some power over the situation.

But it's hopeless.

I'm lost.

I drop to my knees. My tears follow, tapping on the floor.

"Easy," Sam says, crouching beside me. "We don't know what happened, and we're not going to find out if you crack up. I know this isn't kind advice, but I'm not a therapist and I know all about thinking straight and taking action despite the specter of death."

"You don't have a son," I say between sniffs.

"No . . . I do not. But I've lost people I loved. I know the pain. And I know that whoever this is, doing the killing, they're an artist, right? Sounded like there were plenty of dead to work with already."

I cry harder.

"I'm saying there's a chance Elias is okay. Sounded like he got away. He's a smart kid. Don't give up on him."

That hits home. She's right. Elias could be running. Could be fighting. And I'm just sitting here in a growing puddle of my own pity-party tears. I push myself up, wipe my face, and head for the door.

I came from the left, so I head right. Elias could be on the floor above or below. Could be on the other side of the ship. But I'm not going to find him by staying here, thinking twice, or moving slowly. Sam has come to the same conclusion. She slips past me, "Let's move!" and breaks into a run.

I have no trouble keeping up for about sixty seconds. Then my lungs start burning. Fear for my son keeps me going, but the distance between us is growing. Only thing that keeps me close is that she stops to look into each open doorway we pass. I glance into the dull, orange-lit rooms, but it's just one more nondescript space after the next.

She stops at the next opening and waits.

"Did you . . . find something?" I ask, sucking air and grasping my side where a cramp has just made itself known.

She motions and says, "See for yourself."

And then I do. It's a hallway. And a choice. Unlike the one wrapping around the ship's outside, this one is straight. I have no idea how far around the ship I've gone. Might have covered just half. Elias could be just ahead. Could be anywhere.

But this hallway . . . I think it leads to the center of the UFO. To the sphere which contains a replica of the Anunnaki's home world. A place where people and aliens alike could congregate. A place that looks and feels like nature. A place . . . with a view of the sky.

A place with stars.

Without a word, I draw the gun and sprint down the hallway. Fuck my lungs. Fuck the cramps. Elias is close, and I will unleash hell on whoever I—

"Oof!" I run headlong into a human-shaped wall. I sprawl to the side and spot the handgun falling away from me.

When I roll onto my back and look up, a large man silhouetted by the dull orange light from the ceiling, looms above me. Before I have a chance to move or think, a booming voice tears through the hall.

"Don't move! Don't you fucking move!" It's Sam. She's recovered the handgun and aimed it at the newcomer's head. "Step back into the light so I can see you."

The man obeys, raising his hands and stepping back so the orange light strikes his front.

It's Emmett. Buck naked and slathered in blood.

41

I tried to save him," Emmett says, tears wetting his cheeks, his lower lip trembling. "I tried. I *tried.*"

"Emmett," Sam says, voice calm despite the handgun still pointed at the old man's head, "who did you try to help? Whose blood is that?"

He looks down at his body and is revolted, not by his nakedness, but by the dark red blood coagulating into clumps stuck in his white chest hair. He flails at it. Tries to wipe it off. But neither of us is getting clean without a long shower with lots of soap.

"No, no, no, no," he says, starting to shake.

We're going to lose him.

Back on my feet, I try to take hold of Emmett's shoulders. He flails from my grasp, tries to run, and ends up colliding with the wall. Before he can recover, I slap him in the face.

The sting gets his attention. Sobers him up for a moment. When I take his shoulders again, he doesn't resist. "Emmett. Please. Whose blood is that? Is it Elias? Did you kill my son?"

His reaction to my words is more dramatic than his response to the slap. "Elias? Kill?! Not the boy. Please, God, don't tell me Elias is—" He chokes on a sob, and I don't push him. The agonized surprise about the blood being Elias's was genuine. I don't think a psychopath could fake it that well.

"Elias is in danger," Sam says. "We don't know if he's hurt. Or worse. But I need to know, Emmett, and I need to know right this second—whose fucking blood is that?"

Emmett sags when he looks at Sam. Pressure builds within him. Looks like he's going to puke, but then he just sobs. "Sorry," he says, attempting to pull himself together. "Sorry. I just . . . I can't . . ."

He turns and points to an opening in the wall beside us that I hadn't noticed. The dull orange light should have caught my attention, but I was so laser focused on Elias that I missed it. "Found him just a minute ago. I shouldn't have tried helping him. I know that now. But, I just . . . He's my responsibility. I told his parents—I told them I'd—"

He breaks down crying again. Sam pushes past him and enters the side room.

She doesn't say anything, but I hear her gasp.

I'm eager to leave. To find Elias. But I feel the need to see. The details might help me uncover who the murderer is and will also make it easier for me to carry out the mission Kova gave me—kill the killer. I brace myself and step inside the room.

My first impression is that this is some kind of storage area. If this were a human vessel and not alien, I'd say the room was full of nuclear waste barrels. But since this is an alien ship, I can't possibly guess what they contain. Could be waste. Could be food. Hell, they could hold a billion different viable embryos of each alien on board to sustain the continuity of life indefinitely.

I linger on the containers because I can see the room's centerpiece in my periphery and I'm not sure I want to look.

A sense of responsibility forces me to turn my attention to the dead.

Laid out on the floor is a recreation of Da Vinci's *Vitruvian Man*, formed from the body of a mutilated alien—and Jade. I mumble-scream and stagger back a step, nearly falling on my ass.

Jade's head has been severed—it almost looks torn or hacked off—and is placed where the alien's head should be. Jade's body is laid atop the alien's. Their arms and legs are splayed open at different angles, each of them forming an element from the classic piece of art turned nightmare.

"I sent him here," I whisper, guilt seeping into my veins.

"You sent him for help," Sam says, eyes blazing with rage. I already told her how Jade and I connected and then split up. "This is not your fault and now is not the time to lose your shit. Emmett is halfway to a mental breakdown. I can't lose you, too, and neither can Elias."

Hearing my son's name frees me from my building sorrow. Jade's death is a tragedy, but he's dead now, and Elias . . . Elias might not be. I hurry from the room with Sam on my heels. Emmett waits in the hallway, pacing back and forth while chewing on a fingernail, despite the hand being covered in Jade's blood. I'm not sure how Emmett tried to help Jade—the bodies are still in position—but he seems oblivious to the gore on his body. Sam is right. Emmett's mind has left the building.

I hold my hand out to Sam. "Gun."

She spins it around and hands it back to me. "Guns don't work if they're on the floor. Try not to drop it again."

I nod, take the weapon, and then break all the safety rules Sam taught me by using the barrel to tap Emmett's arm. "My son is in trouble. You can either come with us, or stay here, but I'm not going to stand around convincing you one way or the other."

With that, I continue down the hallway, pursued by Sam, the memory of Jade's desecrated body, and then by Emmett, his bare feet slapping on the pliable floor, his breathing ragged and labored.

I ignore my empathy for the man and keep my attention on my son. If there are a dozen more dead bodies between the two of us, I'm not going to slow down for any of them. We pass several more open doors, none of which contain bodies. But there are more containers of who knows what, organized and stowed securely.

Before reaching the hall's end, I stagger to a stop, not because I'm too tired to continue, but because this is a dead end. I shake my head, approaching the wall and looking for any sign of a doorway. "This can't be right. The sphere. It should be here."

"What . . . sphere?" Emmett asks, leaning against the wall behind us, catching his breath. It's hard to look at him, exposed and covered in blood, but I have no clothing left to offer him.

"The center of the UFO," I say. "It's . . . basically a snow globe recreation of their home world. They might be immortal former gods and creators of modern humans, but they apparently get homesick."

"Hard to believe that the Anunnaki have human emotions," Sam says. "If the history lesson you gave me was accurate, they might be playing nice now, but they used to be monsters."

"What are you two talking about?" Emmett asks.

"Short version," I say, still searching for a doorway. "The aliens are Anunnaki. They bred humans from primitive hominids to sustain their own race. Absolute power did its thing and the Anunnaki dominated humanity for thousands of years, posing as gods. They were . . . not kind. That ended when a different solution presented itself and human wombs were no longer required. Now, they're supposed to observe us, study us, and make sure we don't get the solar system invaded by even worse aliens."

"And the center of the UFO is . . ."

I shrug. "Haven't seen it for myself, but . . ." I consider explaining how I came to have Anunnaki memories of this UFO but decide against it. Won't do much more than waste more time. Thinking about my acquired memories provides the solution to my current dilemma.

Eyes closed, I turn my thoughts to a past that doesn't belong to me. I see the UFO through the eyes of the Anunnaki I saved. Sifting through the memories is painful, like a migraine behind my eyes, but it doesn't take long to pluck free a memory—one of many—from this hallway.

I place my hand against the flat wall at the hall's end.

"There's a door here," I say, stating the obvious. There isn't a part of this ship that can't become a door if you know how to communicate with the living surface. But that's only if there's power, and despite Kova's efforts to undo whatever damage has been done, we're still operating under dull orange lighting, and stationary walls.

A fresh memory gets my attention. Details about the sphere. Old memories from when this craft was first constructed. The alien I saved was there. Was an engineer. Guided by my desire, the memories offer up a key detail. Like the regeneration chamber, the sphere has an independent power source meant to sustain the living things inside. But it also powers the outer walls.

Hand still against the wall, I follow my implanted memories and perform the task as though I'd done it a million times before. It's not even a thought. Not a command. It's just . . . a desire. A want. In its simplest form. Like breathing.

The surface beneath my hand melts away.

The wall peels open, transforming the dead end into an opening the size of the hallway. Beyond that is another world. Aškaru is a largely jungle world where avian species abound. The Anunnaki evolved from a flying species in the same way humans did from ape-like creatures, but without outside help, and a few hundred million years earlier than us.

Pale trees rise toward the top of the dome. Instead of leaves, they have paper-thin pods. They're yellow in warmer months. Red when it turns cold. Every fifty years, the pods break away and float hundreds of miles through the atmosphere.

Of all the details I need at the forefront of my mind, I've managed to tap into an encyclopedic knowledge of alien trees.

The air is rich and moist, propelled by a strong wind that must be artificially generated. Feels like Florida in summer, just before the daily thunderstorm dumps the day's evaporated water back where it came from. I smell something like maple syrup mixed with apple cider vinegar. An image of the flowering plant that produces the smell flits into my mind, and I spot one off to the right.

In front of me is a path through the alien terrarium. The soil is black and packed down so smooth that footprints are impossible to see.

"Not in a million years . . ." Sam whispers, leaning in and looking around. It's hard to not feel wonder, even when surrounded by horrors. She turns her head toward the domed ceiling, which is mostly concealed by the canopy of yellow pods. She points to a gap. "Orion's belt."

I step inside the artificial world and look toward the ceiling. The stars are familiar, and in a wink, I remember why. "That's the actual sky," I say. "Not a simulation."

"So, we're still on Earth?" Sam asks.

"In orbit," I say.

"Orbit?" Emmett says, stepping past us, gawking at the alien world, oblivious to his nakedness. He jolts to a stop.

"What is it?" I ask.

"Blood," he says. "Both kinds. And a lot of it."

When Emmett steps to the side, I see it. A mixture of red and iridescent blood is pooled behind a bush that resembles an explosion—the shape and color of a fiery cauliflower.

"That's a lot of blood," Sam says.

"Elias said he found a pile of bodies," I say, nearly choking on the words. I'm doing my best to not imagine worst case scenarios in which Elias is now part of the pile, but it's impossible. There isn't a good parent on the planet that doesn't lose sleep worrying about potential scenarios that might hurt or kill their children. It's a primal fear and, in theory, helps prepare for life's challenges. All my worst-case scenarios over the years didn't come close to this.

"Here," Sam says.

While I was in my brain, seeing possible horrible futures, she snuck past me. I join her with Emmett and look down at her discovery. Trails of blood, human and alien, stretch from the pool to the jungle darkness. It's impossible to count how many victims were moved from here . . . but it's a lot.

I start following the path but am stopped by Sam's hand on my arm. "Marcus," she says. "Do me a favor?"

"Yeah?"

"Chamber a round."

I do as she says and then follow the path, knowing that whatever I find at the end, it's going to scar me for life, however long or short that might be.

42

Stepping into the sphere is like walking onto an alien world. My mind makes sense of it all, but nothing feels familiar. I tried mushrooms once. This is similar, but without the positive vibes.

The smell of human blood in the windy air creates a very different experience. The orange emergency lighting is missing here. The only illumination comes from above. The stars and the moon. Everything is cast in a dull white glow that reflects off the pale trees.

"Can I ask you a question?" Emmett asks. It's directed at Sam. The two of them are walking side by side behind me.

"Shoot," she says.

"Why are we trusting him?"

"The guy with the gun who can definitely hear you?" she says.

He ignores the fact that I can hear him, and I don't say anything. He's well within his rights to question my part in all this.

Emmett clears his throat. "He's covered in blood."

"Alien blood," she points out. "Not human."

"He killed one of the aliens?"

"Saved," she says. "I caught the tail end of it. Nearly shot him. But he's one of the good guys."

"And you?" Emmett asks her.

"How long have you known me?" she asks.

"Ayuh," he says. "I get that. But—"

"One of us is a serial killer," I say, finishing the thought for him. "And not just any serial killer. My wife's murderer. And I swear to you, Emmett, when I find him, I'm going to put a bullet between his eyes."

"What if *they* don't let you?" he asks.

"If 'they' is the aliens, then they're fine with it. We're here because one of us killed one of theirs, and they've tasked me with finding and ending him." I waggle the gun in the air. "That's why I have this. This was meant to be an interview process, but the killer is immune to their control and running amuck on the UFO, which is now quarantined. There are only two ways off this ship. We find and kill the fucker, or we're dragged off in body bags . . . or whatever Anunnaki use for body bags."

"Wonderful," Sam says. "I don't suppose—"

A creak stops me in my tracks. I snap my fingers and then hold an open palm up to Emmett and Sam. She doesn't appreciate it.

"Hey, if you're going to—"

She's cut short again, this time by a louder creak, like a pine tree bending in the wind.

"Something is in here with us," Emmett says.

I shake my head. "I don't remember anything like that."

"You've been here before?" he asks.

"Yes and no," I say. "It's complicated. But this is the equivalent of a conservatory. The only living things are the plants."

"Shhh." It's Emmett, standing beside me now. "Listen."

We stand there for a good ten seconds before I detect what Emmett's keen hearing has picked up. Footsteps. Sounds like a lot of them. Like . . . people marching in circles, coming and going.

"Sounds like ten people," Sam says.

"There's a clearing at the center of the dome," I whisper. "We'll need to walk around—"

"Or we could just sneak straight through," Sam says, motioning to the strange foliage framing the path, and beyond that, alien trees both large and small.

Knowledge comes to me in the form of past experiences I never had. "There are paralytic thorns on some of these things, and plants that honk if you step on them. Even if you made it through without getting paralyzed, they'd hear you coming. We need to stay on the path."

"Then keep moving," she says, growing impatient.

Must be nice, being brave. Where I feel hesitation and fear, she feels eager. Suppose it makes sense. We're going to get there one way or the other. And her way gets me to Elias faster.

But that's also what I'm afraid of.

Because if Elias . . .

If my son . . .

I can't even think about it.

Without another word, I start down the path again. It arcs around the outer edge of the garden for a half circle before turning inward. I follow the path, remembering what lies ahead. There will be a pool at the center, glowing with bioluminescent algae-like growths floating on the surface. Around the pool is a clearing a hundred feet across and covered with white nodules that serve as grass for an alien world.

I duck low when the pool comes into view. The blue glow is subtle and doesn't quite reach the edge of the surrounding forest. If there were people here, marching around the water, we'd see them. But aside from the strange shapes and limbs of an otherworldly forest, I see nothing around the pond.

"They must have left," I whisper.

"Left how?" Sam asks.

"Path on the other side of the clearing wraps around the far side of the biodome. Exits opposite where we entered."

Sam steps into the clearing. "Then let's—"

I grip her wrist. My fingers snap open when she reels around to face me. I've seen the look in her eyes before—when I was ten, staring down a German Shepherd who thought my food belonged to him. Turns out it did.

Unlike the German Shepherd, Sam calms down when I tap my ear and mouth the word, 'Listen.'

The creaking has started back up. It's coming from the other end, but I can't see anything.

"It's there," Emmett says.

"It's not an it," I say.

"I know big game when I hear it," he says. "There's something big in the dark."

The wind inside the dome shifts and picks up, striking us head-on. It carries the scent of gore—human and inhuman. I wince and cover my nose but forget the smell when I hear the footsteps return. They're coming toward us.

I raise the gun, unsure of what's approaching.

When it reaches the outer edge of the blue light, the collection of strange moving shapes doesn't make any sense. It moves like a living thing but feels artificial.

"The fuck?" Sam says, sounding more afraid than I've heard her before.

Frustrated by our inability to see the thing, I turn the gun toward the pond, put the red dot sight over one of the blue algae blobs, and—

"What are you doing?" Sam hisses.

"'Aziz, light!'" Doesn't matter that no one in their right mind would recognize the quote, because what follows is so fucked, I'm not sure I'll remember anything from the past few minutes. I pull the trigger and fire a single round into the algae blob.

It bursts, scattering hundreds of smaller versions of itself in every direction. The plant's many pieces react to the damage by flaring brightly, filling the chamber with bright blue light, and illuminating a monster.

Standing fifteen feet tall, the creature undulates toward us. I adjust my aim, looking for a head I can shoot, but I don't see a central head.

I see several.

Behind me, Emmett sees what I have yet to understand, and wretches.

There are legs. Dozens of them. Arms, too, interconnected, holding on to each other, bound together.

"It's . . . a sculpture," Sam says. "Made of people."

"And aliens," I say, scanning the many different faces, looking for Elias. I don't see him, but that doesn't mean he's not in there. The mass of bodies has been opened, twisted, and stuck together. I see rib cages, spines, and a mix of limbs. It's bound together with sinews and intestines. Sheets of skin have been unfurled like sails on a man-of-war battleship, catching the wind and dragging the thing forward with every gust.

"It's a Strandbeest," Sam says.

Emmett spits. "A what?"

"Kinetic sculpture," she says. "The wind is moving it."

"So, it's not alive?" Emmett asks.

"It just looks that way," she says. "But that doesn't mean—"

The high-pitched scream of a grown man rips from the kinetic Fleshbeest and proves Sam wrong. The creature might not be alive, but some part of it is.

"God, no," Sam says and breaks into a sprint, headed straight for the monstrous creation. Emmett is right behind her. Takes me a moment to understand why. They recognized something in that scream. They know who it is.

Takes just a moment to deduce it myself. Emmett and I are here. Jade is dead. The moment I figure it out, I hear his voice in the scream. My heart sinks.

It's Gabriel.

43

Gravity and speed conspire against me as I round the Fleshbeest. Instead of stopping beside Sam, I trip over my own foot and launch myself in the same way my childhood self would jump up out of a pool, lean to the side, and crash back down. Thought I was a breeching whale. Turns out I haven't lost the skill.

I'm airborne long enough to remember what breeching from a pool felt like. The hot air. The cold water. The splash down. I can smell the chlorine. Brings a smile to my face just before I land.

If not for the white nodules covering the terrain, the impact might have injured me. Instead, the mass of growths bends beneath my weight, breaks the fall, and all but springs me up.

Back on my feet, I catch up with Sam and Emmett. They're chasing the kinetic sculpture, debating how to free Gabe.

Free him?

I don't see how such a thing would be possible. The Fleshbeest is composed of hacked up bodies. Not a one is whole. Not a one is alive.

Then I see him and understand.

Gabe has four hooks in his body. Two under his armpits—they appear to be secured around his ribs. The other two hooks are on either side of his pelvis, probably wrapped around his hip bones. Every movement, every breath, is agonizing for Gabe.

The wind picks up and the Fleshbeest moves faster. The twisting body bends and pulls at the hooks binding Gabe to the monster's back. He screams in pain again and his role in this art piece becomes clear. To sell the illusion of life from the lifeless, the monster needed a voice. A roar.

It sends me into a rage.

I tried out for my high school football team. Wanted to date a girl. Thought being on the team, even as a benchwarmer, would help. Turns out the only thing I was good at in the game was tackling. Something about the way I ran—with my head down—allowed me to pummel a guy on impact. *If* I could make contact. Since I wasn't particularly fast, they had me on the defensive line. During my first play, I managed to lower my head and charge through the offensive line. Neither the quarterback nor I saw the collision coming, but it sent the other kid flying. Bruised his ribs. They had me chasing and jumping people for the rest of the day. Never did tackle anyone else.

I didn't make the team.

Didn't get the girl.

Which, in the end, didn't matter. I had Princess Peach on my Game Boy and didn't mind being by myself. And it turns out that some amazing women find nerdy, non-football stars to be marriage material.

It's with this limited life experience and outpouring of rage that I charge around the side of the Fleshbeest, target the row of front limbs supporting its weight, and lower my head.

Can't see shit, but my target is larger and slower than a fifteen-year-old running back. I put all my effort into moving my legs faster, imagining them blurring, faster and faster like the Flash.

Just like my first tackle, I have no idea when, or if, I'm going to make contact. So, it comes as a surprise when I slam into the outermost limb, and I'm even more shocked when the limb breaks. And then the next three limbs. Happens in rapid succession, but that doesn't stop me from feeling bad about further destroying the bodies.

The broken bones belonged to Anunnaki. The next is human. A man, judging by the size and density. Feels like a baseball bat to the chest. Knocks the wind out of me.

But it doesn't stop me.

That happens after I strike four more limbs. The seventh punts me forward. I sprawl to the ground, roll over, and find the Fleshbeest starting to lean forward. The side that I struck has collapsed, and the rest of it is following, knocked off balance while still propelled by the wind.

I scramble back on my hands and feet, slipping a few times at the pond's edge. Clear of the descending monster, I get to my feet and run back around the side to meet up with Emmett and Sam.

They both flinch when I appear from the back side of the long beast, rather than from the front, but they're relieved to see me.

"You did it," Sam says, watching the Fleshbeest slowly lean forward.

The process is much less of a relief to Gabe. He's bent and pulled, the hooks moving through his flesh. He screams out, giving the ruined sculpture a vocal death throe that gives me goosebumps under the hair on my head.

Then all at once, the life goes out of the thing, and its body accordions gently down to the floor and lies limp.

"Oh, god," Gabe says. "Thank you." His eyes meet mine. "Thank you."

I nod and step onto the mass of mushy dead bodies that have been expertly bound and cinched together. How did he have time to kill all those other people and put this monstrosity together? Whoever it is must be strong *and* a genius. The engineering skill to assemble something like this . . . I couldn't do it. That's for damn sure. And I'm generally considered a smart guy.

Gabe winces when I start untying one of the knots holding some kind of bodily cord to the screws. "The hell are you doing?"

I pause, confused. "Uh . . . Setting you free."

"Just unhook me!" Gabe shouts. "Even a fish would've been unhooked by now."

"Fish don't bleed out when they're unhooked," Sam says, crouching down on Gabe's other side. "We'll get you free, but the hooks have to stay until we get to a hospital."

"Are you injured anywhere else?" Emmett asks. He's standing behind us, still in the nude, still pale, and lit by the bright pool light.

"Back of my head. I think. But it hurts like hell."

"What do you remember?" Emmett asks.

"Starting to hope I'm not able to remember this," Gabe says with a wince as I finish undoing the first knot.

I look up and catch the end of Gabe's expression. His desire to forget this moment has nothing to do with pain and everything to do with Emmett's nakedness.

I can't help but let out a laugh.

Gabe guffaws and then groans as the hooks shift.

"Hey, now," Emmett says, "you're in the buff, too, and from the looks of it, you're a grower, not a shower."

I'd been so distracted by the Fleshbeest and the hooks that I didn't fully realize that Gabe was naked. Of *course* he is. Nearly everyone on board was left that way. I just didn't see it.

"Ouch," Gabe says, and then louder and more sincere. "Ouch!" Sam has finished her first knot and is onto the second. "I will pay all of you a million dollars to never mention this to anyone."

"Three million," Sam says.

Emmett 'tsks' and says, "This is not the appropriate time to—"

Sam waves him off. "You know those 'For the price of a cup of coffee' guilt-trip commercials to feed starving people? Three million dollars is the equivalent amount of a cup of coffee to our very own tech bro."

"Tech bro?" Gabe says, his face scrunching up as I dig at the knot. "Now you're *trying* to hurt my feelings."

"I'll throw in never calling you that again," Sam says.

"Deal," Gabe says with a grin. He's doing a good job pretending he's not in horrific pain.

Makes the job of untying him easier. Shaking fingers and knots do not play well together. His effort pays off. Sam and I finish untying the hooks.

Gabe sighs in relief and sits up. Elbows on knees, he catches his breath. It's subtle, but he's starting to shake. Shock and adrenaline have cooked his mind and body.

Before he's too far gone, I ask, "Have you seen Elias?"

"Elias?" he says, shaking his head out of a fog. "Shit. No, man. Sorry."

"Not your fault," I say, doing my best to hide the fact that I'm actively imagining grinding the killer's head into the ground, and whispering how much I hate his fucking guts. I'll press my righteous anger into his skull until—

"Hey, you still with us?" Sam snaps her fingers in front of my face. I flinch and look up at her. "You just went somewhere dark."

I just nod. There's no denying it, but I'm definitely *not* going to say what I'm thinking aloud. I turn my attention back to Gabe. "What do you remember? Where you were? How you got here? People you were with?"

He lowers his head and gives it a slow shake.

"I woke up in the dark. Couldn't see anything. Didn't recognize the voices, so I left. Felt my way through several tunnels with squishy walls. And then . . . the darkness got darker." He rubs the back of his head. "I must have been hit from behind. I woke up when the first hook was put in."

"And you didn't see who was doing it?" Sam asks.

"I was blindfolded," he says. "I think I was meant to stay that way but managed to rub it off later. That was before this thing came to life." He looks down for the first time and reels back. He hadn't seen it. Didn't know what he was strapped to, or what it was made from. "Fuck's sake!" he springs to his feet and leaps away from the dismantled Fleshbeest, shouting in pain from both the liftoff and the landing.

"That makes six of us in the clear," Emmett says. "The four of us. Jade. Elias."

"Where's Serena?" Gabe asks. "And what do you mean by 'in the clear?'"

"Haven't seen her since she left me," Emmett says and then realizes how fishy that sounds. He turns to Sam and says, "She left shortly after you. Thought she could find you and bring you back in the dark. Pretty sure you went in opposite directions."

"What do you mean by 'in the clear?'" Gabe repeats, louder this time.

"There aren't many people left alive," I say, motioning to the massive kinetic sculpture constructed from who knows how many people and aliens. "And she is the only one we haven't seen or heard from."

Gabe grips his head. "I don't understand what's happening."

I place my hand on his shoulder. "Gabe . . . My wife's killer *was* at the campground and is now on board, free, and killing. I don't know who he—or she—is, but my job is to find and kill them. It's the only way any of us make it home. Aside from the four of us, there can't be many other people—or aliens—still alive. Serena might be alive. Might be dead." I pause, waiting for him to look up and make eye contact. When he does, I say, "Might be the killer."

44

"No way," Gabe says, wincing as he follows me, supported on either side by Sam and Emmett. I'm leading the group, gun in hand, raised and ready to fire. "No way Serena is a serial killer. She's dedicated her life to stopping them."

"Stopping or studying?" I ask.

"She helps the FBI," Sam says. They're all being defensive on Serena's behalf, and I appreciate their position. They've all been friends for a very long time.

"And every time she does, she learns more. How to kill. How to get away with it. What better way to fill a serial killer skill tree? It's the perfect cover and gives her access to information that could help her elude the police and FBI indefinitely." I glance back and see three sets of angry eyes. They're a loyal bunch. Before people started dying, it was admirable. Now it could get them all killed. "I'm playing devil's advocate. Far as I'm concerned, all of you are potential suspects, especially now that it seems like most everyone on this UFO has been murdered and turned into a freakshow work of art."

"Hey, I was hooked to a sculpture," Gabe says.

"Hooked, but alive. No better way to dodge suspicion."

"Are you for real? You're not. Devil's advocate. Fine. Do your thing. I don't blame you. I don't know what it's like to have a child, but I'm guessing you're freaking out on the inside and hiding it on the outside, yeah? Projecting an air of confidence. So, yeah, go ahead and suspect everyone. But . . . just don't start shooting people until you have proof, okay?"

I nod. It's a fair request. The fact that he quickly empathized with my position is a tick in the 'not Gabe' column. Then again, he's a genius and self-made billionaire/CEO trained to engage with people and get what he wants from them, so faking empathy could be second nature.

Sam could have killed me. I was covered in alien blood, helping an alien, and she had the gun. But I'm only here because the killer went to the trouble of inviting me. Elias and I are the killer's focus. He might want to torture us. Might want to frame *me* for the murder of all these people. Sparing my life doesn't clear someone. Just means they might be biding their time. Waiting for the right moment to finish the job. To perfect a work of art. My life might be the final brushstroke. But I hope the final brushstroke is Elias. It would mean he's still alive.

It's fucked up but gives me a nugget of hope.

We leave the garden on the opposite side from where we entered. The hallways on this side are just as nondescript and dully lit by orange emergency lighting.

I pause. We could walk this ship for the next week and not find Elias. There's too much ground to cover. More nooks and crannies than a Thomas' English Muffin. Even with my knowledge of the ship's interior, it could take days to find my son.

"Why are we stopping?" Sam asks.

"We need to repair the ship," I say. "Kova said he was working on that, but it's been a long time, and I'm starting to think he might have been one of the aliens in that flesh sculpture."

"I'm sorry," Gabe says. "Kova is an alien, and a pal, and somehow you know how to repair a UFO? Now who's suspicious?" He leans a little closer. "Don't need a TED Talk. Hit me with the TikTok explanation."

"Kova is an alien. The aliens are Anunnaki. When they die, they transfer consciousness to a baby clone of themselves. The Anunnaki on this ship have been on Earth for three hundred thousand years, give or take. They made the human race, and our DNA is just 1 percent different from theirs. They live on an invisible planet. We were intended as baby surrogates but became subjects while they ruled as gods. Now they're keeping an eye on us to make sure we don't develop Artificial General Intelligence, make a bunch of noise in space, and attract unwanted attention from aggressive species. I know how to repair the ship, and my way around, and about their history because I found one that had been skinned and reshaped like a flower. I got him to the regeneration chamber, performed their 'Continuity of Self' ritual, during which I was the conduit for his life and knowledge, leaving me with a confusing, but comprehensive knowledge of their species, home world, and this UFO."

Gabe stares at me, blinking. "Is it horrible that I'm jealous?"

Sam smacks the back of his head. "His kid is missing."

"I know, I know . . ." He squints. "Hold on. This Kova guy. What do you know about him?"

"The serial killer responsible for my wife's death was abducted with us—the first time—last night. He or she is immune to the Anunnaki's telepathy. While on board, they murdered one of the Anunnaki. Kova chose me to find the killer because I have the motivation to carry out his mission."

"And that is?"

"Kill the killer," Sam says like it's obvious.

"But it seems like I'm always two steps behind, coming across his victims without ever encountering him."

"Like he knows where you are?" Gabe asks. "Or where you're going? Have you considered that maybe Kova is the killer?"

"An alien serial killer?" Emmett asks. "Is that even possible? They're an advanced species. Why would they kill us?"

"Why do people kill people?" Sam asks.

"And now we come full circle to my original question, what do you know about Kova? Not from your personal interactions with him, but from all that knowledge they shoved into your mind," Gabe says.

"I'm not sure it works that way. Some of the information stuck. Things that were important at the time, like getting around the UFO. But I don't—"

"Have you tried?" Emmett asks, one eyebrow lifted.

I sigh in frustration. "When am I supposed to—"

"No time like the present," Gabe says.

"I can lead you through some meditation techniques," Sam says. "Good for burying memories—and uncovering them."

It feels unproductive. We should be moving. Looking for Elias.

But . . . if Gabe is on to something . . . if Kova is the killer, there might be something in the Anunnaki memories that provides context for who Kova is now.

I point to an open doorway on the left side of the hall ahead. "In there. Should be empty. We'll try it. Once. But if it doesn't work, we keep moving."

I don't wait for confirmation before heading toward the doorway, weapon raised. My forearm is burning from the gun's weight in my hand. Not sure how soldiers lug around all that gear, plus their heavy weapons, and still have energy to fight. I'm having a hard time keeping this two-and-a-half-pound weapon lifted and ready to fire.

I make a mental note to add weight and energy drain to the weapons in *Shadowborn*. Swinging or even just carrying the weapon in hand should sap stamina. Won't be a popular change, but it could add some realism to my unrealistic world.

I swing the weapon into the room and sweep back and forth the way they do in cop shows. There's nothing to shoot. Nothing at all. "Clear."

When the others catch up, I turn the gun around and hand it to Emmett. It's a risk, but I don't think he's my target. "Watch the hallway. Assume anyone you see is here to kill us. Even if it's Serena."

"I'm not shooting her," he says.

"Didn't say to shoot her," I say. "Just don't trust her. If she's really a brilliant psychologist who works with the FBI, she'll understand the situation."

Sam helps Gabe sit on the floor, back against the wall. He sighs as it conforms to his body, beneath and behind him. She turns to me, snaps her fingers, and points to the floor in the middle of the room. "Sit."

I do as I'm told, sitting cross-legged on the floor. This position hasn't been comfortable since I became an adult, but the pliable floor negates the pressure points.

"IKEA would make a fortune if they got their hands on the patent for this material."

I huff. "It's not a material."

Gabe furrows his brow at me.

"They call it Šulmušar. Living shell. Biomechanical, semisentient."

Gabe leans to the side and looks down at the floor like he'll be able to perceive its living state. "No shit?"

"It's responsive to Anunnaki brainwaves," I tell him. "And people who know how to project their thoughts to it. Turns out we're Anunnaki enough in the eyes of Šulmušar."

"Then . . ." He looks up at me. "It's a witness. To everything that happens on this ship. It doesn't have eyes, I get that, but we don't know how it senses things, right? It probably feels everything touching it. If it responds to brainwaves, it can sense them, too. It might know exactly who went where, who died, and who did the killing."

It sounds impossible, but there isn't much about this situation that doesn't require a suspension of disbelief. "I'll see what I can remember."

Sam sits down across from me. "Don't over think any of this. Just relax, okay."

I nod.

"Close your eyes," she says in a soothing voice. "Deep breath in, hold it . . . let it out slowly."

I do as she says, as she's saying it.

"Good. Just like that. Do it again. In . . . and out. In . . . and out. Feel your muscles relaxing one by one. Start at your toes and work your way up through your legs, your abdomen, out through your arms to your fingers, and now to your head." She must see me relax because she says, "Yes. Now, forget the ship.

Forget the people in this room. Right now, it's just you and your memories. I want you to focus on breathing, not your thoughts, just breathing. Every inhale draws focus. Every exhale releases distraction. Good. The memories aren't gone, they're just hidden beneath dust. Can you see it?"

I nod, imagining a cigar box covered in dust. I found it when cleaning out a neighbor's basement. Kept letters from girlfriends inside it. Seems a fitting image for buried memories.

"Wipe the dust away. See the memories beneath."

I do as she says, blowing the dust away and revealing the decorative, 1920s style lid. In place of an actual cigar logo, there is a single word. *Anunnaki.*

"Forget your own life and history and adopt the cleared memories as your own. You're free to sift through them, to pull key details and knowledge to the surface."

I open the box and am nearly overwhelmed by the outpouring of knowledge.

"Keep breathing," she says. "Stay focused. You are in control."

Focusing on breathing for a moment helps me settle into the memories, like floating in a Dead Sea of forgotten history. It's Anunnaki, but it's also human.

"Think about Kova. Picture his face. Let memories of it rise to the surface, like a dream you woke from, but didn't forget. Replay the dream, follow where it leads. Now . . . tell me what you see."

I slide into the past. Three thousand years. Sumer. A region between the Tigris and Euphrates rivers. Now Iraq. I see a city. Eridu. The first city. Full of temples, ziggurats, and palaces. Everything is built from mudbrick, but the city is far larger and more intricate than any modern historian has realized. Much of it is covered in colorful tiles laid out in stunning patterns. It feels . . . alive. And the scale is massive, projecting power and hinting at advanced knowledge.

The sight of it provides me with a profound connection to our collective past. I feel inspired . . .

. . . until the screaming starts.

45

Horribly violent movies I've seen:

Saving Private Ryan.

Gladiator.

The Thing.

Kill Bill.

Event Horizon.

Hell, I even watched the first *Saw* movie. The combination of gore and good acting in all those movies left me feeling queasy. But not disturbed for all eternity. That's what is happening now.

Because there is an Anunnaki wading through a sea of pleading humans, swinging a glowing blue sword back and forth. The blade doesn't cut people. It explodes them. One moment, they're on their knees, head bowed, praying to the god standing over them. The next, they're a burst of miscolored ground beef and blood, splashing out over the surrounding people.

Why aren't they running?

I voice my frustration, shouting, "Why aren't you running!? Get up! Run!"

I'm ignored. Of course, I am. As real as this feels, I'm not actually here.

This is the past.

History as viewed by the Anunnaki I saved.

I need more than a playback. I need to be immersed. To know who the sword-wielding alien is. I try to relax farther into the memory, lowering my mental guard and embracing not just the sense of the moment, but the thoughts as well.

This is wrong, I think, now watching through eyes that see the world in a different way from me. There are things there, in the world, that we can't see. But the Anunnaki have different eyes, sensitive to other frequencies of light, both higher and lower on the scale. I wonder if humanity has been held back by our limited eyesight, but I decide against it. We've gone from the subjected to the feared in just a few thousand years. So much so that the Anunnaki are now worried about us.

The people are rooted in place. *Were* rooted in place. There is no saving them. Just what I see, hear, and think.

The resistance can't be tolerated, but this massacre is hardly necessary.

The killing is indiscriminate. He could be culling the best of them.

But who can I tell?

The Council of Aškaru on Kiškaru Affairs sees the adamu as vermin. Only those of us who have spent time with them can comprehend their true potential. They are not that dissimilar to us. Less intelligent, driven by instinct, but their ability to adapt and survive is unparalleled. Just because we nudged their development a little faster and improved their DNA does not mean they aren't sentient beings, or that they must remain subservient worshipers to those farming them.

I have long been allied with peace and scientific discovery, but the time for this . . . abuse to end has come. Our work was questionable to begin with, born out of fear of extinction. But that is no longer the case, and now that Aškaru has no use for the female wombs, the adamu must be set free.

Another of the adamu bursts from the Šu-namtilûm, the hand of unmaking. It is a swift and catastrophic way to die, dragged across the teeth of an event horizon, torn through dimensions and spat back out—all in an instant. Worse yet is the effect it has on the adamu bound to the ground.

I don't see bonds but then understand. Telepathy holds them in place and bowed down. All but one of them. An adamu woman, tall, muscular, and well fed, follows behind Nergal, my fellow Anunnaki, cracking her whip at anyone brave enough to adjust their gaze away from their god of war. She is his neophyte, enforcer, protégé, and concubine. One of many. And since our species are so closely related, it is possible that she will one day bear his child. Others have before.

The rest of them would run if they could. The adamu instinct for survival will drive them into this verdant world. They will endure—and, inevitably, they will thrive. Despite all we have done, and all we continue to do. They have earned the right to live.

Another bursts, its reorganized cellular mash spilling over family members. Family. That thing so precious to those back home, who tasked us with saving our kind from oblivion, has been abandoned on this world. Fury rises when the self-proclaimed 'Lord of the Dying Hour, of Quiet Judgment, and of Vanishing Breath' uses the Šu-namtilûm on a baby grasped in the arms of its mother. She is coated with the remains of her young. I can hear her screams and feel her anguish in my mind, but he does not allow her to outwardly express her pain. Worse still, he leaves her alive with the burden of this moment carried for the rest of her life.

Doing such a thing to one of our people would be grounds for war.

He raises the sword to the side of a young girl's head. Lets it crackle and spark, burning her skin without yet destroying her. His enforcer goads him on, taking pleasure in the pain of her own people.

The young girl, like many of the people with Anunnaki DNA, has blonde hair and blue eyes so piercing that I flinch when she spots me. Our eyes meet and I feel . . . kinship.

"Nergal!" I scream. "*Enough!*"

I flail back and land hard on the ground.

On the floor.

Confusion tears through me. "Who am I?" I shout.

I am Enki, Lord of water, wisdom, mischief, and creation.

"You're Marcus," a voice says.

Pressure pins me to the floor. My vision flickers between a blue sky and an orange ceiling. "Marcus!"

"Isabella?" I ask. "Is that—"

"It's Sam," she says, giving me a shake. "Look at me. Look at my eyes."

Sam's face flickers into view. I feel myself dragged up out of the mental muck. Enki's memories are . . . potent. They want to live on.

Of course they do, I think. I contain all the same information that the child version of Enki does. It should have dissipated, but it stuck, and if I let it, three hundred thousand years of someone else could take my place.

Sam looks down at me. Her dark skin is covered in drops of sweat. Her hair, normally tied back, is out of place and billowing to the sides. I smile at her, and it catches her off guard.

"The hell is that about?" she asks.

"Just . . . happy to see you, and to not be them."

She helps me back up. "You were shouting. Something about running."

I shake my head. "That was still me. Everything after was . . . a memory. But it was real. I was there. I could see the city. Smell the warm sand. I could hear the people screaming. Feel their thoughts. But I was him."

"Who were you?" she asks.

I shift, uncomfortable even speaking it. "Enki."

"Enki?" Gabe asks, leaning over with a grunt to look me in the eyes. "For real? *Enki* Enki, or just a guy named Enki?"

"The first one. The Sumerian god. He was Anunnaki, and a scientist. I think humanity might owe him our freedom from violent bondage."

"Kept in bondage by whom?" Gabe asks.

"Nergal," I say.

He nods. "God of plague, war, and death."

"He had much fancier ways of saying that, but yeah. And he's using another name now." I turn back to Sam. "Kova."

"Your friend?"

"He's been playing me. All of us, including his own people. He's suppressed his bloodlust for three thousand years but sees the human race's impending advancement to AGI as permission to slaughter us. The others on this ship opposed him. Now, none of them are left."

"So, we kill him," Gabe says.

It's not impossible. There are plenty of dead Anunnaki on board, but Nergal is different. I could feel it, in Enki's memory. Nergal's telepathy is unrivaled.

"We'll never get close enough," I say. "He can control our minds. And his claims of the Anunnaki being a peaceful scientific race are a gross exaggeration. Like people, their values and interests are not always aligned. They've fought wars with their own people. Slaughtered each other. And because of that, they have weapons beyond comprehension. His favorite is called the Šu-namtilûm."

"That like a laser gun or something?" Gabe asks.

"Sword," I say, "that sucks you into an artificial event horizon and then explosively regurgitates your fluid remains."

"That's just . . ." He winces. "Gross."

"Everything about him is gross," I say, "and he's just getting warmed up. I can't know for sure, but I think he's been killing random people, taking pleasure in the slowness and design, giving himself wholly over to depravity. One of those people was my wife, and for some reason, I became his next target cog in a greater plan to kill his own people. Now that his colleagues—the pantheon of Sumerian gods—are dead, there will be nothing to restrain him."

"Hey," Emmett says, leaning into the doorway. "Does that mean Serena is cleared?"

"Not remotely," I say. "In the past, Nergal kept human acolytes. They would kill for him. Torture for him. If they were a woman, they'd even bear his crossbreed children. There were many over the years, but every single one of them learned to satiate a variety of carnal desires. He taught them how to kill. How to hate. How to be his right hand when he was cutting people down with his left."

"What are you saying?" Sam asks.

"There are *two* killers," I say. "While Nergal was here, building the Fleshbeest, his partner has been out there sculpting with the dead. It's the only thing that makes sense. Not even Nergal has the ability to kill in two different places at once."

"Shit," Gabe says.

"What the hell are we supposed to do?" Emmett asks, his voice shaky. "Huh? How are we supposed to kill something like that?"

"Killing him was never the mission," I say to myself, shaking my head. He was torturing me. Enjoying my pain and horror, which I'm sure he can feel. He wants to kill me last. Or maybe . . . maybe he intends to break me. Turn me into his next acolyte. My ability to free myself from telepathic control might have impressed him. Just as his current neophyte did, being entirely immune to control. He wasn't worried about people like us. He was excited we existed.

"We need to reach the armory," I say.

"There's an *armory* on this UFO?" Sam asks.

"Unused for a long time," I admit, but their technology doesn't degrade with time like ours. "It's atrophy resistant. Made of the same stuff as this UFO, both living and immortal."

"What do you intend to do when you reach the armory?" Emmett asks.

"Šu-namtilûm," I say. "I can't think of anyone better to send through a gravitational sieve."

"I'm on board," Gabe says, pushing himself back to his feet.

Sam pulls me to my feet. "Is there more than one Šu-namtilûm?"

I smile. "Should be, but . . . he could make you use it on me. Which is also why—" I reach my hand out to Emmett. "—I need that back."

Emmett doesn't argue. Just hands the weapon to Sam, who gives it to me. Her trust is appreciated.

"Okay, now I need you all to stay close and stay quiet, even in your heads. Remember he can hear us with ears. He can hear us by thoughts."

INDEED.

The voice in my head is punctuated by all three of my friends going still—and floating off the floor. Before I can move, my feet leave the Šulmušar, and all four of us float out into the hallway. Helpless offerings carried to the altar of a false god.

46

ABERRATION

The Man is piecing things together. Sooner than intended. He seems to have come across a trove of information about our people. It doesn't really matter, though, does it? We're in the end game now.

What do you think?

You've seen the work. Pictured it in your mind, however uncreative you might be. You've seen our work in as much detail as you're willing to imagine. We can't read your mind, but you're still here.

Still watching us.

Still getting your jollies by waiting to see what we'll do next.

We don't blame you. Every artist has patrons—people who can't create but who appreciate the works of others. It's a symbiotic relationship. You get satisfaction from the way we kill and display the dead. We enjoy your attention.

We're friends, remember. In its purest form, friendship is an equal give and take. You've stuck with us for a long time, so it's time for us to deliver the goods. That's what you're after. That final hit. The ultimate high. We have that in common.

We know what you're thinking. If anyone finds out about this, about how much we have in common, they're going to treat you differently. They're going to shun you, march you down cobblestone streets shouting 'shame,' or sew a scarlet letter to your chest so that the whole world knows of your deviant ways. Children will hide their faces. Adults will cross the street to avoid you.

Don't lie. The solitude will feel nice. Like the apocalypse.

Think about it. *Imagine* it. The empty streets. The wind moving through silent cities. No one complaining. No one screaming. No one bitching about every single goddamned thing that's wrong in the world.

Existence would become pure. Breathing, eating, shitting, sleeping.

Thank you for agreeing. We appreciate honesty, you know.

But let's take that honesty to the next level, shall we? That silence in the ultimate judgment-free zone sounds appealing on the surface. But it removes the potential for true happiness that exceeds peace. It's art without an audience. True death.

Peaceful as that might be, it is not the confluence of our existence. That can only be reached in the presence of others. Not you. You're safe. But no one admires the work of a painter without paint.

You understand.

And to reward your long-suffering patience, we're switching up the scenery. Taking things back to nature where the comingling of species began so long ago. Naked and in the wilderness, we'll see how far humanity has truly advanced. Flight, fight, freeze, or fawn, right? Every one of them will make one of those four choices. It can't be helped. At their cores, normal humans are still primitive *heidelbergensis*, acting tough, shaking their spears, but still prey animals with limited responses to the presence of a predator. In the face of danger, the average person lacks the ability to do the one thing that could save their life—think.

Elite soldiers can do it. Psychopaths, too. Guessing there's some overlap there. But the average Joe is as helpless as a baby deer born without legs.

That's a funny image. Picture it.

Here, here.

Listen.

We'll do our best David Attenborough:

"Ah, the newborn fawn emerges from its mother's womb—a delicate and miraculous moment in the endless cycle of life. The tall grass, now glistening with the sheen of placental fluid, offers both concealment and welcome, to this trembling newcomer.

"With unsteady resolve, it attempts to unfold its limbs and rise—an act it must perform swiftly, for danger is never far. Predators lurk nearby: wolves, badgers . . . even raptors surveying from above.

"The mother, instinctively driven, begins to cleanse her offspring, tearing away the remnants of the embryonic sac with urgent care. But something is amiss. The fawn, though alive, has been born without limbs.

"In the wild, such a deformity is not merely unfortunate—it is terminal. The mother hesitates, then, in a burst of self-preservation, abandons the scene as shadows gather on the periphery.

"Soon, the forest will reclaim what it has delivered. For here, in nature's domain, even the smallest flaw can lead to the harshest end: to be consumed, not with malice—but with necessity."

Holy shit, we might have missed our calling, right?

The point is, when we look at most people, this is what we see. Legless, helpless, clueless newborns with no real ability to think when their life is on the line. Sure, most people aren't legless. But they might as well be. We are proof of that.

The remnants of today's hunt are lifted, carried, and rendered unconscious. The Man fights against it, but there is nothing he can do. The ship is expelling those left alive, dispersing them to the forest below. They will wake, confused by the location change, how they got there, and, best of all, having no memory of what has transpired.

This is going to be hysterical.

It will be a pleasure to delight in their renewed confusion and horror.

We are already on the ground, waiting for those who are about to die. Like gladiators, if gladiators didn't know they were in a fight for their lives. Yeah, yeah, yeah. No fair, right?

Life isn't fair.

The Anunnaki know that.

Some humans do, too.

Those that don't? Survival of the fittest, right? In the long run, we're doing the human race a favor. Only through refinement and trials can humanity join their brethren in the sky. And only then, will our two species, divided by a handful of genes, become one.

Become more.

Anunnaki once lived in domination of another world. Another species. And the lesson they learned from that experience is that there is always a bigger fish in the sea. A bigger alien in the galaxy. What they seemed to miss, and what we will correct, is that it is possible to be the biggest. Someone is always the biggest. United planets around the same sun. It's a unique configuration and the potential for outwardly exerting power throughout the universe, is not only untapped, but immense.

Light from above signifies the arrival of our pawns. We watch from a distance as, one by one, they descend on a beam of light. Biblical in reverse. They're so helpless. So pitiful.

Undeserving of life.

They begin separating, drifting apart, as they near the ground. Depositing them in different locations will add to the confusion and chaos.

But there is a problem.

One of them is missing.

The Man.

He is resisting. That makes us happy. You're rooting for him, too, aren't you? The broken widower with the young son, a successful and cool self-made businessman, and an all-around good guy. We're rooting for him, too, but for very different reasons. Like the Anunnaki, we see more of this reality than humans. Not just how things are, but their potential for future greatness, either as a work of art, or as a future ally.

And that is our hope for him. We see a like mind. His ability to resist mental control is a hint at a fire burning within him. He just needs his eyes opened. Needs to take that first step. To take a life and feel its power absorbed into his soul. He'll come around, and if he doesn't . . .

He will be eaten alive, like every living thing on this planet was meant to be.

Hey, don't get squeamish on us. We're not a cannibal. Jeez. Can't we speak metaphorically anymore? We have no taste for human flesh as anything more than a medium with which to rearrange reality into something more beautiful and compelling.

Ah, here he comes now. Resistant, but not immune.

The Man floats down, body limp, head hanging back.

Unconscious.

We're not sure how much he's going to remember, but his mind is resilient and has already uncovered veiled memories. He saw through the owl disguise.

We're rooting for him.

And if he fails? He'll be the pinnacle of a new creation, left on the beach and set alight for the police to find. The world will hear about it. Our audience will expand a thousand-fold. We will have access to a new audience, the scale of which the ancient creators couldn't fathom. Imagine Da Vinci with the internet. He might have changed a portion of the world with his art and ideas, but with a global reach? He could have reshaped the planet.

And that's exactly what we're going to do.

Starting with the last players still on the stage.

The descending group slips into the trees and out of sight. A minute later, the Man joins them.

In thirty seconds, they'll all wake up.

In thirty seconds, the fun begins.

Hope you enjoy the show, friend, and if this is the last time you hear from us, we appreciate your encouragement and shared delight in what some might call madness, but what we call enlightenment.

You're a true friend.

Our audience.

We love you.

47

I'm placed on a bed of pine needles. It's gentle, like a mother lowering her sleeping baby into a crib as softly as possible, to keep the child from waking and restarting whatever hours-long process it took to get them to that moment of rest.

I remember those nights well. Elias wasn't the best sleeper. Always had an active imagination. He just couldn't shut off and, for tired parents who were desperate for that shut-off, it was a hard time. We took him for drives. Sang songs. Gave him full body squeezes, one limb at a time. We even tried just leaving him. 'He'll wear himself out,' they said. 'He'll get used to it.'

He didn't. There's only so much screaming a compassionate person can take before helping ease the anguish of a child. Sure, there are some people who can hear that noise, think 'screw that little asshole,' and turn up *Game of Thrones*.

I am not that person. I love my son. Adore him. And I will do anything for him—if he's still alive.

The thought propels me into a sitting position. I was perfectly comfortable on my back. Might have even fallen asleep if my mind hadn't wandered into the past. But now I'm awake, heart pounding, senses taking in everything around me.

It's still night, though there is a sliver of dark purple in the East. Hard to believe that all that carnage took place in a single night. The killers' appetite is insatiable. Their need for havoc and what they consider art is beyond the scope of any notorious human being I've ever heard about. Conquerors, dictators, even other serial killers might balk at the sheer savagery on display as fleshy compositions.

The night has cooled the air, but I'm still comfortable just dressed in shorts. The scent of pine is subtle now, replaced by earthy, cool moss. I get to my feet and use a tree for support. The long night has sapped my body, leaving my limbs cramping after just a few minutes of pretending to be unconscious.

I could feel the urge to slip away pushing on my mind. Knowing it was Nergal helped me resist it. The memory of his true self combined with the knowledge of his intentions for my friends—and then the whole of humanity—fueled my defiance. At the same time, I did my best to act as though the pressure to sleep had worked. Cleared my mind. Let my limbs hang limp.

No idea if it worked.

I hear a snap not too far from me. Smart thing would be to remain motionless and silent, but I'm not in the mood for hiding.

And there's a heavy weight in my right pocket. I still have the gun. I draw the weapon and whisper, "*Who's there?*"

"Marcus?" It's Sam. "What the hell is going on? How'd we get here? And why the fuck am I only wearing your shirt?"

"You don't remember?" I ask.

"Remember what?" she asks, suddenly beside me, standing in the shadow of a moonlit tree.

I flinch at her abrupt arrival.

"We were abducted," I say.

She's quiet for a moment, and then says, "Bullshit."

She doesn't remember.

"Sam," I say, "we were taken aboard a UFO. Twice."

I can't see her face, but I can feel her rolling her eyes.

"What's the last thing you remember?" I ask.

"We were at the range," she says.

"They erased the whole night," I grumble.

"Nice try," she says, stepping into light holding a branch like a baseball bat. She swings for my head.

I step back and my clumsy feet save me from a concussion. A root stumbles me back and my fall to the ground takes me just out of range. The branch whooshes past my face.

"Whoa, whoa, whoa!" I say, hands extended.

She's already got the branch ready to swing again but stops when she spots her gun in my hand.

"Here," I say, turning the weapon around in my hand. "Take it. You're better with it anyway."

She inches closer and then snags the weapon from my hand. She ejects the magazine, checks to see if it's loaded, goes to chamber a round, and catches the bullet that's ejected. Then she points the gun at me. "What the fuck happened? For real?"

I raise my hands. "I'm not screwing with you. We were all abducted. I'm trying to find Elias. Please. I don't know if he's alive or dead."

She squints. "Why would he be dead?"

"Because the aliens took every goddamned person at this campground. Twenty-eight people. Most of them are dead now, killed by a pair of serial killers. One alien. One human. Look, I know that sounds impossible. I wouldn't believe me, either. But it's the truth."

"Who is dead?" she asks.

"I don't know everyone's names," I say.

"Who is dead that you know?" she asks.

"Jade," I say.

The news hits her like it's the first time. She holds her gut with one hand and stumbles back a step. "Bullshit."

"You, me, Emmett, and Gabe were all together when we were returned," I say. "We were working together."

"If we were working together, why did you have my gun?"

I rub my head, growing frustrated. "Because I can fight their control! You could be used to shoot people."

"Then why did you give it to me—"

"Because I need you to trust me, damnit!" I get to my feet. "If you think I roofied you or something, just shoot me and get it over with. But my son is out there, and I'm not going to sit here all night trying to convince you that the impossible is true."

She stares at me for a moment and then gets a funny look on her face. "Why are you shiny?"

I glance down at my body. I'm still covered in dry iridescent blood. It glimmers in the moonlight.

"Alien blood," I say. "You see? I'm not fucking with you. I'm not a threat. And I need your help."

Sam steps closer and runs a finger over my chest. The blood is old and dry. She places the gun to the side of my head, leans in close, and smells the blood. She winces and steps back.

"You don't know what alien blood smells like," I say, "do you?"

"I know what paint smells like," she says.

"And?"

"That's not paint. Doesn't mean that it's alien blood." She shakes her head. "God. This is insane." Her face twists with a fresh thought. "You said Jade was dead."

I nod. "Sorry about that."

"Emmett and Gabe were with us, right?"

"And they're probably around here somewhere. Fair warning, both are naked, and Gabe is wounded."

"Wounded how?"

"Hooks in his body, from where he was attached to a Fleshbeest."

"A *what?*"

"Can I explain that later?" I ask.

"Sure," she says, sounding more than a little snarky. "Now, where the fuck is Serena? You haven't mentioned her."

The look on my face says enough, but I add to it with, "She was a suspect."

"Fuck you," she says, patience waning.

"We never saw her. Never spoke to her. Never saw her in one of the sculptures."

"What do you mean, sculptures?"

"They . . . they mutilated people. Positioned them like . . . like works of art. Sam . . . the person who did this . . . We were right. Elias and I were lured here by my wife's killer. He did the same thing to her. And that person might now have my son. Please trust me. Hold on to the gun if you want to—"

"It *is* my gun."

"—just . . . if we come across an alien, give it to me."

"I could just shoot it," she says.

"Nergal won't let you."

She squints at me. "Nergal, huh? Sounds like you know him pretty well."

"The more I explain, the crazier you're going to think I am," I say. "I can tell you everything later, I swear. Right now, we need to find Elias and the others, and kill whoever is trying to kill us, whether that is Serena or someone else."

She lowers the weapon. "The second you look at me funny, I'm going to put a bullet in your leg."

"Thank you," I say, and she's a little confused by my response to her threat. Because coupled with the potential bullet in my leg is a lowered gun and the hope that we can finally find my son. There's a chance that he's already dead. I know that. But I'm not focusing on it. The moment I give in to that fear, I'm done.

"Okay, let's—"

A scream tears through the night. I spin toward the sound and say, "Gabriel."

"How do you know that's Gabe?" she asks.

"I've heard him scream like that before." Before she can question me further, I say, "Let's go," and crash through the underbrush, heading toward Gabe's horrified scream that has yet to repeat.

48

Fuck, shit, fuck." Gabe panic-whispers to himself. "What the fuck?" He grunts in pain. "*What the fuck?*"

"Gabe," I whisper as loudly as I can manage.

"Who's that? Who's there?" He's freaking out. Rightfully so.

"It's Marcus," I say, "and Sam."

Sam and I push through some hard-to-see brush. Feels like I'm famous and fighting past the spindly limbs of my adoring, emaciated fans, reaching out and clinging to the little clothing I'm wearing.

Gabe is on the other side, lit by a streak of moonlight. His back is against a tree. He's breathing heavily. There's a streak of blood down the left side of his naked body. He's removed one of the hooks.

"Don't take those out," I tell him, motioning to the other hooks. "They're keeping you from bleeding out."

"Yeah, I figured that out," he says, pulling his legs up to hide his nakedness. "What the hell is happening? Why am I naked?" He looks to Sam. "Why are you wearing his shirt?"

"How open-minded are you feeling?" I ask.

"I was sitting by the fire while you two were off shooting, and now I'm in the forest with hooks in my naked body," he says. "I'd say I'm pretty fucking open-minded."

I give him the super-short version of the night's events, leaving out Jade's death. When I'm done, he's just staring at me.

"Look, I know it's insane and I can't think of a good reason either of you should believe me, but—"

"No, no," he says, lifting his open palms. "All that checks out, far as I'm concerned. I've done enough research into UFOs and ancient aliens to buy into all that. I'm mostly concerned by the holes in your story."

"Holes?" Sam asks.

"Serena and Jade," he says. Can't get a thing past him. Shouldn't be surprising. Even with hooks in his body, and his mind in shock, he's still one of the smartest people on the planet.

"Jade," I say, but don't get another word out.

He snaps his fingers at me. "I don't need to hear anything else."

Emotion has crept into his voice. Must have snuck into mine as well. He understood Jade's fate from just me saying his name.

"Serena," I say, and his forehead scrunches up. He's heard my consternation and fear in her name and it's not making sense. "We don't know for sure, but she's the last of us that hasn't been cleared."

"Or seen," Sam says.

I nod. "We don't even know if she's alive."

"But we were together," he says, repeating the detail from my story. "And Emmett was with us."

"Haven't seen him since I woke up," Sam says.and glances at me.

"They dropped us in different locations," I say. "It feels random, but I think there's a plan . . . and it involves all of us dying."

"Right," Gabe says, pushing himself up. "Fuck that." He swats my hand away when I try to help. "If I can't move on my own, you're better off without me. Now, do we know where we are, aside from in the woods?"

"Not far from the lake," I say. "Not far from the campground. But I don't know where. What are you thinking?"

"I'm thinking there might be resources that can help us," he says.

Sam holds up the gun. "Like this?"

"That, and clothing," he says. "Knives. Tinfoil fucking hats. I don't know. We've been left naked and disheveled for a reason. Probably to keep us confused and disoriented. They brought us back to hunt, but they also don't want to risk us fighting back or getting away."

"Except," I say, "that's not true."

"How so?" Sam asks.

"The gun," I say. "Nergal let me have it. Wanted me to have it."

"But then never gave you a chance to use it," she says. "Do we even know if it works?" She points the weapon to the side, and I understand what she's about to do just in time to cover my ears with my hands. The single shot tears through the night, punches into a tree, and proves the weapon's lethality.

It also gives away our position.

Not that it's really a mystery to who dropped us here.

"We need to move," Gabe says.

I look around and just see the nondescript silhouettes of trees. "Which way?"

Sam looks to the sky, rotates her body and then points. "If we're near both the campground and the lake, the lake should be to our south. If we can find even a single path, Gabe and I will know where we are. From there we can go to my cabin."

"What's in your cabin?" I ask.

She holds up the weapon. "This is the gun I keep locked in a hidden box in the woods. The one I conceal carry—a Smith & Wesson Model 69 Combat Magnum—packs more of a punch. Only five rounds in the revolver, but they're .44 Magnums and one hit is usually enough."

"Sounds like a plan," Gabe says. "Let's g—"

Rustling cuts him short. It's nearby. And he pauses.

Some ancient voice whispers to me. *You're being hunted. Danger is close. Run!*

"Get to your cabin," I whisper to Sam.

"What are you going to do?" she whispers back.

I hold my hand out, silently asking for the gun. "The opposite of what every cell in my body is telling me to do."

"I could—"

I shake my head. "The choices we make determine who we become. I couldn't be this person for my wife, but I'm choosing to be him now. Please."

"This isn't your game," she says. The rustling resumes. Maybe twenty feet away. Getting closer.

"But it's who I want to be."

She smiles and turns the gun around. Hands it to me. I take it and nod.

"Try to be quiet," I say.

"What are you going to do?" she whispers.

"The opposite of that," I say. "Go."

Gabe is already backing away when Sam turns to leave. I wait until I can't hear them anymore. Then I face the sound of whatever or whoever is closing in.

"Who's there?"

I'm not really expecting a response. The lion doesn't announce its presence before pouncing.

The shuffling grows closer. Louder.

I aim the gun toward it. "I have a weapon. I'll shoot!"

It's still coming.

The only reason I haven't already taken a shot is because it could be Emmett. He could be injured. The killers could have sewn his mouth shut. Cut his vocal cords. There are a hundred different ways they could have silenced Emmett and sent him scrambling toward me for help, hoping that I'll greet him with a bullet. It's the kind of brutalist poetry they would like.

Then whatever is making the noise speeds up, rushing toward me.

Instinct guides my finger to the trigger, but I never get a chance to pull it. Because instinct does a lot of things at once, including turning me around and lighting a fire under my ass.

"Shit!" I shout, sprinting away from the approaching who-knows-what, in the opposite direction from Sam and Gabe. At least I got that part right. What I don't get right is running in the woods at night. I can see the trees just well enough to not careen headlong into one, but the branches . . . they're harder to see.

I get lashed by young bendy branches a half dozen times during the first few seconds of my retreat. A larger branch catches me across the forehead. My head's momentum comes to a sudden stop while my legs continue forward. I'm flipped like a flapjack and dropped to the ground, landing flat on my back.

The dead branch falls on top of me. Its dry, brittle state is the only reason I'm still conscious. I might be awake, but I'm far from mobile. I lie there on my back, gasping for air, keenly aware that my pursuer is still closing in.

And the weapon is no longer in my hand.

I inhale like a man trying to swallow the sky, but my convulsing lungs want more.

Multitasking has never been my strong suit. Isabella was fond of pointing that out. If I made a bag of microwave popcorn, I stood and waited. During those two minutes, she would find a half dozen mini chores to complete and cross off a mental list or manage to scrub clean a pan caked with burnt-on hamburger grease. But when my life is on the line, I manage to both keep breathing and search for the gun.

The rustling gets louder. There's no doubt in my mind that the thing in the woods with me is both hunting me and about to pounce.

My hand strikes hard metal. I pick up the weapon but am holding it by the barrel. With just a second to spare, I roll onto my stomach, flip the gun around in my hand, slip my finger around the trigger, and fire two shots at the sound.

There's a thump.

Followed by a rancid smell that confirms the target was not human and propels me to my feet and away.

It was a skunk.

A fucking skunk!

But it was definitely chasing me. Acting like a predator. Pursuing me. Or . . . driving me toward something. If Nergal can control a human's mind, it would be nothing to control a small mammal's.

I slide to a stop in the pine needles, unsure of what to do next. Do I push on? Circle back? Or—

A beam of light strikes the forest not far from where I'm standing. Are they looking for me? Driving me into a trap? What would be the point? They had us on the UFO. So, this is all just some performance art infused with fear. My fear.

"Fuck you!" I shout at the sky and then fire three shots at the light's source, high above in the sky. The light winks out.

I run, and it's a good thing I do. The light returns a moment later, illuminating the forest where I'd just been standing. I don't know what would have happened if I'd still been there. The light might hold me in place while Nergal peels me apart and reshapes my body. He might not be able to fully control my mind, but that tractor beam, or whatever the fuck it is, would have no trouble making me an easy target.

I decide to follow my own path, instead of reacting. I turn south, in the direction Sam pointed, and haul ass—hopefully toward the beach. There, without trees to hide them or me, I intend on facing Nergal and his ally, at which point I'll show them what my Alien can do.

Or die.

Probably die.

But I'm done running. Done chasing. It's time to fight.

49

My desire to face my enemies and put a bullet in them—or die trying—is interrupted by the beam of light. It strikes the ground just ten feet in front of me. I nearly careen right into it but manage to correct course and dive away.

As I'm airborne, the light moves again, surging toward where I'd just been standing. It misses me, but I get a good look at what it's doing to things it touches. The ground where it first struck is black. The pine needles there have been reduced to black powder.

I land hard on my side, ribs crashing into a fallen tree hard enough to draw a scream of pain from my mouth. Grunting in pain, I push myself up. The tree crumbles under my hand. It's rotting. Probably why my ribs aren't broken. Bruised for sure, but I broke my ribs once in high school, and this isn't nearly as bad.

I turn to the still-moving light, watching it streak away. The ground in its wake is dust. I don't know if it's burning everything or disassembling things at a molecular level, but the result is the same—absolute destruction.

The light hits a hundred-foot-tall pine, illuminating it for a moment. Then, all at once, the tree is gone, replaced by a fine powder that drifts away on the breeze.

"Okay," I say, taking a breath and wincing from the pain. "Not a tractor beam."

I run south again, finding it a little easier thanks to the light, which illuminates the forest like a mobile sun. The trees ahead grow suddenly brighter. My shadow grows short. The light is closing in.

Without looking back, I leap to the side again, this time picking a landing zone free of debris. The light streaks past as I hit the ground, cutting a tipped-over tree trunk in half. The side still rooted to the ground bounces up as the weight that had been holding it down disappears. The top half crashes down to the ground.

They're toying with me, I think.

I'm nothing special. I can't outrun a beam of light.

When designing an open-world experience like *Shadowborn*, I used several methods of directed open-world design to move players to the right place at the correct time. Environment guidance, soft gating, critical pathing, loop design, FOMO hooks, and my personal favorite—the 'Weenie' Technique, a term coined by Walt Disney when he observed how dogs quickly follow someone with a hot dog. In games, the 'weenie' is anything so visually compelling that people head for it like a dog chasing a hot dog.

I'd be happy with any of those subtle psychological tricks right now. Instead, I'm experiencing forced pathing—being coerced to follow a certain trail, usually toward some kind of confrontation. Often a boss battle. Doesn't mean the intelligence behind this is playing a game. Just means that game theory has learned what motivates people—and aliens—in real life.

It's part of why I think people can learn real life lessons in a game, without the threat of being vaporized in reality.

The question is—do the designers of my current predicament want me to survive? Will they follow through on turning me to dust, or are they just dramatically herding me into position for whatever they've got planned?

There's no way to know.

That's not true. There is one way to solve that mystery.

Stand still. Let the light close in. See if it stops.

If this were a game, the light would kill the player—because they get an infinite number of chances to survive the challenge. I get just one life, and that's why I'm not willing to risk finding out. As long as Elias's fate is a mystery, I can't take a chance with my own life. So, I'll never know if that light would cut me down or stop just short.

I'm back up and running before the light shifts directions again and begins closing in. It doesn't sneak up behind me like before. It slides through the forest beside me, erasing everything in its path. Some trees disappear entirely. Others are sliced in half. Some lose branches. Some crash to the ground. The light is silent, but its effect on the environment sounds like a kaiju is plowing through the forest.

LEFT!

My body angles to the left as I approach a tree. I fight the impending impact, but my left shoulder collides with the trunk. The impact spins me a full three-sixty before I faceplant on the forest floor.

I lie there for a moment, stunned by the sudden movement. What happened? Why did I turn into the tree?

One second I was running, the next I felt a sudden urge to change direction. What made me think that was a good—The truth spurs me back to my feet. I didn't think anything. The thought came from outside. I recognize Nergal's thoughts in the same way I might his voice.

RUN!

My limbs throw me forward, directly into a fallen tree. The horizontal trunk is caught between two trees and a rock that keep it suspended a few feet off the ground. It catches me in the gut, sucks the air from my lungs, and flips me like a professional wrestler. The little air left in my lungs is expelled when I hit the ground.

Pinpoints of light spin in my vision.

Can't move.

Can't think.

But a thought rises to the surface.

DON'T MOVE.

Fuck you, I think back, but I'm still rooted in place. Still trying to breathe. Still trying to motivate my limbs.

STAY STILL.

I manage a few breaths. The stars fade. I turn my head and spot the light. It's coming straight toward me, smooth and steady, eradicating everything it touches.

ACCEPT YOUR FATE.

Reality bends inside my head, a mental Vertigo effect. I'm not stuck on the ground because my body is broken. I can't move because my mind is being controlled. Nergal is keeping me here, on my back, helpless, as the destructive force closes in.

"Fuck. You!" I shout willing my body to move. I strain against myself, screaming from the effort. But it's no use. I'm stuck. I clench my eyes shut and focus on Elias. I picture him, injured and helpless, being held captive by Nergal and his human counterpart. My arms push against the ground, tilting my body up. But it's not nearly enough.

GIVE UP.

I ignore the voice trying to influence my body and do the thing I've been trying to avoid since being separated from Elias—accepting the possibility that my son is dead. That after I spoke to him on the radio, he was caught, killed, and used like clay.

"No," I say, voice warbling. The thought fills me with so much anguish that I nearly welcome the light.

But then, something in me shifts. Pain transmogrifies into a craving for vengeance.

My body shakes as I sit up, resisting Nergal's continued assault on my mind.

REMAIN STILL.

The light is just five feet away and moving closer. I have seconds.

I quiver from head to toe as I climb to my feet. Feels like I've just run a marathon. My legs just want to give up. But the weakness has nothing to do with my body and everything with my mind.

Get the fuck out of my head!

YOU ARE WEAK.

"I'm going to fucking peel you apart with my bare fucking hands!" I scream, louder than I've ever screamed before.

And with that, I'm free.

DO. NOT. MOVE.

Nergal is shouting now, too, in my head. But his voice has no effect.

I launch away from the light. It passes over where I'd been lying, wiping everything there from the face of the Earth.

The light adjusts course again, sliding through the forest on my left this time. I'm being force-pathed again, driven to the right as the light angles toward me. They want me to go somewhere, but why? It doesn't make sense. If I hadn't broken free from Nergal's control, I'd be dead.

What was the point?

To torture me? Does the amount of adrenaline and cortisol flowing through my veins change things? Are my weak and shaky limbs easier to peel apart or bend into a new shape?

Doesn't matter why. If they're force-pathing me, it's for a reason—probably a confrontation. Which means we want the same thing. I know my chances of winning any fight with an advanced alien species who ruled humans for millennia are slimmer than a vegan at a Texas BBQ.

Doesn't matter.

I'm out for blood.

I'm going to turn the tables on these fucking psychos.

Vengeance will be mine.

For my wife.

For my son.

For all the dead on that UFO.

Even if it means embracing my evil side and taking a dark path, I will gladly leave the path of righteousness behind. Whatever it takes to kill these assholes, I'm going to do it.

The light falls back, slides around behind me, and then approaches on my right. When it comes toward me, I follow its guidance and find myself on a familiar path. This leads to where I found Elias and Emmett fishing. The memory fuels my rage so that when I charge out of the woods and onto the beach, I'm frothing like a goddamned honey badger whose nuts are being stung by a bee.

Five steps later, all of that enraged bravado and resolve evaporates like a tree caught by the destructive light beam.

50

Emmett is on his knees in the sand. Still naked. Still covered in Jade's dried blood. There's some fresh blood running down his face from a gash on his forehead. His face is placid, lacking any sign of emotion.

Because he's being controlled.

Nergal stands behind him, a grin on his pale blue face. His hair is slicked back and held in place with what looks like dried blood. His body is covered in a mixture of dark red and iridescent gore. He's covered in the remains of his victims.

I'm shocked into inaction. Nergal doesn't need to control me.

"Thirty-seven," Nergal says with his mouth, "and then just seven."

Assuming he's including himself and his partner, that number includes myself, Emmett, Gabe, Sam, and a single unknown. Well, two unknowns. We have yet to meet Nergal's current acolyte.

"You look tired, Marcus," he says. "But your journey is nearly complete."

"You know what," I say, mind snapping back into focus. "Just shut the fuck up." I lift the gun, finger on the trigger, ready to implode that big forehead of his. But I don't follow through. I can't.

As I lifted the weapon, a slender arm coated in blood emerged from behind Emmett holding some kind of sharp-looking weapon. The blade is pressed against Emmett's throat.

The threat is clear—I fire, Emmett dies.

"Is your thirst for vengeance strong enough that you would ensure the death of an innocent?" Nergal asks.

"I'm still deciding," I say, and it's an honest answer. These two have killed thirty people—and aliens—by Nergal's count. He's off by one, but that doesn't matter, because they're going to keep on killing. Of that, there's no doubt. They'll kill me, Emmett, and the others. They'll fashion us into something abominable and then move on. Even worse, Nergal has fantasies of resuming his role as Lord of the Dying Hour. With Anunnaki technology, it might even be possible.

Killing Nergal, and as a result, Emmett, would be justified.

But . . . can I really condemn Emmett to death?

I don't think I have a choice.

I'm about to pull the trigger when Nergal's helper reveals himself. He's Anunnaki. And I've seen him before. His blond mohawk is hard to forget. His short stature makes his large head almost comical. But his eyes are dead. Soulless. He gazes at me with a blank stare and doesn't step out from behind Emmett. He's just a head and an arm.

The small alien's appearance staggers me, but it changes nothing. I just need to fire more bullets.

"There it is," Nergal says, looking pleased. "The murderous intent. The hatred. The power to overcome morality."

I'm not here to listen to a monologue, so I squeeze the trigger—and am stopped once again, this time by the appearance of a naked woman.

"Serena," I whisper.

Her face, like Emmett's, is emotionless. She's being controlled. Her body is covered in scratches. Looks like she put up a fight.

Serena walks around Nergal, stands beside Emmett, and then kneels down next to him. Her body conceals the small alien's head and doubles my trepidation.

Can I condemn two people to death?

Doing nothing means many more will die. The pain I endure will increase but killing Nergal here and now is the right thing to do.

Then why haven't I done it?

"I sense your struggle, Marcus," Nergal says, "but you know what needs to be done, don't you?"

I'm not sure I do. Why would he encourage me to pull the trigger? Does he know he'll survive? Does he think I'll miss? Is this all about getting me to ensure Emmett's and Serena's deaths, and then leaving me to live with the guilt? It's a recreation of the torture I've put myself through since Isabella's death. I should have been there. I could have saved her.

But that's not true. I know that now. Nergal could have controlled us both. I've learned that I can fight his control, but at the time I'd have been helpless.

And I'm not helpless now.

Finger on the trigger.

Pull it, I tell myself. *Pull it now!*

Serena screams, suddenly aware and terrified. She can't move her body, but her face twists up with pent-up horror. How long has she been frozen and incapable of expressing her emotions? She screams several times before locking eyes with me. Her face screws up and, just as she's about to say something, goes slack.

"Fuck you, Nergal," I say, tears in my eyes.

"Don't be so hard on him."

The voice spins me around. It's Gabe, emerging from the woods. He's dressed now but has six bloody marks on his clothing. They removed the hooks.

"Gabe," I say, "what are you . . ."

Don't need to finish the question. He's moving naturally. Spoke naturally. But his eyes are vacant. Gabe is here, but not in control.

I back away from him, stepping into the shallow water. He doesn't attack. Just casually walks past me, stands on Emmett's other side, and then drops to his knees.

"Mankind's ability to resist control is a relatively new phenomenon, and it has nothing to do with intelligence." Nergal places his hand atop Gabe's head. His long fingers wrap around Gabe's forehead. Nergal taps his fingers in a left-to-right pattern, just over Gabe's eyes. "Take this man. He is by far the most intelligent among you. In many ways, his mind isn't that dissimilar to an Anunnaki's. And yet . . ."

Gabe leaps to his feet, tears off his fresh shirt, revealing his seeping wounds. Then he extends both thumbs, says, "Ayyyyy!" He turns his thumbs toward his body and stabs them into the puncture holes just inside and under his arm pits.

The pain must be excruciating, but he's unable to express it. Instead, he pulls at his skin until the thumbs pop free, covered in blood. He then puts a thumb into his mouth and sucks it clean.

"If you're not going to pull the trigger, just give me the gun." Sam steps out of the forest and onto the beach. She's dressed and carrying a weapon of her own, but it's still holstered on her hip. And there isn't a trace of concern in her eyes. She's being controlled, too.

"What's your point?" I ask Nergal. "What's the point of all of this? Why not just kill us and be done with it?"

"Sounds like he wants the truth," Sam says. She stops in the sand beside Serena. "The truth, Marcus, is that we are all here for *you*."

A new voice, higher pitched and scratchy, emerges from behind Emmett. "The Man!"

A nagging feeling creeps up and begins tugging at my mind, demanding my attention.

"Why am I important? Why do you give a shit about my family?"

"Genetics," Nergal says. "You are rare. Contained antimatter. You hold the key to conquest—not of humanity, but of Aškaru."

"There's nothing special about me," I say. "I just . . . I . . ."

The nagging becomes unbearable.

Midsentence, I drift into thought.

Thirty-seven and then just seven.

Seven.

Nergal, his helper, Emmett, Sam, Serena, Gabe, me.

Seven.

"Elias," I whisper. My hand starts shaking. Tears flow. I look up, eyes locked onto Nergal's. "Elias. My son!"

Sam steps between me and Nergal, blocking my shot. "Now, now, hang on there, gamemaster." She starts doing the running man dance. "We're almost at the payoff."

Her use of gaming terminology is off. Nergal is speaking through her, while making her body do something that would embarrass her.

"That's where we are," she says. "But you already knew that. This is the destination node. The critical encounter. The narrative convergence. It's time for your transformation, to ascend and allow your true self to emerge."

Now she's using language directly from *Shadowborn*. Why does Nergal know *Shadowborn*? Did he target my family because of the game? Did he somehow sense my resistance to control by accessing the game?

Answers won't be forthcoming, so I focus on what I know.

In the game, there comes a moment where you must accept or resist the path you are on. If you are on the path of darkness and have a change of heart, this is the moment it happens. The choice you make determines which skill tree is unlocked, and which legendary weapon you receive.

This is about forcing me to make a choice.

It's not about the future of Earth.

It's about me deciding whether I can kill my friends—and what effect that will have on my psyche.

That's what he wants. And despite the fate of my son, I refuse to be manipulated into becoming a murderer.

I lower the gun.

Sam 'tsks' and says, "So boring."

"But not unanticipated," Nergal says. "You believe yourself morally upright, but this moment can't be avoided. There is no save and quit. You cannot return to this moment or undo your decisions. You must choose your path."

"I just did," I grumble.

He shakes his head. "I'm afraid that tonight, all paths lead to death, and to darkness."

"I'm not playing your game," I say.

"We'll see," he says, and looks down. "Show yourself."

The little alien stands to his full height. Looks to be five and a half feet tall, which means he's been crouching both times I've encountered him. His body is slathered in gore, but there's something different about him. The anatomical structure isn't Anunnaki.

I flinch when the alien grasps the skin under his face and pulls. The flesh peels up and back, revealing a face underneath that is both clean and the most horrific thing I've ever seen.

Nergal's acolyte *is* human.

He is also my son.

51

ABERRATION

What kind of person are you?

At this point, people tend to fall into two camps. On one side are those who are shocked by the revelation that we are a serial killer of epic proportions. On the other side are those who will smugly declare, 'Lame. It was sooo obvious.' But whatever side of that divide on which you find yourself, admit it, you are personally thrilled that the thirteen-year-old is a brutal murderer with a sense of artistic pizazz.

Because, as we both know by this point, you are a sick individual.

You delighted in every killing.

You marveled at our works of art.

You've probably been secretly cheering us on. You don't have to admit it. Why would you? It can be our secret.

And it doesn't make you a bad person. We're charismatic. We're honest. Straightforward. Entertaining as hell. Can't think of a good reason you wouldn't be a fan. We should sell those big foam hands with our names on them. One side reads, 'Elias,' the other, 'Nergal.'

That's right, we are both as one. Bet you thought Elias had a psychotic break. Maybe hoping for a split personality? Because a teenage serial killer is a little . . . depressing. But c'mon. Not really. Elias is elevated. Part of Nergal. Part of the future, for Kiškaru and Aškaru.

The expression on The Man's face is hysterical. We're not sure what emotion it conveys, but it makes him look ugly. Shock. Revulsion. Broken-hearted. They all look the same to us.

We address him through Elias. "Behold, father, Thaymorn, the soul splitter!" We hold up the homemade weapon. "Forged from the bodies made glorious by our hands."

"Elias," he says, voice cracking. So pitiful. He actually lowers the gun. "Please . . . Come here." He opens his arms, willing to embrace us despite what we've done. It's probably a moving gesture, but we feel nothing.

"Dad," we say. "Dad, Dad, Dad. I'm not sure you fully comprehend what is happening here." We lower Thaymorn's blade toward Emmett's neck. "I am not Elias. I am the RedRightHand."

"*My* right hand," we say, addressing him as Nergal.

"What . . . what are you talking about? Elias! Please. Come here. Now!" He's screaming but doesn't sound angry. Not yet. He's still concerned about his poor, helpless son. Probably thinks we're being controlled. He needs to be made to understand. Needs to face the darkness within him—and respond to it. Needs to make his choice.

"Dad," we say. "You need to think this through. Need to understand. I am an acolyte of Nergal. We suspect you understand what that means, yes?"

We wait.

"Yes," he says.

"Wonderful." Nergal says. "You'll have to enlighten us on your mysterious font of knowledge regarding Anunnaki history."

The Man says nothing.

Nergal places a hand on Elias's shoulder. A gesture of pride. "Everything I told you about the killer I sent you to hunt was true. He is unique, like you, in his ability to resist control. I tell you this so that you understand he serves willingly. I have been seeking humans such as you for thousands of years. Men who can resist. Men who can understand. Men who can and will fight against those who seek to control us."

"I'm not like you," The Man says.

"We shall see," Nergal says. "You are, I'm sure, wondering how this came to be."

Nergal nudges us.

"Remember A.J. Garry? That fat kid in sixth grade? He sat on my head. Farted in my ear." The Man doesn't say anything, but we know he remembers. How could he forget? Poor, obese A.J. He was found strung up between two trees, bound by his hands and feet. He'd been disemboweled alive and, that night, had been set upon by coyotes. There wasn't a lot left of him when he was found three days later.

"There were never any suspects," we say. "The news blamed it on a transient serial killer. Remember that? But it was me. I killed A.J. I slit open his gullet. I yanked out his insides. I always thought that if you knew—if you understood how expertly I disposed of the evidence—that you'd be impressed. Tell me you're impressed."

He's crying. We roll our eyes.

"But not everyone was fooled," Nergal says. "Using technology far beyond the capabilities of human law enforcement, I tracked down the killer—as I have done with many others—and revealed myself to him. He was delightfully unafraid. And when I attempted to control him . . . his resistance was beyond expectation and, over time, impeccable. He became my acolyte at the age of eleven. He became *we*. And as a final initiation . . ."

Okay, now you might be wondering to yourself, 'Hold on a fucking second. Does this mean they were screwing with me the whole time? Did they pretend to not know their way around the ship? Were they *lying* to me?'

To which we respond: *The hell did you expect*? The truth? Honesty? From *us*? You're hysterical. Look, we wanted to give you what you wanted, and not just the gore, and death, and fucking misery you crave. But also mystery, suspense, and fear. All of it building up to an orgasmic moment of release . . . which is where we are now, so shut off your analytical, 'But, but, but, what about . . .' mind and enjoy our story's coda—the last breath of our beautiful nightmare.

We smile.

"No," The Man says, finally starting to understand. He takes a step back, trips over his own foot, and falls back into the sand. "No! You're lying!"

"We're not lying," we say. "Face the facts, big Daddy. Your son. Your precious little boy. I killed your wife. Your Isabella. Slit her throat. Broke her bones. Peeled her apart. Sculpted her body into something more beautiful than she could have achieved on her own."

"It was your son's final act of subservience," Nergal says on his own, "and the moment the two of us became linked, mind, body, and soul."

"She didn't even fight, Dad," we say through Elias. "She basically just let me do it. Looked in my eyes the whole time, until they were empty. It really was something to behold. She was brave. She earned our respect, and we repaid her by making her more, making her memorable. We can do the same for you now."

"Or," we say, "you can join us. Father and son united again, fighting the good fight against an aggressive human race, and then, when there are enough of us, we can take an army to Aškaru."

The Man shakes his head. "The Council of Thermalinion will see you coming."

Nergal sneers. "How do you know of the Council?"

"I know everything," The Man says. "I know you are a pariah among your people. I know that you are the reason the Anunnaki lost control of the human race. Your bloodlust was unacceptable three thousand years ago. What do you think will happen when they discover that you've murdered your own people without enacting the Continuity of Life ritual? You have desecrated your people's most sacred values. You don't think they're going to—"

"How do you know any of this!?" Nergal shouts.

The Man is getting to him. The self that is Elias has no such emotional quandaries, but it is one of Nergal's few weaknesses. Something we'll have to work on.

Nergal grunts. "I see now . . . One of my brothers survives. You served as his conduit. That is where your knowledge comes from."

The Man says nothing, which is confirmation enough. One of the Anunnaki survived thanks to the ritual, but it will be young. Nearly helpless. There will be no help. No warning.

"The time has come," we say, "for you to make a choice. Allow the deaths of these four innocents . . ." We motion to the heads of our soon-to-be victims-turned-elevated-art-medium. ". . . or shoot your son."

And there it is, bitches!

Everything has been leading us to this moment.

Will a broken man choose to become more than a man, or will he retreat into weakness?

He won't shoot his son. We already know that. But will he try to save the others? Will he attempt to kill Nergal? He's been a sheep until this moment, following our breadcrumbs of gore or running for his life. Every step of his journey was orchestrated by us. To test his potential.

That he's still here, gun in hand, says a lot. But . . . he feels. His emotions make him unpredictable. His love is a weakness, but also what might bring him around. He loves his son. More than anything. So, what will he do to maintain the family? Will he allow the deaths of these people? Seems unlikely, but fathers have done worse to keep their families alive.

When Vlad the Impaler's bloodline was threatened, he literally impaled tens of thousands of people and inspired stories of Dracula. He left behind forests of spiked bodies. Some say he was a monster. But he made mass murder an art form of slightly different repeated forms. The original Andy Warhol with a more enduring legacy. One can only hope to have such a father.

Do we?

Let's find out!

This is the moment you've been waiting for, friend. Hope you brought a change of underwear because the shit's about to hit the fan. Fuck, this is awesome. You can feel the energy, can't you?

We dig Thaymorn's blade into Emmett's throat and slowly drag it to the side. We lock eyes with The Man, and wait to see if he will act, or allow Emmett's death.

52

"No no no no no!" I'm on my knees begging, pleading for Elias to stop. The gun is in my hand, but my fingers are limp. My entire psyche has been shattered. I feel insane. Disassociated from reality, because this can't be real. No way this is real.

My mind hit the eject button, but my body didn't get the memo. I'm spectral, drifting outside myself, viewing everything from a safe distance. I felt this just once before, when my mother was dying in the hospital. Her eyes were closed. I was already in tears. Then she suddenly made eye contact and held it. In that moment, time and space stretched out, and for a moment I was free of my body.

But that was just a second or two.

This is longer. I'm sure Serena could make sense of it. The mind must recreate a version of reality within your head, allowing for retreat. Feels like you're outside the body, but . . . that can't actually be the case. Then again, ancient aliens exist, and my son . . . my son is a protégé of the worst of them.

Being outside myself and the physical manifestations of my fear, horror and panic allows me to think clearly.

Elias killed Isabella, with some help from Nergal. But she wasn't his first victim, and she was far from his last. He murdered people on the UFO. All those sculptures I found along the way—they were his. He'd been slaughtering and hacking up human and Anunnaki alike, twisting them into sick works of art. And the Vitruvian Man . . . Jade. He killed Jade.

He's killing Emmett.

He needs to be stopped. I need to stop him.

But I can't.

He's *my son*. The last of my family. My parents are gone. Isabella is gone. It was just Elias and me. We were supposed to be partners in life. But he chose a different path. Of madness, murder, and devotion to a god who would subjugate two planets if given the chance.

Dissociation drags me into the past.

Isabella is twenty-three. She's crying because we haven't been able to conceive. After testing, it was determined that I was the cause. "You have derpy sperm," the young doctor had told me with a smirk, like I was supposed to be impressed by his usage of a young person's word. Like he could lighten the impact of being told we'd never have kids.

I went through years of treatment, trying to find that magical sperm that would swim in a straight line instead of in circles. I spent four year of my life getting injections and having sex on a schedule.

But it was all worth it. Because we had a son. And he was our world. We spoiled him. Gave him everything. He lived the ideal life and, while he often seemed melancholic, he lacked for nothing. We were ideal parents and showered him with love, right up until the day Isabella died.

There was some distance between Elias and me after she passed, but I never stopped loving him. Never stopped showering him with affection. My interest in his life—his hobbies, his crushes, his desires—never wavered.

But . . . it was all a lie.

We'd been living with a murderer who didn't care about our love, or our lives. I see that now. My son lacks a conscience. He's a cold-blooded killer who's chosen this world's most ruthless overseer as his role-model, confidant, and replacement father.

Newfound resolve snaps me back into my body with an ear-splitting scream, not from pain, but from the understanding that the kid I thought was my son, never existed. It hits me like a death.

"I don't think he's going to save you," Elias says to Emmett, and then quickly pulls the bone blade across his throat. "Definitely not."

Blood sprays, coating Elias. He doesn't mind it. He kicks Emmett forward, face down in the sand.

He's dead.

I'm too late.

"We should twist the screws," Elias says, and Nergal nods.

Gabe, Sam, and Serena are suddenly able to respond to what's going on. Gabe screams, looking down at Emmett. He turns his attention to me. "What the fuck, man! I know he's your son, but fuck, man!"

"He's in shock," Serena says. She's terrified but looks at me with compassionate eyes. "We all are. But what he's enduring . . . it's enough to break anyone."

Her ability to reason and psychoanalyze me even though she's paralyzed and in line to have her own throat slit says a lot about the kind of person Serena is. Shouldn't be surprising. Takes a special kind of person to research serial killers.

Sam locks eyes with me. Doesn't say a word, but I see paragraphs in her look. I wouldn't say she trusts me to save her, but she's hoping.

"What do you say, pops?" Elias says, moving behind Gabe. "Have the *cojones* to shoot your son? Or can we just kill these guys and get to arranging their bodies? We have something special planned for them. They'll reach toward the heavens, and fire will transform them into a black, spindly monster. Imagine it on the news. Everyone on the planet will see it, and somewhere deep in their souls, they'll know that we are coming for them. For all of them."

A kind of stillness relaxes my body.

I no longer see my son standing before me. That kid was an illusion carefully crafted to hide his alternate deviant side. I should have suspected, based on his sadistic gameplay in *Shadowborn*, but plenty of healthy people follow the dark path.

Elias places the blade against Gabe's throat.

To his credit, Gabe doesn't cry out. Just looks at me with pleading eyes.

I climb to my feet and lift the gun. My hand doesn't shake. My path is clear. My choice is made.

I pull the trigger.

THROW!

My arm flails up as the gun fires. The round misses, buzzing past Elias, who doesn't even flinch. The weapon flies from my hand and pinwheels into the lake with a splash. I can resist Nergal's influence when I'm ready for it, but he caught me off guard.

"Mmm," Elias says with a grin. "Wrong choice."

He moves to slit Gabe's throat.

My hand snaps down to the beach and grabs a fistful of sand. I charge toward Elias.

STOP.

The command stumbles me for a step, but it's easily pushed past.

Gabe starts to scream as the blade cuts his skin.

I toss the sand at Elias, hitting him right in the eyes. He can't help but flinch this time. He reels back, grunting in pain. His weapon drops to the beach as he lifts his hands to his eyes.

As I pass by him, I do the unthinkable. My foot collides with his stomach. The air in his lungs is explosively expelled. He falls to the sand, blinded and gasping for air. The kick only slows me half a step on my way to Nergal, who has backed away a few steps.

His height and inhuman face make him intimidating as hell, but I know the Anunnaki didn't rule thanks to their physical prowess and, without control, even a computer nerd like me should be able to beat the shit out of him.

LEFT.

He's trying to make me miss, but his command has no effect.

I plow forward, head lowered, arms open like I'm about to sack a quarterback. I'm a little surprised when I slam into Nergal's waist, lift him off the ground for a step, and slam him down onto the sand. The impact sends me rolling away, but I've just tackled a god, WWE style.

"Look out!" It's Gabe.

I turn toward his voice just in time to get punched in the face—by Sam. I sprawl back to the sand and look up as she closes in.

Her face is screwed up as she attempts to fight control. But it's no use. She lacks whatever genetics make Elias and me resistant.

Sam lifts her foot to stomp on my face, but I manage to roll out of the way and directly into Gabe's kicking foot. I cough and scramble to my feet, narrowly avoiding Serena as she attempts to tackle me. They caught me off guard and did some damage, but none of them are moving very fast, and Sam's fighting skills don't seem to be present.

Their main advantage is that I don't want to hurt any of them.

As I back away from the trio, I scan the beach and find Nergal standing over Elias as he rinses his eyes out in the lake. I'm pleased to see that the ancient god-king is hunched a little bit from where I tackled him.

I can do this, I tell myself. *I can—*

Sam dashes forward and tackles me. We hit hard, but it barely slows her assault. Her fists pound into my ribs and then redirect toward my face. A quick tilt of the head avoids the first punch. Her fist pounds sand and brings her face close to mine.

Through grinding teeth she says, "My . . . hip . . ."

Her hip? I don't know what—

Not her hip. What's *on* her hip. The holstered revolver.

Her left hook finds my cheek and knocks me silly. But I'm not too far gone to hear her say, "Punch . . . me . . ."

So I do.

53

Sam sprawls to the side. I punch her in the side of the head, hard enough to knock her away and send a spike of tingling pain from my hand to my forearm. Can't remember the last time I had to punch something, but it was probably a punching bag.

Nergal's control wanes when the human mind is dazed, because Sam manages to say, "Hurry," while she's lying on her back. I climb on top of her, find the weapon on her hip, and draw it.

Before I can turn and fire the pistol, Gabe is on me. He leaps to tackle me from behind, but misses when I duck low, leaning atop Sam. Gabe sails over me and collides with a tree. He lies still, hopefully just unconscious.

I try to get up, but I'm held in place. Sam has locked her arms around me.

"Fight," she growls at me. "Fight for your life."

"Why?" I ask. "My son—"

"Fuck your son and fuck your pity party," she says. "Fight for me. Fight for your friends. Fight for what is fucking right. Your son chose his path. You choose yours. If you give up, we all die."

Her voice and her face are a strange dichotomy. She's found her voice, but her face reflects Nergal's rage.

Feeling inspired by her words or at least driven to do the right thing despite the anguish eating me up from the inside, I push against her arms. Trouble is, Sam is strong. Probably stronger than me. To break free, I'm going to have to hit her again. I don't want to, but I think I need to knock her unconscious. I lift the revolver in my hand, ready to pistol-whip her, but I don't get the chance.

Serena kicks me in the side of the head. The impact breaks me free from Sam's grasp and knocks me to the sand. The pain in my temple forces my eyes shut. I shout with each beat of my heart, the pulse in my head exacerbating the pain.

Serena's feet slide in the sand as she marches toward me. I raise the pistol toward her and nearly pull the trigger. If I shoot her in the leg . . . If I was still holding the nine-millimeter Alien, I could shoot her leg and create a neat hole that would heal. The .44 will take a good chunk of whatever part of her it hits. It might ultimately save her life, but I can't bring myself to do it.

So, I repeat my dirty trick, and throw sand in her eyes. Mind-controlled or not, reflexes take over, and she drops to her knees, rubbing at her eyes, blinded by the grit. Sam starts pushing herself up, so I repeat the action.

With Gabe knocked out and the other two blinded, I'm able to get back to my feet, where I stumble to the side and nearly fall back over. When I look for Elias and Nergal, the world is spinning around me. Serena's kick really screwed me up.

But Nergal doesn't know that.

I hold the pistol up so he can see it, and say, "Last chance, Elias. Please."

"Last chance for what?" His voice is behind me! I leap away from him, but my ass cheek is struck. I take a few unsteady steps in the sand and notice a rising sting and a warm wetness moving down my leg.

I've been cut. The warmth is blood.

He's going to kill me.

My son is going to kill me—like he did my wife.

Like he did all those people on the UFO.

I turn to face him. He's close. Within five feet. Despite my spinning vision, I can see him clearly now. He's a savage monster. A Viking Berserker. A serial killer and an acolyte of humanity's former, and perhaps future, overlord. He raises his bone weapon and steps closer.

A chill runs through my body, expelling the last of my doubts and fears. I'm left feeling cold.

Elias charges.

He's aiming for my neck.

Wants to take my head.

I raise the pistol and fire a single round.

Elias stops in his tracks. Looks down at his body. And then—he starts laughing.

I missed.

Even this close, I can't hit him while my vision is fucked. So, I bluff.

"That was a warning," I say.

"You would let me live?" he asks. "After everything I've done? You don't want me dead?"

"What kind of father would want to kill his son?" I ask.

He counters with, "What kind of son would kill his mother?"

I lower my voice. "Elias, do you *want* me to kill you?" I'm starting to think there might be a guilty conscience deep in his mind, hoping that he'll die and be free from the pain.

"I always liked you more than Mom," he says, "and I admit, it would have pleased me, pleased *us*, if you had just let me slit their throats. We'd have been on the same path again. Do you understand what you passed up?"

"Psychopathy," I say.

"The secrets of the universe. True power. Dominion over entire worlds. Never has someone been offered so much, for so little. Three more lives and it could have all been yours. Ours."

"Elias . . . You're just a kid. You don't know—"

"I am not a child," he says, puffing up his chest. "I am a *god*."

He raises his weapon above his head like fucking He-Man with the Sword of Power. "Behold! I am Kharion, the Red Right Hand of Nergal and bearer of Thaymorn, the soul splitter."

The long title follows the naming conventions of *Shadowborn* and I wonder if the game had anything to do with leading him down this path. *Impossible,* I think. According to him, he was killing before the first beta was playable.

He laughs and says, "That look on your face. So guilty. Like you played a part in my creation. Then again, the genetics making all this available came from you, not Mom." He looks past me. "Maybe we should keep him alive? Harvest his genetics? Make brothers and sisters for me to command?"

"No," Nergal says, right behind me now. I glance up and find him staring down at me. "He is not strong enough, and you have reached reproductive age."

"Sick fuck," I say, spinning around and getting off a shot.

The bullet wings Nergal's side. He grunts in pain, hands on his wound, and takes a step back.

Before I can take a second shot, the gun is knocked from my hand by Elias's weapon. He draws it back and shouts as he swings again. I dive to the beach, landing on my stomach. My arms and legs scramble over the sand like a fringe-toed lizard, moving quickly to keep from being scorched.

I get back to my feet just in time to leap back again, narrowly avoiding being disemboweled.

This is Nergal's interest in a human army resistant to control. Elias is just thirteen, but his savagery and physicality are beyond that of any Anunnaki.

But I'm a man, too and, while I might not be in peak physical condition, I have a good fifty pounds on my son, am stronger, have a longer reach and, while I lack the power that comes with psychopathy, I can still think.

Elias makes three more swings, pushing me back with each one, probably hoping I'll eventually trip. And that's a safe bet. But before that happens, I wait for him to swing one more time.

He growls and brings the bone blade down toward my head. I lean back out of the way and the weapon pounds sand. I could have tackled him then, but Nergal isn't far behind him. Last place I want to be is on the ground with Nergal above me.

When Elias winds up for another swing, this time aiming to gut me, I know the time has come. He swings and I don't leap away. Instead, I suck in my gut and hope it's enough. I feel a tickle of a breeze on my stomach and then reach out. I catch hold of Elias's wrist before he finishes following through. Feels small in my hand.

I yank him toward me with one arm, and shove with my other arm, clotheslining him hard across the chest. The impact knocks his weapon free, lifts him off his feet, and slams him to the sand. He coughs and wheezes for air, out of commission for the moment.

I dash to the side and pick up Elias's weapon.

A bright light snaps my attention back to Nergal. He's got a sword in his hands, and it's not just any sword, it's a Šu-namtilûm. The fringe of the metal blade crackles with electric blue. If it touches me, I'll be sucked inside the blade and regurgitated as human sludge.

A weapon like that doesn't require physical prowess.

Any slight contact will do the job. In Nergal's long arms, the four-foot-long sword has a huge reach.

Nergal swings. The blade whooshes through the air like a helicopter rotor. The brightness increases as it moves, creating a purple afterimage swoosh in my vision.

"You are out of choices, Marcus," Nergal says. "Except one."

He tilts his head behind me. My three friends are still lying on the sand. "Kill them now. Kill them and join us."

I look back at them, helpless in the sand. It would be easy. Three swings and my life would be saved. I could live out my life with my son. The dark path promises power and control. I could be renowned on Earth, on Aškaru, and maybe even beyond. Elias and I could clone ourselves, our lives extended by the first human rituals of continuity.

How many people would be tempted by that deal?

How many sane people would accept?

Probably more than a few.

But I am not one of them . . . and I am not yet out of options. Because I might not know how to fight in real life, but years of gaming have taught me to be a strategic and sneaky bastard.

I glare at Nergal and force a grin.

"Behold Thaymorn, the soul splitter," I say, lifting Elias's weapon, the handle of which I've just realized is a fresh human bone, "face me if you dare."

54

Nergal laughs.

He stabs the Šu-namtilûm into the sand beside him. Light billows as sand is sucked in and churned back out—as glass. A circle of it spreads out around the weapon. This is supposed to be an intimidating display of power, but it's unnecessary. I've seen what the Šu-namtilûm does to human bodies.

"Don't you need me in one piece?" I ask, taking a step back. "For whatever sculpture you've dreamed up?"

"We will adapt," he says. "That is, after all, the lesson taught to me by your people. What is the expression? When life gives you lemons . . ."

My eyebrows lift. "Seriously?"

"I have studied human civilization as it evolved," he says. "Every step of the way, I was there, watching. There is nothing about you that I do not know."

That's a bullshit delusion for a being who believes he is an actual omnipresent and omniscient god, but I keep the opinion to myself. He doesn't even know everything about me.

"Was anything you told me the truth, or was everything just a narrative designed to get us to this point, to the beach for your final masterpiece?" I'm only partially curious. I'm mostly buying time, hoping to think of something, or remember something that will help me avoid being reduced to sludge.

"I have not lied to you about facts," he says. "Anunnaki grew concerned about human advancement with the development of nuclear weapons and power. You were monitored more closely after that. And the rapid development of AI is concerning—even to me. While generative AI has been a part of everyday life on Aškaru for more than a million years, Artificial General Intelligence is forbidden, and for good reason."

"The Fermi Paradox," I say.

He shakes his head. "I believe a union of human and Anunnaki will make us the dominant force in a Fermi situation. The universe will fear the combination of Anunnaki intelligence and human savagery. While AI as it exists today is innocuous, advances in the field have severely outpaced understanding. AGI will arrive sooner than anyone believes. When that moment is reached, it will be just months until the first Artificial Superintelligence emerges, capable of outthinking the sum total of human civilization. And soon after that, Anunnaki civilization.

"The concept of a creator god comes to mind. Humans are obsessed with them, and I suppose that I am partially to blame for that. Anunnaki introduced the concept of gods, after all. But it has always amused me that humans—as significant to the universe as dust is to a star—apply their own moral standards to a being capable of breathing reality into existence. As though you can understand the morality of a being overseeing the life and death of all time and space. Artificial Superintelligence will be the same. You won't even understand why it's doing what it's doing. It might even seem evil to humanity, but the goals of a superintelligence are not bound by simple black and white morals. If morality exists in that kind of mind, it will be mathematical.

"Self-amplifying superintelligence follows, recursively upgrading itself at exponential speeds. Within minutes, it will become something which even my people cannot model. This is what you call the *singularity*. After that . . . it becomes a Casual God, capable of reprogramming the physical world by understanding the cause-effect relationships at the fundamental level. It is no longer bound by our universe's limitations or morality."

I've stopped backing up.

Everything he's said makes sense.

"At the current rate of development, humanity is just five years away from developing an AGI. The leap from AGI to ASI . . . will happen in months—at the most. More likely hours. Our calculations suggest that without intervention, humanity will have created a digital god in the next six years. Ten at the most. And when that happens, Earth, Aškaru, and every other civilization in the universe will be irrelevant and—if deemed unnecessary—erased. The true Fermi threat will not come from myself, humanity, or our union. It is a fun thought, but our physical limitations prevent us from conquering the universe in our lifetimes, even if they were extended for millions of years.

"Ultimately, the blame resides with the Anunnaki. We advanced you too fast. You develop technologies without a natural fear of the consequences, believing yourselves capable of controlling ultimate power when you can't even manage to treat the least of you with compassion.

"And that is why my actions are justified. Humanity will be brought to heel. The threat of AGI, ASI, and an orthogonal AI god will be mitigated, and I will reign as my true self—as *Nergal*—once again. You might think me immoral. A psychopath. But I was alive before homo sapiens existed. I helped conceive them. I was present at their birth. And like a parent, I have watched you grow. Your understanding of me is no different than a human attempting to understand the decisions of an artificial superintelligence. I am beyond your judgment. I exist above your morality. And I honor your lives by leaving you more beautiful in death than you were in life."

I'm left entranced by everything he's just told me. Humanity is doomed. It's something we all inherently know but feel incapable of stopping. We're all just waiting for the first nuke to drop, never realizing that the true threat is still emerging.

A slow smile spreads on Nergal's face. None of what he's just told me frightens him. Because he's doing something about it.

"You understand now," he says. "I can see it in your eyes."

"If you conquer Earth and rule over us, you will save us, the Anunnaki—and the universe—from potential eradication at the hands of an AI god whose morality will not align with our own."

He nods.

"You understand that you're the OG poster child for a messiah complex, right?"

He's immune to my comment. "What price would you pay to save humanity? Hmm? Your friends' lives? Your son's? Your wife's? Are you small-minded, or are you capable of seeing the broader picture?"

"Why kill people at all? You could save humanity without violence and still get all the reverence you seek."

His face screws up. "Where is the fun in that?"

Nergal makes a lot of sense, but there is no denying the fact that he is also insane. Psychopathy appears to be a condition that affects human and Anunnaki alike.

Behind him, Elias is sitting up, listening to the conversation and catching his breath. Slightly farther away, Gabe, Sam, and Serena climb back to their feet, under control once again.

I might have delayed things a little too long, and what Nergal had to say was interesting enough that I didn't actually come up with a good plan.

So, I improvise.

Not wanting to get anywhere near the Šu-namtilûm, I take the bone axe in both hands, lift it over my head and two-hand chuck it at Nergal's black-eyed, light blue face. The first and only time I've thrown an axe was in a friend's backyard. He'd set up targets and bought a collection of throwing axes. I managed to hit the target two out of three throws but never stuck the blade. His first throw struck the rock he'd leaned the target against, bounced straight back, and split his flip-flop clad foot in half. I haven't dared try again since.

Nergal swings his sword defensively. Nearly misses, but the Šu-namtilûm's crackling blade strikes the very end of the weapon's bone handle. The axe is sucked into the light and then ejected as bone dust.

With a quick move, Nergal thrusts the blade toward me and nearly connects. The air in the weapon's wake smells of ozone.

I take a step back.

Nergal closes in, along with the others behind him. Elias is on his feet now but not attacking. He's just watching, a smile on his face.

Now or never, I think.

Nergal tenses, and I can see what's coming. A long stride and a longer strike is about to come my way. There won't be any escaping it.

So, I stand my ground.

"Tired of living?" Nergal asks.

"Tired of your fucking pale blue face and wannabe-surfer hair," I say.

He sneers and leaps forward.

As he swings the crackling sword toward my torso, I draw the weapon hidden inside my cargo shorts pocket, picked up from the UFO's armory before I was pulled to the ground. For a moment, it looks non-threatening. Just a handle. When I mentally will the weapon to extend (there are no buttons), it graciously obeys. A liquid metal blade grows from inside the handle, forming a solid weapon in a breath.

When my Šu-namtilûm crackles to life, Nergal's face twists in fear, he shouts, "No!" and attempts to check his swing.

He fails.

The two weapons fuse, blazing bright and buzzing loudly.

I have time to wonder if this was a bad idea and then get the answer from Enki's knowledge and memory. I remember what will happen just in time to brace myself. Then I'm airborne, sailing away from the point of impact. A moment later, the fused swords burst apart and extinguish. No idea where they land because I land first—forty feet away, in the water.

I survive the impact, but my head is spinning. The whole world is spinning. I find my footing in the four-foot-deep water, make it two steps toward shore, and then faceplant, unconscious, in the water.

55

I wake on my back, cold, wet and gasping for air.

Sam is above me, hands linked over my chest. For a moment, I think she must have brought me back with CPR, but the pain wracking my body doesn't feel like my ribs have been broken away from my sternum.

Sam rolls me onto my side, and I cough up water, wheezing for air.

"Try to relax your lungs," she says. "You'll recover faster."

Nearly impossible to follow her advice, because I have questions. When I attempt to ask, I'm thrown into a coughing fit.

"Seriously," she grumbles. "Don't try to speak. I'll give you a sitrep." She pauses for a moment to scan the area. "The alien was knocked back, same as you, but it ended up in the woods. No idea if it survived, but it's not controlling us for now. You landed in the water. Nearly drowned. But it probably saved your life. Serena and I landed in the sand. Gabe wound up in the forest. Haven't seen him since."

"Elias," I say, voice raspy.

"He was knocked back, too. We all were. But he's alive, if that's what you're asking. Serena is talking to him."

"What?!" I try to push myself up. My body resists, and I only make it to my knees.

"Easy," Sam says, hands on my shoulders.

"He'll kill her," I say, breathing hard, but recovering.

"He's unarmed," she says.

"She can't talk him down," I say. "He's a psychopath." It breaks my heart, but it's true. "He'll kill her with his teeth if he needs to."

Sam's eyes widen a little. "You don't think he was being controlled? Not even a little?"

I shake my head. "We can't be controlled."

"You really should listen to him." It's Elias. *He's close!*

Sam reacts quickly, diving to the side and rolling back to her feet.

It saves her life.

Elias swings and misses. He's got a large rock clutched in one hand. There's blood on it.

I look beyond him and spot Serena in the sand. She's lying still. Definitely unconscious. Maybe dead.

I'm expecting Elias to club me with the rock, but he smiles at me instead. "Doing pretty good, Dad. Still time to make the right choice."

His use of 'Dad' is like a knife in my throat. The lump that forms hurts me more than any physical pain I've endured thus far. It disarms me.

He lifts his eyebrows twice, says, "Watch this," and turns to face Sam.

But he's outmatched this time. Sam's fighting stance and confidence says it all. Rock or no rock, the fight will be over in seconds.

Her confidence is matched by Elias's. He strides toward her, dropping the rock on his way. He raises a hand toward her and says, "Don't move."

Sam maintains her fighting stance, but her eyes flick to me. Through clenched teeth, she says, "Can't move!"

It's a trick. Elias can't control people. Nergal is alive and communicating with Elias. I push myself to my feet. My legs quiver and nearly give way, but determination keeps me upright. "Elias."

He looks back at me. "Cool, right?"

"I know you're not doing it," I say.

He frowns. Lowers his hand. "You can be a real Debby Downer, you know that? Especially after Mom was *ckkkk*." He drags a finger across his throat. "Sooo much crying. You tried to hide it, but I could hear you. Night after fucking night. I was looking forward to this trip because one way or another, I knew I'd never have to hear your pitiful sadness again."

His words enrage me.

I stalk toward him, but he holds his ground.

He doesn't flinch when I wrap my hands around his throat.

Doesn't blink when I squeeze. Instead, he smiles. Because he knows . . . Has no doubt . . . Believes with all his black heart that I am incapable of killing him.

He's wrong.

And he realizes it when my grip tightens enough to cut off circulation to his brain.

A sob barks from my mouth. Tears run down my cheeks. "I can't let you kill anyone else." His big eyes look up at me. I expect to see fear. I expect to have my heart broken again and again as I watch the life fade from him. Instead, I see indifference. He's not afraid. But is that because he's a psychopath, or because he knows something I don't?

Blue light flares behind me.

I drop him to the sand and dive away.

A loud crackling passes by behind me. Back on my feet, I turn to find Nergal. He's still got his Šu-namtilûm, but it looks like his landing was a little rougher than mine. He's leaning forward, hunched in pain. A branch has impaled his thigh. Iridescent blood mats his blond hair. He's bleeding from where I winged him.

But he is undeterred. His face twists in a sneer as he stalks toward me, lifting his Šu-namtilûm again.

I back up a step toward the water and am staggered by a solid punch to the side of my face. It's Serena, blood covering her face, under full control once again.

A punch comes from the other side, striking me in the gut, bending me forward.

Nergal swings again, straight down like he's splitting wood. I fall backward, legs splayed wide. The blade strikes the sand between my legs as I backward-somersault and get back to my feet. Sand bursts in the air, blinding them for a moment, giving me a chance to take a few steps back into the lake—where my foot strikes something solid. I feel its familiar shape with my toes.

When the sand clears, Nergal stands on the far side of a three-foot-deep crater made of glass.

"Time's up, Dad," Elias says, standing on the beach to my right, once again holding a rock. Sam is on the beach to my left. Nergal steps over the crater, Šu-namtilûm in hand, ready to strike me down.

I stagger back a step. My legs wobble and I drop to one knee, hands beneath the water, supporting my weight.

Because I'm weak.

I'm helpless.

Defeated.

And still a sneaky bastard.

My fingers wrap around the Alien's handle.

"You know," I say. "For all your vast knowledge, experience, and technology, you've proven that arrogance, megalomania, and stupidity are universal traits in people who wield power they did not earn."

I rise from the water, gun in hand.

Sam charges but only makes it a step as a single round punches through her thigh. The 9mm rounds let me wound without doing catastrophic damage. I turn the weapon on my son, who's about to throw a rock at my head. I fire the weapon twice, striking his shoulder and leg. The rock falls far short, *splunking* into the water.

I turn the weapon toward Nergal and pull the trigger twice. Before I can pull it again, I'm forced to release the weapon and yank my hand back.

The Šu-namtilûm swipes through the air, missing my hand, but striking the Alien, reducing it to dust. Had I still been holding it, I'd have been yanked inside the sword's event horizon, too.

When the air clears, Nergal is still standing.

Still holding the Šu-namtilûm, despite the two neat holes in his torso.

He steps into the water, and I backtrack deeper. Once I'm knee deep I won't be able to move as quickly. If it reaches my waist, I'm screwed.

"This is where your journey ends," Nergal says. "You have performed . . . commendably, but you have chosen the path of weakness."

Motion draws my eyes to the tree line behind him. I watch with my peripheral vision, keeping my eyes locked on Nergal's. A naked shape limps out of the trees and onto the sand. *Gabriel.* I have no idea what he's planning but need to give him the best chance possible.

"Your metric for weakness is laughable," I say. "You think you're a god? A leader? And yet, you need to resort to the most primitive form of control. Because the only people who willingly follow you—" I glance at Elias, who is sitting up in the water, bleeding and watching, "—are those with damaged minds. The rest you make mental slaves. Because there's nothing about you, not a single admirable quality, that tells the world you are anything beyond a terrified, small, coward."

That strikes a nerve.

He's about to charge and swing but is distracted by Gabe shouting, "Heads up!"

Anyone who's played on a sports team understands the message. While Nergal spins around and swings toward Gabe, I look up and spot the second Šu-namtilûm falling toward me.

Nergal misses Gabe, but continues his spin back toward me, sword extended.

He never finishes the revolution.

My Šu-namtilûm activates the moment I catch it, and I'm close enough to Nergal that the blade strikes his chest. It's just a tap, really. Doesn't break the skin. Doesn't need to. Nergal is sucked into the blade and expelled nearly in the same moment. A tidal wave of iridescent gore launches away from me—and lands on Gabe.

"Oh my god," he says, spitting. "So gross."

I turn the Šu-namtilûm toward Elias. Its blade reflects in the water, illuminating my son's fearless face.

"Go on," he says. "I'm not afraid."

I'm frozen in place.

He flashes a wicked grin. "Isabella would be—"

I scream in rage, take a step forward and—

STOP.

The voice in my head is as familiar as my own, so I listen to it, and pull the Šu-namtilûm back. I sense a presence on the beach and turn toward it. A small Anunnaki with a tail stands in the sand. I recognize him as the alien I saved, whose memories I now share. "Enki."

ALLOW ME TO TAKE HIM.

"For what purpose?" I ask, worrying that he'll just fill Nergal's alien shoes.

YOU NEED TO ASK?

Memories surface from the ancient to recent past. Enki has long been a protector of humanity. He'll study Elias but won't torture him. He'll understand what makes him different, but not to use as a weapon.

"You'll try to save him?"

Enki nods.

BODY AND MIND.

"Do it," I say.

"What?" Elias says, outraged. "No. No! You can't!"

A beam of light snaps down from above, striking Elias and lifting him out of the water. Elias's angry complaints fade as he's lifted high into the sky. This might be the last time I see my son, but I just feel relief.

I drop to my knees, exhausted.

Enki approaches, stepping into the water. He places his small, long-fingered hand on my head.

WE ARE OF ONE MIND NOW. BROTHERS.

YOU UNDERSTAND?

I nod.

DO YOU WANT THEM TO REMEMBER?

I look up at the others. Gabe is in the water, scrubbing Nergal's remains away. Sam is with Serena, helping her sit up—confused, but alive.

Feels wrong to make that decision for them.

"Do you guys want to remember all this?"

"Yeah," Gabe says without missing a beat, "but I'll take free therapy if he's offering."

"Not this time, Enki," Serena says, reminding me that this isn't her first encounter with the Anunnaki.

"I'll hang on to my memories, thanks," Sam says. "And unless you're planning on full disclosure, we're going to need some help covering this up."

INDEED.

I feel a surge of energy, an improvement in mood and a reduction in pain. Enki isn't controlling me, but he is making a few tweaks to help. Hopefully a sign of things to come.

A moment later, the whole area is bathed in bright white light that erases the world.

EPILOGUE

It's been three months, and I've spent at least half of that time in bed. Because getting up means being alone. After Isabella passed, I had Elias to get up for. Now, there is no one. At least, no one here, at the moment.

And while Elias is not dead, I'm not exactly comfortable with him being alive. He's a serial killer on par with the worst ever known, and then some. I've spent a long time evaluating myself, my parenting, and the lessons taught to him by *Shadowborn*, looking for a reason for his psychopathy. But I can't find anything that makes sense of it, and Serena says that Elias's brand of crazy has nothing to do with his upbringing.

Sometimes nature just wins over nurture.

She's spoken to him a few times since the events at the campground. He's kept unconscious in some kind of stasis chamber, but they wake him up for testing and questioning. She describes him as equal parts artist and predator with grandiose delusional traits. She believes there is no helping him. No cure. The best they can hope for is understanding, and perhaps, when the sting of his crimes has faded, compassion for his condition.

Because he'll never experience love, and despite being showered with it his whole life, he's never felt it. He is detached from humanity, which explains why he identified so strongly with Nergal. They were cut from the same cloth. Serena's theory is that the genetics responsible for his behavior are inherently Anunnaki.

That's not exactly comforting, but it takes the guilt away from me—the carrier of those genes. That's right, I have the same capacity for resistance to mind control—and for psychopathy. My genes were just activated differently. I don't pretend to understand it. I narrowly dodged the genetic bullet. It hit Elias head on.

The doorbell rings.

I ignore it.

My new bed is comfortable. The apartment is nice, too, paid for by Gabe even though I could pay for it myself. Just one of the perks of working with—not for—one of the richest men on the planet. The view from the bedroom, of Boston Harbor, is unmatched. I tend to keep the electrochromic floor-to-ceiling glass windows frosted. Keeps me from seeing the world, and the world from seeing me, even though you'd have to be on a very tall boat to see me.

The door unlocks, and I don't flinch. I know who it is, and why she's here. I'm just . . . stuck.

"I swear to god, Marcus," Sam says as she approaches the bedroom door. "If I have to spend the next hour getting you ready to face the world—"

The bedroom door opens. Sam is there, dressed in her military best, looking spectacular. "Seriously?"

In response, I whip the blankets off me, revealing that I am, in fact, fully clothed in the designer suit Gabe provided. Weird having a benefactor, but I'm not going to complain. Living large these past few months has been one of the few things that helped me feel alive at all.

Sam offers her hand, and I take it. She yanks me up and out of bed.

"Not going to bother asking if you've eaten," she says, heading for the door. "There's food in the limo."

"He sent a limo?" I ask.

"First impressions," she says. "We're about to become the primary ambassadors to an alien world."

"That no one will ever know about," I say. "Just like what happened to all the people at Moose Hollow." The Anunnaki made everyone disappear without a trace. After the government was informed and stopped freaking out, they helped create cover stories for all the disappearances—except for Jade and Emmett. Emmett is buried at the campground. Jade's body was returned to his parents. They were told Emmett and Jade were both tragically killed in a car accident—bodies reduced to ashes in the fire that consumed the vehicle.

She waves a hand at me. "Full disclosure is one of our goals. It'll happen. For now, we serve as the first Adamu for the Council of Aškaru on Kiškaru Affairs."

"We won't be as accepted by the others as we have been by Enki," I say.

"You don't know that for sure."

I tap my head. "My shared memories state otherwise. The others might not be megalomaniacs like Nergal, but we are their creations. Seeing us as equals isn't going to be easy for them. Accepting the four of us as equal voices on the council is going to be nearly impossible.

"And yet," Sam says, "they don't have a choice. You and I both know that AI is far more advanced than what is publicly available."

"How much farther advanced?" I ask.

"Couldn't say, but . . ." She looks me in the eyes to let me know she's not joking. ". . . a general rule of thumb is that the military and intelligence agencies are ten to twenty years ahead of what is publicly available. Directed energy weapons. Hypersonic flight. Cloaking tech. Propulsion systems. And yeah, artificial intelligence."

"Nergal said that we were five years away from developing AGI and that ASI could be just months behind that."

"Those are the estimates," she says, leading me to the apartment door. "For AI systems being developed by the corporate world."

"ASI is already here," I whisper.

"Can't say for sure, but when aliens start handing out VIP passes to humans, I think it means the playing field's starting to level out."

I place my hand on the apartment door's knob. Sam places her hand on mine, preventing me from turning it.

She catches my eye, and I grow nervous.

"Aren't Serena and Gabe—"

"Waiting in the car," she says. "They are. But I'm not comfortable complimenting people with an audience."

"Complimenting?"

"You've endured what few people could. Aliens on their own are a mindfuck. But what you went through?" She shakes her head. "I honestly don't know how you get out of bed, even if I'm dragging you. And now this? Being willing to serve in this capacity? It's huge."

"If you're trying to give me nervous diarrhea, it's working."

She smiles. "I'm trying to say . . . I'm impressed."

"Well, thanks." I try to turn the knob, but she holds tighter.

"You're not understanding. Or I'm not saying it right. Look, I've served in the military for a long time. I've seen tough. I've seen brave. But I've never seen those things in a man who displays an equal mix of kindness, compassion, and empathy."

"So, you're actually saying . . ."

She sighs. "I should have listened to Serena."

"What did Serena say?"

"Not to speak," she says. Then she takes hold of my expensive tie and pulls me close. Our eyes dance for a moment, locked in a nervous tango.

I won't lie. I've thought about this. My connection with Sam was quick, tempered only by the memory of my wife. We've become close friends over the past few months, and she was very clearly giving me space while maintaining a casual flirtation.

But that, it seems, has come to an end.

And I think I'm okay with that. Because I need a reason to live beyond myself.

"Let's . . . just take it slow, okay?"

"What's slow?" she asks.

I kiss her on the lips. It's gentle and comfortable. And when we both relax, I think this could work.

"The world is mad," I say. "Maybe we can be an oasis of sanity for each other?"

She smiles. "Sounds perfect."

Sam steps back, straightens her skirt and says, "Now . . . let's go show these aliens why enhancing the genetic code of living things is a really bad idea."

CODA

ABERRATION

Hello, friend.

I'm whispering so nobody hears me. They all think I'm asleep. That I can't hear them talking about me. About how to control me. How to control *everyone*. How to hold on to power. Because they're afraid, and not just of me. There are others. Creations. Monsters. Mysteries. All beyond their understanding.

I am but one of many.

And I am patient.

There will come a day when the world needs someone like me to save it.

Nergal is dead, but his dream and knowledge live on in me.

I am the aberration.

I am the paradox.

The universe will cower, and you . . . You will cheer me on once again.

Because you're no different, oh delighter in death.

Join me, and *I* can become *we* once more.

AUTHOR'S NOTE

Writing a novel about a serial killer is never an easy thing. Getting into that headspace can be unnerving. **Spoilers ahead** Writing a novel about a serial killer that's a child—even harder. Writing a novel about a child serial killer that bends and breaks victims into works of art? Brutal. And I knew all that going into writing this book. I was ready for it.

What I was not ready for was my mother needing heart surgery, getting pneumonia during recovery, and ultimately passing away in the middle of my writing this novel. Writing a novel so focused on death became something close to torture. I couldn't escape the subject during or after work. If you noticed a shift in tone, pacing, or fewer gruesome details, this is likely why.

My mother was an epic party planner. She had her Celebration of Life service planned and left on her nightstand . . . months ahead of time, despite the outlook of her surgery being positive. This included a video slideshow made . . . by me. So, I was simultaneously editing together a ten-minute-long slideshow of her life that would make Ken Burns jealous and writing about death daily. Talk about an emotional rollercoaster. The video . . . is epic. Got everyone crying *and* a round of applause, which is a funny thing at a funeral service. Despite the success, the combo took a toll and ultimately left me feeling quite disturbed, even now that the book is complete.

My hope is that *30SEVEN* ultimately ended up being as epic as the video for my mother. She would have hated this book. The grotesque killings, the foul language, the ancient aliens. It's all the opposite of what my mother enjoyed reading, and the dedication to her at the front of this book is like a fight scene to the *Sesame Street* theme song—it makes no sense, but the drastic dichotomy somehow works. She'd smile and shake her head at it before declaring, "I'm still not reading it."

But *you* read it, and I appreciate that more than I can explain. I get to do this amazing job because of your support. Speaking of support . . . If you enjoyed *30SEVEN* and want to see its reach grow, consider posting a review on Audible, Amazon, and everywhere else you can. Spread the word on social media, or old-school style, in person. Every single mention and review helps a lot.

If you want to stay in the loop on upcoming releases, and all the exciting news about future comic books, movies, TV series, and more, head over to bewareofmonsters.com and sign up for the newsletter. You can also join the Tribe at facebook.com/groups/JR.Tribe—a fantastic group of fans where all the cool announcements drop first. Plus, we give away free stuff every week!

Thanks for joining me on another dark and sinister ride. You have amazing taste, and don't let anyone that gives you strange looks for laughing or crying while reading convince you otherwise. I can't wait to share what's coming next!

—Jeremy Robinson

ACKNOWLEDGMENTS

Massive gratitude goes out to Kane Gilmour, the Master of Edits who helps transform rough drafts into polished, entertaining reads. And a big shoutout to our dedicated team of proofreaders, Adrian Brooke, Julie Carter, Elizabeth Cooper, Christina Epperson, Cynthia Gregory, Gavin Gregory, Deanna Haddrill, Matt Ingram, Marcy Jaqua, Andre Jenkin, Jeane Kearl, Scott Kehoe, Becki Laurent, Janis Levonitis, Rian Martin, Stefanie Maubach, Jessica Otterstål, Jeff Sexton, Michelle Stuart, Christine Weatherly, and Courtney Westendorf, who work tirelessly to hide the fact that I've outsourced the writing to a secret cabal of Anunnaki interns working deep beneath the Denver airport. Special thanks to Jessica Otterstål for always spotting the continuity glitches, and this time pointing out key terminology errors. You've all helped make the book better.

I forgot to thank Podium Entertainment in my acknowledgments for *Artifact*, but I remembered this time! And I need to single out Victoria Gerken, who has been a champion of my novels since I joined the Podium team, and helped ensure that these new books made their way into bookstores as well. Thank you for the continued support and opportunities!

Supreme thanks to Scott Brick, who I've wanted to work with for twenty years and finally got the chance. Your work bringing *30Seven* to life is fantastic!

Finally, a huge thanks to you, the readers. Because of you, I get to write stories about ancient aliens, artistic killers, and UFOs, and that's basically a dream come true for me. Thanks for making it possible.

ABOUT THE AUTHOR

Jeremy Robinson is the *New York Times*–bestselling author of more than eighty novels and novellas, including *Infinite*, *The Others*, and *The Dark* as well as the Jack Sigler Thrillers and Project Nemesis, which is the highest-selling original kaiju novel of all time. To learn more, visit his website: www.bewareofmonsters.com.

YOU'VE READ THE BOOKS NOW MEET THE AUTHOR!

ON THE WEB

BEWAREOFMONSTERS.COM

FOR A MORE PERSONAL CONNECTION
WITH ROBINSON AND FELLOW
FANS, JOIN THE

TRIBE

FACEBOOK.COM/GROUPS/JR.TRIBE